CW00932930

THE AMERICAN ADVENTURER

Brick Rustin, down-on-his-luck news correspondent, hoped that the Ararat story would put him back in the headlines. Instead, it will put him in the front lines of an international conflict in which one man's life counts for nothing.

THE DEADLY SEDUCTRESS

Livia Lo Presti knew how to make a man do whatever she wanted, and Brick Rustin, obsessed with having her, will serve her purposes very well.

THE BEAUTIFUL REVOLUTIONARY

A woman marked by the Soviets for death, Selma Sabri is committed to a cause she's willing to die for. She's also in love with the American newsman who'd be willing to die for her.

Other Avon Books by
Robert Houston

CHOLO
MONDAY, TUESDAY, WEDNESDAY!

ARARAT

ROBERT HOUSTON

AVON
PUBLISHERS OF BARD, CAMELOT, DISCUS AND FLARE BOOKS

ARARAT is an original publication of Avon Books. This work
has never before appeared in book form.

AVON BOOKS
A division of
The Hearst Corporation
959 Eighth Avenue
New York, New York 10019

First Avon Printing, November, 1982

The author would like to acknowledge the loving, lasting friendship and aid of Erkut and Günay, Atilla and Feriha, and the *çocuklar*. And most especially to acknowledge the intrepidity of Erkut on the machine-gun-tea-party-fraught road to Ararat.

For Claude
My father, the first storyteller,
With love.

ARARAT

BOOK I

Prologue

Later, when it was too late for it to matter, Brick knew he should have spotted the phoniness of the letter from the tone of the first ten lines. It was chirpy, forced. Roger could be cynical, brilliant, maudlin—but never chirpy. Not unless he had something he was unnaturally anxious to hide.

Brick opened the letter and shook the check out first—fifty bucks that would take a month to clear the Turkish banks—then read it through quickly for the assignment. The second time he read slowly, trying to make sense out of what Roger was offering him. From time to time he looked from his desk out over the dark waters of the Black Sea, where the gray sky had been playing at rain all morning. He pictured Roger with a dictaphone in his neat office just off DuPont Circle in Washington, D.C., blue-

3

penciling a story and talking at the same time. It was an image Roger liked. Brick shrugged away a quick moment of envy.

"Dear Brick, old brick," the letter began, the joke Roger had made a thousand times since college. Roger had given him the name, in fact, had claimed that Broderick Rustin was no name for a Christian gentleman in the year of our Lord 1966 in a liberal though properly proper and exclusive New England college like Middlebury, God save the Mark. Brick had put up with it, had come to like it as he had Roger, had kept it all through Viet Nam, then Air Force language school and the tour in Turkey. Now, back in Turkey again, it was more himself than the name his father had plucked off the family tree for him. "Lo, I bring glad tidings of great joy. We ran your piece nearly unedited in the last *Middle Eastern Desk,* and it was picked up by both Pacific News and Zodiac. Stringer *extraordinaire, mon ancien!* The Kurds are very fashionable nowadays. Anything else you can dig up on them will be endlessly appreciated.

"That's a hint, by the way. I haven't had anything from you in six weeks. What's up? I ran into your Agèd Parent the other day at the 1784 in Georgetown (he looks as hale and grave as an assistant deputy director of the National Security Agency should, by the way), and he said you sounded all at loose ends in your letters of late. He thought you needed a change, that the Turks were giving you the works. So, presto! Self-interest and brotherly love combine. Old Roger is here to offer you large sums of money, fascinating companions, adventure, fame, and all he asks is a story from you. To elucidate: on the last day of this month of July, some persons of my recent acquaintance will arrive *chez vous* in Trabzon on a

boat from Istanbul called, for God's sake, the *Ege*.
They will be in need of a cultured, young-
ish, outdoorsy sort who happens to speak Turkish,
English, a smattering of Kurdish and—don't ask me
why—Russian. Purpose, you ask? They are the lat-
est in a long line of Ark seekers. They've got gobs
of Canadian dollars to mount an expedition to find
the remains of Noah's Ark up on Mount Ararat, a
cause dear to the heart of every slightly cracked and
religious-minded archaeologist in civilization."

Brick put the letter down and reached for his tiny
tea glass. Even tea was a pain to get hold of here
during Ramazan, this holy month of daytime fasting.
The very act of breathing had seemed a pain lately,
which made him aware and ashamed of his boredom.
No, he didn't like the jolly, almost silly tone of
Roger's letter, and he wasn't at all sure of what he
was being asked to do. But the thrill of pleasure he
felt at the letter's hint of some kind of break in his
boredom told him just how desperate he must be.
Anything to spend even a few days away from this
red-roofed town that spread like a stain from the
mountains to the waters the ancient Greeks had
called the Unfriendly Sea. He cradled the tea glass
in his palm and studied the rind- and bottle-littered
beach. Below him, two Turks with snap-brim caps
slowly loaded black sand into the panniers of a patient donkey. He envied the donkey's patience.

And yes, he knew about the expeditions to Ararat
so far—the Turkish one, the Russian one, the French
one, the American one just a few years ago. He also
knew about the other American one, the phony one,
which had tricked the Soviets just after the war and
made them angry enough to build their endless border guard towers. His father and his friends at NSA

had laughed about that one. The Americans had left their own artifacts behind them then: a string of antennas all through the mountains to spy on the Soviets with. Back when the Turks still liked us and looked to us as the hope of the glowing, technological future.

There would be no more of that this time, he bet. He sipped the now tepid tea almost wistfully before he went back to the letter. He let his mind linger for a moment on Roger's mention of the need for Russian. But that could be nothing. Roger's archaeologists could simply be guessing that since Ararat lay almost in Russia they might run across Russian speakers somewhere on it. Not likely.

"So far as I can tell there is nothing nefarious about them. What they want, they say, is someone who knows the area and who can handle some incidental translating chores. They will be bringing a Turkish army officer from Istanbul to smooth things past the martial law checkpoints. I'm sure there will be a thousand details you'll want to pore over (that's the phrase, right?) with them when they get there, so I won't go into any. They are all right honorable sorts, a Canadian couple resident in London, plus an Austrian-born chappie with a Ph.D. who reminds me of whichever one of Mutt and Jeff it was who had the moustache. The couple's name is Lo Presti, Tony and Livia, and they're about our age (you're still thirty-two, aren't you, you swine; I hit thirty-three last month). The Austrian's name is Brenner and I suspect there's a great deal more of the tribe of Abraham in him than of Austria. He's *really* middle-aged, not just toying with it as we are, and is my contact. More I can't tell you. Brenner showed up in my office one day with a much-appre-

ciated song and dance about my being the brightest
editor of a Middle East publication in the country,
and that I would surely have all sorts of invaluable
contacts for him. I told him about my old friend and
stringer Brick who might just be able to take a few
weeks off from his job as head of the U.S.–Turkish
Binational Center in Trabzon, and he was delighted.
Two thousand big ones in it for you, oldest pal. And
I'll want a feature on the Kurds. Sounds Kipling-
esque, no? I've already promised them you'll take it.

"I'm off to the cottage in Vermont for a few
weeks—will even be giving a talk at the alma mater
while I'm there. Claire won't be going. Did I mention
we were divorcing? Cheers.... Your Secret Admirer"

Jesus. "Did I mention we were divorcing?" That
was a zinger: the damnedest part of a damned odd
letter. Brick watched the two Turks slide through
the sand with the loaded-down donkey, making their
way through the first raindrops toward the packed
huts in the ravine by the Roman wall. Roger had
often made him feel like the donkey, too heavily
laden, losing half his momentum in the sand while
Roger moved lightly ahead of him....Roger and
Claire, both perfect in English woolens and soft Italian leather. He had been with Roger when he met
Claire at a talk on some sixtiesish thing like the
New Politics thirteen years ago. In front of the fireplace at the pleasant, tweedy, teacuppy campus, they
could have posed for a *New Yorker* advertisement.
Had time and chance happened so damn quickly to
that?

Roger had always seemed to be able to anticipate
the exact center of any political issue on campus and
place himself there; Brick had seen the sense of what
the radicals were saying in those days but couldn't

find a center anywhere in them. Roger had managed to hang on in graduate school until the thing in Viet Nam was over and he was safe from the draft. Brick had simply closed the door on the confusion and dropped out of college in his junior year. His father talked him into trying a semester at the American college in Mexico City—had hoped that would "pull Brick together." But he found less sense in that rich-kid's last-chance saloon than he had at Middlebury, and hitched north again. When the choice of the draft or Canada hit him, he joined the Air Force. Canada would have killed his old man. He figured he'd rather kill Vietnamese, though he knew it was a rotten choice to have to make. Then, while Roger spun off from the staff of the *Congressional Review* to found his own small Middle Eastern news syndicate, Brick finished his tour and came back to get done with college. A month after registering he was safely back in the Air Force. He had been as out of place on that postwar campus as a Studebaker at a new-car show.

This time his old man put in a word, and he was off to military language school in California, learning Russian. His father had gotten him an analyst's job at the National Security Agency for a time, but Brick asked to go back overseas. Washington overwhelmed him, so he had wound up here in Trabzon, at an Air Force Security Service listening post on the Hill of Martyrs overlooking the city. On clear winter mornings he could see the mountains of Russia across the sea and the clean snow on the Turkish mountains behind him. He decided he had found peace in a place that had changed less since Rome ruled it than Washington had since Truman. When the time for his discharge came, he decided he wouldn't make the same mistake twice. He took his discharge in Turkey.

By then he had enough contacts to get a work permit and sign on as a "local hire" to run the backwater U. S. Information Service Library and Binational Center in Trabzon. He learned fluent Turkish, read, hunted, and played chess with Father Dinato, the only other Westerner for three hundred miles, except for the two Jehovah's Witnesses who came through every six months. Roger began throwing him assignments as a stringer at about the same time he started leaving bright, blond children in Claire. He sent pictures. They bought a town house in Georgetown.

And now Roger and Claire were over, before he himself had even gotten started at anything, and with no explanation. And Roger was writing strange letters volunteering him for quack expeditions to Mount Ararat. What in hell was happening to the last of his certain certainties? He shoved back from his desk, all but feeling the warm rain that had begun in earnest now. Roger's letter was a signal for something. He had felt it coming for months, had sensed the peace turning into emptiness, had felt at last a gnawing Protestant guilt at being bored, had heard time juggling the books in the night while he slept. Always he had told himself that he had escaped from a world that didn't make sense, that he was as much of his generation as Hemingway and that crew had been of theirs when they ran away to Paris after their war. Except that he was tougher: he was here at the end of the earth, not in Paris. But no. They had *done* something, for Christ's sake. He hadn't escaped, he had fallen overboard.

"Ibrahim, *gel burya!*" He shouted for his Turkish

assistant director and stood watching the sea whip in the rain until Ibrahim's fixed smile and gold tooth appeared beside him.

"Efendim?" Ibrahim said, all Turkish deference and politeness.

"I have two weeks vacation left and six days sick leave coming. If I took it all at once, could you keep this damn place from sliding into the sea?"

Ibrahim's rodenty face brightened. He brushed his peroxided hair back militarily. Brick knew how he would relish the chance to play sultan in the office, and disliked him even more than usual. "With difficulty, but...yes, I think so."

"In the morning we'll go over the schedule." Brick forced a smile. "You may have to be brave and handle things."

One

Mustafa at the Özgur Hotel—the only one foreigners would be likely to be booked in—had them, reservations sent by a travel agency in London, Highgate Voyages. A double for Mr. and Mrs. Anthony Lo Presti, a single for Dr. Wolf Brenner, arriving the thirtieth on the weekly mail boat from Istanbul, the *Ege*.

Roger's letter had come four days ago. Ibrahim was briefed and ready. But as Brick stood on the dock and watched the passengers' gawking faces along the rails of the white ship, he realized he really was no more convinced now that he should go with these people than he had been on the day the letter came. He didn't know them from Adam's housecats. What would he do with the two thousand dollars when he had it? By now he had learned to live on his piddling salary as well as any Turk. Did he really want to go climbing around among the stone huts of that dry, cold mountain again? Hadn't once been enough—the time he had nearly lost a toe to frost-bite? Yet the letter had been a signal, that much he had grown more and more sure of. He would follow it up; he owed it that.

Taxis, donkey carts, and trucks fought for inches of dock space. The tugs and the ship hooted at each other like market women. Green-uniformed officials yelled hopelessly at the surging hawkers of pretzels, fruits, sugar cookies, American cigarettes, and blew their whistles against the families who elbowed their way close to the gangplank to beat out the porters who would grab their relatives' suitcases and bundles before they could be shoved away. Every week it was the same chaos, every week since Jason and the first Greeks had put in here to make off with the Golden Fleece. Still fleecing, Brick thought, pleased with the notion, as he tried to pick out the three archaeologists among the faces at the rail.

Brenner was easy. Roger had been right about the moustache. And with the moustache went a pair of glasses that made the eyes behind them look twice their size. Brick could see even from his safe watching place here below on a bale of hazelnuts that the eyes were never still. They darted like humming-birds from the lowering gangplank to the crowd to the town on the hill beyond the dock. Once it seemed to Brick they met his, but they didn't linger long enough for him to be sure. He had a feeling that they never would. Brenner's pointed face swept back from the eyes like a fox's. Above it, stiff graying hair fought the wind. Brick let his look travel to Brenner's paunch. Nope. That one would never make it to the glaciers of Ararat. A desk man, a data man.

The Lo Prestis weren't so easy. Lo Presti was an Italian name, so they would probably be dark. He glanced along the rail for a young dark-haired couple. Aside from those couples from the mountains—the women in their veils and striped tribal aprons—the Lo Prestis could have been half the couples on the ship. He leaned down to Ibrahim, who stood beside him, and pointed Brenner out. Ibrahim would see to it that the right porter got Brenner's bags. Their equipment could be sent for later when the deck cranes had brought it up from the hold.

Brenner and Ibrahim's porter, a short fierce man who had a death grip on Brenner's bag, were stumbling in silent, precarious battle toward the edge of the dock by the time Brick reached them. Brick took Brenner's arm. "Dr. Brenner? It's all right. I'm Brick Rustin. He's my man."

Brenner looked startled and tried to back away from Brick's grasp. The porter saw his advantage and gave the bag a final jerk. Brenner lost his grip and the porter, triumphant, ducked away into the squalling, shoving crowd.

"I don't care if he's your bloody father." Brenner's speech was a mixture of Vienna and Oxford and vexation. But the edge of his anger seemed softened with relief at seeing Brick's light-complexioned face among the milling moustaches of the Turks. "He's a villain. Where's he going?"

"My car." Brick pointed vaguely toward the Iran-bound sea-land containers his old Peugeot waited behind. "His name is Genghis."

"Hah! Naturally." Brenner smiled. "Will he make off with Tony and Livia's bags, too?"

13

Brick answered the smile. "If you'll point them out to me he will."

Brenner squinted at the gangplank. "There. The only white couple. Should be obvious."

Brick looked to the swaying steel stair. Yes, it was obvious after all. Tony Lo Presti's sandals and Levis and bush shirt made him stand out among the Turks like a man circled in an FBI photo. Brick didn't think he had been at the rail before. He bumped down the gangplank with two heavy bags, one ahead of him and one behind him on the narrow steps. His thinning hair clung to the sweat on his forehead. Brick placed him in his late thirties, slim but not skinny. The intensity with which he concentrated on keeping his balance knitted his dark brows into a V and gave him a slightly Mephistophelian look. Brick guessed it wasn't an unusual expression for him, and it was the one major flaw in a handsome face. But he should have no trouble on the mountain, if he had shoes other than those damn sandals.

If Brick decided to take these people to the mountain, that was.

When he saw the woman, Livia, Brick was certain she hadn't been at the rail before. He wouldn't have missed her. She wasn't beautiful in any way he would define the word. But still, no man would have missed her. Her thick hair, parted in the middle and as glistening black as an Arab's, hung in long waves that half hid her face. She was not thin: the loose khaki shirt she wore to hide what she probably thought were too heavy shoulders failed as a disguise. Nor did it hide the full breasts that gave the lie to the shape of the man's shirt, or the posed swimmer's movement that took her down the steps, carrying only her shoulder bag, behind her husband.

14

Robert Houston

As she came closer Brick saw that her face was too wide, her nose not quite straight. But somehow the combination of herself, the way she looked up through her hair, her half smile, her motion, wiped out details the way distance did to mountains. The effect was what mattered, and he thought it was breathtaking.

Tony didn't fight for his suitcases. With relief, he let the porter snatch them away and then took Livia's shoulder bag from her. "Brick Rustin, I assume." He put out his hand. The accent was pure North America. "The man with the famous name. Livia, brighten up. We're met!"

Livia took Brick's hand firmly, and her eyes focused on him as if he were the only other human being for miles. "Well met, too, I'd say." Her voice was deep, controlled. There was a heavy lacing of London in her own American accent.

Brick held on to her hand too long, and she took it back from him with a slight pressure. But her smile did not disappear.

"Would you like me to have my man go to your cabin for anything else?"

The voice that answered came from beside him. It was hollow, a little husky, and Turkish. "I'll have the rest seen to, Mr. Rustin, thank you. And if you'll please follow me to the hotel, my people will also see to the unloading from your car. I've dismissed the porter."

Brick turned, not startled as much as puzzled. The hollow voice came from a gaunt man with deep, sad eyes and a matching sad smile below his wide moustache. On the shoulders of his green, regular Turkish army dress uniform Brick made out a leafy crescent with a star between its tips, a major's insignia. Two

15

enlisted men in frayed wool uniforms and worn boots flanked him, M-16s slung over their shoulders.

"No need for that, Major," Brick said, careful to keep his tone neutral. He had never seen this kind of treatment before for anyone as clearly unofficial as these people were supposed to be. "No trouble."

"Major Özpamir is our military escort," Brenner said. His eyes bounced from Özpamir to Brick, worried. "He's been kind. We've put ourselves in his hands, Mr. Rustin."

"Well, then. I'm happy you're so well provided for." He held his hand out to the major. "Feel free to drop by the center while you're here."

Major Özpamir took his hand warmly. "It's not like that, what I imagine you're thinking. We are all pleased—the government is pleased—that you're joining Dr. Brenner's party. I take charge only because I have ways of...smoothing things. You understand Turkey, Mr. Rustin. No?"

"I haven't quite joined anything yet, Major."

Özpamir's sad eyes cut to Brenner a moment, then back to Brick. "I see. I had not understood that clearly."

"But you will join us," Livia said. There was a tag of forced cheer in her voice. "Roger promised, and we've counted so on you."

Brick turned to her. "You know Roger, then?"

"Oh, not really. Wolf—Dr. Brenner—told me that. I only met Roger briefly in London."

"In London?"

"Yes. We just left him there."

"Oh? I understood he was in Vermont."

"Well...perhaps he is now. He was on his way there, I believe. Yes. He was. Is there any gin we could talk this over over?" She threw her hair back

16

and reached for Tony's hand. "Western civilization *über alles,* you know."

"I've arranged for wine from the ship," Major Özpamir said, and laughed. "But gin? In Trabzon during Ramazan? With great fortune a little *raki,* perhaps. Gin and Western civilization both we left behind in Istanbul, I'm afraid, Mrs. Lo Presti." He laughed again absently, offered her his arm, and led the way toward a waiting staff car. The two men with M-16s shoved the crowd away in front of them. No one protested.

Brenner lowered his head and bulldogged after them. Tony's eyebrows reknit; he shrugged at Brick and sauntered behind Brenner. After he had gone a few feet, he turned. "What the hell can you do? See you at the hotel?"

Brick considered a moment. Livia was stepping into the staff car through the door Major Özpamir held for her. If this was all part of the signal, there was something in it he wasn't at all reading yet, as if he had picked up a novel with the wrong dust jacket. "Right. What the hell," he said. Even if it was the wrong book, somebody else's, it was at least a book, not the blank pages of his own life. One chapter, what the hell. He could always put it down.

From his stool in the dim corner of Atilla's hardware shop, Brick watched the woman, Livia, move slowly past the palms and pines and mimosa of Taksim Square. She was wildly out of place here in her man's shirt and pants. The bored, unshaven men who sat at the tables of the open-air teahouses under the trees—closed now for Ramazan—should have told her that with their stares. Atilla, one of his oldest friends in Trabzon, reached up with a ruler

17

and turned down the volume of a radio on a shelf above his head. He watched her, too, with his firm Asian eyes that some ancestor had left him as a remembrance of his homeland on the Mongolian steppe.

"That's the one?" he asked.

"That's the one."

"Does she know it's Ramazan? She shouldn't be out like that, without a man."

"She knows."

Atilla shrugged. The shrug said, Praise Allah that she's one of your people, not mine. Brick shrugged back, denying the kinship with such ungodly ways. Atilla nodded, accepting the denial, and began to slowly weave a pencil in and out among his fingers. From his stool in the corner Brick had watched that gesture through a thousand long afternoons.

"Next she'll light a cigarette," Atilla said. Brick had met Atilla his first week in Trabzon, nearly ten years before, when his widowed father ran this tiny crowded store on Shop Street. Atilla had worked on the American air base then, before the Cyprus war and the student riots had closed it down. He had taught Brick Turkish, had showed him how to pick wailing Turkish tunes on the long-necked *saz,* had taken him to the government whorehouse, and had poured him his first glass of *raki.* Then Atilla's father had declined in health, turned the shop over to Atilla, and died while Atilla first moved into his chair, then into his bedroom as he married and began to fill the rambling house on the mountainside with new children. But the shop hadn't changed. High rises had begun to litter the coast toward distant Istanbul, and factories had begun to obliterate it toward Russia, a few miles away. The bright striped wooden fishing boats were nearly all chopped up for firewood now, and the donkey carts that remained dodged shiny Ulusoy buses and Murat automobiles and Chrysler pickups. Brick knew of only a dozen *hamals,* the human donkeys with baskets on their backs, left in town. Women were beginning to wear lipstick; a few even worked. Allah was vanishing back up into the mountains he came from, toward Iran and Arabia. Not long now, the old people said, until Trabzon would be as lost and unholy as Istanbul. Brick agreed, and decided the stool was as safe a place to watch it from as any. Or to watch the other from, the chaos that the Turks lived in fear of that could sweep down on them from Iran, beyond the mountains. As much as they embraced their religion, they knew there was something to fear in it, too.

Livia paused, pulled a cigarette from her bag, and lit it. "Allah, Allah," Atilla murmured. A *hamal* with his huge basket strapped to his back watched her, too, from a corner of the square. When she took the first puff from her cigarette, he spit. Brick had never seen him before. The man didn't take his eyes from Livia.

"So are you going with them?" Atilla asked.

"I don't know."

"What have they told you?"

"Not much. Last night we went over their maps. For archaeologists they know damn little about them."

"That's why they need you."

"Maybe. The officer says he's going only as far as the foot of the mountain, to Doğubeyazit, with them. Says the last thing they need among the Kurds is a Turkish soldier."

Atilla nodded slowly. "The Kurds would arrange

19

an avalanche for the lot of you. If there were such
things as Kurds." Brick waited patiently. Atilla took
his politics seriously, and Brick had learned to nod
no matter what outrageousness Atilla lectured him
with. It was one of the unspoken understandings of
their friendship. "In Turkey now, there are only
Turks. If there was once a Kurdistan, it is now just
eastern Turkey. If there were Kurds, they're now
mountain Turks."

Brick watched Livia move with her swimmer's
motion through the traffic that squealed around the
square on the cobbles. The *hamal* still hadn't taken
his eyes off her. So, Brick thought. Click! Snap your
fingers and the Kurds went away. He had heard
Atilla's argument before: it was the official Turkish
one. Simply redraw the maps and rewrite the history
books, and no more problem. Except that the Kurds
didn't look at the maps or read the history books.
They went on revolting now as they had for the past
four hundred years.

Livia stopped in front of a small *kebap* restaurant
catty-corner from the square. She stood back from
it a moment, scanning the windows as if she expected
to find a menu posted. Brick smiled. No, lady, it
wasn't a Paris boulevard cafe. Then she looked up
and down the street as if she were expecting someone
to come along and tell her if she should go in or not.
On the corner of the square, the *hamal* adjusted his
basket, threw his shoulders forward for balance, and
stepped off into the traffic. He moved with the flat-
footed pace of a man who, from living like a mule,
has learned its deliberateness. His shaven head set
his direction for the restaurant. Livia went in.

Atilla nodded toward the restaurant. "Namik's
got every fundamentalist in the province down on

him. He says he'll keep his restaurant open when he damn well wants to, Ramazan or not. Says that leftist outfit he belongs to, that Dev Yol, will look after him. What do you think?"

Brick didn't think. He watched. The *hamal* stopped by the plate glass of the restaurant and peered in. Then he gave the sidewalk a quick check in either direction. Slowly he bent and slipped his long basket off his shoulders and leaned it against the building. Then he reached inside a moment. When he straightened up, he had taken nothing out of the basket. Again he looked up and down the street. He backed away from the basket a few paces, turned and walked to the corner. As he rounded the corner he broke into a run.

"Christ!" Brick said. He vaulted Atilla's counter. A display of power-saw blades went ringing out onto the street ahead of him. An old man with a cane and the skull cap that advertised he had been to Mecca toppled as Brick glanced off him. Brick threw himself past the taillights of a swerving *dolmuş* collective taxi and caught a glimpse of Atilla at his heels. A quick fantasy of his high school track coach cheering him over hurdles leapt through his mind as he spun a lemonade seller into a vegetable vendor's cart.

Livia sat in a folding chair stubbing her cigarette out and trying to make sense of the handwritten menu when Brick burst through the door. She opened her mouth for a question that never came out. Brick took her arm and pulled. She resisted. "God, Brick, what—"

Whether he grabbed her hair from fear or judgment he wasn't sure. He only knew that she had to move and not talk. She screamed and stumbled from her chair. The table skittered across the floor and her water glass smashed. Atilla was in the restaurant shouting for everyone to get out. The waiter and his only other customer slammed past Brick and Livia. Beyond Livia, Brick could see Namik, the restaurant's fat owner, standing dumbfounded beside his rotating *döner kebap* spit with its layers of smoking lamb, wiping his hands on his apron.

At the door Brick let go of Livia's hair and shoved her ahead of him. She fought him and he wrestled her down behind the vegetable vendor's cart. She kicked at him. Atilla slid to the cobbles beside them, then threw his body over hers.

When the shock of the explosion hit the cart, tomatoes, cantaloupes, watermelons cascaded over them and past them into the street. A watermelon smashed against the side of Brick's face, like a blocked punt. He felt himself rolling, snatching at things that wouldn't stay still. His head buzzed, and the world swirled past him in slow motion. Then there was a moment of shattering near-silence as slivers of glass and pieces of stone rained clattering around them.

When Brick raised his head he saw a traffic cop standing in the middle of the street, stunned and staring at a Renault rocking on its side in front of the restaurant. Beyond the Renault, the front of the restaurant gaped, open and bare. Inside, rafters swung down into the emptiness. Chairs, tables, counter, all were gone. And Namik, fat Namik, was gone.

Atilla rolled off Livia. She didn't raise her head, and Brick could see her jerking with sobs. He crawled to her, touched her shoulder and said her name.

"Where's Tony?" she wept into her shirtsleeve. "I want my husband!"

22

"I'll go," Atilla said in English.

"They know we're here," Livia said and rolled over, her eyes wild. "My God, they know we're here."

Brick squeezed her shoulder. "Who knows you're here, Livia? That explosion had nothing to do with you."

"Yes it *did*."

"It was the goddamn rightists. I swear to you."

"Oh, Christ, oh, Christ," she said and pushed to her feet. "Tony!"

Brick looked behind him. Tony Lo Presti and Atilla wove running through the tables in the square. Livia ran to meet Tony and buried herself in him. People swarmed into the smoking restaurant now. A barefoot kid ducked out of it with a handful of *döner kebap*. Yes, Brick thought, yes. So this was his peace, his place where time would leave him alone. It wasn't signals he was getting: it was orders.

Tony Lo Presti caught up with him outside the Binational Center, just as Brick was turning into the carved stone Byzantine doorway beneath the crossed Turkish and U. S. flags. Tony had been running, still wearing those damn sandals.

"Rustin!" he shouted.

Brick turned slowly, dabbing at the sticky watermelon juice in his hair with Atilla's handkerchief. How in hell could he be jealous of a woman's own husband, especially a woman he had known since only yesterday? He set his face in as friendly an expression as he could muster.

"Jesus, Rustin. Thank you. I feel like an ass not being able to say more than that."

Brick let his hand be shaken, not disliking the man, really. "Fine. Don't say anything, then. It's OK."

"She's totally freaked, you know."

"I figured that."

"I mean, she's saying things that don't make sense even to me."

"Who knows you're here, *ağabey?*"

"Oh...well, lots of people."

"That's not what I mean."

"I'm sorry, then I don't know what you do mean. What did Livia say?"

Brick opened the door and motioned Tony inside. Ibrahim was vanishing down the hallway as they stepped in. "He listens. To everything. Damned if I know what he does with it. It's in the genes."

Tony gave a short, nervous laugh. Brick offered him a chair in his office, a moldering yellow room with slick mohair couches, bookshelves, and a desk the Russians had left behind a hundred years before. "We need you, Rustin," Tony said. "We're babes in the wood here. You just saw that."

"How about your army officer?"

"Some things he just can't—or won't—explain. Cultural gap, I suppose."

"You picked a hell of a time for an Ark hunt." From his desk he took the last bottle of the case of Scotch he had had a trucker smuggle in to him from Iran before the revolution. "Martial law here, a lunatic in Iran, the Soviets paranoid, everything from here to India going to hell."

Tony held his palm up in a kind of shrug. "When it's already gone to hell, it'll be worse."

Brick sat. He poured them both a shot of Scotch in Turkish tea glasses. "Granted. Are you leveling with me, Lo Presti? You're really an archaeologist?"

"Not much of one. I minored in it at McGill. Brenner's the man. He's worked at Masada, Chan Chan,

24

Altun Ha...everywhere. I raise money, and Livia's
been playing with graduate work in archaeology at
Cambridge. I'm along for the ride. I'll write a report
and scrounge more money for a full expedition if this
pans out."

"How come?"

"I love my wife. And I got tired of making money
publishing Canadian cookbooks."

"And her? Why this Ark business?"

"Brenner's idea. She worked with him in England.
And, well, she's Jewish, you know. Stout Zionist parents who'd love to see the Ark stuff add up. They
came out of the Warsaw ghetto and figure they owe
something." He took a sip of his Scotch. "Maybe they
do."

Brick studied him, adding things up himself. The
need for Russian, the tight military escort, Livia's
hysteria—all of it could be explained. He could accept that, or he could sit here all afternoon giving
this man who seemed harmless a third degree, which
wasn't to his liking in any case. One thing he had
come out of Air Force intelligence with was the
knowledge that big pictures grew out of little pieces,
but that to make a picture out of too few pieces could
be deadly. If he was going to get out of here, ever,
he had to learn to take chances again. He may not
have decided he did want to leave for good, but he
was sure he wanted to know he was still able to
choose.

And then there was the final, most persuasive
argument. He trusted Roger.

"I know what you're thinking," Tony said.

"A hundred lira says you don't."

"You're remembering that American expedition,
the phony one. Hell, Brick, do I look like a cloak-

and-dagger type? Do any of us? Brenner's a poor shmuck who wants to play Schliemann at Troy and make the big discovery. My wife's a romantic. And me? I love my wife."

"You said that."

"Often," Tony said, the Mephistophelian look creeping back over his face in spite of his slight smile. "Will you come? I'll make it three thousand."

Brick let the Scotch settle into a warm spot in his stomach, to spread its well-being through his body. To hell with the money. He took a deep breath and held it, then let it out in a long sigh. "Sure. Why not?" he said. Then he raised his voice and said to the closed door, "Ibrahim, you get that? It's all yours!"

The clang of a coppersmith's hammer in the bazaar followed Brick along the street like an artillery barrage, and his hangover fuzzed the world like the morning mist that crept up between the stone buildings around him. The jostling crowds in the twisting, cobbled street were subdued today, and yesterday's bombing had shut the doors to even the clandestine teahouses. The military authorities, themselves sick of it all, had agreed to allow a silent protest march through town in the afternoon. They, Brick, and everyone else knew that it could turn into more than that. The soldiers were already stationing themselves at street corners. Tension leapt from face to face in the crowd like electric sparks.

Today they were going. Three jeeps—private, rented ones—in a convoy. Nothing military would do, nothing to spook the Kurds. Brick and Tony Lo Presti had taken the Scotch back to the dismally modern Hotel Özgur last night to seal the bargain.

Livia, recovered but shaky still, and Brenner had joined them. Major Özpamir, whom Livia had taken to calling Erkut after her second Scotch, stayed with them only long enough to agree on a schedule, then left for the military base on the Hill of Martyrs. In spite of their initial run-in, there was a kindness, an intelligence in his face that Brick liked, something oddly unmilitary that didn't go with his perfectly tailored uniform. Another piece to throw into the jigsaw bin, he thought. When his head was unfuzzed, he would deal with that, too.

Livia and Brenner had given up after dinner. Brick took Tony on a tour of the dim streets of the old city, full as a carnival after dark now because of Ramazan. Nothing by mouth during the day, the Prophet's prescription ran. But when the old Russian cannon on the Hill of Martyrs boomed at the exact second of sundown, the gorging began. Hot stuffed peppers, *shish kebap,* ground lamb *köfte,* fresh, eggy yellow pita bread, *döner kebap,* steaming ears of corn, pilaf, fluffy *laz börek* pastries, all the things a hungry imagination dreamed of during the day showed up on tables and menus after dark. Once at sundown, then again for the midnight meal. And in between those times, after prayers, the clubs and teahouses filled with men whose hands kept the backgammon dice and chips clicking with the constant swift clatter of rain on a tin roof. Brick had talked Mustafa, the hotelkeeper, out of a bottle of licorishy *Yeni Raki*—tiger milk, the GIs had called it. He and Tony had pitched the empty bottle off the dusty promenade into the dark sea near midnight. They had meant to last through the midnight meal, but failed. Tony threw up on the climb back to the hotel.

Just after daylight, Brick had stumbled out of bed and managed to stuff a week's supply of jeans and socks and shirts into a backpack. The sleeping bag, parka, insulated underwear, and climbing gear he had bribed his way in with from London two years ago, he would carry separately for now. Brenner had assured him they had the rest—the tents and stoves and mess gear.

The jeeps idled in front of the hotel. Brick knew that if he weren't so unsteady, he might well find the courage to change his mind again and go back to bed yet. Only a few taxi drivers sat at the stands in their huge, ancient Chevrolets yet. The smells of Trabzon—faint urine, black tobacco, cement, the sea—hung lightly in the air. The hotel doorman was asleep on his feet. Behind him, Tony stood miserable and useless. Major Özpamir crisply directed the loading of the jeeps, one piled with crates and canvas bags, the other two for the climbing party. Brick dropped his gear beside the supply jeep. Özpamir would drive one jeep; Brick had agreed to drive another. Özpamir's men would handle the supply jeep. By tonight, they would make the stone garrison city of Erzurum, on the cold plateau. By the next night, dry, windswept Doğubeyazit at the foot of Ararat, or Ağridağ as the Turks called it. From Doğubeyazit, there were only three places to go: through the border crossing into Iran, over the mountain passes into the Soviet Union, or upward to the glaciers of Ararat. Brick's mistreated stomach churned at the alternatives.

Brenner, eyes darting, bounded out of the hotel. "Ah, Brick," he bubbled. Brick was sure his cheer was malevolent. "Had your breakfast yet? Coffee?"

Brick swallowed. "Neither."

"We have Nescafé. Have a cup. Can you imagine, a coffee shortage in Turkey of all places?"

Brick nodded and stepped inside the hotel. Or tried to. A soldier blocked him with an M-16. Christ! The lobby was full of them. Brick turned to Major Özpamir. Now he saw that beyond Özpamir, in the street and on the stone wall along the square, nearly a score more soldiers were ranged. He hadn't noticed them in his hangover fog before. Özpamir flicked his hand to the soldier to let Brick pass. "Precautions," he said.

"Against what?"

Özpamir nodded toward the street by the square where the bombed restaurant gaped.

"Why here?" Brick said.

"We are particular of foreigners, Mr. Rustin. You know Turkish hospitality." He smiled. Brick was in no mood to answer the smile. He was on the verge of turning around to leave when Tony took his arm unhappily to lead him into the bar for coffee. Brick let him, trying not to concentrate on the gnawing sense that he should run, that the stack of pieces was growing high enough for him to begin to put them together into a picture that was terribly, wrenchingly out of focus.

Half an hour later, it didn't matter. Major Özpamir, in civilian clothes, eased his jeep out into the growing morning traffic ahead of Brick's. Brenner, his attention buried in guidebooks, sat beside him. Brick tested the unfamiliar clutch and, with a jerk, dodged a Murat sedan to hug Özpamir's taillights. Tony moaned in the backseat. Livia turned in the seat next to Brick and absently rested her hand on Tony's knee. As before, she wore a man's fatigue shirt and jeans, though this morning her cascading hair was held back by a pale yellow scarf. In spite of himself, Brick's glance fell momentarily on her hand. The sight of her thin gold watch, painfully feminine against the dark skin and shirt cuff, slashed him with jealousy. He hoped neither of them had seen him. He checked the rearview mirror for the supply jeep. It cut off a bus to swing in behind them, two of Özpamir's men in civilian clothes, rifles hidden, jockeying it.

As they worked past the harbor, heading toward the brutal road that would take them through the mountains to the interior, Livia eased her hand away from Tony's knee. Tony had made a pillow out of his parka and stretched out on the seat. His mouth was open, and he was breathing heavily. Livia dug a *Samsun* cigarette out of her shirt pocket. "You seem to be in better shape," she said to Brick. She smiled and looked at Tony.

"I'm a veteran," he said. "Besides, a little goat cheese and black olives for breakfast does wonders." He smiled back.

"Ugh." She made a face. "My hair hurts today, you know."

"Sorry," he said.

"God, don't be. I think I'm still a little in shock."

"You have a right." In the jeep ahead, Brenner's attention had left his guidebooks. His eyes leapt ahead, to the side, behind him, as if only his constant vigilance kept the world around him intact.

"No. I said some stupid things." She waited for Brick to follow up, giving him an opening if he wanted it. He concentrated on easing the jeep around a Mercedes truck loading tea leaves from a small plantation on the hillside. If he asked questions, he might get answers, answers he didn't want to know

now. After a time, she went on. "I don't really even know what all that was about."

"Neither does the government. The right wants Turkey to be another Iran. The left wants it to be another Soviet Union. Most people want it to be Turkey and try to keep their heads down when the right and left start blowing each other up. You didn't know about the head-down part, that's all."

"It's really all that simple?"

"No."

"And you? How do you feel?"

"It should be Turkey. The Turks are good people."

She held her cigarette up so that the wind over the windshield blew the ashes off. "A lot of people don't think that these days."

"A lot of people don't understand them. If you know how to keep from crossing them, they can be the kindest people I know. They're a little like the Irish that way."

"And if you cross them?"

"Ask the Armenians. Or the Greeks. Or the Kurds."

"I didn't think they'd left any Armenians to ask, back when they decided to exterminate them."

"Not many." He shrugged. "I don't excuse genocide. But I can't hate the Turks. That was half a century ago."

She stubbed her cigarette on the floor of the jeep. "I suppose I should try to understand that. I'm Jewish. So's Dr. Brenner. They say we shouldn't hate Germans these days."

"Do you?"

She stared straight ahead through the windshield. "Not the ones I know. Some of the money for this expedition is German."

"And you'll find Noah's Ark on Mount Ararat with it." He was conscious of the edge of sarcasm in his voice. If she too was conscious of it, she was beyond it. Her attention was fixed on Brenner's swiveling head in the jeep in front.

"We'll find...something on Mount Ararat. Yes." She turned abruptly and touched Brick's arm. "I'm glad you came, Brick. I think you're a decent man."

Brick glanced in the rearview mirror at Tony, who stirred as they turned off onto the collapsing road by the river that led up into the dark green of the mountains.

"And Tony's a decent man," she said. "God knows why he's here at all."

"He says he loves you."

"Yes," she said flatly. "He does. Sometimes I wish he loved me less. It might be better for both of us."

The road climbed slowly at first, skirting the half-finished bridge of the new highway to Iran that the government dreamed of before it ran out of money. Trabzon dropped away almost immediately, and the forest began. Now and again they slowed through a village that clung to the steepening banks of the river among the trees, or dodged sheep from some farmhouse that sat behind its cornfields where the land flattened for a few kilometers into a valley. Once Livia caught her breath at the sight of a shepherd boy on a hillside. The boy sat playing a high-pitched, sad tune on a set of panpipes. At a stream near him a veiled girl in the bright apron and shawl of her village stood with water jugs balanced at the ends of a pole over her shoulders, head down, rapt. As they eased over the stone bridge across the stream, they passed so close that Brick could see the girl trembling.

Robert Houston

Then the river was further below them, frothing from rapids, and the road narrowed and curved with the convolutions of the mountainside. Across the river valley now, village mosques sent their minarets up from the mimosa and willow and hazelnut trees like bare pine trunks. Here and there, a ruined Byzantine church sat alone on a hilltop. Cleared corn and vegetable fields rose up impossible slopes into mist. As the morning deepened, the mist retreated higher and higher ahead of them into the mountains. The air grew no warmer, and the smell of woodsmoke signaled the villages they approached now. This was the country of the whistlers, villagers who spoke to one another across the valley not with yodels, but with an ancient language of whistling.

Tony slept on. Livia and Brick talked little. He told her about the caravan road on the opposite mountainside and pointed out the remains of it. Xenophon's Ten Thousand had retreated along it once, and for millennia it had carried the wealth of Persia and Armenia and Georgia on slow camels to the Greek, then Roman, then Ottoman ships at Trabzon. Vines grew over its stone guardhouses now, and it had crumbled to a vanishing dent along the cliffs.

She asked him where he was from, why he was in Trabzon. He told her, as briefly as possible. As he talked, he felt again that sense she had given him on the dock that he was the only human being for miles. He asked her about her own background, and she gave it to him as sketchily as he had given her his. Jewish immigrant parents in Toronto, who had taken a small stake from a cousin there and turned it into a string of men's shops, then apartment buildings, then knitting mills in Colombia, then into

33

semiretirement with a condo in the Virgin Islands and a flat in London. She met Tony at McGill in Montreal, and after a stint on a kibbutz in Israel came marriage and dabbling in half a dozen "careers," she called them with a guarded smile. Her Zionist parents had fought the marriage, but at last had decided to be "modern" and bless it. All the time she talked, she kept glancing at Tony as if making sure he wasn't listening.

He wasn't. He slept on even as Major Özpamir's jeep swerved to a stop by a roadside fountain. Brick looked to Livia, puzzled, and pulled in behind. Livia kept her eyes on Özpamir. Özpamir got out of his jeep with a folding tin cup, smiled at Brick, and motioned toward the fountain. "Thirsty?" he asked cheerfully. *"Su var.* There's water."

"God, yes," Brick said. His mouth still felt as if a cat had slept in it. He swung out of the jeep and looked to Tony. "Is he thirsty?" he asked Livia.

"No," she said, her voice low and tight. Brick glanced around them. Nothing moved except the boughs on the great slouching spruces on the mountainside, shifting in the wind. "Let him sleep." From the fountain no different from the hundreds of others along Turkey's roads, steps cut into the rock led upward into the spruces. From far away in the forest, Brick heard the steady rhythm of a woodcutter's axe, and water splashed gently into the marble basin of the fountain. The supply jeep behind them gurgled as its motor died. The quiet, after the noise of the road since early morning, was overwhelming.

Livia climbed out after Brick and took the cup full of icy water Özpamir offered her. As she drank, she followed Özpamir's eyes to the steps, whose edges were chipped and rounded with time. Even Brenner's

incessantly moving eyes were still now, watching
the steps as if he were waiting for the mountainside
to open up behind them. Özpamir seemed to become
aware of the tense silence first, and broke it. "Want
to stretch your legs?" he asked Brick. "We're ahead
of schedule a bit."

"I don't mind," Brick said.

Brenner took a few steps ahead up the road, then
crossed it to look into the valley below. "Magnificent!" he said. "Come look."

Brick reached to help Livia past the mud that
spread from the overflowing fountain. Her hand was
cold, rigid. He felt his own body stiffen in response.
"What the hell's happening?" he asked.

"Nothing," she said. "Look at the view."

Below them, when they joined Brenner, the river
valley fell away so sharply that it appeared as if each
tree grew from the top branches of the ones below
it. They had left the mimosa and hardwoods now,
and were into the land of the spruce and the pine.
The stream was a bright glinting string in the noon
sun a thousand feet or more beneath them. The high
peaked roofs of weathered wooden houses showed
here and there among the spruces far across the valley. At the end of a path down the mountainside,
Brick thought he could make out a swinging bridge
across the stream.

"It's like the Alps must have been a hundred years
ago," Livia said quietly, tension still coloring her
voice.

"What a waste of good scenery," Brenner said.
"With a resort maybe, a casino..."

Brick turned to the sound of the footsteps even
before the others did. There was a clatter of pebbles
on the rock stairs, then a softer thud of boots. He

35

saw first the boots coming from the undergrowth beside the stairs, then the man: slim, in wrinkled gray trousers, with a black wool overcoat slung over his shoulders. With one hand he held the strap of the worn long rifle that hung across his back. With the other, he steadied himself on the spruce boughs.

And from his coiled, flat turban, which allowed one end of the cloth to hang beside his head like a mortarboard tassel, straight blond hair poked. No one spoke to him as he descended. Brick started back across the road, but Livia tightened her grip on his hand. The man glanced at the two soldiers in the supply jeep and then raised his hand in greeting to Major Özpamir. Brick saw his blue eyes then, and heard the accent that confirmed what he had suspected when he saw the blond hair. *"Ahvet,"* the man answered to something Özpamir greeted him with. *Ahvet,* "yes," not *evet.* The accent was unmistakable. It was Kurdish.

The man and Özpamir both turned their back to the others and moved a few paces ahead of Özpamir's jeep. They spoke rapidly in Turkish. "What are they saying?" Livia whispered to him.

"I can't make it out. Damn it, Brenner, who the hell is that man?"

Brenner's fixed, bland smile didn't wilt. "A friend of our guide," he said.

"Crap."

After a moment, Özpamir glanced over his shoulder at the supply jeep. The Kurd kept up his rapid speech. Özpamir nodded now and again. The door on the passenger's side of the supply jeep clicked open. The squat soldier who sat next to it swung a leg out and rested it on the ground. Brick had only gotten a quick look at him before they left—glasses, mous-

tacheless, sergeant's stripes until he changed from
his uniform. He reached behind him in the jeep. His
eyes were on the Kurd. Brick saw the muzzle of his
rifle move smoothly up from the backseat just as the
man's partner, the driver, did. Özpamir turned and,
with the Kurd, walked back toward the supply jeep.
The rifle nosed further out.

"Major!" the driver shouted and slammed his arm
down on the rifle. Özpamir and the Kurd threw
themselves behind Brick's jeep. As they did, the soldier with the rifle flung his other leg from the jeep,
rolled, and hit the road at a crouch, running. His
partner snatched up the M-16 he dropped.

"Chabuk!" Özpamir shouted. "Quickly!" The driver
of the supply jeep swung around to try to sight over
the piled supplies behind him. His foot caught on the
gearshift. *"Chabuk!"* Özpamir shouted again. Then,
"Don't kill him."

The Kurd's long rifle came down in an arc over
the fender of Brick's jeep. The Kurd knelt behind it,
sighting for only a piece of a second after the rifle
was in position. It seemed to Brick in the mountain
silence that the sound of the shot blasted off the rock
face beside him loud as a field gun.

The running man straightened a moment, half
turned, looked back toward the jeeps. As his leg gave
out he screamed. Özpamir and the Kurd and the
other soldier broke for him. Brick saw the bloodstain
on the man's leg, just below his hip, grow as the man
struggled to rise. His mouth was open and tag ends
of screams kept finding their way out. He gained his
balance, turned, and lurched toward the edge of the
road by the valley. His partner reached him first.

But not soon enough. As his partner touched him,
the man threw himself forward one last time. His

37

balance went. He clutched for a cement milepost,
held it a moment, and collapsed toward the edge of
the road. His partner dove for him. The man slipped
away from him, over the edge, like a bag of sand.
Brick ran after Özpamir. From the corner of his eye,
he saw the man slam into an outcropping fifty feet
below him and hurtle outward over the emptiness
of the valley like a skydiver. When he hit the trees
a hundred feet below that, he vanished as completely
as if he had gone into the dark green waters of a sea.

Brick pulled up short, halfway between Özpamir's
group and Brenner's. He listened. There was not
even a sound of wind. Then he heard a truck at great
distance winding down its gears. He looked toward
the jeeps. Tony, blinking, dangled his head over the
backseat. His eyes met Brick's.

"Jesus Christ," he said.

Brick heard a sharp click behind him. Özpamir
was approaching him, a just-cocked .45 officer's automatic pistol in his hand. "We'll have to move now,"
he said in Turkish. "I don't want that truck to pass
us here. I'm sorry."

"You're going to leave him down there?" Brick
said.

"I'll send a detail from Erzurum. Are you willing
to keep driving?"

Brick dropped his eyes to the .45. "No explanation?"

"I'm sorry. Will you drive? I assume Lo Presti
knows how to handle a jeep, so you don't have to."

The nausea Brick had felt when he got out of bed
washed over him again. Even in Viet Nam, he had
been far enough behind the lines that the dead he
saw were hidden in body bags. Once he had seen a
mad dog shot in Trabzon; and he had hunted since

childhood. But this...? The man had to be dead down there. He had to be. But if he wasn't? He could even be conscious, waiting. They had killed even the mad dog quickly. Even the wounded boars he hunted in these mountains he tracked to make sure they weren't suffering.

"I couldn't convince you to leave me here, too."

"No." The truck whined closer. Brick glanced over his shoulder at Livia and Brenner. Livia looked away. Brenner looked everywhere.

"Then I'll drive."

At the jeep, Özpamir handed the pistol to Tony. Tony took it silently. He checked it to see that it was cocked; it wasn't a stranger to him. Livia took the backseat this time. The Kurd leaned over to say a last thing to Özpamir, then trotted to the stone steps. He was halfway up them by the time Brick pulled out behind Özpamir. "He's a long way from home," Brick said to Tony.

"We'll find him," Tony said.

Brick's nausea stilled as the wind slapped at him from around the windshield. What took its place was less physical, but more powerful. It was a mixture of things: anger, an odd excitement, and if he was honest, fear.

"Do I get to know where we're really going?" he asked Tony.

"Ararat," Tony said. "That's the truth."

"Come on, Tony,"

"Please, Brick. Not now. We'll talk in Erzurum, I hope."

"You hope."

"Yes. I sincerely hope."

Özpamir's jeep was vanishing now into puffs of mist. Soon the fog would swallow them completely.

Then they would break through the pass of Zigana, and the mist and the forest would disappear together there, two miles up. Delicate pines would take over in the valleys, but the mountainsides would bear only scrub bushes and dry grasses. And as they descended onto the plateau, the steppe and the desert would fight each other for the land. Beyond Giresun they would climb once again through the even higher pass of Kop, where the snows lingered until June. Then Erzurum. Then Kurdistan, far from the rains of the Black Sea, far more primitive and distant from the civilization these people in the jeep knew than even these misty stone and wood villages they bumped through now. And what in hell would they do there?

And yet, and yet. The jeep plunged into a bank of fog. The trees and cliffs vanished. His excitement quickened.

Erzurum. Haphazard. Cold stone in the gray light of evening. At the outskirts, muddy, twisted streets churned by endless herds of sheep. Crumbling wooden shops whose fronts were hung with a hundred soft shades of wool. Coughing trucks with their windshields tasseled and the ornate letters of *Mashallah,* God Bless, on their cabs to protect them from the evils of the road and other drivers. Cheerless apartment buildings, snap-brim caps and baggy black pants and thick moustaches like uniforms. Hurrying, head-down women in black robes. Flitting girls in patched red-striped aprons and bright, bangled head scarves and veils and plastic shoes. And soldiers. A frontier garrison city against the barbarians for the Romans; a frontier and a garrison still. Beyond here, Brick knew, stretched Kurdistan, the land that didn't exist.

There were thick hunks of bread and goat cheese and boiled eggs and syrupy cherry preserves for supper, eaten alone in Brick's underlit hotel room with the chill of the drizzly mountain night seeping through the window that wouldn't close. The sheets on his bed were gray and unchanged, the toilet down the hall clogged and unflushable. Outside, truckers clustered around the bare bulb of a newsstand, their coat collars turned up, drinking tea from delicate glasses.

No one guarded him. Why should they? Where would he go? To the authorities? Major Erkut Özpamir *was* the authorities. Should he run? At the end of the road ahead lay Iran. Behind him roadblocks would stop him before he even got out of sight of the lights of the city. And on all sides rose the bare mountain wastes where the howls of wolves still kept the night awake.

He handed the bellboy, a smiling dwarf, the supper tray at the door of his room. The hallway was empty, its peeling, fly-spotted gray paint soaking up the dim light from the bulb at the head of the stairs. From downstairs he heard the television testing its lungs for the night. He recognized the theme from *Dallas,* echoing up the stairs like a communication from another planet. Hell shit piss damn. He wanted company. He didn't care what kinds of lunatics the others were. He walked the dozen paces to Tony and Livia's room and knocked. They owed him an explanation: whatever else, they damn well owed him that.

Behind Tony, as the cracked door swung open, Brick saw Livia, Brenner, and Özpamir staring at

41

him as if he were a schoolboy who had walked un-
announced into a teachers' meeting. Özpamir sat in
the room's chair. Livia and Brenner sprawled on opposite beds. Livia's eyes were puffy, as if she had
been crying.

"Brick!" Tony's embarrassment made him appear
silly.

"We were just talking about you. Come in," Brenner said. Brick had decided there was something
inhuman about his constant, Viennese-accented
cheer. Brick stepped past Tony, who closed the door
behind him, then leaned against it. "Take a seat, if
you can see to," Brenner went on. "Can you imagine—there's a light-bulb shortage here, too?"

Brick sat stiffly on the side of the bed beside Livia.
She studied her hands. Özpamir nodded at him. "Did
you have a good dinner?" he asked.

"Delightful."

"Well, Brick, I'm glad you came by," Brenner began, as if he were a loan officer in a bank. "As I said,
we were just talking about you. And you'll be pleased
to know we've reached a decision."

"Delightful."

"You want an explanation of things. Am I correct?"

"I want an explanation of things."

"Of course you do! Major?" He looked to Özpamir.

Özpamir sat forward to pull a wallet from his back
pocket. He spoke in Turkish. "I want to apologize to
you, Brick. To be honest, I'd never have had you here
to begin with. I don't think you're necessary. But
this was all arranged weeks ago, when my friends
here were afraid they would have...communication
problems when they came to Turkey. But you *are*
here, and I'm afraid there's nothing to be done to

42

change that." He handed Brick his open wallet. In it, facing Brick through a plastic window, was an I.D. card with Özpamir's picture on it. The card said he was Major Erkut Özpamir, of Milli Istihbarat Teskilati. MIT, the "National Information Organization." But it wasn't really that at all. Brick knew, as anybody in Turkey over the age of six knew, what MIT meant. Turkish Internal Security, the secret police.

Brick worked hard at keeping his eyes and hand steady as he handed Özpamir his wallet back. He had seen the MIT before, back in his Air Force days. They would come through the base every few months, inspecting. Sometimes in civilian clothes, sometimes in uniform. But always very serious, very efficient, very cold. Later, he had found out that his friend who ran the NCO club, a man whose wedding he had gone to, was an MIT plant. He realized then that the whole elaborate American security system was a children's password game compared to the MIT's. Whatever else he may have thought about them, one thing above all stood out: only a fool wouldn't respect them.

"How much do you know about the Kurdish problem?" Özpamir asked, switching to his impeccable English as he folded his wallet.

"Is it a Kurdish problem—or a Turkish problem?"

"Both," Özpamir said. He slipped his wallet back into his pocket and sat back into the torn plastic upholstery of the chair. He looked past Brick, searching into the dark corners of the room for a way to put things. Brick could imagine him more at home in a seminar room at Istanbul University than in this dingy hole. "We have fought the Kurds, yes—nearly all of us in the Middle East have fought the

43

Kurds at one time or another. Even the Babylonians did, if you believe some historians. And it is true that we have probably killed many more of them than they have of us. That, I'm afraid, is inevitable. They are weak, we are strong, and we surround them. You should understand that, Brick."

"I should?"

Özpamir shrugged. "You probably think I mean Viet Nam. I don't. I mean the Apaches, the Cherokees, the Choctaw."

"Touché."

"I don't intend to insult you by giving you a history that you no doubt already know. What I want to say is a matter of perspective, of asking you to look at something through different eyes for a moment. The Kurds are a romantic people, yes. They refuse to assimilate. They speak a language that is probably the closest thing to Sanskrit we have left. They are full of legends, are wonderful horsemen, foolish but magnificent fighters. I admire them, whether you believe me or not. But they do refuse to assimilate, which I realize is part of their attractiveness to you people in the West. They may live in Iran, Iraq, Turkey, even some of them in the Soviet Union. But except for the Soviet ones, they refuse to be part of any country. They want their own—a homeland— like the Jews, which makes them even more attractive to you. After World War II, your Atlantic Charter supported that notion, back when you were still of the opinion you could make the world reasonable. For a short time, you even allowed a Kurdish Republic."

Brick wondered at himself that he didn't resent Özpamir. He hoped to God he wasn't in for a night of those smug clichés that blamed the United States for everything from the arms race to somebody's grandmother's sciatica. He didn't think he was—not from Özpamir.

"But as I say, you know all that. You know how the Shah supported them in Iraq until your Kissinger told him to stop, that it was bad for business. And then once the Shah was gone and the mullahs took over in Iran, it was Iran's turn. And there, too, more of them have been killed than they have killed. I sat on the border and watched the Iranian gunships bomb Kurdish villages while the men were in the mountains with the flocks—bomb them, then come back over and spray the area with chemicals to keep disease down because they couldn't be bothered to bury the dead. When I see that, I understand why the Kurds fight, why they keep their hate alive. Yet...they refuse to assimilate. And so I understand too why the Iranians bomb them. I am a Turk. No country will give up its territory willingly. Not the Iranians, not the Iraqis, not ourselves—especially for some vague notion of 'autonomy' that would surely turn into much more than that."

"Major..."

"I know. All right. What does this have to do with the soldier who was shot? No more lectures." He smiled the tolerant, private smile Brick remembered seeing come onto the face of his professors from time to time when they realized—or thought they did— how great a gap separated them from their students. "There are rare times in history when justice and policy happen to meet. We shouldn't really take any credit for that; it's pure accident. Now is one of those times." He paused, gathering his words. "There are a few million Kurds—nobody knows just how many. They might not seem all that important to the rest of the world. But they are just now. Follow me. Assume first that the Soviets continue to support the Kurds as they have off and on, and that the leftist faction of the Kurds takes credit for that. Then assume that the Kurds win in the most likely place, in Iran, where the government is weakest. What are the possibilities? They begin with a new Soviet Autonomous Republic of Kurdistan, in what was a part of Iran that already borders the Soviet Union. At best, we can expect a Soviet client state, which would spend its time stirring up trouble among the Kurds everywhere, including Turkey.

"Stay with me now. Both Iran and Iraq are dangerous to Turkey, for different reasons. Yet we would be foolish to openly antagonize either of them if we could avoid it. Far better to keep them occupied, keep their energies directed elsewhere. As long as they're fighting against a Kurdish rebellion, that's just so much less energy and fewer resources they can use to stir up trouble elsewhere. So think about it. The Kurds are actually our *allies,* though God knows we've taken long enough to see that. We can offer them a safe haven here—very quietly, of course— in return for their goodwill within Turkey."

"Whose thinking is that?"

"Partially mine, partially a few others'."

"And what if the Kurds actually win in Iran?"

"Then we have an autonomous Kurdistan that's *not* Soviet and that's grateful to Turkey and the West for its help, at least for a while."

Brick looked to Livia and Brenner, then to Tony at the door. Brenner nodded and smiled hopefully at Brick. "And you?" Brick said to Livia. "No Ark?"

"No Ark," she said, lifting her eyes. "Sorry."

"Then why?"

"Do you know who supplies most of the Kurds' arms, Brick?"

"I've never asked."

"Israel." She watched him for a reaction. He gave her none. "I told you about my parents, and that I spent some time on a kibbutz. I picked up some loyalties along the way."

"To the Kurds?"

"I'm serious, Brick. Israel's interest in keeping the asses in Iran and Iraq occupied is just as great as Turkey's. Greater, if the major will forgive me. And God knows we could use an ally in this part of the world if the Kurds win."

"And that's why a man was shot and left in the woods today."

"No, damn it, that's not why," she said, her voice rising. She slid off the bed. "Show off to somebody else. I'm going to...to, oh, hell, I'm going to watch *Dallas.* I think I'd rather put up with that crap than this."

Tony stepped aside, almost a dance step, and opened the door for her.

"Mrs. Lo Presti," Özpamir said. She paused without turning to him. "I wouldn't go outside now. It's Ramazan."

She slammed the door behind her. Tony crossed the room and flopped onto her place on the bed beside Brick. "She had commando training in Israel," he said. "Makes 'em uppity."

"Christ," Brick said. "Then in that restaurant..."

"She could have broken your back."

"Sufficiently confused?" For once, Brenner's cheer was controlled.

"Sufficiently," Brick said.

"Have you heard of a man named Mullah Mustafa Sabri?" Özpamir asked him.

"I think so. The man in Iraq."

"The man in Iraq—and elsewhere. He led the Kurds, as much as anyone could be said to lead them, through their last rebellion. He was the nearest thing they had to a national hero."

"I remember him."

"He died—what?—three years ago. In Washington. He spent many years in exile in the Soviet Union."

"A man of clear loyalties."

"Yes, he was, if you understand the Middle East. Mustafa Sabri has a son, Ali Sabri. I met him in Tehran once, when the Shah was supporting the Kurds. He could well turn out to be a stronger leader than his father, if he has the chance."

"And that's why you and I are here in this godforsaken room?"

"Yes." Özpamir dug in his shirt pocket for an unfiltered Bafra, and lit it. The heavy, sharp smoke hung in the close air like the damp chill. "Are you a political man, Brick?"

"Only as much so as I have to be to survive."

"That means different things at different times. Now you must be political for a while." He leaned forward. "Ali Sabri followed his father's example. He went into exile in the Soviet Union when the Shah withdrew his support. And now is the time he should come back."

"He won't?"

"He can't. He has discovered that he's a guest of the Soviet people until it's decided that he can be useful. For the moment the Soviets don't want to upset the Iranians. And no matter what great horsemen the Kurds are, or how magnificent fighters, they simply can't go swooping into the Soviet Union to bring him out. They have too much to lose. The only people who have no new enemies to make in bringing him out are the Israelis. And even they don't want to anger the Soviets if they don't have to."

Brick started to interrupt, but Özpamir held up a hand. "Let me finish now. We're almost there. The Soviets do know that the Israelis are supplying arms to the Kurds, many of them coming through 'smugglers' that we allow to pass through Turkey. And they know that those arms come through a middleman, based in London, though they don't know who that middleman is. Suppose, now. If a known Israeli sympathizer were found inside the Soviet Union attempting to bring out Ali Sabri, and if that man could be identified as a supplier of arms to the Kurds, who would be to blame? Wouldn't it be relatively simple for the Israeli government to blame that man's greed for the rescue attempt? After all, the wider the war, the more arms that can be utilized, no?"

"You're telling me—or trying to tell me—that you're actually going to cross into the Soviet Union, locate a man the Soviets no doubt have under heavy guard, bring him out, and stay alive?" Brick looked to Brenner and Tony. Brenner's peaceful face showed him nothing. Tony carefully wadded a corner of the faded bedspread, then unwadded it again. "You'll forgive me if I don't accept that right off."

"*We're* not going in, no. I'm waiting behind in Doğubeyazit; that part was true enough. Remember no one must be connected officially with any government or movement. Only Dr. Brenner, Livia, and Tony will cross the border."

"On the outside chance that this were to be true, Brenner, why in the name of God would you do it?"

For a moment, it looked as if Brenner's cheeriness might slip up on him again. But his face remained calm and serious. "I'm the perfect man," he said. "I do have some reputation as an archaeologist, you know. When we put it out in the right places that I was taking on this expedition, no one raised an eyelash. You say that, yes? 'Raised an eyelash'?"

"No."

"No matter. I'm also a businessman. In the event that I get caught, it wouldn't be difficult to establish that I'm the arms middleman, too."

"That's not enough."

Brenner shrugged. "So? What do you want, Brick? I'm a patriot. You couldn't understand that unless you had been with me in Palestine after the war. In Israel it is still fashionable for my generation to be patriots. Put it that way. This is a cheap, efficient way to do something important for my country."

"And Livia?"

"Brenner's generation doesn't have a monopoly on patriotism," Tony said. "Believe *that* or not, too. Livia's parents are known Zionists. We carry Canadian passports. None of us has any direct link to Washington. We just might have a better chance to survive that way. And me? Hell, you know why I'm here."

Brick thought a moment. "Yeah."

"Which has brought us to your question, Brick: the man who was shot," Özpamir said. "The Kurd who met us on the road had come from Iran the night before. He has worked for MIT often and is reliable. The soldier was a Shiite Muslim, a supporter of that mindless stupidity some people try to dignify by calling it an Islamic Revolution. The Kurd brought me the news that my man had managed to get a message through to the Iranian authorities that I was coming toward Doğubeyazit. How much he knew at the time he sent the message, I don't know. My guess is that he was going to give details when we reached Doğubeyazit. If that's the case, we're OK. The Iranians won't have had enough to pass on to the Russians."

"And if it's not the case?"

"What the hell?" Tony said. He flung himself off the bed and tried to look out the dust-blinded window. "What's one more calculated risk at this point? Suicide is suicide."

"Shut up, Tony," Brenner said softly.

"Where is Ali Sabri?" Brick asked.

"In Erevan, just across the border," Özpamir said. "Not so bad."

Tony turned from the window and began to pace. They all watched him, as if he were doing something vital and marvelous. At length, Brick said, "And me?"

"I apologize," Özpamir said gently in Turkish. "I have to make clear to you your position. You're in this country at the sufferance of the Turkish government. Your permission to leave it is at the sufferance of the Turkish government. There is martial law throughout eastern Turkey. So let's say your options are...limited. As are mine. Dr. Brenner and the others have asked that you be allowed to continue with their expedition as far as the Soviet border. With an American nationality it wouldn't be wise for you or this...project...if you crossed the border. I've agreed to that."

"And if I don't?"

"You'll remain in custody of the Turkish army here in Erzurum."

"For how long?"

"Until it's safe and wise to release you. I'm sorry."

Tony paced past. "For God's sake, will you be still," Brick snapped. Tony stopped in mid-pace. Brick looked past him to the fly-specked walls of the room. They were as gray, as dismal as the fog that he knew swallowed the town beyond the windows. As dismal as the walls of a Turkish army prison. God help him. Brick felt as if he were breathing through a thick wool blanket. He believed Özpamir. If he had had a man shot, how much less would it take for him to see another man in a prison for a few days, weeks, months? And Brick granted him the necessity for it, that was the damnable thing. What's more, he believed what the man had just told him about this cockeyed, long-shot scheme to steal a Kurdish tribal headman from the Russians and turn him into a revolutionary leader. Was it really any wilder than the Germans' sneaking Lenin *into* Russia? Things happened that way. A cockeyed idea that somebody convinces somebody else might, just might, work. There's always that somebody in a ministry who plays enough horses to believe in the inevitability of long shots. And there it is, Lenin's in Russia or the triple reverse play works and the game's all over. Cheap and efficient, Brenner had said. A government's dream. A sane man's nightmare.

Tony came and sat beside Brick again, now perching stiffly on the edge of the bed. "We would have had to tell you sooner or later," he said. "Roger said you'd be with us. We thought that if you got as far as Ararat, we'd have time to tell you slowly. At least I thought that. You'd trust us by then. And Livia truly felt better knowing somebody like you would be along."

"Oh, I see. Fine! Make the wife feel better and throw the man a few thou. He's not really needed, but why not? Does it fuck up his life? Well, accidents happen. Say you're sorry." Brick stopped himself by an act of will. He slipped his hands, trembling with anger, beneath his thighs. "Major, I would have thought better of the MIT, at least."

"So would I have," Özpamir said, his sad eyes finding Brick's. He was still speaking in Turkish. *"Anliyormusunuz,* Brick *bey?* Do you understand? There was money involved. A great deal of money. And this is Turkey."

Özpamir folded back into the shabby chair, wearily massaging his temples. No, hell. It wasn't Özpamir's fault. All the professional integrity he had been able to maintain in this timelessly corrupt country must have revolted against the notion of even as important an operation as this one being tamperable with, bribeable. He pitied the man, in spite of himself. *"Anliyorum,"* he said. "I understand."

"Well, then," Brenner said, with his loan officer's forced cheerfulness again. "Now you know our decision."

"Now I know."

"And do you have one for us?"

"No. I don't know. Do you mind if I just don't talk for a while?"

"Want a drink?" Tony said.

"Jesus!" The force with which Brick threw himself off the bed surprised even himself. Only when he closed the rusty bolt behind him in his own room did he stop to take a long, clean breath. How much better

53

off he would have been with his own company than with *that* conversation! So that's the first chapter, he thought, the one I could stop after. He walked to the window and rubbed a clear spot in the dust. Below him at the newsstand, Livia stood cradling a glass of tea. Half-a-dozen truck drivers gawked, wishing for courage enough to try to speak to her. She ignored them, put down her tea glass on the counter, and started slowly for the hotel. The droplets of water on her hair made it shine in the streetlight like freshly broken coal. Signals! Taking charge of his own life! Jesus. He was an even greater damnfool romantic now than he had been when he was twenty-one. Roger knew him, all right, knew he would be here tonight.

But from here? In a Turkish prison cell he would at least be alive. He had two separate stories from these people up to now. Yes, he believed Özpamir, as far as he had gone. But how far had he gone? What had he left out—if anything?

The Kurds were all right; that much he knew. They had been screwed soundly, and kept coming back. Did that give them some sort of moral edge, he wondered? He walked away from the window and stretched out on the bed. A tick made its slow way along the bedspread toward him. So it was moral, now. Would that be his next excuse?

He listened to her steps coming up the stairs, tired, deliberate steps. The television was quiet now, *Dallas* over. Down the hall he heard a door open and Brenner's voice, then Tony's. The footsteps on the stairs paused. The door closed, then another opened and closed. Brenner and Özpamir were in their room. The footsteps resumed, reached the top of the stairs, started down the hall. Then they stopped again. The

knock on his door was as slow and deliberate as the
footsteps had been. Without knowing why, Brick tiptoed to slide open the bolt.

"You weren't asleep?" she asked. Her voice was
cigarette husky.

"No."

He stepped ahead of her into the room. She seemed
nervous as she reached into her shirt pocket for a
Samsun; her eyes darted around the room deciding
where she should sit. Brick slid the chair away from
the scarred Formica desk for her. "They gave you
the story?" She sat, looking grateful.

"Chapter and verse."

"Well?"

"Well. Is it true?"

"It's true. Are you coming?"

Brick sat on the sagging bed beside her chair. "It's
truth time, right?"

"Truth time."

"Why did you want me to come? You went to a lot
of trouble. And you didn't—don't—know me from
Eisenhower."

She inhaled her smoke and held it. "All right. I
took a chance. You sounded OK—normal. And I
wanted somebody OK and normal along who could—
help out, if need be."

"Tony?"

She chose her words carefully. "Tony is my husband. I...care for him...very much. But do you remember what I told you in the jeep today? About
wishing Tony loved me less?"

"Yes."

"Tony is terrified of losing me. I know that. If
things get tight, he'll think of me first, not the expedition. I don't want that."

55

"And Brenner?"

"God, who's ever known Wolf Brenner? He's involved in more things than Howard Hughes was. And Wolf is, oh, fifty-seven, fifty-eight. What if something should happen to him?"

"Before or after the border?"

"Pardon me?"

"I don't go past the border. Remember?"

"Oh. That was the deal?"

"That was the deal."

She leaned back in the chair and let a smoke ring drift toward the ceiling. Damn, Brick thought—from the formality of "pardon me" to spraddle legs and smoke rings. He liked her, even though he didn't want to like her just now. She watched the smoke ring get caught in a draft and scatter. As it did, she grinned, and the grin turned into a giggle. "Did you know," she said, "that I knew a girl in school named Toora Loora Lipschitz? How's that for being a long way from Erzurum, Turkey?"

"That's nothing, madam." Brick answered the grin. "In Virginia, there lives a worthy gentleman name of Doodle Pigg. And if you'll investigate the Birmingham, Alabama, phone book, you'll not only find one Vesuvius Bobo, but a genuine Vaseline Caffee. Top those."

"Where on earth...?"

"A hobby. I collect names. Want to hear some more?"

"Yes!"

"Were you really trained as a commando in Israel?" He knew he was a son of a bitch as soon as he said it.

Her eyes left the ceiling. The brightness he had

seen kindling in them faded. "I was. I taught Tony weapons."

"What are you carrying across with you?"

"Machine pistols. Ingrams." She dropped her cigarette to the tiles of the floor and ground it out. Her voice had hardened, as if she were bargaining in a marketplace. "What else, Brick?"

"Nothing. I've got more than I want."

Her hand reached for his. He gave it to her. She laid both of them on his leg. "Be my friend?" He was as acutely conscious of her hand as if it had been a piece of dry ice.

"I'm your friend."

The hand left his and moved along his thigh. "Thank you."

"Even without that, I'm your friend."

The hand stopped. "Will you stay with us?"

"For a while maybe."

Her hand slid slowly off his thigh. He covered it with his own just before he lost it completely.

"If you were my husband," she said, "would you have left everything behind and followed me here?"

Brick thought a moment. "I would have tried to talk you out of the whole thing."

She squeezed his hand. "A diplomat's answer. But I do think you might have tried."

"And if I hadn't been able to?"

She released his hand and stood, brushing her hair back from her face. For the first time, he noticed a small mole on the right side of her forehead. He thought for a moment that his hand would rise involuntarily to touch it. "Oh, hell, I probably would have come anyway. But I would have loved you for trying." She regarded him a long moment, head cocked, then bent and gave him a quick, soft kiss.

"Careful," Brick said.

"Careful? Careful's for London, not Kurdistan."

She let herself out. Brick lay very still when she had gone, every cell of his skin sensitive and alert, the way it was when he had a fever. So. Tomorrow he would be behind the wheel of a jeep again. This time he would know where he was going, though for Christ's sake not why. It didn't make sense. But maybe he could find his own kind of sense in it. Hadn't that been what he was after all along—his own kind of sense, one way or the other? He let his hand trail down to his crotch. He hoped Livia hadn't noticed his erection. Shameless, Rustin, he told himself, shameless. She was a married woman. Great fried damn.

The last of the day's trucks, air brakes puffing, pulled in at the newsstand outside. The truckers would sleep there, safe, with hot tea waiting and nothing to be afraid of in the night. Like himself, for this night. How many more nights after this one would he be able to think that? He told himself as honestly as he could that, if he was being had, he wanted to be had. No more pretending to turn back now. Whatever came, came. He had bought the book.

Two

A haze, as if the earth were steaming, seemed to hang over the entire Anatolian steppe. The day was cloudless, yet, behind them, the mountains vanished quickly into the blue bowl of the sky. If it held that way, Brick knew, they wouldn't be able to see Ararat until they were almost upon it. They made better time than yesterday along the great flat stretches of the steppe, and the pavement was less likely to be washed away than it was in the rainy forests of the coast. Now and again, they passed middling, donkey-biscuited towns, as often as not lorded over by the ruins of a castle. Now they were into the lands that had belonged to the fierce Seljuk Turks before the Ottomans had conquered even them and created their empire. The Seljuks and the Armenians, whose strange squat towers with their high peaked roofs

59

ruled here instead of the delicate arches of the holy buildings in the rest of Turkey. It was a colorless land that had been crossed and recrossed by the armies and caravans of every great and petty conquerer since before the beginnings of history. And now they were here, too, Brick thought with more than a touch of irony as he watched Livia doze in the seat beside him and Tony snap pictures of herdsmen, like a tourist.

They saw their first Kurdish villages on the banks of the River Araks, which leapt down through the mountains, gathering strength to form a long part of the border, then spill out into the Caspian Sea beyond Baku, in Russia. The low stone huts seemed to grow out of the brown and gray land itself. Goats grazed on their grassy dirt roofs. Stretching around the huts like fences, or piled into small copies of the ancient Armenian towers, the winter's supply of neatly molded dung patties for fires waited and grew. In a treeless world, they were salvation. At the river, noisy with rapids, naked children splashed or filled buckets with the nearly turquoise water to carry home. The women who watched them from the doorways of the huts were as heavy with bangles and belts and broaches as gypsies. Livia's eyes seemed to take in every detail of them with a remote, generic jealousy.

That first village had been a herdsman's village, Brick knew. Now most of its families were in tents in the higher mountain meadows with their flocks. But in the larger villages that they passed beyond the headwaters of the Euphrates, the Kurds were settling, civilizing. Sturdier, broader, mud plastered houses marked the places where the villages were turning into towns. Among them on the rudiments of streets sat hay trucks, and no goats grazed on roofs. Instead, great stacks of hay surrounded each roof's smoke hole, the sign of nomads beginning the long journey through farming to the tenement world of Istanbul.

"It's terrific insulation in the summer, if you don't smoke nearby," Brick said to Livia as she craned to get a last glimpse of the haystack-roofed village they had just passed.

Livia laughed, and her words were nearly swept away by the wind as they gained speed. "I thought Erzurum was the end of the world," she said. "But I have a feeling I ain't seen nothin' yet."

"Next person who tries to tell you the twentieth century has something to do with time, don't you believe him. It's all geography."

Just outside Iğdir, they saw the Soviet border for the first time. Livia looked at it when Brick pointed it out to her, but quickly turned away. The road passed within a third of a mile of it, and they could clearly make out the unbroken double fences that stretched out of sight along the river on the Soviet side. They were parallel, with smooth-swept sand between them. Concentration camp–style guard towers were ranged along the fences every kilometer or so into the distance like oil wells. A narrow road dropped away from the highway to the only crossing the entire length of the border. The nondescript white Soviet border station sat alone in a stand of pines, ominous in its emptiness.

"The Turks tell me they don't bother to patrol the border," Brick said. "The Russians do a good enough job by themselves." Livia didn't laugh. Tony took a picture.

The steppe swept away from them everywhere.

61

Along the rare rivers, poplars grew like refugees from another, vanished world. Grasslands colored the land a dozen subtle shades of tan, up to the stark hills where here and there tall walls of white and pink clay had been carved by the weather into lacy folds like curtains. And then, as they wound up out of a long, sounding river canyon, the snow-blanched peak of Ararat took shape from the haze. They had seen it first as that: a ghostly white form in the blue haze, like an afternoon moon. Now the whole uneven cone, three miles high, was before them. Humped ridges ran toward them from its skirts. Over its shoulder they could make out the faint outline of Lesser Ararat, toward Iran. As the road climbed through the foothills, the mountainsides around them turned watercolor shades of pale violet and magenta from billions of tiny August flowers. Tony snapped madly.

"You know you can't take that with you," Livia shouted back to him.

"I'll have it sent for!"

As they swayed through Doğubeyazit in the endless wind of the high plateau, evening shadows were turning the weary mud town a uniform dun. Robed women lingered at wells for the last of the day's gossip. Shepherd boys and cowherds chased their animals across the highway in front of the jeeps, eager for home. Ragged children peered from over crumbling mud courtyard walls. Behind the town, on a peak in a blind canyon, the ruined palace of Isak Pasha turned a faint rose in the last rays of the sun. Between the town and the palace, barbed wire and faceless sentries surrounded the tanks of the Turkish army's border divisions. Brick translated the sign above the gate for Livia: Defense of Honor Begins on the Border.

A lonely stork nested on a telephone pole at the far edge of the army post. While Major Özpamir checked them through the final roadblock, black and gray crows cawed into the windswept dusk around them. The last hotel of their trip lay just ahead. Tomorrow night they would sleep on the mountain. Beyond the hotel, hidden by a brown hill, was the Iranian border station. The end of the road.

"You'll meet your guide in the morning," Özpamir said as they gathered over stuffed eggplant and hot lamb soup in the empty dining room of the modern hotel, built for the tourists who didn't come now. "You can trust him. He's a half-Kurdish, half-Azerbaijani Turk smuggler—mainly into Iran, but now and again into the Soviet Union, too. You'll go by jeep to there..." He pointed through the window toward a dim cluster of lights on the lower slopes of Ararat. "There's a road of sorts that far. From there it's horseback to the border, and from the border—"

He darted a quick glance toward Brick, then turned back to Brenner. "Well, you know the arrangements." Brenner's cheer seemed completely gone now, and he only picked at his food.

"But I won't," Brick said.

"You'll camp at the border with the supplies. Do you really want to know the rest of the details?"

Brick cut a piece of the honey-heavy baklava the waiter set in front of him. "No. How long will I be there?"

"Two days."

"Short trip."

"Would you want it longer?"

Tony answered for him, brows nearly touching. "No. God, no."

When the waiter set Brenner's baklava in front of him, Brenner pushed it away and stood. His face was pained, then he spoke with an effort. "I think I will say good night to you now."

"Are you all right, Wolf?" Livia asked.

"Oh, I will be, yes. I think the altitude is a little...well, some sleep is the thing, *ja?*"

Livia pushed back from the table. "I'll go up with you."

Brenner managed a wan smile. "No, no. Please, I'll be fine." He moved away unsteadily. Livia followed and took his arm while he tried to wave her away.

The others watched them leave the dining room. "Glory," Tony said, his face as long as an August afternoon. "Just what we need."

"If it's altitude sickness, it should pass by morning," Özpamir said. "Does he have blood pressure problems?"

"I don't know. Wait, yes, he takes pills."

Özpamir sighed and poked at his baklava absently. When he spoke, his anger was poorly disguised. "He should have told us that. I'll have a doctor sent from the post."

"Will that do any good?" Brick asked.

"Bilmiyorum. I don't know. I'm not a doctor." He cut his thick baklava with such force that half of it skittered out of the plate onto his lap. *"Eshek oğlu eshek!"* he cursed. "Son of a bitch!"

Brick looked beyond him to Ararat, framed in the window as in an airline poster. It rose huge and solitary from the treeless plain. A nearly full moon

washed the snow of its peak blue. Somewhere far off
in the corridors of the echoing hotel, the wind
slammed a window. Oh, yes, he thought. *Eshek oğlu
eshek*. Son of a bitch. Son of a bitch.

"He'll catch up," Özpamir said, breaking off from
his huddle with the doctor in the lobby. Morning sun
slashed sharp and hard across the blue carpet. "We'll
take him to the post and do some tests. The doctor
can give him something for the altitude if his blood
pressure's all right." He looked to Brenner, who
gasped discreetly on a couch. "He forgot to take his
pill." There was an edge of disgust in his voice.

"Catch up? God, how?" Tony said.

Özpamir nodded toward a man standing alone,
sipping tea, by the empty fireplace. He was a short
man, no more than five-three or -four, with a bull
neck, a nearly shaven head, and arms that hung to
only an inch or so above his knees. Brick had yet to
meet him and get a clear look at his face. "Your
guide knows where you'll camp tonight. You'll leave
now and set up camp. One of the jeeps will stay
behind. We'll send another man up with Brenner by
noon. They should make your camp by dark."

"Why don't we just wait a day?" Brick asked.

"There are...arrangements...on the other side
of the border, I'm afraid. You go today, or cancel."

A young lieutenant, natty in dress fatigues and
neck scarf, trotted into the lobby and saluted. Outside, two of the jeeps sat idling. *"Mohamed bey."*
Özpamir raised his voice to the man by the fireplace.
"Shimde." With a smooth, unhurried motion the
man put his tea glass down on the hearth and crossed
the carpet to Özpamir. Brick saw now that his face
was far gentler than he would have imagined: thick,

wide lips, high forehead, and liquid, almost Spaniel eyes. A sensitive, intelligent, nervous face. The man answered Tony's outstretched hand with a curt military bow. Brick knew the meaning of the gesture; handshaking was a decadent Western custom—the man declined to acknowledge it.

"Colonel, I believe you know Mr. and Mrs. Lo Presti." Brenner tottered over to join them. "And Dr. Brenner. You don't know yet Mr. Broderick Rustin. Brick, Colonel Mohamed Rize, formerly of the Imperial Iranian Police."

Hell, Brick thought. No bargain basement smuggler for this expedition. He did a poor imitation of the man's bow. "You've met the others before, Colonel?" he said in his rough Kurdish.

"In Munich," the man answered in perfect but slightly accented Turkish. "My wife and daughters live in Munich now."

Brenner broke in feebly with something in German. The colonel answered him as tersely as he had Brick. It was clear that Brenner was trying to apologize, and that the colonel wasn't impressed.

"Well," Özpamir said. "I don't anticipate any problems with Dr. Brenner's joining you. But if there should be, let me repeat: do not continue without him. Your whole story will fall apart unless he is there. And Brick must stay behind. An American citizen with you would complicate things beyond anything my government is prepared to deal with." He looked at Brick. "Or to take responsibility for, Brick. Do you understand what I'm telling you?"

"I think I'd better, Major."

"Do you want a gun?"

"No."

"Good." He drew himself up and zipped his jacket,

a signal the conversation was ended. *"Kismet,* then. Good luck."

Even in the sun, the morning air was cool enough in the open jeeps for jackets. Brick and the colonel took the lead, bouncing straight across the plain on a dirt road toward Ararat, leaving a rooster tail of dust behind them for Tony and Livia. At the two checkpoints they passed—one just off the highway, the other where the plain began to break up in the foothills of the mountains—they were waved through. They had been expected. Brick got little from Colonel Rize. Yes, no, or a thin smile to most of his questions. Yes, he had been in the Soviet Union before. Why? A smile. Was it difficult? No, not very. Did he think this time would be difficult? No, but this time was very different—and the thin smile.

By eleven o'clock they reached the village Özpamir had pointed out the night before. It was as primitive as anything Brick had seen anywhere on earth. Stone huts dug half into the hillside, no electricity, no roads beyond it. A well. Sheep trails off into the mountains. The constant wind. Nothing more.

Except for the horses, the sandaled children, and the blond Kurd who had met them on the road outside Trabzon. He rose from a rough stone bench in front of a hut as they drove up, and flicked away the butt of a home-rolled cigarette. He was dressed in the same clothes as before, the end of his headscarf hanging to his shoulder, Kurdish fashion. He looked the jeeps over for a moment, then greeted the colonel. *"Merhaba, Mohamed bey,"* he said. "The other man?"

"He is ill. He will be along with Refik later. Can you get him to our camp?"

"Tabi. Of course."

The lean, small mountain horses were saddled

67

with Western-style military saddles without markings. They cropped at the sparse grasses while the
blond Kurd and a half dozen of the larger children
transferred the baggage to pack mules. Brick let his
eyes wander among the haphazard huts on the hillside. Empty, all empty, so far as he could see. That
wasn't right. Even if the men were in the hills with
their flocks, or in Iran fighting, there should have
been more women and children than these. If the
soldiers at the checkpoints had been expecting them,
so had the Kurds. But expecting them to do what?
Did they suspect a trick? Or was it just centuries of
mistrust exercising itself, flexing?

And did he blame them? *Was* there a trick—was
he being set up again? One thing he could be certain
of: the Kurds were not far away. The men with their
long, ancient rifles and their new black-market automatic weapons were somewhere in the rocks of this
mountainside.

He took a few steps up the wash toward the center
of the village, then felt a touch on his arm. He forced
himself to turn slowly. A woman in the long-sleeved
blouses and brass-belted, striped apron of a villager
stood pointing to the hut the blond Kurd had been
sitting in front of. From the horses, the man called,
"Rest out of the sun, *efendi*. There'll be plenty of it
to go around later."

The hut was furnished with a rough table, worn
cushions, and a spectacularly woven carpet that covered all but a foot at the edges of the packed dirt
floor. Livia and Tony sat on adjoining cushions;
Brick winced when Livia crossed her legs, a nearly
unforgivable insult here. But the woman pretended
not to notice as she poured lemon-scented water into
their cupped hands to refresh themselves with. Then,

using sign language, she offered something to drink, studying Livia's every movement. They asked for water. The woman vanished through the door of the hut. A scorpion dropped to the dirt floor and scuttled back into the stones of the wall.

"Welcome to the Kurdistan Hilton," Tony said.

"Don't be a snob," Livia said. "She's doing her best."

Tony flipped a corner of the carpet over to check the weave. "I'd buy this from her in a minute. Wonder where she got it?"

"She made it," Brick told him. "Find *that* in a Hilton." His eyes met Livia's. She laughed softly. Tony looked from one of them to the other and dropped the carpet.

When the woman came back, she carried a tray with a water glass, a pitcher of water, and a bowl of ice. "Ice?" Tony said. "How in hell do they run a refrigerator here?"

"Where did the ice come from, *hanem?*" Brick asked the woman.

She pointed out the door and up toward the glaciers of Ararat. "It comes down in the streams," she said. "The children gather it."

Brick felt a rush of love for this place, these people. They were being offered the greatest delicacy this woman had: ice, in the desert. If there was any kind of sense to be made out of why he and the others were here, it had a hell of a lot more to do with that basic decency than with client states and buffer zones and balances of power. If that was romanticism, then so bloody be it.

The woman served the men first. As she offered Livia the tray, her eyes didn't leave a ring Livia wore on her little finger, a small garnet cluster in gold. Only when she was afraid Livia would catch her staring did her eyes move away. Then, her open, tough face screwing itself up to a decision, she said, "It's beautiful."

"She's admiring your ring," Brick told Livia.

Livia flashed the woman a cocktail-party smile. "Thank you."

The woman continued to stare. Brick watched the smile and the stare face each other down, then laughed. "She wants it," he said.

Livia's smile hung on as she turned to him. "What?"

"The ring. When a Kurd admires something that way, you're supposed to give it to him."

He laughed harder at the discomfort on Livia's face. The Kurdish woman shot him a vicious look from beneath the tassels of her scarf. Livia furiously worked the ring from her finger. Tony caught up Brick's laughter. This, too, Brick thought, this, too, you had to be able to love. If the Kurds gave, they knew how to get also. If you didn't know that about this revolution, you were a romantic far too damned lost to ever understand it. He felt better about himself, and about his chances of surviving this incredible week.

The trail led along a dry wash from the village, sloping gently upward for a mile or so. The colonel rode ahead. As the wash cut into the mountainside, they lost sight of the peak of Ararat. Brick hadn't been on a horse in years and sat uncomfortably on the hard saddle. Then, as they left the wash and scrambled over the loose stones of a path that sliced sharply up the rough mountainside, he clutched the horse's flanks with his knees like a kid at camp. The rope to the pack mules jerked as they climbed, and by the time they reached the ridge of the first hill his shirt beneath his jacket was soaked with sweat. Ahead of them was a wasteland of humped, dry dirt and stone. The grasses here were even too sparse for grazing. There was no living thing in sight, though he knew that boar and wolves were hidden, resting out the day's heat, beneath a hundred shady overhangs. The trail ahead of them was a faint line, tan against brown, over the broken, hilly land.

And then the wasteland was behind them in the heat of the afternoon sun. The land descended in a broad sweep to a small valley with stunted trees. A stream fed by the glaciers of Ararat glittered in the sun among the trees, and the trail followed the stream upward again, but more easily now. There were signs of campfires. But the Kurdish shepherds who had built them were as hidden now as the boar and wolves.

By three o'clock, they stopped. At a place where the stream bounded between two huge boulders in half rapids, half waterfall, the colonel reined his horse up in a small meadow, marked with the stones of many campfires. A huge, solitary oak hung over the water, and would provide shade for the sweated horses. Behind them, the afternoon sun threw shadows of the jutting rocks into the narrow valley.

"Home?" Tony said over the sound of the rushing water. Sweat plastered his thinning hair to his forehead as it had the first time B⁓ick had seen him on the gangplank of the boat. He failed at looking pleasant. Rize dismounted as easily as if he had only jogged his horse around an exercise course.

"Sweet home," Brick said. He rose up in the saddle

a couple of times to let the blood circulate before he risked dismounting.

Livia turned to look behind them, then up at Ararat, its frozen peak less visible here behind the stark rock ledges than it had been from the hotel at Doğubeyazit.

"You climbed that?" she asked Brick. Circles of sweat stained the shirt underneath her arms.

"Only to the snowline once. And not from here."

"Once?"

"That was enough."

Livia's look left the mountain and moved over the remains of the campfires in the clearing. "I don't like it. It's too public."

"But lovely," Tony said as he swung from his horse and came to help her dismount. "Now you know why there was always water in these people's vision of paradise."

"Is the border far?" Livia asked Brick, clearly not interested in paradise now.

Brick asked the colonel. "Over that," Rize said, pointing to the ridge that paralleled the stream to the north and hid them from the border. "Over that and down. We will see to the animals, make camp, then I will show you." In spite of his liquid eyes, for the entire weary trip the muscles of his neck had seemed to remain as tense and rigid as bridge cables. He began to work at the knots of the ropes that strapped the tents to his pack mule. The mule brayed and bent to the stream for a drink.

Livia, who evidently had supervised the packing and knew what was where, now supervised the unpacking. "Careful," she said as Brick unstrapped two wooden crates from her mule. "Get some help on those."

Brick gave her a questioning look. She tried to answer his look with a silly, light one. "A few hand grenades, some ammunition and stuff," she said. "Nothing serious."

Nothing serious, Brick thought. Tony's blithering about paradise, Livia's silly look: both doing their best to pretend to each other and themselves (and to him, too?) that they were on a day-camp outing. Only the colonel, who worked steadily and silently, seemed to accept what they were doing, where they were. Beyond that ridge lay Armenia, *Soviet* Armenia. They were going to cross the border of the most paranoid nation on earth, here—somewhere— in the Caucasian mountains. Then they were going to steal a man from somewhere in a Soviet city. And then come back to somewhere in these mountains. Alive, supposedly.

But as he and Tony lifted the crates gingerly to the ground, Brick saw Tony's hands. They trembled.

Long evening shadows cut black swatches out of the clear stream below them by the time they had made camp and reached the top of the ridge. Loose rocks from the crumbling land bounced behind them to the water a hundred feet below, and the constant wind ground the dust into Brick's very pores. The colonel motioned them to stay low. He pointed toward a watchtower in the plain below them, far to their left. "Soviet binoculars are good," he said, sounding a little impressed.

The landscape dropped away from them sharply at first, then in a miles-long slope broken by low hills. At the beginning of the long, easy slope, the Araks River—the border—sliced a sharp canyon out of the tan land. Only here and there was the river itself visible as it twisted into a bend. Running into it from the north was another, smaller river. Brick tried to remember maps. That river should be the Zanga, dropping down from Lake Sevan in the north. And on it, thirty miles or so ahead in the vast, dusty, bowl of the plain of Ararat, would be Erevan, the capital of the Soviet Socialist Republic of Armenia, the city built new by the survivors of the great Turkish massacres.

In the dusty haze, Brick could only make out what seemed to be thicker clouds of dust, smoke from factories that marked the city. Here and there the land was cut by canals, and beside the canals stretched darker patches of cultivation. Collective farms, he imagined. He could make out only two roads, one that ran vaguely east—west like the Araks, the other that headed north toward Erevan.

"No fences here," he said to the colonel. "No guard towers."

"Would *you* attack across Ararat?" the colonel answered. "Mounted patrols watch for a few smugglers like me along the river. That's all. And they don't watch too hard. We leave them presents sometimes. They understand."

Livia and Tony studied the mountainside below with binoculars. Livia at length lowered hers and turned to Brick. "Ask him if the checkpoint is there, where the road crosses the river."

Brick asked. "Just beyond it," the colonel said. "A kilometer past the checkpoint there is a dry wash into the hills. The car will be there. They will find it."

"You're not going?" Brick said.

"I leave them when I get them across the river. Then I come back here to wait with you."

Brick translated for Livia, then asked her, "What time do you leave?"

"After dark."

"Not much of a moon tonight."

"Enough to see by, not enough to be seen by—we hope. It was planned that way." The wind carried her words away so that Brick had to strain to hear her.

"Horseback?"

"To the river. Then by foot."

"Can Brenner take that?"

There was a moment of silence. Livia's voice was hard, matter-of-fact. "He damn well better."

At the camp—three tents, the horses and mules, a Sterno stove—Livia dug out tin dishes and Tony heated some cans of stew. The whole stream bed was in shadow by the time they ate. No one spoke much. From time to time they all sneaked looks at their watches. Brenner. Brenner should be here by now. Yet no one said it. On the mountain slopes around them, thin lines of smoke rose to be scattered by the wind almost as soon as they appeared. The unseen Kurdish shepherds were building their dung supper fires. A chill came from the little waterfall. The sun dipped out of sight above the ridge they had climbed. Brenner.

"Brenner was to have handled the translation with the colonel," Tony said to his stew. "In German."

"Is to," Livia said.

"What?"

"*Is* to handle the translation. When he gets here."

"Yeah," Tony said. He glanced up at her sharply. "Is to."

The colonel lit a Coleman lantern. The sky above

them, clear with just the slightest touch of haze, turned a pale magenta to the west. In the east, it darkened to a shade between blue and black. The ghost of a moon appeared, with Venus beside it. Tony stood and flung his dish away into the stream. "Shit!" he said.

"Tell him to sit down," Rize said, squatting beside the Sterno stove. "He is being a child."

"How long do you have?" Brick asked.

"Forty-five minutes, an hour at the most. If we leave after then, it will be too late." The colonel shrugged.

"Can they go without Brenner?"

"As I understand their plans, no."

"You don't care much."

"I'm being paid. I like the Kurds. But no, I don't care much."

Brick rinsed his plate in the dark stream. The ridge above them was a line against the dim sky now. He stood, walked past the fidgeting horses, and started up it. There was just enough light left for him to retrace the path they had taken earlier. When he reached the top, stars were thickening the sky. Now below him in the distance he could see the lights of Erevan making a pinkish glow in the sky over the city. Here and there there were brighter red spots, blast furnaces he supposed. It was a city, a real city that spread out into suburbs and was crossed with boulevards and ringed with apartment buildings. A city such as he hadn't seen for months. He shook off a feeling close to homesickness. On the road by the river, infrequent headlights crawled. A few turned north toward the city.

Somehow he had known all along. The excitement he had felt and denied since he had first read Roger's

Robert Houston

letter had meant this, these lights, that dark Armenian plain. The signal had pointed him toward this crumbling ridge on the massif of Ararat. And now it drew him toward that unknown city on the plain like the very force of revelation. It was as if all his life he had been pacing in a train station, waiting for a train, not knowing why he was waiting for it nor where it was going when it got there. Until now. Now that this idiotic, impossible possibility had chuffed into the station.

His excitement quickening on fear, he half slid, half climbed down the steep trail from the ridge. In the bright circle of light from the Coleman, the others still sat, Tony chucking stones toward the darkened stream. Brick paused a moment, composing himself before he stepped into the light. "No Brenner?" he said.

"No Brenner," Tony answered.

"You know what that means," Brick said to Livia, who sat shredding the leaves from a dry, brittle bush. He tried to keep the excitement out of his voice and, apparently, failed.

"Özpamir said under no circumstances, Brick," Livia said.

"Can the two of you do it alone?"

"There's an outside chance."

"How outside?"

"Over the horizon."

"Özpamir's in Doğubeyazit. He only said he couldn't be responsible. I'm not asking him to be responsible."

Tony left off his rock pitching. He nodded toward Brick. "There's no time to fill him in on things," he said to Livia.

"As long as one of us was always with him, we wouldn't have to."

77

"That would be a burden."

"Do you want to try to translate? Or to get into that house by yourself?"

Tony considered. "I can't."

"I know that."

"Özpamir will shit."

"By then it'll be too late."

Tony picked up another rock and sailed it toward the stream. "Do what you think best. Brenner's responsible."

Again, Brick had the sensation that he was being discussed as if he weren't there. Livia looked up at him. Her face was half hidden by the shadows her loosened hair cast in the Coleman light. *"None* of us can be responsible, Brick. You understand that."

"I understand that."

"What does the colonel say?"

Brick asked him. The colonel shrugged, his eyes averted.

Livia opened a pack beside her tent. She handed Brick a worn dark suit and a white, much-washed dress shirt. "It's Brenner's size," she said. "Too small, but so much the better. What size shoe?"

"Ten."

"Brenner's a ten and a half. You'll make do." She pulled a pair of cracked black lace-up shoes from a pouch on the pack. "Bury your wallet here, and any other identification you have. I don't have anything phony to give you, but nothing's better than what you've got. And come here." She fished in her own pack.

"Why?"

"I'm going to give you a haircut. Yours is too long. When I'm done I want you to find some gravel and

78

rough up your fingernails. Split a couple, like a farm worker's."

"You're serious."

"And when I'm finished with you, Tony will cut my hair." She looked away.

They left the mules tethered. The colonel would be back at the camp by midnight. He rode in the lead. Tony, dressed much the same as Brick, came behind. Livia wore a plain skirt and bright flowered cotton blouse, and socks inside her plain, peasant's shoes. A scarf wound around her head and covered the lower part of her face, Armenian style. She had scrubbed away her makeup and carried a string shopping bag with a bleak, long coat in it. Brick allowed his horse to pick its own way among the stones of the path behind her, and prayed. All along the border at regular intervals, flares from the watchtowers lit the sky like slowly falling skyrockets.

They saw the first light in front of them not more than a hundred yards along the dark path: a quick flicker from a match, bright, then snuffed. Brick started. And then there was another, the same quick flicker, like a firefly, twenty or so yards beyond that. Brick looked past Livia and Tony for a reaction from Rize. There was none, except that he seemed to steer straight toward the spot the light had been. Almighty God! Brick let his hand slip into his coat pocket, to the .38 police revolver Livia had talked him into taking. She had wanted to give him a machine pistol, but he refused. The revolver, at least, he knew how to use. He was glad he had taken it now. If the Shah's former colonel had set them up for something, if he got no further than this, he had the small comfort of knowing he had had some chance. He tensed, leaned forward, close to the horse's neck, less of a target.

A low voice came from behind a boulder beside the path as they reached the spot where the light had been. Brick couldn't make out what it said. *"Soğul,"* the colonel said, equally low. Thanks.

Ahead, two more lights flickered. The colonel headed for them. The low voice came again from beside the boulder as Tony, then Livia passed. Neither of them answered. Then as Brick passed, he saw a man squatted beside the boulder, a Kurdish shepherd wrapped in a dark coat, his crook held up beside him. *"Mashallah,"* the man said. God Bless.

"Soğul," Brick said. These were the men whose cooking fires he had seen, then, the men who had been so absent from the landscape during the day. And now they were here, lighting the way down the mountainside. They knew why he and the others were here, and this ritual was a kind of thanks, a kind of blessing on the expedition. Brick felt tears start, then vanish in the mountain wind. As they passed each of the men down the twisting, steep path, the greeting was always the same: *"Mashallah."* God Bless. *Mashallah. Mashallah.*

Three

In less than an hour they were down the mountain-side. Brick checked his watch. Eight-thirty. What-ever they had to do, they had to do before daylight. That much he had been able to find out, and not much more. He heard the faint rush of the Araks in its canyon ahead—the canyon they had to cross, somehow. The last couple of shepherds followed them to the edge of the canyon to take the horses. Brick stared into the nearly utter darkness of the canyon. "Allah, Allah," he said to the colonel.

The colonel took a few steps along the rim of the canyon, as if he were checking to see that nothing on it had changed. "It seems darker from here. Once we start down, your eyes will adjust."

"You actually smuggle things across here?"

Rize laughed softly in the darkness. "Not things.

81

People. The things I take across south of here, near
Lake Van, into Iran. Only people come and go from
the Soviet Union." From his small backpack he un-
coiled a nylon rope and wound it mountaineering
fashion across his body from his shoulder. "Tell the
others," he said. "Make no move until I say so."

Fifty feet down, Brick found out why the colonel
had taken out the rope. The path simply stopped,
ran out against a wall of rock. The colonel held up
his hand, then tied the rope to an outcropping. "It's
no more than ten meters," he said. "Tell them to
take it slowly, hand over hand. They will find the
level spot easily, and from there we can go on with
no rope." Without waiting for questions, he launched
himself into the dark. Brick held the rope until its
tautness relaxed. The colonel was down.

"Next?" he said.

"You go, Tony," Livia said. She tried to bring back
the lightness to her voice. "If I fall, I'd rather it be
on you."

"Charmed, I'm sure," Tony said and edged by
Brick to the rope. He was down it nearly as quickly
as the colonel.

"Livia?" Brick said.

"Brick, listen. I want to say something. You're a
damn fool for coming along. You don't have any of
the details of what we're about to do, so this is all
doubly unfair. But God only knows we need you.
Don't let Tony—or me—try to make you do something you don't feel is sane, OK? I told you before
in the jeep I might have to depend on you. Now I
really mean that. For all our sakes, be tough. All
right?"

"Whatever that means."

She touched his arm. "You'll know when the time

82

comes." She took the rope and moved out over the cliff.

And as she did, Brick saw the silhouettes.

There were half a dozen of them, men and horses a single creature against the faint sky, moving slowly across the rim of the canyon on the Soviet side. The canyon wall there was much lower than on this side, Brick could see now. The horsemen were almost level with him. It would be no shot at all from there to here. "Livia," he said. There was no answer. The rope was still taut in his hands. "Livia," he tried again, louder. "Stop moving, for God's sake."

"Brick? Did you call me, Brick?"

"Stop moving!"

"Stop what?"

When the spotlight came on, it struck the cliff fifteen yards beyond her. Brick flattened himself on the path. The rope quivered in his hand and was still. He could feel more than see the spotlight coming closer as the tan dirt of the cliff face brightened almost imperceptibly. There was a shot, then another. And then the rope went slack. A trembling began somewhere in his legs, and worked its way up.

"Livia?" he said.

Nothing.

"Livia!"

The light was fully on the cliff face below him now. He turned his head away into the dirt and held his breath.

And then he felt the brightness diminishing. The light was moving on! He turned his head back toward the other cliff. The light swept quickly by again, then flicked off. But he still lay without moving, his breath heaving now that he had let it out, until the

horsemen reined around and trotted off along the
cliff. Then, without calling to anyone below, he slid
over the edge of the cliff.

He saw the others by the time he was halfway
down the slope. Livia was crouched against the rock
face, throwing up. "Goddamn stew," she coughed.

"I thought you said the patrols didn't look hard,"
Brick exploded to the colonel, knowing Tony should
be doing it instead.

"They don't. If they were looking hard they would
have seen us."

"Then what in hell were they shooting at?"

"A jackal, perhaps? A hyena? Something to break
the monotony."

Brick felt his anger rise higher. A jackal, a hyena?
Goddamn it to hell and back, he felt like a fool. He
turned on Livia. "Then what the hell happened to
you? Why did you let go?"

Livia's head was between her legs. "To get down,"
she said miserably.

"You could have missed the ledge and broken your
goddamn neck."

"I took a chance. I take chances. They might have
seen me on the rope."

"Easy," Tony said. "You did the right thing."

"Easy!" Brick said. "Goddamn if..."

"Yeah, easy, Brick. Back off. She's my wife."
Tony's voice was sharper than Brick would have
imagined it could be. He was startled into silence.

"Yeah, she is," he said at length. "Colonel, more
patrols?"

"Probably not. We should have time to cross before
that one comes back if we leave now."

Brick ignored Tony. "Ready, commando?" he
asked Livia. She took a deep breath and held her

hand out. Brick let Tony take it and help her to her feet. Strike one, he thought: you let yourself damn near panic at some shepherds with matches. Strike two: you let a bored border patrol shooting at shadows tip you into pitching a fit at everyone around you and making a mammoth fool of yourself. And you haven't even crossed the border yet! God help you when something *really* happens. Hero.

The descent and river crossing—an easy ford through the summer-low waters—cost them another hour. Brick had expected something more when he looked behind him in the middle of the river and realized he was in Soviet territory. There should have been trumpets, and kettle drums. But now there was nothing but the feel of the cool water rushing above his knees, the sound of it splitting itself around a boulder in its path.

When they slogged close to the black bank he saw that Rize was leading them ashore just upstream from the junction where the Zanga flowed into the Araks, a smaller canyon chopping into a larger. As he sloshed onto the pebbly bank the colonel waved him and the others near to the low cliff, out of sight of anyone passing above. "They should know the route—in theory, at least. Tell them to follow the Zanga, and keep a sharp watch. Stay in the trees, when there are any. The valley flattens out a kilometer or two ahead, and you'll be more visible but the walking should be easier. Remind them that the military checkpoint is just beyond the bridge. You *must* pass it in the dark, keeping as low as you can. The wash you'll look for will lead off to your left, and you'll recognize it by the ruins of a stone house. The car will be there at four A.M. and will wait until four-fifteen, no later. Do you speak Armenian?"

"No," Brick said.

"You can speak to the driver in Kurdish, then. He is a Kurd. Later, if anyone speaks to you in Armenian or Russian, answer them in Kurdish. If they speak Kurdish, answer in Russian. You're blond enough to be either a Russian or a Kurd, and your accent will be less likely to be noticed if you're using a language that's not the speaker's native one. In a pinch, you can use Turkish, but try to make it sound Azerbaijani Turkish. Questions?"

"What happens after the car picks us up?"

The colonel motioned toward Livia and Tony. "Ask them. By the way, the car will be an old one, an *emka* from before the war. If it's anything else, don't get in. Understood?"

"Yes. And yourself?"

"I will be here at this spot by two A.M. tomorrow morning."

"Then so will we, I hope."

"Kismet. Good luck."

"Soğul."

The colonel shook Tony's and Livia's hand in turn, solemnly, and said *"Auf Wiedersehen"* in a bad accent to each. They all stood and watched him splash into the river through the dim moonlight and into the darkness. Brick felt left in a much greater darkness. They were on their own now. Totally.

"It's a long way from a colonel in the Shah's police to this," Livia said. "I could pity him."

"Sic transit gloria," Tony said without feeling.

The Soviet water in the Zanga sounded just like the Turkish water in the Araks, Brick thought as

they moved along the river, now crunching through
the pebbles of the banks, now moving into the shallow water when the cliffs pressed too close. Sometimes paths climbed from the river into the hills, and
once they came across a straggly cow that bounded
off up one of the paths as they approached. The valley
widened, the hills became gentler, and the land grew
brighter from the starlight. As they rounded a long
bend, they passed the small stone houses and garden
plots of a commune village. Only in one of the houses
did a lonely night-light burn, wavering through the
stand of poplars that shielded the village from the
winds of the river valley. Village dogs yapped, echoing into the starlit hills, and they crouched as they
passed, certain that the sleepless farmer with the
night-light would discover them.

Tony spotted the bridge first. It was a steel span,
two lanes, that hung starkly against the stars, black
on black. He motioned them down, and they squatted
behind a clump of low bushes, watching. Just beyond
the bridge was a white concrete blockhouse, only
partly visible because of its elevation. Floodlights lit
the road in front of it and the area to its sides and
back. It needed painting.

"They're asleep. Or dead," Tony whispered.

"No such luck," Brick whispered back.

"Damn. Do they go on patrols or come out back
to take a leak in the river or anything?" Livia said.
"Do we just trot past it and hope?" From her string
bag, she unwrapped the machine pistol.

"Put that away," Tony said. "You want to start
a war?"

"Yes, if I have to. Better dead than red."

Tony giggled nervously. Livia sputtered a laugh
into her scarf, and Brick, in spite of himself, felt a

giggle fighting its way out of his chest. Oh, hell yes! Now was the time. A case of nervous giggles all around, and the Soviets would find them doubled over in the river splashing water on one another with machine pistols. No trumpets and kettle drums, and now to die tittering! No, it wasn't supposed to work this way at all.

A solitary truck rumbled across the bridge above them, and they flattened themselves out of the line of its headlights. The giggles vanished as the truck squonked and rattled to a stop in front of the blockhouse. A door slammed. From the far side of the blockhouse, two figures, a man and a woman in uniforms of identical gray, walked leisurely to the cab of the truck. A man in the cab of the truck poked his head from the window and shouted a greeting. The woman smiled and waved.

"Now," Brick said. "Stay low, move fast."

Livia was on her feet before he finished speaking. The idling motor of the truck and the rush of the river covered the crunch of their feet on the gravel. They sprinted in a half crouch past the bright blockhouse, keeping close to the eroded bank. Within fifty yards, the lights of the blockhouse were blotted entirely by the bushes.

"Well," Tony said, panting, as they paused for breath. "We passed Go."

Livia checked her watch. "Three-forty. We're early."

"Good," Brick said. "I'd rather see who's in that car before he sees us."

The ruined stone house and the dry wash on the left were just as the colonel had said they would be. The banks to the wash were steep, so they moved along it openly. It ran only a few hundred yards before it intersected the road, crossing beneath the road in a concrete culvert. Just beside the culvert, the ground sloped toward the wash gently enough for a car to maneuver from the road to the smooth bed of the wash. So far, it all fit. Once a car was in the wash, it would be hidden. Livia, her machine pistol still loose, climbed one bank of the wash twenty or so yards from the road. Tony climbed the other bank. Brick stayed in the wash. He would meet the car, would be both translator and scapegoat.

He sat on a tuft of dead grass a few feet up the side of the wash, and forced himself not to think. He could feel sleep creeping up on him now. It would be all right at dawn. But now, in this last hour of darkness, after an all-night walk, he knew he would have to battle the drowsiness. When he finally saw the headlights jouncing wildly along the edge of the wash, he realized he'd been losing the battle. Bloody hell! He had been so far gone he hadn't even heard the car turn off the highway. He thrust himself in anger off the tuft of grass to wake up. He had planned to wait until the car had passed to approach it, but now, groggy, he found himself flat in front of the headlights. Bloody hell!

The car, shock absorbers long gone, swerved and bounced as it tried to stop. Brick could see nothing past the glare of the headlights. Was it an old *emka*? Would he know one if he saw it? Too late, he thought, too late. Instinctively, he squatted below the headlights.

He and the car sat facing one another like football linemen for a long moment, the clatter of the engine filling the wash. Then a voice broke over the noise. Brick made out one word in what he took to be Armenian: Brenner.

"No. I am Dr. Brenner's friend," he answered in Kurdish.

Gears ground. The car lurched backward. "No!" Brick shouted. "It's all right, wait." The car careered up against the side of the wash, then plopped down again. It moved forward a few feet to get a new start. Brick leapt out of the beam of the headlights. And then all movement stopped. Now, away from the glare, he saw Livia standing beside the driver's window, her machine pistol level with the head of an invisible driver. The pinging, knocking engine died.

"Brick," Livia said in a whispered shout. "Get the hell here."

Brick scrambled beside her. Inside the car cringed a sandy-haired man, mid-forties, Brick guessed, with a small, sharp profile and wisps of hair shooting from under a bald crown. He wore wire-rim glasses and stared in utter terror at the muzzle of Livia's weapon. "It's OK," Brick told him. "Brenner's sick. You know the others who were supposed to be with him? Livia Lo Presti, maybe? Tony? They're here."

The small head nodded. "I am an intellectual," it said. "I am a Kurdish nationalist. I am a socialist but not a Party member. My name is Burhan. Please don't kill me. I believe you."

Tony's head poked through the shotgun-side window. "Nobody behind him," he said.

"What kind of car is this?" Brick asked.

"An *emka*, please. It belongs to the Workers' Social Committee at the observatory. I'm the head of that committee."

"Put the gun away, Livia," Brick said.

"No."

"Put it away, damn it. He's our man. You want to scare him so that he runs us into a ditch?"

Slowly, Livia lowered the gun. "Thank you," the small man said in thick English, then switched back to Kurdish. "I hope Dr. Brenner will feel better soon, *inshallah*."

"He will," Brick said. "May we get in?"

"There is some hurry, yes. My risk is huge, you understand?"

"Your risk." Brick opened the door for Livia and realized how odd it must look to be opening the door for a woman with a machine pistol. Livia's bare arm brushed him as she got inside. He had never seen her in a skirt before this one, awful as it was. He liked the notion of the skirt, liked it too much, he knew. He slid in beside her on the worn mohair seat. Tony crawled in next to the driver.

"There is coffee on the seat beside me," the little man said, his hands still plastered to the wheel. "And cakes. I thought you would need them. Please, you in truth aren't going to kill me?"

"Not as long as you brought coffee," Brick said. "We never kill people who have coffee."

The half light of dawn came in pale shadows over Ararat. On the road into Erevan they passed one car, two farm trucks, and a single oxcart. Even as they swung past the country dachas of Party officials set back in the fields on the outskirts of the city, the traffic became only slightly heavier: one or two new Volgas bouncing along the dirt roads toward the highway with executives who wanted to get an early start at work. And when they hit the suburbs, which were neat stone and brick houses with half-grown trees lining broad streets, the streetlights were still on.

"How far?" Brick asked Burhan as the suburbs

became thicker with nondescript apartment buildings that seemed all to be built out of the same pink
tuff stone, with the same striped awnings on their
west-facing windows.

"Through town," he said. "On the northeast."
They roared around an electric bus with a huge
chrome star on its nose. Row on row of factories and
warehouses lined the road now, broken here and
there by office buildings and schools. On a high rock
toward the river, the ruins of a castle with the tall
spire of a mosque inside it were visible in the breaks
between buildings. A city, Brick thought, a Euro-
pean city here on the fringe of Mesopotamia. What
a strange kind of oasis.

By the time they had crossed town on the wide
boulevard, past a fountained, tree-thick square that
Burhan told them was Lenin Square, the streetlights
were off and the streets were filling with cars—far
more cars than Brick had expected to see. In places,
they ran into the neanderthal beginnings of traffic
jams.

"You *want* to do this all in daylight?" Brick asked
Livia.

"Yes. In daylight."

"Why?"

"Did you see how absolutely quiet this place is at
night? Imagine how any commotion at all would
stick out."

"The options aren't very appealing."

"No," she said flatly.

"Want to tell me how we're going to do it now?"

"It sounds idiotic. But as you say, the options
aren't very appealing."

"Go on."

"This much we know. Ali Sabri fled to the Soviet

Kurds at Alikochak. But that wouldn't do for the Russians. He was a potential troublemaker. So they brought him here to Erevan, where he would be surrounded by Armenians. Armenians and Kurds have never had much use for each other, so he's not likely to start anything here or to find much sympathy for Kurdish causes. Besides, they can keep him here as a 'guest' less obviously. Put him in a nice suburban house in a city of nearly a million people, keep a couple of Russian policemen stationed in the house, and who notices? So. Our problem becomes how to get him out of that nice suburban house on a quiet street without attracting the whole neighborhood's attention. Which lets out grenades, guns, and that sort of thing. So I'm going to have a baby."

"I work fast," Tony grinned from the front seat.

"It goes like this," Livia said. She took the ugly overcoat from the string bag, put the bag in one of the pockets of the coat, and hiked her blouse. "Tell me when it looks reasonably natural," she said as she began stuffing the coat into her blouse and skirt, which she unbuttoned. "It doesn't have to be perfect."

"Brenner was to be her father, and me her husband," Tony said. "Brenner rushes up to the door of the house, yammering in Armenian while I help Livia go into labor on the front steps of the house. You'll be, oh, a brother now, I suppose, and yammer in something else. Just three peasant farmers in town, looking for some relatives in the suburbs. They get lost. The woman goes into labor. They hit the nearest house, knowing that Armenian hospitality can't let them down. There's confusion. We're in the house. It's all over."

"You're right," Brick said. "It's idiotic."

Burhan broke in. "Five minutes more, maybe. You are prepared?"

"More or less," Brick said. "Are you?"

"I am an intellectual and a Kurdish nationalist and a socialist. Of course I am prepared."

"He's ready," Brick said to Livia. "He's also an intellectual, he says."

"God help us. He's to give us twenty minutes. Does he know that?"

Brick asked. "Twenty minutes, of course," Burhan said. "Please, may I borrow your watch. I have a good sense of time, but just to be sure..."

"I left it behind," Brick said. "It was American."

"No matter. I have a good sense of time."

"Twenty minutes," Brick told Livia. "He knows." She looked satisfied. God help us, Brick thought.

This suburb was newer than the one they had passed through on the south of town—trees just planted, freshly dug gardens, tin-roofed, two-storey box houses, some with cars in the drives. Not all of the houses had glass in their windows yet. Not picturesque, Brick thought as they pulled up on a side street. But not mud huts with dung fires, either.

Ahead, a woman wheeled a baby along in a carriage. Far down the street, a trolley crept around a corner. Already the heat of the day was making itself felt in a flat, quiet, dull world. Livia was a good actress. She let Tony help her from the car, and she waddled to the curb. Brick took one arm, Tony the other, and they pretended to fuss over something about Livia's comfort as the creaking *emka* smoked from the curb. They were alone now, on a street in Erevan, the Soviet Union. Tony had two machine pistols—his own and Livia's—under his coat, and two hand grenades. Brick had one revolver. When he tried to speak, his throat tightened as if it were corked. Yes, idiotic, start to finish. "Where now?" he managed to force out.

"Around the next corner, third house on the right," Livia said.

As they turned the corner, Livia began to stagger and moan. Every few paces she would stop, as if a contraction had her. Brick tried to keep shoving her forward, sure that some kindhearted Armenian woman in one of the first two houses would see her and come rushing to help. In front of the third house, no different from any of the others except that it had no garden, Livia lurched onto the front walk. "Now, damn it!" she hissed at Brick.

If he was trembling, so much the better. If he stuttered, so much the more convincing, Brick told himself as he stepped onto the small stoop of the house. He banged his fist on the door. And oh, Christ. He hadn't even decided what language he was going to speak! Russian? No. They would surely be Russian guards. Kurdish? His Kurdish was so weak that he had to rehearse what he was going to say first. Turkish? How in hell did he fake an Azerbaijani accent? He wasn't even sure he recognized one.

A curtain pulled back from the window beside the door. Livia stumbled against the stoop, and sat down, moaning. The curtain held itself open a moment, then flapped shut. Brick heard fumbling at the latch of the door. It swung open a few inches, then a few more. A burly man in a gray uniform with red stars on the lapels asked in brusque Russian what was wrong, what did they want.

Brick let the words out in a tumble, "My sister,

my half sister. Is there a telephone? We're visiting relatives, you see. She's..." He stopped, terrified.

He was speaking English.

The man in the uniform looked at him dumbly. *"Ne ponimayu,"* he said. I don't understand.

"Moya sestra!" My sister! Brick shouted the Russian at him in panic and pulled the door away from his hand. Strike three. Livia let out a doleful cry. From behind the burly man another, younger man in the same uniform, with a sensitive face, pushed his way onto the porch. He muttered, "Oh, my God," and took Livia by the arms. She stood and staggered toward the door. The younger man shoved the big one out of the way and let Livia's momentum carry them all into the house. As he did, Tony grabbed Brick's arm and hustled him after them. Before Brick was even certain they were all in, Tony, with a cat's quickness, had slammed the door and had whipped out one of the machine pistols. He flipped the other one to Livia, who elbowed the younger policeman in the stomach and backed away. Surprise and pain fought each other on his face as he struggled for breath. The bigger policeman lunged for Tony. Brick, hearing his pocket rip, brought his .38 up in a single motion with all his strength into the man's face. The man grunted, threw his hands to his face and careened away from Tony. Blood spurted from between his fingers. Tony unsnapped the man's military holster and jerked his pistol from it, then sent it clattering along the tile hallway.

"Ali Sabri," Livia said to the younger man.

"Ne ponimayu," he gasped.

"The hell you don't," Brick said to him in Russian. "Where's Ali Sabri?"

"Kto Ali Sabri?" Who's Ali Sabri?

"Screw your mother," Brick said. He turned to the doilied, dark wood living room behind him. Empty even the knickknack shelves empty. "Upstairs," he said to Tony. Tony took the stairs two at a time.

"Empty," he called from the top of the stairs.

"Is there a basement?" Livia asked.

"Not likely. I'll check the kitchen," Brick said.

In the kitchen he found a door, locked, that led either to a basement or a pantry—there was no way of telling which. He turned to look for a knife, a screwdriver, anything to pop the small padlock with. And as he did, he saw Ali Sabri.

Alone, stretched in a wooden lounger in the unfenced backyard, his shirt open to the sun, eyes closed and a fantastically carved Turk's-head meerschaum pipe hanging from between his lips. He was no more than forty, with thick black hair, a sharp, hooked nose, high cheekbones, and a runner's body. And he was asleep.

Carefully, Brick turned the handle and eased the back door open. He scanned the rest of the yard. There was no one. Only a slim girl a few houses away hung out laundry and was totally absorbed in it. Brick stepped softly down the back steps onto the rocky dirt of the yard. He waited until he was a pace away before he spoke quietly. *"Bay* Ali Sabri?"

The man didn't move. After a time, the pipe twitched. Then the heavy-lidded eyes opened. They seemed to be already fixed on Brick, as if the man had located him through his eyelids. The man cleared his throat and took the pipe from his mouth. "British?" he said in English.

"American," Brick said.

"I'm surprised." There was cockney in the accent.

"Somehow I always imagined that if anyone came it would be the British."

"No," Brick said. "I don't think the British do this sort of thing much anymore."

"Pity," Ali Sabri said as he sat up. "They were good at it. Are my hosts inside?"

"Yes."

"You are CIA?"

"No. My name is Rustin. I'm not anything."

"Two surprises, then. Are we leaving? Do I have time to get some things together?"

"Not many."

"I don't have many things. I'm a Kurd. Are there any women with you?"

"One. The wife of my friend."

"Another pity. I'm randy as a goat." He swung off the lounger. "You don't have to hold that pistol. I'm plenty ready to go without that. Where *are* we going?" He moved off toward the house.

"Turkey first. Then Iran." Brick followed, holding the pistol limply.

"The first one I don't like. The second one I do." He opened the door for Brick. "My hosts are rather decent. I hope you don't hurt them." Brick stepped through the door. As he did, Ali Sabri slammed it and ducked out of sight beneath the pane. Brick whirled and tried the latch. It was locked—Ali Sabri must have locked it while he was holding the door open. Brick fumbled at the cockeyed Soviet lock. Goddamnit! It was as complicated as everything else in the Soviet Union. He drew back his pistol to smash the window, then thought better of it. That much noise would surely bring neighbors. He took a breath and reached for the latch again. A press, a turn to the left, and it clicked!

As he stepped onto the back stoop again, Ali Sabri appeared around the corner of the house, heading toward him. Brick jerked the .38 up. Ali Sabri's expression didn't change. Behind him sauntered Tony, his coat flung over his arm—and, Brick was sure, the machine pistol underneath that.

"You took a long time. I came around front to check," Tony said. "Found him strolling away down the street."

"What the hell was that all about?"

"Never trust a Kurd," Ali Sabri shrugged. "Ask the Turks."

"Where did you think you were going?"

"Home."

"That's where we're taking you."

"How do I know that? Would you trust a strange foreigner who showed up with a pistol and said he was taking you home?"

Brick considered. "No."

"I don't either."

"Look. Do you know a man named Burhan, from the observatory? He says he's a Kurdish nationalist."

"I know him."

"He'll be here in...almost right now. He knows us. Will you accept that?"

"It will help."

"What do you have to take with you?"

"I'll go with him upstairs," Tony said. "We'll take care of that. You and Livia see to the gendarmes."

Inside, Livia had both Russians seated across from her on the tacky flowered couch. The one Brick had hit still held his nose, though a handkerchief stanched the blood now. "I'm sorry," Brick told him. The Russian grunted. Brick turned to Livia. "What do we do with them?"

Livia kept her eyes fixed on the big man with the bleeding nose. "Kill them, I think."

"Shit."

"No. I don't like it either. But what else?"

"You could do that?"

"I have done it. In Israel."

"This is different."

"Oh?"

"Hell, yes. These poor bastards aren't going to sneak back into your village or kibbutz and blow up some kids if you let them go."

"I've thought about it ever since we left London. What if something like this comes up again? What if I'm tracked back to London? I can be identified now."

"Livia? Do you realize how remote the chances of that are?"

"Not remote enough."

"Look at me, Livia."

She turned slowly toward him. Her eyes had a glazed, fatigued look to them.

"Do you see what I'm doing, Livia?"

"You're pointing your pistol at me."

"Keep aiming that thing of yours at those men. They're going to get up and go into the kitchen with us."

"Don't, Brick."

"You told me to stop you if you did anything that wasn't sane. This isn't sane."

"Don't, Brick."

"Stand up now." He motioned to the Russians to get to their feet. *"Idite,"* he said. Move.

In the kitchen, he fumbled in the drawer he had begun to search when he had spotted Ali Sabri. In a back corner his fingers found a key. Pistol still on

Livia, he unlocked the padlocked door he'd found earlier. It opened onto stairs that led down into what smelled like a root cellar. From a nail beside the back door, he lifted a coil of clothesline cord. "Put your gun down now," he said to Livia. "No, give it to me." Still with glazed eyes, she handed the machine pistol to him. "Now tie them. Tightly. You learned knots in Israel, right?"

"No," she said. "Girl Scouts." She tied the hands of the big man first, roughly, then his feet. She was gentler with the younger man. "Tell him," she said to Brick, "that he was very kind to me when I was pregnant."

Both men hopped down the stairs. When they were down, Brick had Livia tie them to the bannister. "They'll be loose at shift change, you know," she said.

"We'll be gone at shift change."

"But not out of the country. It's a risk."

"It's a risk."

They reached the living room just as Ali Sabri and Tony clumped down from upstairs. Tony saw the machine pistol in Brick's hand and Livia ahead of it. "What the hell?" he said.

"Tell him, Livia," Brick said.

"I wanted to kill the two guards."

"To what? To shoot them?"

"No, that would be too noisy. Some...other way."

"Livia, are you all right?"

"No. Yes. Brick stopped me." She lowered herself heavily onto the couch. Tears came, but no sobs. "I'm very tired now, I think. And I'm hungry. Would you have let me kill them, Tony?"

"Don't be stupid. I don't know."

Ali Sabri, looking embarrassed, walked to the

window and pulled back the curtain slightly. "Burhan, I think," he said. "A black prehistoric car?"

Brick picked Livia's coat up from the floor of the living room. "Better leave the way you came in. In case." Wearily, almost automatically, Livia stuffed the coat under her blouse again. Brick handed her machine pistol to Tony, who put it back under his coat. He put his own .38 back into his coat pocket, but left his hand loosely on it. Ali Sabri stayed at the window.

"No, wait," he said. "He's leaving."

"Leaving? Who?"

"Burhan. He's seen something."

Tony was beside Ali Sabri in two steps. He looked through the crack in the curtains that Ali Sabri held back for him. "Oh, God."

"Oh, God, what?" Livia said.

"It's another one. Another guard. He's turning up the sidewalk."

"No," Ali Sabri said. "Not just another guard. He's a captain, the supervisor. He comes to make sure I'm 'comfortable.'"

"Nobody said anything about this," Tony said angrily. "Two guards, they said. Eight-hour shifts. Nobody mentioned when any goddamn inspector would come by."

"Nobody knows when," Ali Sabri said. "He comes when he feels like it."

Brick stepped to the window beside them. The hugely overweight officer, middle-aged, middle-height, stopped to tie a shoelace. A house away, under a tree almost high enough to give shade, a car and driver waited.

"Shit, oh, shit," Tony said.

"Let him in," Brick said.

"Let him *in?*"

"You want to go meet him?"

"No. You're right. Inside."

Ali Sabri let the curtain flop closed and backed away from the window. They waited for the knock. It didn't come.

"Pavel Ivanovich?" The officer's voice sounded just outside the door. No one moved.

"Pavel? *Slyshaete?* Do you hear me?"

"Answer him, goddamnit, Brick," Tony whispered.

"Why in hell doesn't he knock?"

"He never knocks," Ali Sabri said. "He expects them to see him coming. It's his test."

"Brick!" Tony said.

"Pavel, *chort vozmi! Slyshaete?* Damn it. Do you hear me?"

"Da, slyshayu," Brick said. Yes, I hear.

"Now," Tony said. "Open the door and I'll grab the bastard."

Brick took a last quick peek through a crack in the curtains. The officer backed off from the door a pace and scanned the front of the house. "Pavel," he said. *"Gde Ali Sabri?"* Where is Ali Sabri?

Brick tried the first thing that came to his mind. *"Lezhil spat."* He's asleep.

The officer backed off a step more. Then, his face set in a look of frightened comprehension, he turned to run. "He's leaving," Brick yelled.

Tony pushed by him to the door. "Son of a bitch," he mumbled. "Son of a bitch, son of a bitch..."

He fired his first burst as the officer reached the end of the sidewalk. The man's sheer bulk seemed to hold him up for a moment. He spun in an easy, graceful pirouette, as surprising to Brick as a hippo toe-dancing. Tony fired another short burst. The man clutched for one of the new saplings beside the walk. The sapling bent beneath his weight, then snapped as he collapsed with it underneath his arm.

His chauffeur opened the door, stepped halfway out of the car, then slammed the door again. Tony was running toward the car by the time it began to move. He fired three short bursts and it lurched, swerved, hit one curb, then another, and lugged to a halt. The driver slumped forward. Brick was on the stoop now as Tony turned back toward the house. Down the street, the girl Brick had seen earlier hanging out clothes stood, hand to her mouth, by the corner of her house. Tony didn't see her. She whirled and slammed through her front door. Brick looked up at the telephone poles. A phone line ran from one of them to her house.

"Get them out!" Tony shouted.

"Out where, damn it?" Brick shouted back.

"Out, just out. Anywhere but here."

Brick looked up and down the barren street. This house or another house, what was the difference? There was nowhere else to hide. Livia was beside him now, her face still drawn, tear streaked. Brick whirled. Ali Sabri! Jesus, Livia didn't even have a gun now. What had she done with him? He ran back into the house. In the living room, Ali Sabri stood where they had left him, his face a mask.

"Where is there to go?" he said. "I'm better off here."

"Outside," Brick said.

Ali Sabri shrugged and walked past Brick to the door. As he stepped through it, the black *emka* lumbered around the corner. It slowed, as Burhan apparently saw the dead officer and the car crosswise in the street, then began to gather speed again.

"Tony!" Brick shouted.

Tony turned. With the same quickness that had surprised Brick earlier, he ran for the car. As it passed him, he lunged, grabbed the door handle, and flung himself into the front seat. The car jerked to a stop. Livia leapt a little wire fence beside the walk, and ran. Brick shoved Ali Sabri. They followed her, Ali Sabri outdistancing them all.

Burhan sat eyes-front behind the wheel, frozen. Tony put Livia beside him, and he and Brick slipped into the backseat with Ali Sabri between them. "Please. Do not sit on the sandwiches I have brought," Burhan said to Livia, miserably. "Praise Allah, Ali *bey*. You are free. Forgive me. I am terrified." He ground a gear and the car lurched forward.

Four

Only the rosebushes survived. The rest of the village was deserted, the stone huts clinging to the side of the little valley like petrified goats. The rosebushes had taken them over, too, climbing their walls, threading their vacant windows, arching over their collapsing roofs. Burhan told them the village had supplied roses to the great rose jelly factory in Er-evan once. Then, thirty years ago its people had been "removed" to a larger collective farm, leaving the roses to inherit their village. The *emka* sat like a winded rhinoceros a hundred yards below them, where the rutted road ran out. Tony was asleep on a pile of leaves in one of the deserted huts, the un-bearable sun broken by the roses over his head. All the way here, as Burhan had dodged through the back streets of Erevan, Tony had shaken and made little choking noises in his throat. That had seemed to strengthen Livia somehow, and now she sat near him, casting worried looks at him as they ate the thick sandwiches and drank the tepid tea Burhan had brought.

"As for the car," Burhan was saying. "No one knows I have it. It's not used much. That is no problem for me. It's the getting it back to the garage that is the problem."

"Then don't," Ali Sabri said.

"Don't? Don't take it back?"

"Leave it somewhere. Walk home."

"Oh, no...no, surely. They would find fingerprints or some such things."

"No, they won't," Brick said. He tiptoed to Tony and gently opened his coat. The two hand grenades were snap-hooked near his armpits. He unhooked one. "Pull this," he told Burhan, and pointed to the pin. "Drop it in the driver's seat, where your fingerprints are most likely to be, then run. Understood?"

Burhan took the grenade as if it were a snapping turtle, nodded and settled back to his tea, content. Ali Sabri threw the remains of his sandwich into a rosebush and took a long scarf from his cloth bag. With great care, he began to wind it into a Kurdish turban. "I have been naked a long while now," he said, and smiled.

"Your English is very good," Livia said.

"My father fought with the British in the war. Afterward there were still British everywhere in Iraq, where we were then. And for a while—" He shrugged. "There was the American university in Baghdad."

"You went to the university?" Livia tried to keep the incredulity out of her voice but failed.

"Is that so odd?" Ali Sabri said. "Didn't you go to university?"

Livia reddened. "Of course."

"I was going to be an engineer. But, well, you want to know the truth. I never got to the university. The only place I've been outside these mountains"—he swept his hand toward Ararat and Brick knew he meant the mountains from here to Iraq—"is Erevan. And I don't think so much of that. And, oh, two days in Tehrán once to meet the Shah. But I don't count that."

"Well that's...admirable," Livia said lamely.

"Yes, it is. Now you want to tell me what you want with me?"

Livia seemed startled for a moment. But she glanced at Brick, and began almost as if she had rehearsed this moment. She explained to Ali Sabri about the Turkish and Israeli offers: the safe asylum, the arms, the diplomatic support. She used her eyes a great deal and smiled at every shadow of an opportunity. Brick admired her. He knew how Ali Sabri must feel: as if he were the only human being for miles.

"Reasonable, reasonable," Ali Sabri said when she finished. "And, you'll forgive me, what will you want in return?"

"Friendly Kurds. A buffer."

"And no more?"

Livia took a deep breath. "And the longer you keep fighting, the better for all of us."

"Ah. If we keep dying, you are safer."

"You would keep fighting anyway, wouldn't you?"

Ali Sabri hesitated. "Yes. We always have."

"Then better to do it with friends."

Ali Sabri motioned brusquely for Livia to pour him more tea. Looking a little shocked, she did. "Details? Guarantees? There surely will be those."

"That's why you have to come to Turkey first. To Ankara."

"I never thought I would make that trip. And return."

"You said our offer was reasonable. Why should we take you away from the Soviets just to turn you over to the Turks?"

"Do you know the Hodja's story of the camel and the scorpion, Mrs. Lo Presti?"

"Whose?"

"Nasreddin Hodja. We tell many stories of him in the Middle East. He was a wise man who lived here many centuries ago—or at least they say he did. In any case, the Hodja tells of a camel and a scorpion who came to a river together. At the water's edge, the scorpion said to the camel, 'Dear Camel, I will surely drown if I try to swim this broad river. May I ride across on your hump?'

"'Oh, dear Scorpion,' said the camel. 'If I allow you to do that, you will sting me and I shall surely die.'

"'Consider, dear Camel,' said the scorpion. 'If I sting you, you will sink and we shall both die. Is that reasonable?'

"So. The camel considered, found the scorpion reasonable, and allowed him to ride his hump. And lo and behold, in the middle of the raging waters, the scorpion stung him. 'Oh, dear Scorpion,' the camel said as he felt the poison spreading. 'You have stung me and I shall surely die.'

"'This is true, dear Camel.'

"'But you, too, dear Scorpion, will die with me.'

"'This also is true, dear Camel.'

"'Then tell me, dear Scorpion—I entreat you with my last breath—why for the love of Allah did you sting me?'

"'Because, dear Camel,' said the scorpion as the water lapped at his little scorpion feet. 'This is the Middle East.'"

Ali Sabri took a sip of tea and wiped his mouth. "This, Mrs. Lo Presti, is the Middle East."

"Then you won't come?"

"I didn't say that. I just want you to understand the basis for our friendship. I am told that the Iranians, who were our friends a few years ago, are bombing our villages."

Burhan finished his sandwich and stood, brushing the crumbs from his pants. He had waited politely for a break in the English conversation he had understood none of. "You should all sleep now," he said. "I will watch. I had some sleep last night and will have some more tonight."

"They'll surely come for us, won't they," Brick said.

"Surely," Burhan said. "But we are isolated. I chose this place myself. I used to come here when I was in college, to learn the stars. Sometimes I would stay for a week. No one would come."

"Are you afraid?"

"Much afraid, yes."

"Have you ever done anything like this before?"

"Never. But when my Kurdish brothers from Alikochak came to me and asked if I could get a car, since I know Erevan well, I agreed." He rocked back a little on his heels, as if he were making a speech. "I have no wife. My mother is provided for by the state. Why not? Why not once in your life...well, I believe in a free Kurdistan, too. Do you understand?"

"Yes," Brick said. "The 'once in your life' part, yes."

Burhan looked embarrassed. "Look, there," he said, pointing up toward the upper end of the deserted village. "You can still see it, I think. The goat trail that goes upward toward that little cleft in the mountain."

Brick strained his eyes. "I see it."

"Before nightfall, you will take it. You won't want to try it in the dark. As it goes over the top of the mountain, you can easily see the border. To your right, you will see the Zanga River; to your left, the great Lenin canal. The slope of the mountain is easy, and forested. Descend on the trail through the trees to your right. You should be able to follow it even after dark. Just before you leave the forest, rest an hour. That should allow you to get to the Zanga and meet your colonel by two A.M."

"You know about the colonel, then."

"About the colonel, yes. About it all."

Ali Sabri, who had listened without interrupting, pushed to his feet. He embraced Burhan, who stood a head shorter than himself. "My brother," he said. Burhan turned away. With a dingy, much-used handkerchief, he wiped away tears. Brick, whose own father had never embraced him that way, with such honest emotion, felt a quick flash of jealousy. Annoyed at both the feeling and himself, he shoved it away, as if it were a persistent cat. He looked to Livia, who was smoothing the wispy hair off Tony's forehead. As he lay back, he admitted to himself that he wanted her more than he had ever wanted a

112

woman. The jealousy crept up again, this time with a friend: a disappointment bitter as a child's. So this is the revelation, he thought, the once-in-your-life: a fat bureaucrat of a cop and his poor driver dead in Erevan. Being a fifth wheel in a dead Armenian village. Those were my goddamn signals. He closed his eyes.

"Well?" he heard Livia say. There was seduction in her voice.

"Well?" Ali Sabri's voice answered.

"May I sleep, and know that you'll not be gone off across the mountains when I wake up?"

There was a pause. "I've never seen Ankara. Perhaps it's better than Erevan."

He awoke to sweat, the buzz of flies, and Burhan's hands shaking him. He swatted at both the hands and the flies, and felt the burning sweat trickle into his eyes. "They've come," Burhan was saying. "I did not stay awake. Please. They've come, and I cannot see Ali Sabri." The Kurdish swirled in Brick's head before he was able to put it together and make sense of it. He dabbed at the sweat in his eyes with a damp shirtsleeve, and tried to focus. Burhan's small head was right in front of his, and he was pointing frantically down the canyon toward the road. Brick ducked to see around him, and made out what seemed to be two beetles crawling toward the road across the plain. He dabbed at the sweat again. The beetles became horsemen.

"Who are they?" Brick asked.

"It's *them,* don't you see? They won't find us, no. But it's the car. They've surely got binoculars and they'll see the car."

"Stay calm," Brick said. "They won't see it unless

they come farther up the road than they're likely to."

"I can always run." In his panic, Burhan hadn't heard him. "But if they find the car they can trace me." He stumbled a couple of paces back from Brick. "They mustn't find the car!" He looked wildly around for something on the ground. Brick guessed what he wanted, and lunged for the hand grenade. But Burhan had a yard's head start. He scooped up the grenade and threw himself down the hill. Brick found a footing, then lost it again on the pebbly dirt. By the time he was on his feet again, Burhan was running in a wild, awkward lope toward the car. He was in the clear now. If the horsemen did have binoculars, they had seen him.

"Livia! Tony!" Tony was already moving groggily through the door of his hut. Brick tried to think, to see some order in the jumble of things that were happening. But there were too many things. Ali Sabri—where in hell could he have gone? He took Tony's arm and jerked him from the hut and explained—as best he could—what had happened.

"Sabri?" Tony said thickly. "Hell, Sabri's here. He's asleep in one of those huts up there. I woke up to piss and saw him."

"Get him," Brick said. The sound of the old *emka*'s grinding starter echoed up the canyon. Then the engine roared, and the car climbed the hill beside the road in a tilting, precarious turn. By the time Livia was beside him, it already was jouncing madly along the road toward the horsemen with a huge rooster tail of dust behind it. They had seen it, too. They galloped toward it, hanging low on their horses' necks. Brick saw the glint of a rifle as it came out of the lead horseman's saddle holster.

114

"Why didn't you stop him?" Livia said. She had taken her scarf off, and her bobbed hair, wet with sweat, stuck together in dark strands on the back of her neck.

"I tried. He panicked."

"Who do you think they are?"

"Could be just border guards. Or they could be looking for us."

"Either way," she said. "It's bad."

The horsemen rode in a long arc and intersected the road a hundred yards or so ahead of the *emka*. Burhan kept his course toward them. Then, thirty or so yards away from them, he swerved off the road. There was little difference between the road and the sparse, dry grassland beside it. The *emka* jerked violently back and forth as it hit the dirt—but kept going. One of the horsemen raced to meet it. The other, the one who had been in the lead before, raised his toothpick of a rifle. The distance was too great for Brick to tell just when he fired. He only saw the *emka* veer, sway as it went out of control, then slide sideways into a great cloud of its own dust. Not until then did he hear the distant, small crack of the rifle.

The first horseman reached the car and disappeared into the confusion of dust around it. As the second horseman rode up, the dust cleared enough for Brick to see that his partner had already dismounted and opened the door, and was bending over something in the driver's seat. There was no time for the second horseman to dismount. The car exploded first.

It popped like a dry balloon, soundlessly. Pieces of things spiraled from it into the air, and a thick ring of dust shot along the ground around it. The second horseman was flung backward nearly out of

115

the saddle, and his horse reared, again and again. When the sound of the grenade found its way up the canyon, it was a faraway jet boom, no more. Briefly, Brick wondered if Burhan had even meant it to happen that way, if he had understood about the pin after all. The poor bastard, the poor, skinny romantic bastard. Not so far from himself, Brick thought. And the fourth man to die in this god-awful mess. So far. He wanted the leisure to feel more for him than he could now.

As the horse bucked away from the car, the man on its back flopped like a doll tied to the saddle. He was hurt, clearly, but he was holding on. "Fall, damn you, fall," Brick whispered under his breath.

Somehow, however, the rider managed to bring the horse under control. Yet he made no attempt to slow it. As they reached the road, he let the horse continue its terrified gallop—away from the canyon, toward the highway that ran somewhere out of sight beyond the low foothills.

"Will he make it?" Livia asked flatly.

"I don't know. Depends on how bad he's hurt."

From behind them, Ali Sabri's voice said, "On how badly the horse is hurt, I'd say. The man is no good without the horse."

"That idiot, that damned idiot," Livia said.

"Burhan?" Ali Sabri answered. "Because he panicked? You wouldn't be here without him, and neither would I. Remember that. He did his best."

"Fine," Livia said sharply. "We're here, and we're trapped." She turned to face Ali Sabri and Tony.

"Are we?" Ali Sabri said. His voice remained calm in the still, hot air. "With the border five kilometers away?"

"You'd cross the border in daylight?" Brick said.

116

"I have crossed borders, my friend, in more kinds of light than even God on a good day knows about. Kurds understand borders."

"I don't," Tony said. *"Where* is the border five kilometers away?"

Brick explained to them what Burhan had told him in Kurdish about the paths. Now, in the afternoon shadows, the goat trail was more sharply defined against the canyon than it had been in the morning. Tony shaded his eyes against the glare from the bright sky and studied it a moment. "If that cowboy makes it to the highway, we don't have much time," he said.

"No," Livia said. "You have to go now."

"You? Second person singular?" Tony asked.

"You and Ali Sabri."

Tony turned to her very slowly. Their eyes met and held, sending messages. "And you, love?"

"We'll follow. After dark."

"Oh? You and our new friend."

"If they come back, Tony, there had better be somebody here. If not, they'll go straight for the border. I want you to be across it before they shut it completely."

"Me? Or Ali Sabri?"

"Both of you."

Ali Sabri had listened uncomfortably. Now, as he had done in the house in Erevan, he moved away from them. There seemed to be something about Livia, about the way she and Tony spoke to each other, that embarrassed him profoundly—even to the point of bowing out of conversations that could affect him.

Brick began to follow Ali Sabri down the canyon. In the distance, the horseman crested the top of the first hill. He wouldn't be visible anymore; they'd never know whether he made it or not. But now Brick knew they would have only one choice: to assume he had.

"Brick," Livia said. "Please stay."

"Yes," Tony said. "God knows you should have something to say about this. *Should,* though I'm not sure you will."

"Stop it, Tony," Livia said.

"All right, then. Why don't I stay with Brick, and you take Ali Sabri? Or why don't we send him alone?"

"Tony, look at the man. Who is he? I'm a woman. God knows what macho nonsense he might try to pull to show he's running things if we were by ourselves. He might at least listen to you. And send him alone? What if we didn't make it? Do you really think he'd make contact with Özpamir on his own? Or go to Ankara alone? Please. Now, of all times, make sense."

Defiance, almost like a child's, crept into Tony's voice. "And you'll stay here to head 'em off at the pass?"

"Who, them? The Soviet Army? God, Tony. I want to get out of here. Brick says it's not likely anybody knows about that path over the cliffs. Right, Brick?"

"From what Burhan told me, it's possible that somebody does, I suppose—but not likely," Brick said.

"Then all we've got to do is let them know we're still here until you've had time to make a try for the border. There's a good chance they'll send for reinforcements, or helicopters, or settle in to wait us out—something. In any case they'll feel secure enough not to try to come in for us right away if they don't think they have to, and they'll want Ali Sabri alive. So they'll go easy. Then before dark, as we planned, we can leave. And if they try to come for us in the dark, it'll be too late. We'll be gone."

Tony's eyes, their brows knit now not in any Mephistophelian way, but simply in uncertainty, left Livia. "Brick?" he said. "What do you think, Brick?"

Brick looked after the figure of Ali Sabri, who stood pitching futile stones toward the black smoke that rose from the ruins of the *emka*. "One of you has to be with Ali Sabri, I suppose. I couldn't. I'm not in on your deal."

"Yeah," Tony said, with no pretense of pleasantness.

"Well. There's only one more alternative." He knew as he spoke that he was saying it because he had to, out of some sense of perverse fitness. "I stay alone."

"No," Tony said. "That's rotten. You shouldn't be here in the first place."

Now they all stood, the afternoon's hot wind scattering clouds of gnats, and watched Ali Sabri throw the stones harder and harder, as if he were trying to drive away some presence that hung around the smoldering car. After a time, Livia said, "It's settled, then."

"It's settled," Tony said softly.

Tony waved, forcing himself to clown, just before he passed from sight through the cleft in the rocks. Ali Sabri hadn't protested the decision; he had seemed even to tacitly approve it. Livia waved back at Tony until he was long beyond seeing her. When she dropped her hand, without showing Brick her face she walked beyond him into a ruined hut, one that was almost wholly overgrown with roses. Brick didn't try to speak to her. He sat on a heap of stones and watched the last of the smoke blow away from the skeleton of the *emka*. The bodies of the horseman and his horse lay like forgotten toys a few yards from it.

When Livia came from the hut, she had made some attempt at straightening her bobbed hair, and had tried without much success to brush some of the dirt from her cheap skirt. And the dust on her face was smeared with the remains of new tears.

"How about that?" she said. "I haven't cried twice in a day for years."

"Want to do some more names?" Brick said, not really wanting to say anything.

"You do some. You're better at it."

"OK. Lemme see. Phone books again, swear to God. Dimple Wiggins, Vera Little, Thurlow Snoddy, Warner Grumbles..."

"I couldn't have let him stay behind. You saw what happened to him after this morning in Erevan. He fell apart."

"In the car? Yeah, he was hurting."

"But, God, I was proud of him. We would never have made it out of that damn house without him."

"No, we wouldn't have."

"You know, I think that's the first living thing he's ever killed. He won't even poison mice."

She walked a few paces from Brick's heap of stones and looked off down the canyon. "They should be coming if they're going to."

"Before long."

"I'll tell you something else, Brick Rustin. I almost crumbled up into little pieces this morning, too. You knew that. Thanks."

120

"Happens to the best."

"It's just that we think that everything's so damned orderly. There's a street in a town that's quiet in the morning, with people hanging out clothes and listening to the radio and walking their babies. And then the world falls apart. Somebody starts shooting and cars smash up and everything awful that's really always there so close to the surface is right out in the open. It's like getting mugged, I guess. That terror, that violence, is just always there, so *god*damned close to the surface. And we go on trying to pretend that everything makes sense, like Baptist preachers or TV commercials. That's the really horrible part."

She walked the few paces back up the hill to him. Then she leaned down and kissed him, very gently, on the lips. Brick sat still, his hands tensed on the stones beside him.

"I didn't last long as a commando. Things like what happened to me in the house this morning kept happening to me. I thought too much, I guess." She picked up his hands and put them on her hips. "I don't want to think now, Brick. Please."

"Do you love Tony?"

She kissed him again, longer this time. He tasted the faint salt of sweat on her mouth. He slipped his tongue between her lips. She opened her mouth and rolled her own tongue around his, then pulled away and straightened up. "Tony gave us permission, don't you see. When he said, 'It's settled,' that's what he was giving us: permission. I know him."

"He's done it before, you mean," he said—a statement, not a question.

She hesitated. Her hands slid down her sides and lifted his hands from her hips. She glanced toward

121

the empty plain, then toward the hut she had just come out of. "Please, Brick. We don't have much time." She smiled. "I wanted this to happen before, before...whatever else happens. Do you want that, Brick?"

He stood. "Yes," he said, looking for a smile to answer hers with but not finding it. "Yes."

It was the strangest lovemaking Brick could remember, quick, nearly wordless. There had been almost no touching beforehand, no sense of play, as if the act itself had been too important to be put off. Yet in that quickness, that release, was a greater intensity, too, than he could remember. If before, Livia had made him feel he was the only other human being for miles, in their lovemaking she had made him feel he was the only man on earth. She had consumed him, had surrounded him, had taken all of him into her. When she said his name as they struggled against each other in the bed of leaves she had made for them, her voice made it clear that she was making love to *him*—only him and completely him. He had never felt so bloody—*particularized* before. He knew she was married to another man, and he didn't give a damn. He'd experienced a kind of consummation with her that, in happening only once, he knew had become necessary to him. Whatever he had to do to make sure he continued to have that, he would do.

And now they each lay separately on the leaves in the ruined hut, loosely holding hands and staring up at the tangle of bloodred roses above them. A tangle, Brick thought, like the tangle he had to somehow make sense out of. He could well be in love with Livia, yet what in hell did that mean for him—

and for her? What kind of promises had she made him by making love to him? And soon, very possibly, Soviet troops would be coming up the canyon after them. And four men were dead who wouldn't be dead if it weren't at least partly for this woman who lay naked beside him. And he wanted her as much now as he had before they had made love. And even if the troops didn't come, he and she somehow would have to get over a border that would be crawling with guards. And he knew now that he was where he was, ultimately, because of something he felt for this woman, and not any kind of revelation or morality. And yet, and yet—he couldn't let it be wholly because of her, either.

The light filtered at an evening angle through the thickly twined limbs of the rosebushes. He would have to get up in a few seconds. Nothing would untangle now. There was no time. No time for anything except to try to unentrap himself and Livia, with only one chance at it, from this wilderness of roses.

Outside the hut, he sat on his heap of stones and watched the jeeps and the flat-faced trucks move over the hill below. It was almost with relief that he saw there were only four trucks, canvas-covered, camouflaged regular army troop carriers that lumbered over the remains of the road swaying like fishing boats. They hadn't risked bringing artillery. Livia had been right. At least he knew the two of them wouldn't be blasted out of the canyon before they had their one chance.

Livia came out of the hut tying her hair up in the scarf, Western-fashion now. She stood a moment beside him, watching. He reached out and took her hand. It was tense but steady in his.

"I'd guess they'll come up to investigate first. Then they'll try to work up over the mountainsides around us," he said.

"Unless they know about the path."

"Unless they know about the path."

The same calm tension that Brick felt in Livia's hand was in her voice. "We can't afford to wait until they're on the mountainsides. They'll be able to see the path by then."

"I know that." Brick glanced at the sun, which was balanced on the edge of the canyon rim on his left. "Less than two hours till dark."

"If that much."

"Not much range in those machine pistols. We'll have to get close." The lead jeep bounced off the road toward the *emka*. The second one kept coming, with the trucks behind it. They had ten minutes, maybe. No more than that. "Come on."

"Wait," she said, and ran to the hut. She came out again with Tony's other hand grenade. "I kept this to convince them we had more than pistols."

"I wish we did." He stood. "Ready?"

"Brick?" She touched his arm. "What happened, you know—I'm glad it did. Very."

His kissed her lightly. "Scared?"

"Shitless."

"Know any prayers?"

"Yeah. The kaddish. The prayer for the dead."

They kept to the edge of the village, out of sight of the convoy below. Brick was glad of their one advantage: the convoy was in the open plain, with no way to hide what it was doing. From time to time as he and Livia worked their way down the canyon, Brick glimpsed the troops. The first jeep, like a scouting ant, had nosed around the *emka* for a few minutes then rejoined the rest of the pack, which had stopped at the canyon's mouth. A couple of officers seemed to be checking the village with binoculars while a platoon of troops formed up in front of the trucks. The rest of the men stayed behind the trucks in a loose formation. Brick lost sight of them as he scrambled around a heap of boulders, maintaining altitude on the canyon wall. When he saw them again, the platoon had started up the canyon, staying low and using what cover they could.

Near the spot where Burhan had parked the car before, the canyon, boulder-strewn from landslides, grew narrower. And above that point, the rock had broken away in such a fashion that a small cave— really only a shelf with an overhang—had been left. Brick judged the distance to the shelf. They could be there before the troops reached the narrow spot in the canyon. And they would be almost directly above the troops.

The sun was behind the mountain now, but the sweat had broken out again on Brick—from the climb, or from what they were about to do, he wasn't sure. To get to the shelf without being seen they had to cut straight across the side of the canyon, scrambling on the loose rocks and losing sight of the approaching soldiers. In the moments when the evening wind paused, Brick could hear Livia murmuring something in Hebrew. He hoped it wasn't the kaddish.

They reached the shelf just as the officer leading the platoon was motioning his men to spread out and take the narrow pass in single file. Brick threw himself flat and gave his hand to Livia, who, panting, spread herself beside him.

"How's your throwing arm?" he whispered.

"Damn good, actually," she said.

"High school state championship team?"

"No."

"I was. Give me the grenade."

Reluctantly, she handed it to him. The officer still kept the lead below them and cautiously moved into the boulders. Brick picked his spot. If he missed, the grenade would bounce God-knew-where and manage to blow up no more than a gopher hole or two. He took a deep breath, held it, and got to his knees. He lobbed the grenade underhand and followed through with his swing as if the thing had been a bowling ball.

The grenade glanced off a boulder beside the path, then disappeared. The officer stopped, startled, and looked up at the canyon walls. Brick ducked out of sight and closed his eyes. He counted to five after the explosion. When he opened his eyes, he crawled forward to the edge of the rock, staying as low as he could.

Then Livia was on her knees, spraying the path with bullets. The officer shouted to his men and hit the dirt. Thirty paces or so ahead of him dust still boiled off the path. Brick grabbed for Livia.

"You missed, you son of a bitch," she hissed, and fired another burst at the path.

"No, hell, I didn't. Get down."

A few shots cracked against the rocks, yards away from them. Livia dropped down and slid off the shelf; her firing had let the troops know which side of the canyon they were on, but their luck had held. No one had seen precisely where they were. Brick watched the troops a minute more, then slid off behind her.

"Run," Brick said. "Stay out of sight, but run."

She stood her ground. "You did miss, damn you, you did!"

"You wanted to let them know we were here, right? Did I have to kill any of the bastards to do that? Look!" He stood back to let her see around the rock shelf. The troops were backing down the path. A couple fired randomly at the rocks to cover the rest. But they were leaving—retreating! "We've got what we want. They'll take time to get themselves back together—maybe not even before dark. Now move, damn it!"

"You son of a bitch," she said. He shoved past her and scrambled toward the goat trail. A few steps away from her, he turned. She was following. "So move, damn it," she said.

They stayed on the mountainside and intersected the trail above the village, near where the last of the rosebushes clung to the dry, rocky land. Brick picked one of the stunted roses and offered it to Livia. With an odd, not happy smile, she stuck it into the barrel of her machine pistol. "God help me," she said. "I hope that's the last thing that fills up this barrel."

She kept up with him as they climbed, and when they stopped to rest it was because he wanted it, not she. The sun had gone far enough down so that its rays weren't even hitting the top of the canyon now. The path was easy enough, preserved by the dryness, and they had no trouble keeping a good pace. The steepest part was just before the top, where the path twisted back on itself to reach a sharp V in the rock that marked the break in the cliff. In the middle of the turn, they had their last glimpse of the village, muted in the shadows now, its roses disappearing as tiny dark-red spots in the gloom. It was still empty.

Ararat was before them, its icy peak the palest of corals in the sunset.

The light slowly left them on the way down the mountain, as if the day's batteries were dying. As they worked their way out of the new growth of the forest—the product of some Soviet reforestation project years before—the wind took on a nighttime coolness. Brick was glad he had held on to the baggy coat. The path had gotten better as they came further down the mountain; forest rangers and berry pickers must have visited it often. Or lovers, young *kolkhozniki* farmers seeking the privacy of the great spruces, away from their communes. Once they surprised a pair kissing, but smiled and nodded their way past them, embarrassed and terrified.

Then the forest ended and the path broke up into three smaller ones at the edge of a vineyard. Only a thin line of gray on the horizon told them they were still heading west as they moved through the even rows of grape frames—that, and the bulk of the Ararat massif over their left shoulders. Leading from the neat houses and meeting hall of the vineyard commune was a dirt road. Brick had visions of search parties and dogs, so they stayed off the road but kept near it as a guide. Within two kilometers, breathless, they found the highway.

Brick tried to remember the land as he had seen it before they dropped down into the forest from the mountain. This highway would be the east–west road, the main one that ran the length of Armenia, not the feeder road to Erevan they had taken before. If that were so, then they should be within only two or three kilometers of the border. So it would be foolish to keep going west to find the Zanga River and cross where they had crossed before. The land seemed flatter here, too, which meant that the Araks canyon would be shallower. They should cut toward Ararat, get out of the Soviet Union as soon as they could. Among the Turkish Kurds, they should be all right. *Should* be, Brick emphasized to himself.

"You willing to try it?" he asked Livia as they crouched in the grasses beside the highway. A military jeep swooshed by them and whined away down the highway into the night.

"To get out of this country quicker? I'd fly if I had to."

They paralleled the highway, starting at even the sound of crickets, until they found a dry steam bed between two low hills. The hills were barren, too dry and rocky for farming. That was good, Brick thought. No more communes.

In half an hour they were beyond the hills. Before them was the canyon of the Araks. And beyond that, on the Turkish side of the river, campfires blinked. Kurdish campfires and safety.

Something in the sight, perhaps the closeness of it, seemed to trigger the exhaustion in Brick that he knew had been building all day but that he hadn't allowed himself to feel. Livia slowed, too, and wordlessly they collapsed into the grasses. In the distance, they could hear the faint rushing of the Araks. The wind rustled the grasses. There was no other sound.

Livia lay beside Brick and pulled him close. "I must smell like fish," she said.

"Probably," Brick said. "I can't tell. I smell like the fishmonger."

Livia laughed softly. "God, I hope that river water is drinkable."

"Depends on how thirsty you are."

"We'll have no trouble crossing it. I'm going to drink the damn thing dry."

"Close your eyes," he said. "Imagine a Big Mac and a quart of Coke. With ice."

"Mmmmmm."

"What will you do?"

She waited too long to answer. "About the Big Mac?"

"About Tony."

"Don't ask me that, Brick. Please."

"Christ! I have to."

"I've stayed with Tony ten years. That counts."

"And me?"

"I've known you less than a week, Brick."

"Will I see you again when we get back?"

"If you want. I don't think I'll be in Trabzon much."

"No. I won't either. And if I keep seeing you—in London, or wherever—could something develop? I mean, would you let it develop?"

"I have a rule, Brick. It goes, 'never anticipate the outcome with the outcome.' Does that make sense?"

"Not much."

"It does to me." She pulled him closer. "Please. No talking now."

"One more question, OK? One I haven't wanted— don't want—to ask. About Roger. How much does Roger know about all this?"

"Shhh! Listen." She covered his mouth with her hand.

The voices that came from the stream bed were low, controlled, the way nervous people talk in the darkness. Men's voices, two or three—Brick couldn't tell for sure. He strained to make out what language they were speaking. As they came closer and he heard the crunch of their footsteps in the stream bed, he recognized the strange consonants of Armenian. Home guards, then. Not Russians. That was a small relief. Home guards would have been rousted from their supper at some commune, probably the vineyard they had passed, to look for a Kurd they could care less about finding. They would only want to make a round and get back to their supper and brandy. Nor would they be trained soldiers.

But could he and Livia be seen from the stream bed? When they had fallen into the grass, he had had no thought of hiding in it. He tried to wriggle further from the stream bed and pull Livia with him. He got only a few inches before he saw that his movements were causing a much greater commotion in the dry grass than they were worth. Livia squeezed his arm for him to be still. Very slowly, she tucked her legs up. Brick glanced down. His shoes stuck out at least a foot into the stream bed. The beam from a flashlight swept the grass only seconds after he eased them out of sight. His dry mouth filled with a stale taste of dust.

As the men passed, he saw that he had been right: two men in civilian clothes and another in the uniform he had seen the border guards wearing at the checkpoint by the bridge. One of them stopped and ground out a cigarette a yard from Brick's feet. Brick smelled the cheap, black-tobacco *makhorka*. Livia was as still and stiff in his arms as a log. He could feel her heartbeat.

The men moved on down the stream bed, which would empty into the Araks. When their footsteps were almost inaudible, Livia whispered, "I won't wait for them to come back. I can't stand that again."

"No," Brick said. As quietly as possible, he turned

in the grass so that he could see along the stream
bed. It cut straight to the river. The river canyon
was so low here that he saw the occasional flashing
of the Araks in the moonlight. At the end of the
stream bed, the men stood and talked a moment,
then turned upstream along the riverbank.

"Give them a couple of minutes," he told Livia.
"Then, Christ, all we've got is surprise. Can you
swim?" He remembered the first time he had seen
her coming off the boat. A swimmer's walk, had it
been?

"Yes."

"Relax then. Gather some strength. When I go, go
with me."

He lay and counted, one thousand...two
thousand...three thousand...until he hit a hundred.
The three men had still not reappeared. He gave it
fifty more counts, each one as long as an hour, it
seemed. Dear God, he thought. One quick run to the
water; it's not much to ask. Please, dear God...

"Go!" he said.

He swung himself into a runner's crouch, grateful
that he hadn't rested long enough for his muscles to
tighten. Then he sprang into the stream bed, running,
with Livia's hand in his. She stayed with him, the
rapid sound of their feet hushed by the loose soil,
their breathing louder than the river ahead of them.
He hadn't run like this since he was a child, full of
the terror of running from a swaying tree in the
night. Yet now the terror was real, waiting in the
vaster night of the Soviet Union behind him, waiting
in the three men who might be only yards away from
the mouth of the stream bed. He stumbled, jerked
Livia's hand. She lost her balance, too, and went
down on one knee. They pulled each other to their

feet. And then they were running again, holding hands and laughing and running like four-hundred hell. He didn't know who started laughing first, only that they cackled and couldn't stop and the river glimmered a dozen feet ahead of them and he didn't give a damn.

Not even when they saw the startled faces of the three men in the moonlight, only a room's length away. One, the guard, stood with a half smile, uncertain. He had his pants unzipped, pissing into the water. Livia shrieked. "Oh, God, he's *pissing!*" she managed between howls of laughter. The other two men were as frozen as boulders. They all stood staring at each other, he and Livia and the three men, for what seemed fully ten seconds. Then Brick leapt.

From the corner of his eye he saw Livia hit the water a moment ahead of him. He wanted to get underwater as soon as he could. But the water was less than knee-deep and he had to fight for each step. It was swifter than he had thought, pulling at his legs like an undertow. He glanced behind him. The guard, pants still unzipped, fumbled with the snap of his holster. One of the other men raised a hunting rifle. Livia struggled a pace behind Brick, her scarf flapping loose around her face. She ripped it away just as he reached back for her, shoved her forward into the water, and dove behind her.

He crawled like a crayfish on the rocky bottom, fighting the current, until his breath gave out. When he surfaced, it was just in time to hear two quick shots. He looked for Livia. She was ten feet away from him now. He shouted her name. She dove again. He kicked forward, back underwater. And when he reached for the bottom, it was gone.

He panicked for a moment, and the moment was

133

enough for him to lose his equilibrium. The current tumbled him like a tree branch, over and over until he hit a rock that shoved him into line with the rushing water. Now he was a projectile, shooting between scraping stones. He put his hands in front of himself blindly and felt his breath giving out. He kicked, trying for the surface. But it wasn't there; the whole world of air was gone.

When he hit the rapids he was dizzy, bursting with held breath. Then he tumbled head over heels in the churning water, felt foam around him, and knew there was air. His hands found a jutting log, and he grabbed. It was slippery, rotting, and his hands only held it for a few seconds. Yet he breathed. One deep gulp, and as he slid back into the noisy water, the mineral taste of it in his mouth, his head cleared.

It stayed clear until he shot from the rapids into the swirling pool of deeper water at their base. He pulled toward the bank, praying it was the Turkish side of the river, and found there was no strength left in his arms. The water swirled him until he lost all sense of direction. He tried kicking, dog-paddling. Ahead, he saw white water in the moonlight again. He had to get to a bank, any bank. He had no strength for another set of rapids. He kicked, he flailed with his weak, cramped arms. He brushed a rock, grabbed, missed. Then another smooth rock was ahead of him and the water wrapped him around it like a bundle of grass. With the last of his strength, he reached past the rock and touched mud.

He moved like a centipede, bending, straightening, until his chest was in the mud. He managed to get to his knees. Ahead of him, to his right, was Ararat. He was in Turkey!

Panting, trying to keep his shaking head still, he looked around him for Livia. He saw the dark pool beside him, the rocks blue in the moon shadows around him, the crumbling gray riverbank rising behind him. The wind flailed at him like a spray of ice water. In the pool, Livia's scarf whirled a moment, then was snatched away by the rapids. He tried to shout, but he couldn't hear the sound of his own voice. He bit at the air, his lungs still not full enough of it, and pitched forward into the mud.

He didn't sleep. He was conscious of time passing, of the night deepening, of the stars brightening and sharpening. He moved in and out of a half doze, always kept just on the edge of consciousness by the wind skimming across his wet clothing. But for how long? When at last he tried his arms and found that they trembled under his weight but held, he sat up. His head was clear, but he felt as generally miserable as if he had only partially slept off a bad drunk. He tried to think. How far downstream had he been pushed? Should he head inland, or try to follow the river back upstream to the point by the Zanga where the colonel was to be waiting for him? Hell fire. It could be far past two o'clock for all he knew, and the others would have given up on him already. But inland? He could wander for days without finding even a shepherd. And the things that came out at night in these hills—the mountain lions, the long-tusked boar, the wolves—guarded their land well. He felt for the pistol in his torn coat pocket. It was gone, somewhere on the bottom of the Araks.

With the help of a root growing out from the bank, he got to his feet. His legs, like his arms, trembled at first. But he took a couple of tentative steps and felt their steadiness returning. No, he couldn't go inland. Nor could he make progress here at the river's edge, which narrowed in places so that he would have to swim to keep going. Above, alongside the canyon, the land seemed reasonably flat, and he could always slip back to the river if he had to. He could follow the river from there, and hope. And look for Livia.

The thought of Livia cut at him like the cold wind. Had she survived even the first set of rapids? Or what about the shots he had heard before he dove under? She was probably a good swimmer—maybe better than he was. But, Jesus, what swimming had been possible in that broken water? If she wasn't here, by this pool, as he was, her chances of having made it were as good as a cat's in a coyote pack.

But if he assumed that, and didn't look, was he any better than Özpamir, whom he had condemned like an unctuous prick for leaving the man behind in the canyon on the way to Erzurum? And this was Livia, not some stranger. What a stinking joke it would be if the main reason he had come on this insane trip were gone even before he made it back. A reason that was the first real reason he had found for anything in four years. A bad, stinking goddamn joke.

He wouldn't—couldn't—let himself think of her as he groped for a climbing purchase on the low canyon wall. No, not refuse to think of her, really, but refuse to think of *her,* the feel and smell of her, the way she moved, the softness of her as he penetrated her. He would look for her as he walked, go to her if he found her body along the river. But not think of her.

The climb was easy here, the cliff no more than

a high bank. But when he was on top of it, he saw that he had been carried only a few hundred yards from the stream bed, not the miles it had seemed. He could see the length of both banks. They were empty. He looked downstream in the other direction. The next rapids was a long one, and beyond it the river spread into a shallow, broken fan over gravel before it plunged into its next canyon. A body would have lodged there if it had made it beyond the rapids.

In ten minutes, he was past the rapids. The easy-rippling water spread flatly through the gravel. Here and there logs rose at haphazard angles, imbedded in the riverbed. Only logs.

He turned back. She wouldn't have survived the first rapids, then. Or maybe it had been the shots. Had she survived those and had she gotten away from the three men on the other side, she would have looked for him. She couldn't have missed him.

He resisted the temptation to turn inland toward the occasional campfire he saw in the distance as he walked upstream. They looked so close, yet God only knew what lay between him and them. Across the river, an occasional flashlight darted along the riverbank, and he saw flares far upstream toward the watchtowers. He ignored them, stayed low, and kept going. A mounted patrol passed, vanished into the night downstream, then passed again. Once he heard shots; another time, wolves. Still, he kept going, walking steadily on clear ground for the most part, now and then scrambling over the remains of landslides or over outcroppings in the smooth hills. The movement warmed him, and he was glad for it.

He was almost upon the canyon of the Zanga before he recognized it. He had come upon it from the other direction before, upstream of it, with Tony and

Livia and the colonel. At first he wasn't sure it was the same place. Yet as he drew closer he made out the flat spot Rize had led them to, the small delta they had walked along to head inland toward the bridge. It was the first recognizable thing he had seen for twenty-four hours. Twenty-four hours? Only that? Dear God, he thought, it seemed like twenty-four years!

He scanned the riverbank in the dimness, all along the section where the colonel had promised he would be waiting. Did he really expect anyone to be there? Only by the purest luck would the hour be anywhere near the appointed one now. Or even if it was, what were the chances that the colonel, knowing that things had gone wrong, would risk being here? He looked now to the long, sloping hill they had come down on horseback to reach the river last night. How long would it take to climb that on foot? How much energy—energy that he might not have? And once he climbed it, what would he find at the camp? He remembered the awful canned stew they had eaten by the Sterno fire there. He would give a year of his life for a can of the vile crap now, for an hour's heat from a can of Sterno. And yet the camp would probably be empty. And then what? If the Kurds knew that anything had gone wrong, what would they have waiting for him? Would they want to wipe out a bad memory?

He rested. His choice was no choice. He could go only one way: up the hill, back toward the camp. And beyond that, home.

No Kurdish shepherds lit the way now. He lost the trail, found it, lost it again. Still in the distance, campfires glimmered. Yet only in the distance. The hillside was as deserted now as in the days before the first creature set foot on it. The strength that had carried him along the riverbank was failing now; each time he lost the trail he had to rest before he set out to find it again. The moon moved across the sky, and whenever he rested he saw that more stars had wheeled beneath the horizon. The night had to be ending, *had* to be. All nights, even this one, had to end. Yet it wasn't until he rounded the ridge he had climbed once to look at the far lights of Erevan that he saw the first glow of dawn rising like an emanation from Ararat itself, the way Noah must have seen it.

He pushed himself the last twenty yards to the crest of the trail. And just below him, colorless in the weak light, the three tents squatted in the meadow like arks.

Near them, the horses and pack mules nodded, and the stream leapt over the rocks as before. All was silent, nothing moving except for the water. He followed the course of the stream along the small canyon with his eyes. It was deserted. Cautiously, he picked his way down the trail.

Tony and Livia's tent was the first. He stood beside it a full minute, listening. He heard nothing, not even the sound of breathing. He pulled open the flap an inch and bent to see inside. Their sleeping bags lay side by side, empty.

He closed his eyes and calmed his breathing, then stood. The colonel's tent was next, only a few steps away. Again he waited beside it, listening for the sound of breathing. And again he eased open the flap to find a flat, empty sleeping bag.

At his own tent, he didn't bother to listen. He didn't care now. He wanted to sleep for an hour, just that above all things, no matter what in hell was around him or waiting for him. He knelt, then flung open the flap. In the near dark of the tent, he saw the machine pistol before he saw that it was Ali Sabri holding it.

"You made more noise than a horse," Ali Sabri said quietly. "If I hadn't been worried about making noise myself, I would have shot you before you touched the tent flap."

"Where are they?" Brick said. His unused voice cracked.

"They? Your colonel is probably where an Iranian colonel ought to be, in a whorehouse somewhere. I haven't seen him. My friend Tony was asleep in his tent last time I saw him."

"He's not now."

"Is his wife with you?"

"No."

"What happened?"

"I lost her. In the river."

"Dead?"

"I don't know. I think so."

Ali Sabri lowered the machine pistol. "Allah, Allah. I tried to tell him that on the way back here. She was no woman for this kind of thing."

"Shut up," Brick said.

"Oh," Ali Sabri said after a pause. "I see. I didn't understand."

"No, you didn't."

"How far is it to the village her husband told me about?"

"Maybe four hours' ride."

"Have you slept?"

"Some. Not really."

"You sleep. I'll watch awhile and make coffee.

140

Maybe find my friend Tony. But I won't tell him about his wife. You do that."

"Where do you think he is?"

"Are all the horses here?"

"Yes."

Ali Sabri shrugged. "Then he's probably shitting somewhere, *inshallah*. You sleep."

"I don't need to sleep," Brick lied.

Ali Sabri snorted. "I'll not have you falling off a horse on the way. One hour's sleep, until it's warm enough to ride." He crawled off the sleeping bag. "Here. Yours is the best bag. I tried them all."

Brick backed out of the entrance to the tent as Ali Sabri brushed by him. He wanted to protest more, but knew he wasn't capable of it. He had to concentrate just to breathe.

"You're still wet," Ali Sabri said. "You have clothes in there?"

"Somewhere."

"Then take those things off before you sleep. Nobody sleeps when he looks like a wet Armenian peasant."

"What will you do?"

"I told you. Look around. Make coffee."

"No. I mean after that. If you don't find Tony."

Ali Sabri studied the ground. "You trust this Turkish major—what's his name?"

"Özpamir. I think so."

"And the other man, Brenner?"

"I don't know."

Ali Sabri looked up. "Then we find Özpamir. Turks I can understand. Israelis—who knows?"

"Why don't you just go to Iran now?"

"Empty-handed? That's the way I left. My own people I understand, too. If I come back with arms

and an arrangement with the Turks, I'm still a chief.
Empty-handed, I'm just a...what do you say?...a
symbol." He tapped his forehead and smiled. "I've
thought about it. I'll take the risk. Now sleep."

Stripped, Brick folded back the sleeping bag, pro-
longing the moment. Did he believe Ali Sabri? Had
the colonel simply not been there when he and Tony
showed up—or had something happened to him *after*
they arrived? Or, for that matter, had Tony made it
back at all? He tried to remember little things about
his conversation with Ali Sabri. In the dark, he
hadn't been able to see him well, to gauge his expres-
sions. Had there been anything menacing in his
voice? Not that Brick could tell, anyway; the good
humor that had been there since he first found him
at the house in Erevan hadn't failed. But what did
that mean, really? If he slept, would he wake up?
Ali Sabri said he was worried about making noise.
Why? If there was no one but Kurds, his people, in
the hills, why would he be worried about noise? But
given that Ali Sabri *was* worried about noise, was
he just waiting for him to go to sleep to...do whatever he was going to, damn him.

Brick settled into the sleeping bag. Somehow, he
felt safe. Maybe because he trusted Ali Sabri, even
though there was no good reason he should. But
maybe, too, because he felt a perverse kind of un-
touchability. It wouldn't happen this way, not in a
sleeping bag, not after what he had survived in the
past thirty or so hours. No, Tony had made it back,
as Ali Sabri said. When he woke up, he would feel
better and Tony would be here and they would all
ride back to the jeeps, then a hot shower and a meal
in Doğubeyazit. Then to Trabzon, and Ibrahim's gold
tooth and peroxided hair.

But where in hell *was* Tony? Or Rize? Or Brenner, or Özpamir?

Or Livia.

He wasn't going to think of her. No. He fought for sleep, for the not-thinking.

He could have been asleep all day, or ten minutes, when he became conscious of the gunfire. At first he was in Trabzon, and the cars were backfiring as usual. But then the filtered light of the tent, the olive nylon above him told him he wasn't in Trabzon. And there were no cars here. His head hurt. He lay with his eyes open, trying to locate the hurt and still only half believing he had heard gunfire.

Until he heard the second round: a burst from a machine pistol, then two or three single shots. Not nearby, but close enough to come to him clearly and wake him fully. He shoved the sleeping bag away from himself, his headache shifting like water in a jar as he moved, and crawled to the tent flap. Outside, Ali Sabri squatted beside the Sterno stove, which had a pot of water on it and an open can of Nescafé beside it. He was absolutely still, his head cocked like a dog's, staring toward the trail from the village. His eyes were as intense as if they were seeing through the rocks that blocked his view of the trail. Above, dawn had shaded into early morning, but just barely.

Ali Sabri motioned for Brick to be still. Brick settled, half in and half out of the tent, and waited. Ali Sabri held a totally intolerable position for a minute, two minutes, three. Then he eased to his feet and glanced at Brick with no real interest, as if he were only making sure he was still there.

"Tony?" Brick said. "Did you find him?"

"No." Ali Sabri said. "Do you have that pistol still?"

"No."

Ali Sabri checked the slopes of the valley around them. "Get dressed, quickly. I'll be just over the top of the trail, there." He pointed to the trail back toward the border, in the direction opposite the gunfire, then strode away without looking at Brick again. Brick crawled back inside the tent, groping for the backpack he had left his clothing in, fighting to make his stiff, unsteady fingers open the buckle.

Ali Sabri was prone beside the trail, with rocks piled in front of him in such a way that he had only a half-dozen inches of clear space to see—or fire— through. Brick slid beside him. They were just beyond the crest of the hill so that they had only to raise their heads slightly to have a view of nearly the entire stream valley.

"Seen anything?" Brick whispered.

Ali Sabri flicked his eyebrows up and clicked his tongue in the universal Middle Eastern *no*.

"Any ideas?"

"You weren't the first to come to the camp this morning," Ali Sabri said. "I heard somebody else, about two hours before you came."

"Did you see who?"

"Kurds can do many things. Kurds cannot see in the dark, *efendi*."

That explained why Ali Sabri was shy of making noise, then. "How many people?"

"One came. Two left."

And that explained Tony, too, Brick thought. His head felt as if someone had suction cups attached to the backs of his eyeballs, jerking them. He shut his eyes and rubbed them and they hurt worse. When

he opened them, he saw the tail end of a movement—
a shadow, maybe, or only a flash of light inside his
own eye—that appeared to come from the far rim
of the little valley, where the trail crossed. He looked
to Ali Sabri. He was watching the same place.

All was still again, as if whatever they were
watching was watching them, too. They waited.
After a time, something glinted in the morning sun,
just where Brick thought he had seen the movement.
Something metal. Then a figure rose from beside the
trail's protecting boulders and stepped into the open.

Since he had seen her last in her peasant's skirt
and blouse, Brick's mind skipped a beat before rec-
ognition came. But there was no question: the swimmer's walk, the heavy breasts underneath the man's
shirt. No, it was Livia.

She walked hurriedly along the trail toward the
camp, glancing over her shoulder without breaking
stride. Brick started to rise, but Ali Sabri laid his
hand on him to hold him down. Livia crossed the
stream, making no attempt to come upon the camp
quietly. As she came closer, Brick could see her face.
It was haggard, but clean now. He couldn't yet see
her eyes, and that was what he needed. Her eyes
would tell him something, give him a clue. She came
straight to Brick's tent, where Ali Sabri should have
been sleeping. Her left arm was held oddly, as if
hurt, and in her right she carried her machine pistol.
A yard away from the tent, she stopped. The machine
pistol remained pointed at the ground, and she
looked in confusion at the boiling water on the Sterno
stove.

"Let's go," Ali Sabri said. "She thinks I'm in the
tent. She would have used that gun by now if she'd
intended to."

Livia jerked the machine pistol up when she saw them, then lowered it. As they slid down the last few feet of the path, she took a hesitant step toward them, but stopped, still confused. Brick saw her eyes now. They had that same glazed, removed look in them they had in the house in Erevan when she had wanted to kill Ali Sabri's guards. He slowed, and held out his hand for Ali Sabri to slow with him.

"Brick?" she said, her voice just short of hysteria. "Oh, Jesus, Brick."

"It's OK," Brick said, talking as he would to a skittish horse. "Yeah, it's Brick."

"Brick? Where've you been, Brick?"

"Around. How'd you make it back?"

"I swam, swam straight across. I hurt my arm. I thought you were gone. I looked."

"Did you?"

"I did, I swear I did, Brick. I went as far as those rapids and I didn't see you. Then I had to get back. You understand that, don't you?"

Brick watched her. Her face was drawn as tight over her bones as a drumhead. "Where's Tony?"

She took another step toward him, then abruptly turned away. "Tony's shot, Brick." Her voice caught. "I came to get Ali Sabri, and Tony's shot."

"Who shot him, Livia?"

She whirled on him, her face now as distorted with tears as an infant's. "You've always got goddamn questions, don't you. *I* didn't shoot him. Whatever else, damn you, I don't shoot my own husband."

"I know that. I didn't mean you did."

"Then don't ask me. Don't ask me anything else, for God's sake. They sent me back for Ali Sabri. That's what counts, don't you see."

"No. I don't see."

146

She looked from Brick's face to Ali Sabri's, then half turned toward the ridge that overlooked the Araks. She laid the machine pistol down. "Where is it? Shit, where is it?" She took a few random steps, then, excited, walked toward a moss-covered rock the size of a medicine ball that lay just at the foot of the upslope. Brick followed her. When she reached the rock, she stooped and heaved it over. She fell to her knees and, with her hands, scooped the dirt out of the hollow beneath where the stone had been. She pulled a plastic envelope from the loose soil and held it up for Brick to take.

"I'll go back. You've got twenty minutes, at least, when I do. I'll tell them I didn't find you. Unbury your own things, Brick, and make sure you've got your passport. Here, take this." From her shirt pocket, she pulled a ballpoint and note pad and wrote hastily. "This is an address in London, in Highgate. That envelope I gave you has a thousand pounds in it and God knows how many Turkish lira. And there's a passport, a Pakistani one, for Ali Sabri. He can pass for a Pak and nobody's likely to try to find out if he speaks whatever they speak in Pakistan. Get him to that address, Brick. Please. Don't go back to Doğubeyazit. Just...get him out of Turkey, to London."

"From here? God almighty, Livia..."

"*Don't argue, Brick.* You can do it. For my sake— for your own and Ali Sabri's sake, just *do* it."

"What about you?"

"I'll get back. They won't hurt me. I've got to be with Tony. You see that, don't you, Brick." Her eyes were pleading now. Brick reached out and touched her hair. She took his hand, kissed it, and held it to her cheek. "Go, Brick. Now."

Gently, Brick took his hand away. "Livia, listen to me. I don't even know why I'm here..."

"I know, Brick, I know that. If I could undo all this, I would. But listen to *me* now. You'll never get out of here if you don't do this. Please, please believe me."

It was like the tangle of things he had felt in the village in Armenia, Brick thought. Only worse. At least he knew the terms there, understood what he had to untangle. Yet now, with nothing really resolved, there was a whole set of insane new resolutions to make. And all the while a war was happening inside him: battles among joy at seeing Livia alive, fear, anger at being here in the first place, the painful certainty that she hadn't cared enough for him to find him by the river—and, he realized, a stupid sense of responsibility for Ali Sabri, of all things. And how to settle a war in himself, when this woman (a woman he had already risked his life for) was telling him he had twenty minutes to save his life in? And save it from who? Jesus, Jesus, Jesus. London! She might as well have asked him to take Ali Sabri to some address on the moon.

Ali Sabri stepped up beside him. "My friend Brick," he said. "And I tell you as a friend. I think we should listen now."

"And go to London?"

"Well...go from this place, at least."

"Can you get us to Erzurum?"

"We're in Kurdistan. I can get us anywhere in Kurdistan."

Brick held out his hand. Livia took it and stood. "I can promise Erzurum. Beyond that, I don't know," he told her.

"Don't stop in Erzurum, Brick," she said, her voice

calm now, almost cold. "Don't find Özpamir. Or Brenner, or the colonel, or—anybody." She pulled her hand away with same slight pressure she had used the first time he had met her, coming off the boat. She ducked away from him and scooped up the machine pistol. "And don't come after me. If they don't shoot you, I will."

Brick took a step toward her. Ali Sabri touched his arm. "No. I believe her."

Livia, blinking through her tears, backed to the stream. "Thank you, Brick. Whatever...whatever else. Thank you."

Ali Sabri kept his hand on Brick's arm until she had reached the path over the hill toward the village. She didn't look back. When Ali Sabri dropped his hand, he said, "It's impossible, no?"

"It's impossible."

Ali Sabri took the plastic envelope from Brick's limp hand. "Do I really look like a Pak?"

"Enough like one."

"Where will *you* go?"

Brick started to speak, then realized there was no reasonable answer he could give. He watched Livia's retreating figure on the path. "How in *hell* did...did anything?"

"This is the Middle East, my friend," Ali Sabri said.

Brick turned to him and forced a smile. "I'll go back to Trabzon, I suppose."

Ali Sabri opened the envelope and took out a stack of hundred-pound notes. "You'd never make it alone."

"No. I guess not."

"Do you have a car?"

"In Trabzon, yes."

Ali Sabri sighed and stuffed the notes back into the envelope. "Twenty minutes, she said?"

"Yes."

"As I say, I can get us to Erzurum. From Erzurum...well, I'm a foreigner everywhere. It's up to you."

Christ on a pogo stick, Brick thought. "Would you really go to London—assuming that getting to London were at all possible?"

"Tehran, Ankara, London, what's the difference to me? I told you. I can't go home empty-handed, Brick my friend. And if I may say to you something—they tell me this Özpamir is with MIT. If everything here has gone as wrong as it seems to have, you don't want to be in Turkey anymore. Turkey is finished for you. At least until you can decide how to set all this right again."

"It's impossible, all of it."

Ali Sabri shrugged. "Then I'm leaving. We now have eighteen minutes, I suppose." From his shirt pocket he pulled the grotesque Turk's-head pipe he had been smoking in the yard in Erevan. His eyes met Brick's as he put the empty pipe in his mouth. "Coming?"

Brick looked beyond him at the half-hidden peak of Ararat, with the glow of the morning surrounding it like a halo. If he could only start climbing, up and up and up to the cold, clean glaciers, to a place where he could make a new start with a new world, like Noah. A place where he had choices again...

Ali Sabri ducked into Brick's tent and came out with his string bag of belongings. He took a few steps down the valley, then turned again. "Times Square—is that in London or New York? I can never remember."

"New York."

"Ah," Ali Sabri said. "Pity."

Brick took a deep breath, letting fatigue and the pain of his headache wash away thought. That was the key, still: to not think, only to turn the page. Chapter one, end. God, how he wanted to put the book down! Yet—chapter two, begin. And would there be a three, and four, and after that...?

"I have to get my passport," he said. "Goddamn-it."

Five

Sheep. The smell of sheep, the air cluttered with the baaing of sheep, the taste of mutton roasted on spits over campfires as he made his way with Ali Sabri down through the dry foothills of Ararat to the steppe again. At each campfire fresh horses or mules somehow appeared, and with the dawn they set off north again toward Erzurum. They avoided the villages and slept with the shepherds in the high meadows or along streambanks far from roads. While they slept, runners or riders went out to the next herding camp to announce their coming. Even though Ali Sabri had trouble sometimes with the local dialect, he joked or flirted or was appropriately grave around the campfires. He was a politician, Brick discovered, and a good one. No wonder the Soviets had wanted to keep him out of commission; no wonder the Turks and the Israelis took the risks they did to get him back into commission. Brick's respect for him grew.

And then at Iğdir, a shady town that shambled alongside the highway to Erzurum, the sheep buried them. Brick never did understand just how the ride in a sheep truck materialized. But he did understand the heat and the sleeplessness and the fear of the truck's being searched at checkpoints as he and Ali Sabri huddled among the sheep and tried to keep out of the mounting shit all through a long day. By evening, as they crawled through the potholed suburbs of Erzurum, he was half hoping that they would simply be discovered by an army patrol. At least they would stop, would sleep, and there would be no damnable decision to make the next day about where to go from Erzurum—a decision that wasn't really a choice, but only a response, like a rat's in a Skinner box.

There was supposedly a motel here owned by a Kurdish lawyer and nationalist. The plan was that they would hole up there for a few days and "assess the situation." If they only knew more! Who had shot Tony, and why? How much did Major Özpamir know about everything that had happened? He could have been told that the mission had failed—and God knew that was a credible enough possibility—and by now be back in Ankara, dismissing Brick and Ali Sabri as dead and trying to cover his own ass with his superiors. If that were so, no one would be looking for them. It would be easy enough to contrive to get to Trabzon and simply drive out of the country. But what if Özpamir knew more than they did? They'd never even make it past the first checkpoint on the road to Trabzon from here. That was the terrible part: how did you react to a situation when you didn't

even know what the situation was? It was like trying
to make your way through a city in which all the
street signs were in code.

In the dusk the motel was cheerless and bleak, a
baby-blue cinderblock remnant of the tourist boom
of the sixties. A peeling sign with holes for long-
vanished neon tubes hung above the office and a cow
grazed forlornly in the weeds of what once must have
been a flower garden in front. The truck slowed and
drove past it, checking. Brick and Ali Sabri got to
their knees, ducking and craning to see through the
slats of the truck bed, their heads like boats on a sea
of sheep. There were lights nowhere but in the
motel's office and in a room beside the office, but
those were enough. The soldiers there and at all
corners of the building made no attempt to hide
themselves.

"Shit," Brick said as he slid back down among the
unhappy sheep.

"It could be this has nothing to do with us," Ali
Sabri said. "Some local commander raiding another
Kurd's business—maybe not even that. Maybe just
raiding for whores."

"So we know even less than before."

"No. We know we're in Erzurum."

A sheep backed up to Brick and farted gently.
"And now what?"

"I promised to get us to Erzurum. From here...well,
I can always make a living as a shepherd."

"Wonderful."

"We still don't know for sure that they're even
looking for us. Remember that."

"Got any ideas on how to find out?"

"Can you contain yourself until the morning?"

"Not in this damn truck."

Ali Sabri popped up from among the sheep and banged on the truck window with his fist. The truck eased to the curb. Ali Sabri made a quick scan of the street, then scrambled up the truck rails and hung over the top one like something on a clothesline. He and the driver mumbled at one another awhile, then Ali Sabri dropped down among the sheep again. The truck pulled away from the curb. "So," he said. "Tonight we sleep, and in the morning we know something."

Every inch of Brick hurt or cramped. He should ask Ali Sabri just what it was they would know in the morning and how they would know it. But he didn't care. The "tonight we sleep" was enough for now. He supposed he trusted Ali Sabri within limits, and one of those limits would be Brick's becoming a liability to him. So far he didn't think he was—no great help, but no liability either.

"Ali?" he said.

"Efendim?"

"You really think I'm going to get you to London, don't you."

"Not far from here, my friend, the West begins. What you can do there I have no idea. But I do know you can do a great deal more than I can. It's your world. I don't really want to become a shepherd, you know." They bounced in silence for a while. Then Ali Sabri said, "You take your time to make up your mind, don't you?"

They slept with the truck drivers in the loft of an ancient and uneven wooden house near the market. As tired as he was, Brick tossed on his pallet until well after the noise of the midnight Ramazan meal had begun outside. Özpamir was a decent man. Why were they running from him? Because he was a Turk and Livia was a Canadian and that somehow made her more trustworthy? Piffle. So why not turn themselves in and ask to be taken to Özpamir? Because for one thing they had no idea if Özpamir was even still alive. Ali Sabri was right: Turkey was finished for him. Where to, then? If Livia had made it away from Ararat, she would most likely be in London. And why had he gotten involved in this to begin with—what was the payoff for it?

To change his life, to have Livia, to do something that mattered...so many clichés that were real. And could he really live the rest of his life not knowing what had happened that last morning on Ararat? There was only one place now that all those things could be made to meld into some sort of shape.

But oh, Christ, it was a long, long way to Piccadilly.

And when he awoke to the spider webs and dust and the sound of numberless roach feet in the walls, the emptiness of the loft, the vacant spots where the pallets of Ali Sabri and the truck drivers had been, blew even that last hope to hell.

Down an outside staircase, along the narrow alleyway, and into a street nearly as narrow. And now where? He bought a bottle of yogurt-and-water *ayran* from a grocery and drank it in secret, and tried to think. As long as he had Ali Sabri with him, he at least had a place to hide—even if that meant a stone hut or a tent in the mountains. But now...now he had to move, and move quickly. He already knew what the alternatives were behind him toward Iran. That meant he had only two ways to go: toward Ankara, in the interior, or back to Trabzon. Again, a choice that wasn't a choice. If you were afraid of spiders, you didn't hide in their webs. Trabzon was on the sea, at least.

Stares followed him. In Trabzon he was known so well that the staring had almost ceased. But here he was still a curiosity, a thing as out of place as a turban in Des Moines. No, it wouldn't be long until he was stopped. The last thing he should do was merely wander. He circled back through the narrowest streets he could find toward the market and the house he had slept in last night. Did it belong to the truck drivers? Did anyone even know they had been there? He was as little certain of the reason he was heading there as he was of anything else—probably as little certain as the foxes he remembered in Virginia circling back toward their holes, where the hounds would be most likely to find them.

One of the streets he took passed near the hotel where he and the others had stayed on their way to Doğubeyazit. Nothing seemed to have changed there: the newsstand Livia had walked to in the rain, the truckers clustered around it like moths even this early in the morning. He felt a hitch in his chest when he thought of Livia on that evening, her hair glistening in the rain, her husky voice in his room later. He half expected to see the jeeps still parked in front. Jeeps there were, but these bore the emblem of the Turkish army. He kept close to the cement walls and reminded himself that Livia lived in another age, that surviving mattered now, nothing else.

As he turned the corner toward the market, one of the trucks caught his eye, a ten-wheeler Mercedes with a steel sea-land container on its back. The container was from the East German Danube Company—one of the familiar dozens that came in through the Trabzon docks. But the truck was even more familiar: Ulusoy Karadeniz Nakliyat, Ltd., the logo read. Brick stopped and took a few steps back up the street. Ulusoy Black Sea Transport, Ltd. Their offices in Trabzon were no more than a hundred yards from the docks, no more than six blocks from his own office. If the container was on its way back from Iran it might be empty, might be in Trabzon by nightfall.

Or it might be full and on its way to Iran.

Brick scanned the drivers clustered around the newsstand, trying to pick out the driver who went with the Ulusoy truck on the outside chance he would recognize him as a Trabzonan. The faces were all unfamiliar. If the driver was one of them, he would spend a few minutes passing on news of the road with the others, complaining about the craziness in Iran, then maybe sneaking a glass of tea before he hit the highway again. But what if he wasn't? What if he had waited the night out in his truck and was asleep in it still?

Brick moved further up the street toward the newsstand. Did they lock those damn containers when they were empty? If you got inside one, could you even breathe? As he passed the hotel he turned his head away in case the desk clerk might remember him. Already traffic was beginning to clog the broad street that ran between the hotel and the newsstand, and two of the soldiers who went with the jeeps leafed through magazines at the stand. Slink, Brick told himself, and that's the surest way to attract attention. Trying to look bright-faced as a tourist, he bounded out into the traffic.

Mercifully, the truck had backed into its parking space so that the container's doors were hidden from

the street. Brick pretended to read the messy collage
of posters on the stone wall the truck nuzzled its rear
against. A shoeshine boy—head shaved in good
country fashion—veered toward him, but Brick
glared him away. No one else seemed to notice him.
He edged toward the rear of the truck until he could
see the long metal bolt that held the doors closed,
the bolt with the holes for an absent padlock.

Brick held his breath as he slipped alongside the
truck toward the cab. He hadn't felt this jittery since
his teenage days swiping hubcaps in Washington.
At the cab, he bounded lightly onto the running-
board. Stretched out on the seat, snap-brim cap over
his eyes, was the driver. Sleep, friend, Brick thought.
Sleep. Fifteen minutes is all I ask. Time to get my
passport and backpack from the rafters of the loft.

He dodged his way across the street again and
forced himself to walk calmly back toward the market. Shopkeepers' heavy-lidded eyes followed him
from doorways and street urchins trotted alongside
him, their hands out for whatever he might drop into
them. Which of the shopkeepers was an MIT man,
he wondered. He was certain that the gossip network
would pick him up by noon, and then it would be too
late. He sped up his pace.

Long morning shadows turned the stairway to the
loft into a cubist painting as he started up it. A cat
bounded down the alleyway, but nothing else moved.
He heard voices from the house as he ascended, but
they were calm, the kind of tones sleepy people use.
He smelled cornbread baking—morning smells and
sounds that seemed abnormal to him in their nor-
malcy. At the head of the stairs he swung the door
open and stepped into the gloom.

His eyes not yet adjusted to the dimness, Brick

caught at first only a quick movement, like something leaping. He threw himself out of the light from the doorway and onto the dust of the creaking floor. He heard no other sound but his own breath.

"That's twice you have done that," Ali Sabri's rumbling voice said at length. "The next time you don't announce yourself I shall be obliged to shoot you."

"Where the hell have you been?"

"Learning things."

"May I get up now?"

"No. Stay there—as a lesson. Never surprise a Kurd."

"Then what did the damn Kurd find out?"

"That neither the army nor the MIT is looking for us. The Kurd asked other Kurds, who know everything."

"The motel didn't have anything to do with us?"

"No. They claim it was full of Frenchmen trying to buy hashish. Hah!"

"Then they think we're dead."

"Not everybody does. A man was here leaving thousand-lira notes in people's hands for any kind of information. He got a great deal of it, but of course nobody told him the truth."

"Who?"

"A German. He left a telephone number in Trabzon and a post office box number in England. Your Brenner—he's German, no?"

"That's close enough. Was he alone?"

"So far as I could find out."

"We're safe then—for the moment."

"A very brief moment. If your Brenner was asking, the MIT will know about it soon. And who knows

161

that he might not have found an honest Kurd who actually will inform him we're here?"

"Would that be so bad? He's on your side," Brick asked.

"Who knows? They found your Iranian colonel in the Araks days ago. Whose side was he on?"

Brick was less shocked at that news than he should have been. He realized he must have been expecting it; it fit the queer kind of logic events seemed to have been following since the world quit making sense. "He wasn't 'my' colonel. And Brenner's not mine either."

"That's my point. Stop thinking like a Westerner, my friend."

Brick's eyes had adjusted to the weak light that trickled in through a dusty, broken window. He got up and pulled his backpack from the cobwebs of the rafters. "I've found us a way to Trabzon."

"Us?"

"You want to stay here?"

"No. But I don't want to be in Trabzon, either."

"I didn't think so."

"So you have some way to get *from* Trabzon?"

"No. Not yet."

"And you would go to London?"

"I think I'd rather be trapped in London than here."

"So it's not impossible after all."

"Yes, it's impossible." He stopped at the door and turned. "People don't really do things like this, you know."

Ali Sabri got to his feet, slung the machine pistol over his shoulder and draped his blanket over that. "If life is no more than life, Brick *bey*—if it's merely

Robert Houston

real—how terrible that is. Of course people do things like this!"

They rounded the final spit of land before Trabzon just as the last tab of the sun disappeared into the sea to the west. The trucker had taken the back way home, a dirt road that had juggled them around in the empty and echoing container like BBs. They managed to prop the doors open a few inches with shipping flats, but that made it worse. The driver was a fiend. He slid around crumbling curves on the Czar's old supply road through the mountains like a suicidal stunt pilot. What they saw from their crack in the door they didn't want to see: sheer drop-offs on one side, sheer cliffs on the other. Waterfalls eating away at the road, cows bounding off it into foggy emptiness as the truck blasted past them, shepherds leaping for safety against rock cliff faces. And then, as they descended from the mountains through great shadowy spruce forests below the cloud level, dust rolled in far thicker than the fog. The juggling stopped when they hit the new coast road at Hopa, but the swaying as they followed the zigzag coastline was a new torture. When the lights of Trabzon, of home, replaced the vanished sun, Brick was exhausted. He would happily have spent the day with soft sheep instead.

As the truck mired in traffic near the new bus station, they eased onto the lip of the truck bed and closed the container. An astounded traffic cop tweeted and yelled, but they were off the truck and into the first of the twisting streets of the old part of the city before he could do more than that.

"And now?" Ali Sabri said as they stopped for

163

breath outside a bakery where hot, buttery pita bread slid from an oven like pizza.

"Now I eat, and drink gallons of whatever's drinkable." A muezzin began to blast his call for Ramazan prayers through a loudspeaker from a mosque nearby. "On *your* money."

While they gorged on pita bread and *döner kebap,* Brick tried to pretend he knew what he was going to do. They were in his territory now. Not the West, but not Kurdistan, either. A few hours before he had been dependent on Ali Sabri for even such basic things as food. Now, here, it was all turned around. Ali Sabri's smattering of Turkish would make him as alien here as he would be in Sweden. Jesus blithering God. But if he didn't know what they were going to do, he did know they had to do something now, while the Ramazan crowds were still in the streets.

When Ali Sabri had finished shoveling the last of the *döner kebap* into his mouth with the pita bread (à la Turk, as the locals said) in the back-street *kebap* house, he wiped his moustache and looked at Brick expectantly. Hungry as he had been, Brick hadn't been able to get much of the greasy lamb down. Could they risk just driving out of town? He'd prefer that—at least he could take with him some of his books and a few of the small antiques he'd collected. But an American in a Peugeot with Turkish plates and a Pak with a Kurdish turban would send every checkpoint they passed into conniption fits. But what else was there? Wild notions of stealing fishing boats wandered into and quickly out of his head. A bus? Buses stopped at checkpoints, too. He tried to remember the day of the week, one of those things that had ceased to matter lately. If it was Monday, the

164

mail ship that had brought Livia and the others
would be heading back to Istanbul tomorrow. But
no, not that either. They would have to show passports there, too. And if the MIT thought they were
dead, wouldn't it be a pissing fine shock to have their
passport numbers show up on a passenger manifest.

Brick stood, wildly hoping that motion would start
some kind of chain of events. "Ready?"

"For what?"

Brick scowled. "To change clothes. We stink. And
you can't go anywhere looking like an extra from
Lawrence of Arabia."

"You don't sound very confident. Where do we go
in our new clothes?"

"Don't ask."

They kept to the waterfront road that avoided the
square. The road was wider and the few cars still
out tonight would be going too fast to pay much
attention to two figures in the shadows. When they
at last had to cut uphill on the twisting streets by
the government whorehouse and the coppersmiths'
shops, Brick motioned for Ali Sabri to follow him
from doorway to doorway, checking each as they
went, watching the street ahead and the balconies
and windows of the ancient, grim stone houses.
Maybe no one in Erzurum was looking for them, but
this was Trabzon and somebody had shot Tony, the
Iranian colonel was dead, and he'd be goddamned if
he'd walk up to his apartment beside the Binational
Center as if he were only strolling home from the
baths.

They waited for a roast-corn vendor to rattle his
pushcart by on the cobbles before they made the last
sprint to the Binational Center. Brick fumbled for

his key as they pressed into the doorway. Did he even have that anymore? Like days of the week, keys were another thing that had ceased to matter. And as they leaned against the door, he learned that they still didn't. The heavy door swung open, unlocked and unlatched.

Ali Sabri shifted the blanket that covered the machine pistol and slipped it from his shoulder. Brick froze—not on purpose, but with the same feeling that had nailed him to his bed as a kid when he was certain he had seen something move in his closet. Ali Sabri brushed by him.

The musty book smell of the library comforted Brick as he passed it, reminding him of sanity and chess with his friend the priest and rainy afternoons with week-old editions of the *International Herald Tribune*. He ought to be able to simply step into it and flick on the light and sit down to read as if he'd never gone looking for a nonexistent ark. But no matter how much this place, this cocoon of his old life seemed the same, it wasn't and would never be again. The unlocked door behind him told him that. Whatever had been with him on those dry slopes of Ararat had followed him back here, too. Whatever, whoever.

His office was empty and dim in the spill of light from a streetlamp. The classrooms where he gave English lessons were empty. The closet where he stored his sparse audio-visual equipment was still locked. Nothing was missing from the kitchen. But beyond the kitchen, the door that led to his forever damp apartment swung gently in the breeze that washed in from the sea. Whoever had left the front door open hadn't been looking for anything in the Binational Center. They'd been looking for him.

Ali Sabri led again, the machine pistol held in front of him like a flashlight. Brick's shabby, comfortable living room was undisturbed—except that his last bottle of Scotch sat empty on his coffee table with two glasses beside it. Goddamnit. Ibrahim had managed without him all right—had managed to appropriate his life while he was gone. Brick felt relief settle over him like the waters of the shower he so badly needed. The bottle and glasses explained the unlocked doors. He wondered who in hell Ibrahim had found to bring in here—one of the students, a whore, a tourist he'd picked up? He bent and clicked on a table lamp and started to call to Ali Sabri, who had moved on to the bedroom door already, that it was all right.

But Ali Sabri's fiercely motioning hand telling him to turn the light off meant he was wrong, that it wasn't all right.

The room jerked back into its streetlamp-lit dimness. Ali Sabri stepped aside as Brick joined him at the bedroom door. The scene in the bedroom wouldn't resolve itself at first, like pieces of a torn photograph. Rumpled sheets, clothing strewn over the Oriental carpet, and something on the bed that caught a ray of light from the window and gleamed dully. Brick stepped into the room, puzzled. A yard from the bed he made out the face that surrounded the gleaming gold tooth, Ibrahim's face, the dark little rat's eyes still open, the peroxided hair still sweat-plastered. And next to Ibrahim, the lines of the heavy, naked woman's body, one hand clutching the sheet as if she had been trying to pull it over herself, took shape. Instinctively Brick reached out to touch Ibrahim, as if to wake him, then drew his hand back when he understood what the dark stains were on the sheets, the stains that trailed down them into a small black puddle on the carpet.

It shouldn't have been Ibrahim in the bed. It wasn't him they were looking for. God in heaven, if Ibrahim had only been asleep, if he had only not seen whoever it was that stepped into the room looking for Brick. He tried to get a better look at the woman's face, then turned away. He didn't want to recognize her.

Ali Sabri brushed by him and bent over Ibrahim. "Sometime within the past day, I'd say."

"What did it?"

Ali Sabri shrugged. "Shot, that's all I can tell. Was he your friend?"

"In a way." Ibrahim would have brought the woman here during the late afternoon, when classes were over and he could find an excuse to close the library early. If it had been before that, the students would have suspected something. And there would have had to be something like a silencer on the gun; old Ismet *bey,* the honey and butter seller across the street, poked his nose in to check out the noise if Brick so much as dropped a glass. Brick was afraid now, childishly afraid, as if there really had turned out to be some creature in the dark closet. Silencers and machine pistols and unknown hands that held them, side by side with the familiar reasonableness of his library. What had Livia said—we go on pretending that things make sense, that the world is an orderly place? He turned away from the terrible disorder of the bed.

"Don't touch anything," Brick said. "I'll get us some clothes."

Ali Sabri nodded. While Brick stuffed things into

his backpack, Ali Sabri paced, checking the window, the hall, the back door. Brick tried to ignore the bed. Blue jeans for both of them—they would be a little big on Ali Sabri, but no matter. Slacks and shirts and even a tie apiece, walking shorts in case they had to look like tourists. He concentrated on keeping his hands steady. To hell with roadblocks. They would get the car from Atilla's backyard where he had left it (never do to leave it on the streets) and go, just bloody damn go. Once they were out of Trabzon they'd think about where they were going.

Could he just leave poor Ibrahim and the woman here? Three weeks ago that would have been unthinkable. Now he knew that yes, he would just leave them. Like he was leaving his old life.

They locked the door behind them. Ibrahim had family here. Better that the police would have to be called to open the door tomorrow, that they be the first ones in.

They skirted the square again, past the voices and laughter from the backgammon clubs and the teahouses, the families at their Ramazan meals before open windows, the crowds on their knees in mosques—up the street that climbed toward the bluffs of the Hill of Martyrs and Atilla's house. What would he tell Atilla? What could he possibly tell him that wouldn't put him and his family in some sort of danger?

When he saw Atilla's face, he knew that Atilla would want few explanations. First there was shock, then, close behind, worry. He only glanced briefly at Ali Sabri, who stood back in the shadows beside the front stoop, as if Ali Sabri were something he realized he shouldn't be seeing at all. Behind Atilla in the bright dining hall his family—his wife and girls, various cousins and sisters and brothers and their children home for Ramazan—sat at the long table heaped with food and strained to see who was at the door. Brick hoped they couldn't see him. What would he look like to them, filthy and afraid and bringing something loathsome he had no right to bring into that warmth and hospitality that would have waited for him like a brother himself if only— if only there weren't too goddamn many "if onlys" now. His eyes filled with tears, and Atilla was a blur as he stepped out onto his stoop and closed the door behind him.

Atilla took Brick's hand. *"Hamdolsun,"* he said. "Thank God. They said you were dead."

"I am. Don't ask any questions. Please don't. I just need the car."

Atilla didn't release his hand. "I saw the woman and she said there had been a fall on Ararat. You look awful."

"She was here? In Trabzon?"

"Cigarettes and all." Brick wiped the tears away, hoping that Atilla wouldn't notice them. But Atilla was studying his face. "You're in no shape to drive."

"Who was with her?"

"I saw her in the airline office with an army major. They were arranging to have some people taken off yesterday's flight to Ankara so they could get seats."

"Her husband? That other one, Brenner? Were they going, too?"

"I don't know. They needed several seats. I just happened to see her there as I was going by and went in to ask about you. She didn't want to talk. Are you all right?"

"There was a fall," Brick lied. "But I'm all right."

Atilla's eyes moved away from Brick's face. "No,"

he said. "There wasn't a fall, I think. But I'll believe
there was. Where are you going?"

"I don't know."

"Will you come back?"

"No."

"If it's that kind of trip"—he glanced again at Ali
Sabri, who avoided his eyes and fiddled with his
Turk's-head meerschaum—"you're crazy to try to
drive. The terrorists have gone mad this last week.
The military has checkpoints every ten meters on
the roads between here and Ankara or Istanbul. I
think I could arrange for a seat on a plane tomorrow,
booked or not."

"No. I can't."

"Brick, my brother. What in the name of Allah...?"

"Just unlock the gate so I can get the car and I'll
be gone."

Atilla's eyes met his again. "No. I won't let you
do that."

"You won't *let* me?"

"You'll go on the mail ship."

"Atilla, for God's sake, if I can't risk the plane I
can't risk the boat, either."

"Yes, you can." He released Brick's hand. "Trust
me. I won't go with you to the docks. But I'll meet
you there in an hour." He nodded toward Ali Sabri.
"Does he come with you?"

"Yes."

"What is he?"

"His passport's Pakistani."

Atilla snorted. "Then the Kurds—excuse me, the
mountain Turks—have spread farther than I
thought."

"What about my car?"

"I said trust me. Do you?"

Brick's hesitation was short, he hoped too short for Atilla to have noticed it. "Yes."

Ali Sabri followed Brick as patiently down the hill to the docks as he had followed him up the hill for the car they never got. He tugged at the vile tobacco that had materialized for his meerschaum in Erzurum and merely nodded at Brick's explanations. Brick's irritation grew at that. The man was supposed to be a politician, a leader. Now, if ever, Brick needed ideas, argument, confirmation. Yet he got no more reaction than if he had told Ali Sabri that it would rain again next week. Finally he burst out with an order. "And get rid of that damn gun as soon as we hit the docks."

Ali Sabri took a long tug at his pipe and stopped, looking as if he'd just remembered something important he'd forgotten to do.

"Let's go," Brick said.

"My friend, I'm puzzled." Ali Sabri's voice was solemn.

"That's at least something," Brick said.

"It doesn't seem a sign of great wisdom for a man without a gun to order a man with a gun to throw it away. Does it seem so to you?"

"You won't do it?"

"You'll allow me to say that my belief in your basic good sense has kept me from noting that you've been acting one damn great lot like a headless chicken ever since we got to Erzurum. I suppose I should admit I've considered abandoning you more than once since then."

"You've considered abandoning *me?*"

"But now when you ask me to put myself totally in the hands of an unknown Turk with no way to

172

defend myself, I have to inform you that is a crock of shit. With all due respect."

"I'll be damned."

"We all may be. So I'll keep the gun for a while." He tapped his pipe out on his heel, locked his hands behind his back, and strode away. "This is still the Middle East," he called over his shoulder. Brick considered, feeling mulish, and followed.

Ali Sabri consented to having his head scarf and wrinkled dacron Soviet clothes wrapped around a rock and pitched into the oily waters of the port. He marveled as he studied himself in a window of the closed customs house in Brick's old jeans and sneakers and Save the Whales sweatshirt. "Hippies wear these, don't they?" he asked Brick as he craned his neck to see himself from the rear.

"Not quite," Brick said.

"Pity."

But his light mood disappeared as swiftly as a lira into a beggar's hand when the headlights bounced from the twisting road to the old city down onto the open space surrounding the docks. He pulled Brick with him to the other side of the customs house and crouched into the shadows of a dock crane, where they could see on all sides but be seen on none. A couple of hundred yards away the White Boat, the *Eğe*, rode easily against the wharf with only a half-a-dozen night-lights still burning on her. Brick could hear sleepy voices from the deck bar, and envied them.

The headlights cruised slowly out onto the concrete pier. When they flicked off, Brick made out the form of his old Peugeot behind them. Relieved, he stepped from the shadows. Ali Sabri jerked him back. Brick struggled angrily for a moment to break free—

then relaxed into Ali Sabri's grip as he saw first the driver's door open, and then the one on the shotgun side. Atilla was the driver. But the other man, balding and nearly twice Atilla's size, was a stranger, though somehow he seemed vaguely familiar to Brick. They looked along the pier in both directions, straining to see into the darkness, then swung onto the steel steps that led to the promenade deck of the *Eğe*.

"There's an extra key," Brick said. "It's taped behind the bumper."

"Patience, *efendi*," Ali Sabri said.

They waited, Ali Sabri with that impossible stillness Brick had noticed on Ararat, for a quarter of an hour that seemed an hour. At length Atilla and the stranger appeared on the promenade deck at the head of the stairs. With them was a man in a white uniform—the purser, Brick judged. They shook hands and Atilla and the stranger clattered down the stairs. At the Peugeot, they conferred about something and the stranger got back into the car. Atilla looked along the pier again, as if deciding which way to go, then started walking casually toward the dock crane. Ali Sabri's stillness broke as he raised the machine pistol to rest on his knee, pointing toward Atilla.

"Damn it, he wouldn't be coming toward us like that if he had anything in mind," Brick whispered.

"Probably not." Ali Sabri made no move to lower the pistol.

"Stay here." Brick shoved to his feet and stepped out of the shadows. This time Ali Sabri didn't try to pull him back.

Atilla saw him almost immediately and stopped. Brick's footsteps, the thud of his hiking boots on the

174

empty pier, echoed off the old stone customs house as loud as hooves. That was Atilla waiting for him, he told himself. The last man on earth he should connect with fear. Yet he had to force himself to keep an even pace, to smile and give a silly wave as if they were meeting for a game of snooker. He caught a glimpse of the purser leaning over the rail of the *Eğe* and watching them.

"You've been here long?" Atilla said when they were a yard or so apart.

Brick hesitated, and lied. "Just got here."

Atilla hesitated, too. "I see."

"Oh, hell. I didn't know who that was with you."

"It's my cousin from Istanbul. You met him last year at Ramazan. I'm disappointed, Brick *bey*."

"I'm sorry. I'm just…exhausted, I guess."

Atilla took his arm and walked with him along the pier. "You're almost a Turk, but not quite. I've told you you're my brother. For a Turk that should be enough."

"I know. I guess I'm scared, too."

"That part I don't want to know about. You can go aboard the ship tonight. You'll have to stay below in the hold until you clear the port, I'm afraid, but the purser will have blankets and pillows for you. Tomorrow you'll have a stateroom. Take this." He slipped a folded paper from his shirt pocket. "It's a receipt for your car, consigned to my name for delivery from the *Eğe* in Istanbul. Your name's not on it anywhere. The purser will see there's no trouble about it."

"How in hell…?"

Atilla turned so that he was facing him and smiled. "How do all things get arranged in Turkey, Brick? If you remembered my cousin, you'd remem-

175

ber who he works for in Istanbul, and you'd understand."

"Oh, damn. That cousin." A conversation in Atilla's living room last year came back vaguely. A cousin who was some kind of freight agent for Turkish Maritime Lines, going on and on about tonnage and new routes and the price of oil until Brick thought he'd scream. No wonder he'd blocked the man out!

"Your name won't appear on the passenger manifest either. There may be some trouble with a Dutch couple who think they have reservations for your stateroom, but the purser can handle that, too. Oh, and you'll owe him ten thousand lira. If you don't have it, I can lend it to you."

Oh, blessèd, blessèd corruption, Brick thought. He took his arm from Atilla's and embraced him.

Yet even as he did, his mind raced ahead. Was there a more perfect city on earth to hide in than Istanbul? Yet was there a more perfect city to disappear into forever without a trace, too? He looked over Atilla's shoulder toward the shadows of the crane where Ali Sabri crouched. Istanbul was still in Turkey. Ali Sabri would still be with him, and with Ali Sabri all of the people or things that wanted him. He would be leaving nothing behind in Trabzon except the last real help he could expect to get between here and an address in London. There could be no more "arranging."

Akcaabat, Giresun, Ordu slid by as minarets and waterfront warehouses and haphazard houses that rose with a gentle mystery into the green, flowered mountains. It was only after the ship passed Samsun, with its new luxury hotel and wildly modern beach

houses, and the mountains gave way to the flat tobacco fields of Bafra, that Brick was even able to
begin to get a fix on what he felt. By the time he and
Ali Sabri had thought it safe enough to go on deck,
Trabzon was already picture-postcard size behind
them and the *Ege* was slicing through the dark
swells of the open sea. Brick knew that he would
miss Trabzon in time—after all, he had spent more
than a third of his life there—but not now. Now it
meant Ibrahim's and the woman's bodies on his bed,
and fear, and simply more painful things left behind
than he could afford to think about.

In the back of his mind a sense of loss and a sweaty
sort of apprehension nagged to keep him from feeling
real peace, but for the moment he was able to let the
slow rolling of the ship trick him into feeling almost
safe. The *Ege* had seen better days (better years!)
but the hot water worked some of the time and the
food was plentiful and good, the sheets clean, the
officers' white uniforms pressed and comforting, the
bar stocked, and the first-class deck full of easy conversation about nothing in particular and deck
chairs and card games that nobody got very upset
about losing.

Ali Sabri relaxed, too. After managing, on the first
morning, to pass for a Pak with a pair of Welsh
schoolteachers on holiday, he stashed the machine
pistol in the stateroom and took to telling lurid tales
about bandit raids and horse thievery and melodra-
matic escapes from mountain villages that he must
have had to plunder a thousand years of Kurdish
legend for. That they had happened in Kurdistan
and not Pakistan stopped him not at all: he simply lied, substituted outrageous imaginary names of
places in Pakistan. While Brick worked on the ship's

supply of gin, Ali Sabri gathered tablefuls of lis-
teners and worked on the supply of women. As they
put in at Sinop, with the usual melee of taxis and
fruit vendors and porters and stevedores, the purser
came raging to Brick that, by the holy name of Allah,
he'd had enough. Ten thousand lira was too damn
few to put up with his ship being made into a whorehouse, especially during Ramazan, especially by a
Pak, especially with two English schoolteachers at
once in the middle of the afternoon in a decent first-
class cabin and howling so that families on the deck
had to banish their children to the heat of the sun-
deck to hide them from it. Brick listened, finished
his gin and joined them. Ali Sabri gave him the
better-looking one and that night at dinner slipped
the purser another thousand lira.

"Feel better?" Ali Sabri asked him as they stood
at the rail and watched the far lights of shore slide
by and smelled the rain that was coming off the sea
from Russia.

"Some. Not much. This helps." He drained his gin
and flung the glass off into the roiling wake. The
hiss of the wake and the undertone of the engines
softened all sounds but their voices. "It makes it
matter less that nothing fits."

"Yes. Nothing fits."

"Livia and the others weren't even in Trabzon
when Ibrahim was killed. Somebody tried to kill
Tony Lo Presti, but everybody who could possibly
have been involved showed up in Trabzon together
like old friends. Brenner was trying to locate us in
Erzurum—but where the hell was Major Özpamir
then? Christ, I don't even know *what* happened,
much less why."

"And you're worried that I'm not worried."

"Maybe."

"Listen to me, my friend. From the time I could talk and learned that the language I spoke wasn't the language of the people who wore the uniforms and drove the jeeps and told us how we should live, I've been worried. I followed my father from caves where we lived with men who were dying faster than we could replace them, to congresses for Kurdish republics that lasted less time than it takes a woman to have a baby. I saw six Persian holy men allow themselves to be wired with explosives and blown up one day trying to kill my father and me. I went with him into exile in the Soviet Union because there was no place else to go after all the broken promises, and later, after he was dead and there was a new round of broken promises, I went there again on my own. I'm supposed to be a leader, but how can I lead if I'm running all the time? How can I be a leader if all my decisions are made for me in Moscow or Ankara or Baghdad or Washington or, worst of all now, Tehran? And you ask me if I'm worried!"

Voices rose only sporadically now from the cargo deck below them, where the truckers and gypsies and peasant families slept, and the last of the first-class passengers yawned and heaved himself from his deck chair. The purser strolled by and gave them a foul look. The first gust of rain hit. "I'm sorry," Brick said.

"You should want out of this," Ali Sabri said.

"No," Brick said, surprising himself. "I don't. That's the funny thing. I've been had, I've made a fool out of myself half-a-dozen times—I'm being used by God knows how many people right now, even by you. But you're all I've got. I need you, and—the others. Does that make sense to you?"

"Not much."

"Hell, probably not. Look, you know what I knew about my father when I was a kid? That he put himself in a car in the morning and came home at night and couldn't talk about what he did all day. *Codes,* he would tell me when I asked him what he did. I never knew why he did it, or what he believed in, or wanted me to believe in. You probably can't understand it—I wouldn't blame you. I didn't know people were *supposed* to have good reasons for what they did with their lives. And then when I went to college and was told people were supposed to know why they chose to do one kind of thing with their lives and not another, it was a time when everybody around me was spouting half-baked Marx or wearing towels on their heads or shaving their heads and sitting with their legs crossed on the floor or eating blotters full of dope. Christ, that was no better than *codes* for an answer."

The light from a lighthouse slapped at them and was gone. "So then I told myself that I was getting out of the whole mess by staying in Trabzon. God, if that wasn't making the ultimate cliché out of myself! I could be as damned selfish as I wanted and wallow in being lonely and tell myself that it was noble. That stinks, too."

Ali Sabri pulled out his meerschaum and packed it. Brick went on, his voice growing more urgent. "I feel as if everything I've done these past weeks has been in a kind of fever, and I like that. I *need* to know I'm alive again. Listen, you matter. What you want matters, even if you fuck it up when you get it. Figuring out this mess matters, and then later maybe I can even figure out my own life. I *choose* to let it all matter for me, and that's goddamned important. I won't give any of that up, not if I can help it. That may not explain much to you, but it does to me and that's all I give a rat's ass about for now."

"That's very dangerous for you, my friend."

"More dangerous than rotting away?"

"And after London?"

"Maybe there won't be an after-London. Who knows?"

Ali Sabri kept his eyes on the wake. "Understand this. I want to stay alive, and I want this arrangement for the guns and money to come to pass rather more than I imagine you'll credit. I'll go as far as I have to go to make it happen, and there are people who will go as far as they have to to keep it from happening. I'm forty-some-odd years old—I don't know just how many—I've waited all my life and I've learned some patience. Now, if this scheme your friends have brought me works, maybe I can stop waiting. You see, there's another side to being forty-odd and having learned patience, Brick *bey*—I may have learned to wait, but I'm a great lot less inclined to. I can't have the glory of dying young anymore. I've got to have something to show for myself." He leaned over the rail and spat into the sea. "That's what I've got to offer. No solutions, not for you or anybody except myself and my people."

"I didn't ask you to offer anything."

"No, you didn't."

Brick turned to him and stuck out his hand. "Fair enough, then," he said.

Ali Sabri regarded the hand a moment, then took it. "Solutions, Brick *bey*, are like God—no matter how complicated everything seems, they turn out to be far simpler than you thought. Trust that."

Brick smiled. "Kurdish wisdom?"

"Wisdom, period." He let Brick's hand go and stretched. "Istanbul tomorrow?"

"Istanbul tomorrow."

"And from there?"

Brick shrugged. The purser passed again, fussing with deck chairs. The man had a face like a ferret, Brick thought. "Trust simple solutions," he said. "Like miracles."

Istanbul arrived endlessly. The houses began even before the *Eğe* slipped at dawn imperceptibly from the Black Sea into the clearer waters of the Bosphorus straits. Once there had been villages with sheep and cows grazing in the fields around them on the hills that rose up from the waters—Brick remembered that. Now the Bosphorus's shores were one continuous village, all the coves and beaches where the Greeks and then the Romans and Byzantines and the sultans and their janissaries had had their villas. A castle here and there or a palace from the sultanate still was allowed to cling to the rocks or spread with the remnants of its gardens and woods over the flatter land, but the suburbs and the high rises and the restaurants and marinas and factories had inherited Constantine the Great's earth. It seemed to take half a day, with the buildings growing thicker and thicker and older and older, before they moved beneath the new suspension bridge over the Bosphorus, an impossibly high thing that began in Europe and ended in Asia like a thin silver wire put there only to give Kipling the lie.

Ali Sabri had had a bad night. The ship had rolled in the rainstorm like a carnival ride, and he had padded into the bathroom half-a-dozen times. At first light he was up, and Brick at last got a couple of hours of undisturbed sleep. After a breakfast of thick bread and fresh fruit and cheese and preserved cherries, which Ali Sabri skipped, Brick found him leaning over the rail of the forward sun deck gulping the fresh air that streamed at him from the glittering waters and watching the crowded white ferries that scurried ahead of them.

"Try a glass of tea," Brick said.

"I'm hiding," Ali Sabri said.

"Too many schoolteachers on an empty stomach?"

"Something like that." He pointed toward the western shore, where already Brick could make out the Galata Tower of the ancient Venetians on the hill beyond the docks. "That's Europe?"

"That's Europe."

Ali Sabri swiveled to look across the Mississippi-wide straits at the Asian shore. "It doesn't look much different."

"Oh, but it is. Just wait."

"I don't think I like it. You know anybody here?"

"Nobody that could do us any good—or that it wouldn't be dangerous to contact."

"Pity."

"Lots of freighters," Brick said, letting his eyes wander over the forest of masts and deck cranes along the waterfront. "A bribe might get us on one—the car, too, maybe."

"How far is the border?"

"A few hours. You want to drive and risk Turkish customs officers?"

Ali Sabri considered. "No."

"Fine. Then we'll find you a dark place to drink tea, and I'll get to know the docks."

"I'll come."

"No. You stay out of the way for a while." Shoes

clattered on the stairs behind them. The teased hair
and glasses of one of the Welsh schoolteachers rose
above the level of the deck. Brick smiled. "You're
more trouble than you're worth."

As he went down the stairs to have a glass of tea
sent up to Ali Sabri, who was grunting things to the
schoolteacher, Brick felt good. He had no right to,
but he did. The shabby splendor of the heart of Istanbul was taking shape as a tug droned up to guide
them into the docks. A line from a poem pecked at
the back of his mind. "I have sailed the seas and
come to the holy city of Byzantium..." Was that how
it went? Christ, he hadn't read poetry in years. But
let it be a holy city, he thought. A city of miracles.
He needed them. Ahead, the land rounded itself off
into the crowded mouth of the river of the Golden
Horn, and beyond that he made out the walls of the
Topkapi Palace. Images of this city he had wandered
at all hours in all seasons tumbled through his mind:
the dim mussel restaurants that crowded beneath
the Galata Bridge, the thousand spires of the grand
mosques that sprawled over the low hills, the crumbling gray stonework of buildings once elegant that
hunched over never-empty streets, dark stairways
and alleyways that led to gardens or whore
houses or hidden Byzantine churches or fragrant
restaurants or stinking slums or nowhere. The blue
of the Bosphorus as you looked through the trees
from the flower-ringed pool of the Hilton, the calm-
ness of it as you watched it from one of the open-air
restaurants that lined it, the beaches of the Prince's
Islands out in the Marmara Sea with their great
rambling wooden summerhouses and their curlicued
roads that only horses and carriages ever climbed.

Constantine the Great's chariot circus, Justinian the Great's cathedral, Suleiman the Magnificent's mosque—the city that was the center of the world once. That wasn't far from that now.

A city of miracles, he thought as the gloating, ferret-faced purser touched his arm with the revolver and nodded toward the tugboat below them. Goddamnit to hell backwards on miracles he thought as he followed the purser's nod to the figure of Major Özpamir leaning erectly on the rail of the tug. Brick's stomach clenched. Not that kind of damned miracle.

"You are still a guest," Özpamir said to Ali Sabri as the Mercedes honked its way into traffic from the 1940s-style white Turkish Maritime Lines building. "You always have been. I regret that I wasn't able to meet you at Ararat to make that clear to you."

"Then I can leave if I want to," Ali Sabri said.

Özpamir smiled his sad, hollow-cheeked smile. "Not that kind of guest, I'm afraid. As soon as I can make the arrangements, you'll be going to Ankara."

"Ah. So I'm the kind of guest I was in the Soviet Union."

"Not at all. The Soviets wanted to keep you from your people. I want to get you back to them."

Brick's Peugeot pulled alongside as they turned uphill at the Galata Bridge, toward Taksim Square and the center of the city. The air smelled of rotting vegetables, and across the Golden Horn the ornate railroad station that the Orient Express had spilled its stick-pinned and fur-wrapped passengers into for so many years came briefly into view. Özpamir nodded at the driver of the Peugeot, who cut off an antique Plymouth taxi to swerve into line behind them. Brick winced.

"All the arrangements I was told about in Erevan are still in place then?" Ali Sabri said. "That surprises me."

"Substantially in place, yes."

"What does that mean?"

"It means that a number of things have happened that I didn't expect, as you know. I'm only a major—and perhaps not that for long. I can't speak for the politicians. I would hope that things still go as planned. I'll ask you to believe that I wouldn't have found you if I didn't hope that."

"The Israelis—are they the problem?" Ali Sabri said.

"I can't speak for the Israelis, either."

"So they *are* the problem."

"Where are they?" Brick said into the rearview mirror. He was squeezed in the front seat between two of Özpamir's men—wiry, fashionable sorts in jeans and sport shirts unbuttoned too far down.

Özpamir met his eyes in the mirror. He hesitated before he said, "They are no longer in the country."

"Just that?"

"I'm sorry. Just that."

"Did they all leave together?"

"No. The husband—Tony—went out first. He was hurt."

"Bad?"

"He was evacuated from Erzurum on a hospital plane. Beyond that I don't know."

"Livia didn't want to leave with him?"

"No."

"Did that strike you as odd?"

Özpamir hesitated again. "Yes."

"Did she say why she stayed?"

"She said she and Mr. Brenner had some business.

186

I don't know where or with whom, and I was in no position to ask. They traveled with diplomatic immunity."

"Do you know our Iranian guide is dead?"

"Yes."

"And Ibrahim, my assistant director?"

"Yes."

"Do you know how Tony was hurt?"

"I know how I was told he was hurt."

"How?"

The Mercedes pulled over to the curb behind a tour bus loading passengers. The Peugeot stopped behind them. "Brick," Özpamir said. The patient, professorial tone came back into his voice. "I didn't want to involve you in any of this to begin with— you know that. Do you understand?"

"Damn it, that's not fair. I *am* involved."

"All right. I was told you did it."

"Who told you that?"

"I was told."

"Do you believe it?"

"My business is with Ali Sabri, Brick. If you were involved in any of the other affairs, I'm not the one who will investigate that. Personally, I'll do what I can where I can when the time comes, but it may not be much."

"Then am I a guest, too?"

"For the time being. You'll stay here with Ali Sabri—unless he objects—and will go to Ankara. *Inshallah,* things will turn out well there."

"I don't object," Ali Sabri said. "I do object to that filthy purser of yours. And if I am a guest I want my gun back."

The tour bus swayed away from the curb. *"Shimde,"* Özpamir said, and the driver of the car got out to

open the door for Brick and Ali Sabri. For the first
time Brick paid attention to where they had stopped.
As he ducked out of the car with one of Özpamir's
men beside him, he recognized the glass art-nouveau
awning of the Grand Hotel Pera Palas—recognized
it and swore. He looked behind him down the hill.
A hundred feet away an American marine looked
back at him from a glass booth at the U. S. consulate.
Cruel and unusual punishment, Brick thought. So
close, so son-of-a-bitching close...

Özpamir's man stepped back and motioned Brick
toward the Pera Palas, all Turkish courtesy, all
Turkish certainty that he would be obeyed.

While Brick sat in the window of his room on the
top floor of the hotel, watching and brooding, Ali
Sabri explored. The Pera Palas was a museum, the
last of the Levantine grand hotels. It had never failed
to cheer Brick before when he had stayed there, to
tickle some romantic fancy that now was as dead as
the day before yesterday. He wondered if Agatha
Christie had felt as trapped as this while she hid in
the room below his, pretending to be dead and scribbling out her book about the Orient Express to pass
the time. Or if Atatürk had felt as damned hopeless
as this while he paced his private suite on the second
floor and mulled the ways to single-handedly jerk
Turkey out of the Middle Ages and into the twentieth
century. Hundreds of birds wheeled in a great circle
over the Golden Horn while two bored hawks sat on
an antenna at the American consulate and watched
them. From the gable window of a building across
the way a maid watched, too, but closed the window
and disappeared when she caught Brick staring at
her. Even maids wanted nothing to do with him. In

188

the middle distance, a gigantic electric Ramazan banner lit up between two minarets of Suleiman's mosque: "Welcome, Sultan of Months." Floodlights flicked on to light other minarets all over the city, and ships cruised the Bosphorus like sleepy ghosts in the coral twilight. The beauty was almost painful; Brick's loneliness was almost sweet.

But on the street below an antiterrorist squad stopped cars for arms searches. There was nothing beautiful or sweet about that. Poor Atatürk, Brick thought. The nation you made all by yourself is falling apart, and you not in that monumental tomb of yours even half a century yet. Poor Brick, too. Why in hell does it have to fall apart on you?

Why, indeed? Damn you, Rustin, he told himself. You wanted in on this, and when something unexpected happens, you get scared, you feel sorry for yourself, and you're ready to roll over and die. You're terrified of a jail cell in Ankara, and yet you're sitting here and waiting for it. A city as big as the one out that window is damn well big enough to hide a man until he can slip out of it. For all you know Özpamir is as decent as he seems and is keeping you here in Istanbul long enough for you to do just that: find someplace to hide. Then think, think.

He stood and tried to flick on a lamp. On the third try, he found one with a bulb in it. He fumbled in his pockets. He still had five thousand lira—less than fifty bucks—that he had crammed into his jeans before he left Trabzon. All the thinking in the world wouldn't do him any good if he didn't have more than that.

Once Özpamir's people had taken Ali Sabri's machine pistol, they hadn't bothered to search him further. Somewhere on him he should still have most of the wad Livia had left with him. Now that he knew his deal was still more or less on with the Turks, there was no reason in hell he should want to go on to London. But Brick was entitled to some of that money, even if he had to break a Kurd's neck to get it.

As he started for the door, he glanced wistfully out the window at the roof of the consulate, where two men were lowering the flag. No help there— even if they granted him asylum in spite of all of the charges that could be cooked up against him, he'd rot for the rest of his life there before the Turks would agree to let him leave the country. It was Ali Sabri now, or nothing.

Özpamir's man followed him down the hall. The major had made it clear that Brick and Ali Sabri were free to go where they wanted—as long as they didn't try to go unaccompanied. At Ali Sabri's room, the man stood back at a discreet distance with Ali Sabri's guard while Brick knocked on the tall oak door.

Ali Sabri glowed as if he hadn't seen Brick in months. "Ah, my dear friend!" he said and embraced him. "I was just coming for you. What a wonderful place this is! You know about Miss Christie's room?"

"Can I come in?"

"Of course. No! First I show you Miss Christie's room. It's empty at the moment and my friend in the hall has a key to all the rooms. What luck! I learned my best English by reading her books, you know. The British left them behind by the hundreds..."

"Fine. If you don't mind, I'd like to talk to you first." He tried to step past Ali Sabri.

Ali Sabri took his arm and guided him into the hall. "Plenty of time to talk. We'll have tea later, maybe even some *raki*." He mimed turning a key to his scowling guard and dragged Brick along toward the elevator.

"Christ, I've got something important to say, Ali."

"So does Miss Christie. Come along."

Brick's anger cooled as they waited for the grumbling guard to open the door to room 401. Ali Sabri was capable of playing the fool, yes. But he wasn't a fool. Something was happening. He let Ali Sabri go ahead of him into the room, which looked just like his own room upstairs—bigger than it needed to be, with French windows, elaborately carved armoire and desk, overstuffed easy chairs, everything spotless and polished.

"There," Ali Sabri said. "That could well be the same desk she used. And there, under one of these very floorboards they discovered the key to her diary. Wonderful, yes?"

"Wonderful."

Ali Sabri closed the door, as if it were an afterthought. "And look in here..." He led Brick into the bathroom and pointed triumphantly at the massive, brass-fixtured commode. "That, no doubt, is the very facility she used to shit into!"

Brick smiled in spite of himself. "What the hell's this all about?"

Ali Sabri's face turned serious. "Perhaps nothing. But if I were our hosts, I would have microphones all over my room. That was your business once. What do you think?"

"Is that the way you're going to run your country when you get one?"

"Yes. No matter what your Western mapmakers say, this is still the Middle East. Miss Christie would understand."

"What would there be to gain by listening to us?"

"This, for example. Are we still going to London?"

"We?"

"Listen quickly. Without the Israelis, the Turks will have nobody willing to take the blame for their support of the Kurds. They'll have to abandon us. Özpamir still believes the Israelis will come through. But what if they don't? Where will I be left? If I were them, I wouldn't just let me go. Who knows that I wouldn't stir up trouble here, too?"

"Wouldn't you anyway?"

"No. Not for the time being, at least. Why would I want to kill the chicken that laid the golden egg?"

"Goose."

"But if the Turks aren't able to support me...In any case, I can't stay here until I know more. The only people who can tell me more are your people in London. I don't trust them, but even if they aren't any help, I can be more useful from London than as a 'guest' in Ankara. Correct?"

"That makes sense."

"Excellent. You say that it's a few hours to the border?"

"Four or five, depending."

"Where can someone get lost for an afternoon in Istanbul?"

Brick thought. "You can get lost for a year in the covered bazaar."

"Then we tell Özpamir tonight that we hold him to his word. Tomorrow, as a guest of the state, I want to see the covered bazaar. You'll be my interpreter."

Özpamir's sad eyes had grown even sadder when Ali Sabri made his announcement. But Brick wasn't certain that he was worried about letting Ali Sabri

loose on the city as much as he was about something
else. He had shown up for dinner in the hotel's cav-
ernous, white-linen and tuxedo-waitered dining room
already distracted, it seemed to Brick. Each time
Brick or Ali Sabri had queried him for news from
Ankara, he had avoided giving them a direct answer.
He shuffled his food around on his plate but ate almost none of it, and continually asked them to repeat
what they said, as if he were having trouble concen-
trating. When he saw them through the pink, white,
and black marble lobby to the open cage of the elevator, he forgot to wish them a good night.

But that had been last night. This morning when
he checked up on them at the hotel, he seemed controlled again, as if during the night he had put himself at ease somehow.

And now, as they dodged the lame beggars and
the postcard and chewing gum and wallet vendors
who tried to intercept them at the entrance to the
covered bazaar, Özpamir didn't matter anymore. Ali
Sabri forged ahead as if he were already racing the
two limber guards who wove through the crowd behind them.

"Where can we lose them?" Ali Sabri asked Brick
as they plunged through the great arches, past the
marble Ottoman fountains where the poor stopped
to wash and watch.

"In the heart of this thing. The old bazaar is a
labyrinth."

"They'll be expecting us to try. It won't be easy."

"No. They'll be expecting me to try, not you."

"Does that make a difference?"

"It might." The important thing was that the
guards not be sure they had been ditched on purpose.
If they were unsure, they'd want to save face, find

Brick and Ali Sabri on their own first if they could. If they searched for an hour before they asked for help, that was an hour's head start.

Already the crowds were thick in the avenue-sized entrance hall, babbling with vendors in half-a-dozen languages. Ali Sabri slowed and pretended to be interested in the delicate goldwork and heaps of loose diamonds in the plush shops of the Sephardic Jews that clustered near the entrance. Brick stayed in sight but moved slightly ahead of him to the leather shops on the other side of the noisy, echoing hall. The guards split up, too, throwing nervous glances at each other. Good. They were off balance already. Brick deliberately ducked into a shop and watched his guard panic before he stepped back into the stream of bodies, innocent as virginity itself. Half-a-dozen times of faking like that and his guard would begin to lull, to panic more slowly.

But the guards were good: no matter how many glass god's eyes or tasseled satin slippers they had thrust under their noses by vendors, they managed to stay close. Brick fingered leather coats and flight bags and tried on rings and watched merchants roll out Oriental carpets for him until he was dizzy. He would disappear into one of the smaller side corridors where the copper merchants or rug dealers or teahouses clustered, then reappear to sit in an open shop and rest while boys brought him tea on swinging brass trays and his guard unbuttoned his shirt even further against the heat. If he was wearing out, his guard was wearing more quickly under the pressure of having to stay alert. By the time they had fought their way down the mile-long entrance hall to the old bazaar, the morning was all but gone.

Old books, antique camel saddles, junk, broken

pistols, swords, dusty and delicate silver snuffboxes and ivory figurines, intricate meerschaums, Delft plates and Chinese vases, Roman coins and Byzantine bracelets, all the remains of empire that could be ransacked from the attics of Istanbul's collapsing wooden mansions by the Turks and Greeks and Armenians and Jews who sat morosely in the dimly lit shops and waited for those customers brave enough to risk the winding, hilly corridors that once had been the open market streets of Constantinople— that was the old bazaar. The world's first shopping mall, Brick thought as he leafed through a stack of seventy-year-old French comic books in one of the shops. Ali Sabri had lost himself among meerschaums. Brick edged close to him.

"Buy something," he said. "Anything to stall, but stay here."

Ali Sabri nodded and examined a meerschaum carved into a pair of breasts.

As casually as he could, Brick wandered across the narrow corridor into another shop as dim and junk-laden as the first. But this one was on a corner, with doors opening onto two corridors. His guard sidled up to the dusty window so he could keep him in sight. Brick haggled with the shopkeeper awhile over a jade Buddha, then abruptly plunked it on the counter and stepped through the door into the other corridor. He gave his guard a second to round the corner and catch up with him, then about-faced and went back into the shop. The guard looked puzzled; he started to follow, then thought better of it. He was tired, he had watched Brick play this in-and-out game all morning, and he knew that his partner, who was still guarding Ali Sabri in the corridor they had just left, could keep an eye on Brick, too. He would wait this one out. Brick prayed he didn't change his mind as he crossed the corridor toward the shop where Ali Sabri seemed deep in a sign-language battle with the owner over the breast-shaped meerschaum.

But at the door of the shop he brushed past Ali Sabri's guard and kept going up the corridor, trying to seem busily intent on finding something around the next curve. As he turned the curve he glanced back. Ali Sabri's guard was looking frantically around for his partner. Brick stopped so that he could still see the reflection of Ali Sabri's guard in a shop window. The man took a step toward Ali Sabri, apparently decided he was safely busy for the moment, and struck out up the corridor after Brick. City of miracles, Brick thought. Thank God.

Brick checked the shops near him and picked the smallest and dingiest of them to enter. The shopkeeper, an unhappy stump of a man with a scimitar moustache, watched him uncertainly. *"Efendim?"*

No more panic. Not this time. He stepped to the end of the chipped wooden counter and bent down to see something inside the glass beneath it. He pointed to what could have been, inside the scratched glass, either a turtle or a snuffbox. "Let me see that."

"This?" The shopkeeper picked up a silver belt buckle.

"No, no." Brick rounded the counter and squatted behind it. A shadow passed the shop window. "That."

"Ah! The pillbox."

Brick silently counted to five. The corridor slanted uphill and forked twenty paces beyond the shop. Ali Sabri's guard should have taken one of the forks by now. "Pillbox? I thought it was a turtle." He stood up, looking apologetic.

He paused a moment at the door. So much depended on chance now—that his own guard was still waiting for him in the other corridor, that Ali Sabri's guard would take two minutes more to search both forks before he came back to find his partner. Brick stepped through the door. Two hippies with German flags on their backpacks huddled in front of a shop window. There was no one else in sight.

Fighting to control his breathing as much as his pace, he walked back toward the shop he had left Ali Sabri in—strolled, he told himself. Ali Sabri leaned against the doorpost of the shop, stoking his new meerschaum. Except for the shopkeeper, he was alone.

Brick motioned for him. Ali Sabri sauntered toward him, and they met at the base of a narrow flight of stone stairs that climbed between two shops. Ali Sabri peered up the stairs.

"You wouldn't know where that goes, would you?" he said.

"I don't care, either."

Brick led. The stairs rose to the height of the shops' ceilings, then began to curve. As they did, the light disappeared and Brick felt his way along damp stone walls that closed more and more tightly around him, as if he were climbing into a huge conch shell. Why in God's name would anybody build a spiral staircase into the walls of a bazaar?

And then he understood. Nobody had built the staircase into the bazaar. The bazaar had been built around the staircase! They were in a minaret. Centuries ago the bazaar had been only awnings tacked to the side of a mosque, and the muezzin had climbed up this way to wail the faithful to prayer. A minaret!

Of all the miserable damned dead ends to work yourself into, Rustin...

It was a certainty the muezzin didn't come into
the minaret this way anymore since the bazaar had
been covered. There had to be another door somewhere. But how many hundreds of years ago had the
bazaar been covered? How long ago had loudspeak-
ers been installed to save the muezzin his climb entirely? What were the chances that the door would
still work? Not bloody much, Brick thought as his
hands slid from stone onto wood and he traced the
outline of a child-sized door with his fingers.

Ali Sabri stumbled against him in the dark.

"Where would a door halfway up a minaret lead?"
Brick said.

"It depends on who built the mosque. Anywhere."

"Pray that this one leads onto a roof." Brick
pushed at the door. It moved as little as the stone
around it would have. He sat and leaned his shoulder
into it. Still nothing. He twisted himself so that his
legs were wedged against the wall opposite and put
his back against the door. "Sit beside me," he told
Ali Sabri.

The two of them groped at one other in the dark
until each had most of his back against the door, and
good leverage with his legs. Laurel and son-of-a-
bitching Hardy, Brick thought as he said, "Push!"

The door gave a little at first, stuck once more,
then, with a great creak and a splintering of wood
around the hinges, gave way. Brick and Ali Sabri
sprawled through the opening behind it like loose
springs.

They were on no roof. They were on a long balcony,
and before them lay the cool, domed interior of a
mosque. Stained glass let a hundred shafts of light

fall on layers of rich carpets covering the floor—and
fall on the scores of the prayerful on their knees on
the carpets. The sound of the crashing door echoed
back at Brick like trumpets on Judgment Day. The
prayers stopped. Heads turned.

"Take your shoes off," Ali Sabri said. "Don't make
things worse." He slipped out of his shoes and crossed
the balcony to a flight of stairs leading to the floor
of the mosque. There was a murmur from the crowd,
but nobody got up. Brick followed, hating each creak
of the stairs as he descended. When he was halfway
down, the yelling started—first from a man at the
edge of the congregation, then spreading like waves
from a pebble in water. Brick leapt the last three
stairs and hit the ground running.

Ali Sabri was ahead of him through the doors.
They ran down a couple of shoeless old men in the
vestibule, and then they were back in the bazaar
again—the old bazaar. But where in the old bazaar?
Brick had memorized the way they had come into
it before, like Theseus unwinding his string, so
they could get out again quickly. Now in front of
them stretched only twisting, forking corridors that
curled back on themselves like a hall of mirrors.
They struggled into their shoes, then dodged and
ducked past tourists and shopkeepers only to turn
half-a-dozen corners and wind up ducking and
dodging past the same damn shopkeepers and tourists.

How long they ran Brick had no idea. He was only
conscious that he was sweating like a preacher in
a whorehouse, that at last the corridor they were on
straightened and broadened and that they were in
a part of the bazaar he recognized, a newer part, a
section of rug merchants clustered around a foun-

tain. Somewhere there was an exit, he knew—not the main exit, but that didn't matter. He needed sunlight and air.

They broke into daylight on a poor peoples' market street more crowded than the most crowded section of the bazaar. For a half hour they elbowed through bodies that seemed rooted there thick as grass-blades. It was already early afternoon when they at last found a street clear enough for a taxi to risk navigating, and another three-quarters of an hour of traffic before they pulled up in front of the garage of the Pera Palas. But they still weren't clear yet. If Özpamir's men didn't have a guard on the Peugeot, miracles were easier to come by than Brick had ever thought possible.

A story about a lost claim ticket and a hundred-lira tip took care of the attendant at the entrance to the garage. And the Peugeot was easy enough to spot among all the look-alike Turkish Anadols and Murats even in the lightless garage, even as blessedly abandoned as it looked without one of the clean-cut MIT men beside it. For the first time since he had been aboard the *Ege,* the tightness in Brick's gut loosened.

"Miraculous," he told Ali Sabri.

"You think so?"

"Don't you?"

Ali Sabri shrugged. "Perhaps."

"What else?"

"Nothing. Kurds are too suspicious. Find your key."

Brick untaped the spare key from behind the bumper. As they eased into traffic, Brick checked the entrance to the Pera Palas. Two bellhops stood in listless conversation in the doorway. No one else

was visible. Surely if Özpamir's men had given up
and notified Özpamir that he and Ali Sabri were
"officially" lost, half the MIT men in Istanbul would
be swarming over the hotel. How long did they have
now, he wondered, before word went out about Ali
Sabri and himself to the customs station at the Greek
border? Or to the martial-law checkpoints on the
highway? They had lost so goddamned much time
already that their ration of it had to be nearly gone.
No more miracles now. Just driving—fast, hard
driving.

Past the last suburbs and the final camping
ground for the German tourists who flocked to this
Turkish sun like lizards, the road stretched flat and
straight and relatively empty through dry hills and
smooth fields, country that grew more Mediterra-
nean with every hot kilometer they drove. Brick
floorboarded the Peugeot around a maniacal bus
cruising on the wrong side of the road. Already he
missed the cool forests of Trabzon. Ali Sabri, himself
almost like a lizard, appeared to doze beside him in
the seat.

The first checkpoint just outside the city had been
easy. But Brick had expected that: even if they had
been reported, there would hardly have been time
for Özpamir to get the army's gears in motion before
they passed that one. It was the last checkpoint, the
one they had just passed, that puzzled him. They
were less than a dozen miles from the border, and
it was nearly evening. Özpamir had had time to send
messages out to Mongolia, if he wanted. Yet they
had passed through the checkpoint without the
slightest rise of an eyebrow from the young lieutenant who manned it. Brick had been prepared to risk

crashing it, gunning the Peugeot and heading for the border through the fields if he had to. But Ali Sabri had faced the lieutenant as calmly as if the man had been a ticket taker in a movie theater. And now he was dozing, goddamnit! Brick could accept that communications to army checkpoints were slow here in the middle of nowhere. But surely Özpamir would have known where they would head; surely he had simply picked up the phone and called the border station.

"Are you awake?" he asked Ali Sabri.

Ali Sabri grunted.

"Border's coming up. Got any ideas?"

"No. Just stop when you're asked."

"I don't think you heard me. The border's coming up."

"I don't think that's such a problem, my friend."

"You don't think that's a problem."

"I haven't expected they were going to stop us since before we left Istanbul." He pulled his new breast-shaped meerschaum from his shirt pocket and gave it a trial puff. "Have you considered that Özpamir doesn't want us caught?"

"I haven't considered that, no."

"Why was there no guard on this automobile? Why has it taken so long to do something as simple as notify the army to stop two men on a major highway? What we did was very obvious, you know."

"All right. Then why didn't Özpamir just tell us we could go?"

"He doesn't have the authority for that, clearly. He had to make it look as if we really escaped. Right now I imagine he's having a breakdown trying to discover ways to excuse his failing to get the news out about us quickly enough. He's probably more afraid than you are that we won't get to the border soon enough."

"That's—"

"I don't know why he wants us to get out of Turkey, if that's what you're going to ask. Who knows why a Turk wants anything! But I'm sure he does."

Brick pondered. "It's too farfetched."

"Then just say I've spent all my life crossing borders. One more doesn't bother me."

A squad of soldiers resting in the shade of one of the buildings of the stucco customs complex watched them idly as they slowed for the speed bumps that led to the border. How many times had he come in and out of Turkey, Brick wondered. Each time passing customs had always been just a nuisance, a formality. Now, the last time he would ever do it, he was so damned afraid of the idle soldiers and the bored immigration official who waited in the glass booth ahead of them that he couldn't steady his hand to find second gear without a grinding that caused even the sleepy cats on the walk to look up. Why in hell should he have to leave like this? He resented Ali Sabri, who fingered his phony passport in stupid confidence that his cockeyed notion about Özpamir would save them. He resented Livia in London, or wherever she was, for catching him up in this nightmare. He resented himself for letting her do it. He resented Özpamir for finding them in Istanbul. He resented Noah, arks, Ararat, politicians, borders, Kurds, and Ali Sabri's obscene pipe.

He resented anything as long as resentment could take his mind off the shrewd, sagging face of the immigration official in front of him, and off the knowledge that no matter what the man told them to do, he was out of options. He wouldn't turn back.

He watched the man's face for any sign of surprise or suspicion as he leafed through the passports, stamping and scribbling in them seemingly at random. But the man's bored expression remained as fixed as Wednesday. What now, Brick thought. The man would just hand them their passports and tell them to have a good trip and they would drive away home free? He studied the road ahead. Just in front of him was a wooden gate like the ones lowered at railroad crossings. A hundred or so yards beyond that a narrow steel bridge arched over a little river. In the middle of the bridge four soldiers—two Turkish, two Greek, a pair on each side of the bridge— faced off across an imaginary line. Beyond the bridge clustered the low, gray buildings of Greek customs. So close, so goddamned close now. He slipped the Peugeot into gear.

On Ali Sabri's side of the car a customs man, an officer in a dull green uniform and high-peaked military hat, walked slowly along the car, peering into the backseat, poking at the tires with his shoe. As he leaned into the window to speak to Ali Sabri, a phone in the building just behind him rang. He pushed away from the car to go answer it. Brick watched him through the building's plate glass window. The man made hasty notes on a pad, nodding and giving short answers into the phone. After a moment, he looked from his note pad to the Peugeot, back to his pad, then abruptly hung up.

The immigration official in the booth tapped Brick's arm with the passports. Brick started as if the man had stuck a burning match to him, then tried to look sheepish. "What are you bringing from Turkey?"

"Nothing," Brick said, and took the passports.

"A pipe," Ali Sabri said and held up his meerschaum, grinning.

The official bent over to see the pipe and leered back. He raised his hand to wave them through, but never finished the gesture. His eye caught something behind the car and he froze. In the rearview mirror, Brick saw the customs officer trotting toward the booth from the building where the squad of soldiers had been lounging. Half a dozen of them trotted after him. The officer was making chopping motions in the air with his hand, clear signs. *Hold them,* they said, *hold them.*

"I think perhaps Major Özpamir ran out of time and excuses," Ali Sabri said.

"For Christ's sake, what do I do?"

Ali Sabri glanced back at the soldiers, who were a dozen paces from the car. He threw his hands up.

Brick popped the clutch just as the customs officer drew his pistol. Tires squealed as the Peugeot slid sideways, and from the corner of his eye Brick saw the immigration man dive for the floor of his booth. That the customs officer fired at them he knew because of the two holes that appeared suddenly in the windshield, but he heard nothing except the sound of the old engine's clattering pistons and the splintering gate. A sliver of the gate sailed in through the window and Brick felt it slice against his neck. He swerved. The car bounced off the road and over a curb. He jerked the wheel and kept the gas floored. When they hit the roadway again he felt the thump and the wallow in the steering that told him they had blown a tire. He grabbed the wheel with both hands, dropped low in the seat, slammed the transmission through second and into third, and aimed for the bridge. He figured he had maybe half of his control of the steering left. A camel through a goddamn needle's eye, he thought as the narrow bridge rushed at them.

The astonished Turkish soldiers on the bridge dropped to their knees and struggled to get their rifles unslung. The two Greeks stood in a wild amaze, then, as the Peugeot glanced off the railing and onto the bridge, ran. Brick was flung across the seat into Ali Sabri but managed somehow to keep his foot on the gas pedal and one hand on the steering. Ali Sabri shoved him back into place behind the wheel. The front fender was gone—Brick could see that much. And the steam from the sprung hood told him the radiator was mortally wounded. But they were on the goddamn bridge, and they were still moving.

They slammed back and forth between the railings like a pool ball. Brick knew his shoulders and chest were being beat all to hell, but he couldn't feel it yet. One of the Turkish soldiers got off a wild shot, yelled something, then disappeared over the railing into the river. The other one threw his rifle at the Peugeot like a spear and vaulted behind him. Something exploded softly under the hood and the car's power whooshed away like a breath held too long. Brick pumped at the dead gas pedal and swore, then slapped the transmission into neutral. "Coast, you son of a bitch, coast," he yelled.

And then there was no more bridge. Ali Sabri was whooping and tousling Brick's hair, a dozen men were running toward them from the Greek customs station, the Peugeot was rolling gently to a stop in

the middle of a Greek road, and they were home free,
Brick thought, home free—fifteen hundred miles
from London, bleeding and no doubt full of busted
ribs, and with no car or clothes and probably under
arrest, but home free. Praise Allah.

Six

Ali Sabri strode beside him through the great gray cavern of Victoria Station like a disapproving prophet, outraged at the wickedness of cities. Brick knew he was nervous and angry, fuming that even his new Greek clothing and luggage hadn't been enough to keep the British immigration people from treating him like a wog at Gatwick Airport. That was the Pakistani passport's great drawback: no matter if he owned half the city of Karachi, in the mother country of the Commonwealth he would never be free from the curse of wogdom. Now, glowering, he popped his meerschaum into his mouth and glared at a matronly woman queued up for a telephone, defying her to glare back while Brick began the battle for a cab.

That Greeks and Turks hated one another so consummately had been their salvation. The Greeks were eager for any excuse to refuse to discuss extradition with Ankara. A vaguely worded telegram from Brick's father at NSA, a cock-and-bull story about Ali Sabri being a political refugee (the Pakistani passport had almost sunk that until Ali Sabri had convinced a friendly Greek official that Kurds could be born anywhere), a few pounds pressed into the right palms, and they were on a plane for London within a week. By then Brick's cuts were beginning to heal, his bruises (no broken ribs after all) less painful. And the warm Thracian nights he spend drinking iced fruit drinks on Thessaloníki's promenade beside the Aegean had done fair to begin the restoration of his soul, too.

But he had passed most of his free time rolling the events of the past weeks around in his mind, chewing and rechewing them like cud, trying to reduce them to something simple that he could digest. He accepted that Özpamir had deliberately allowed them to get out of Turkey. But all the reasons he could come up with didn't really explain why he had done it; Özpamir was a professional—he might act out of compassion when he could, but never at the expense of doing his job. He had acted secretly and on his own when he let them go. There was no conceivable way that a military man could think of that as doing his job. He took a huge personal risk in the expectation that something would come of it. That was as far as Brick could take it. Whatever Özpamir was expecting to happen would have to happen, in which case Brick would know what had been on Özpamir's mind—or not happen, in which case he would never know.

As for the rest, the part Livia and Brenner and

Tony had been involved in, he had resigned himself to knowing no more until he got to London.

And this was London.

Ali Sabri could have been on Mars. While Brick haggled with cabbies, he strolled the sidewalk as if he expected to buy it, rocking back on his heels to read the advertisements and the graffiti on the walls, stopping in front of a bench to stare at a blue-haired punk rocker as if the kid were an exhibit in a wax museum, scowling at Arabs, trailing a gang of leather-jacketed skinheads, peering down plunging necklines until Brick was convinced they were both going to be hauled away to Bedlam, or wherever they hauled such people to nowadays.

"You don't seem impressed," Ali Sabri said when they at last settled into a cab. His new clothes— Qiana shirt, dark slacks, loafers—made him stand out even more than Brick's old jeans would have. He was out of place in them, as if he had put on somebody else's skin. His slicked hair and rawboned horseman's hands and moustache and tanned face against those clothes made him look more a migrant worker on the make than a Kurdish chieftain. Brick felt a flash of anger at whatever it was that had dragged Ali Sabri here as if he were a new specimen for the Queen's Park Zoo.

"I've been here before."

"And you actually came back."

"I like it."

"Pity."

"You're right."

"You're hoping to find the woman here, aren't you?"

Brick bristled. "I don't know what the hell I'm

expecting to find. Mostly somebody to take you off my hands so I can go home."

"You won't talk about her at all, will you? Why not?"

"She's somebody else's wife, for God's sake."

"Does that stop people here?"

"No, but it makes things damned complicated. Look," Brick said. "If something happened back there in the wilderness, it probably doesn't mean a damn thing here. We may not even recognize each other."

"Friends should talk about those things."

"Friends should, yes."

"Are we not friends?"

"Yeah, we're friends. But I don't want to talk about it." He didn't want to think about it, either. He had been pretty successful at that, he believed, even from the time he thought she had been lost in the river. She had always been there somewhere in his mind, of course, like old love letters in a trunk; but when he began to actually think about her, about what might or might not happen when they saw each other again, he had most often been able to find something else more pressing he needed to think about. It was a good trick, but a trick nonetheless. The stupidity of what he was doing should have stunned him: showing up out of the blue at an unknown place in London with a man like Ali Sabri, not having the slightest real idea who might be waiting for him at the address Livia had scribbled for him as she knelt on a mountainside in Soviet Armenia. But instead of that—or instead of being afraid—he was excited at the notion that, whatever was waiting for him, she was most likely included in it. He'd probably bore her silly within a week here—or vice versa. But he had to have that chance to find out what would happen, had let wanting it shape everything he had done since he had first agreed to follow her to Kurdistan.

They climbed a long hill and the neighborhood turned posh: ivy-covered stone walls with the lead roof of an old mansion visible behind them here and there, or the sharp shake roofs of modern town houses. At the ends of cul-de-sac side streets, Brick could see the beginnings of forested parkland, which he took to be Hampstead Heath. And beyond that, London spread into the distance. At night the view would be magnificent. Whoever they had been sent to find wasn't likely to be selling pencils for a living.

The place had been an estate once, or maybe a mews. Inside the old walls, the stables or main house long torn down, two dozen glass-heavy brick town houses sprouted among perfect lawnettes. Jaguars, Mercedeses, even a couple of Rolls and a Bentley snuggled beside one another on the cobbled parking areas. The gatekeeper pointed the house out to Brick, staring at Ali Sabri as if he were memorizing him well enough to pick him out of a police lineup. Ali Sabri pretended not to notice.

"It's been a long trip," Brick said to him as they went up the fieldstone walk to the door.

"I wouldn't want to make it again."

"We won't."

When Brick rang the bell, he felt like a damn teenager. He was imagining Livia's voice already, enjoying her relief and surprise already. Yet when the door opened the surprise was all his, but none of the relief. He had heard the voice that spoke to him only a score of times since college, seen that face even less. The man they belonged to had come to exist for him almost solely as a steady torrent of hasty letters and small checks.

Flushed and awkward, Roger stuck out his hand with a false heartiness that embarrassed Brick. "Why Brick, old brick," he said.

Brick studied Roger as he puttered at the bar making bright, empty small talk and drinks. The setting was right for him. The whole southern wall of the town house was glass, cut halfway up by an interior deck, with the heath and London framed as if they were a landscape painting. There was plenty of rich wood—stairs, bannisters, paneling—and the furniture was antique, each piece very deliberately chosen. But everything else was Connecticut suburban, from the unheard-of-in-England dishwasher in the kitchen to the deep synthetic carpeting and the indirect lighting and air conditioning. A shotgun wedding of the authentic and the convenient, Brick thought, the parents of my bastard generation.

Roger himself seemed not to have aged; he could have stepped right out of their Middlebury yearbook into this town house, allowing for a few changes in hairstyle. His clothing was still woodsy and woolen and expensive, his hair still thick and auburn, his smallish body still almost adolescently lithe. He probably jogged or something, Brick decided, or whatever else was fashionable at the moment.

It was his eyes that were different. There had been humor in them in college, and a kind of bland confidence. Now they were too busy, glancing at you to see if you were watching him instead of comfortably resting on you as they had in years past. It was as if he were mentally looking over his shoulder, were preoccupied with something you couldn't see.

"...so if you'd simply called I'd have come round for you at the station," Roger was saying. "I hate like hell to think of you and Mr. Sabri fighting for a cab on a day like this one. They simply refuse to come this far out."

"We didn't have the phone number, Roger," Brick said. "Livia was a little rushed."

"Oh. Well," he said and raised his glass. "Welcome. This is very much an honor for me, Mr. Sabri. I admired your father very much."

"So did I," Ali Sabri said and sniffed suspiciously at the Scotch Roger had given him.

"I thought you were in Vermont," Brick said.

"I was indeed," Roger said. "Just popped over last week."

"This your place?"

"Yes. You like it?"

"Did you give up the house in Washington?"

"Oh, no. Claire and the kids have that."

"The house in Vermont?"

"Not that one, either. I want to keep it in the family."

"The magazine's doing pretty well, then." The coolness and the Scotch were padding Brick's nerves, but he was nursing anger now. Roger was so fucking...well kept.

But at the moment he looked uncomfortable. "Oh, the magazine's far too small...I've been fortunate, Brick. I've come into some money—elsewhere."

"How's Claire?"

"Fine—the last time I saw her. She'll be thrilled to hear I've run into you."

"I like Claire. I was surprised to hear about you two."

215

Roger studied the ice in his glass. "Frankly, so was I."

Ali Sabri slipped out through the glass doors into the garden, leaving them in privacy. Brick was grateful.

"It wasn't my idea," Roger went on.

"Did it have to do with the money you came into?"

"No. Well, partially, I suppose."

"Or maybe the way you came into it."

"What's that supposed to mean, *mon cher?*"

"You tell *me,* goddamnit, Roger. You sit there and blather like I've just dropped in for a drink on my way to dinner, and here I am at the end of the most god-awful trip any man since Moses ever made, with a Kurd standing out there in that garden that I've damn near been killed half a dozen times trying to bring here—and I don't even know why I'm here! And you ask *me* what something's supposed to mean?"

Roger went to the bar to make himself another drink. "Rough trip, huh?"

"Oh, for the love of—there are seven people dead behind me, Roger. Seven people!"

Roger turned and leaned against the bar. "Brick, I've gotten myself into something unpleasant. That's pretty obvious. I'd like to get out of it, but I can't yet. Try to understand—how much money do you think I was making off *Middle Eastern Desk?* Lord, the old man was bankrolling every other issue—probably would have had to keep on doing it until he died. I'm thirty-three, and I was stuck. Where could I have gone? Editor of *Foreign Affairs* or something like that? I'm no scholar, Brick, you know that. I had simply gone as far as I could. But at thirty-three? Roger, golden boy, becoming the one they ask 'What-

ever happened to old Roger?' about at class reunions?
I couldn't have borne that. I owed myself more—we
all owe ourselves more than most of us have the
courage to take, Brick. So when this—opportunity
came up, I took it. Claire didn't see it that way and
I'm deeply sorry. I love her. I'm also deeply sorry I
involved you. When Livia asked me if I knew somebody like you, I had no idea it would turn into what
it did. Believe me."

"Seven people, Roger. Why?"

"Oh, don't moralize, Brick! *I* didn't kill them.
Look, I've been trying to figure out what to do ever
since you came. Nobody even knew if you would turn
up, much less when. Let me...let me make a phone
call."

"It's your house."

Roger seemed relieved to get away from Brick as
he trotted up a flight of stairs from the entry hall.
There was a phone on the table beside Brick. He was
tempted to listen, but he'd had enough of listening
to other people's conversations in the Air Force. He
looked around the room for a door that would be
likely to lead to a bathroom, something he hadn't
seen since Gatwick. He found one off the entrance
hall.

When he discovered the makeup case and dressing
gown there, he supposed he should be glad they were
only in the guest bathroom. The lavender dressing
gown could have been any woman's, but the silver
initials on the makeup case identified them both:
LL. And now what Roger had said made sense—
"When Livia asked me if I knew somebody like
you ..." *Livia* had contacted him, not Wolf Brenner,
as Roger had claimed in his letter. Roger's busted
marriage. Livia and Roger and London. Brick had

never known you could feel betrayed from so many directions at once. He sat on the padded commode lid until the sick feeling in his stomach went away, letting the water run in the basin to block out any other sounds.

In the living room, Roger waited for him looking no more at ease than before. "Everything come out all right?" he said lamely.

"What did you find out?"

"Not in. They'll call back."

"They?"

"One of them."

"Tony? Brenner? Livia?"

"Not Tony. Tony's back in Canada."

"That must make it convenient. You should introduce him to Claire."

Roger sat down heavily in a chair opposite Brick and stared at him blankly. "So Livia left her makeup case again. Damn it, I half think she does it on purpose."

"Marking her territory."

"She had nothing to do with Claire and me, Brick. This all happened—afterward. And there's nothing to it, really. I couldn't handle Livia, I know that. I think she just uses me for—recreation—among other things."

"Her husband doesn't seem to do too well at handling her, either."

"Better than anybody. He..."

"I don't want to know about that. Who shot him? And why?"

"Did something happen between you and Livia out there?"

"Who shot the poor bastard, Roger? And who tried to blame me for it? Quit changing the subject."

"My God. I should have known she would have..."

"Roger, goddamnit!"

"No, goddamnit *you,* Brick. Don't you understand that I can't tell you anything! You want to see me dead, too? Just wait, please wait. They'll call, I promise."

Brick jerked the phone up on the first ring. He did it without thinking, without giving a damn. "Roger?" The cigarette-husky voice was unmistakable, even over the telephone.

Brick took a breath and glanced at Roger, who was already halfway out of his chair, before he answered. "No, Livia."

"Brick? Dear God, it is you, isn't it?"

"How are you?"

"We hadn't heard...anything. I didn't even know if you'd gotten off that awful mountain or not. Are you all right?"

"Never better."

"I'm so very glad, Brick. And—and Ali Sabri?"

"He's here."

"Oh, I knew you could do it. Listen, don't go anywhere. I can't come right now, but I'll be there by...what time is it now, five? I'll be there by seven."

"I'm not going anywhere." You're as witty as a rhinoceros, Rustin, he told himself. But he was using all the strength he had to keep his voice even and the hand that held the receiver steady. Christ, he hadn't expected this—this falling apart at a voice on a telephone. He had to toughen somehow. "How's Tony, Livia?"

There was a silence. "Tony's better off at home. He has to convalesce, Brick." There was another silence. "I have a lot to explain to you."

"Don't bother to bring makeup. There's some here." Asshole!

"That's not part of what I'm going to explain to you."

"I didn't think so."

"Brick, I'm glad you're here. Hear that: I'm glad you've come. And not just because of Ali Sabri. Do you understand what I'm saying to you?"

"I want to, Livia. I don't think I'd better try to talk any more just now, all right? I'm not doing so well at it."

"At seven, then. May I speak to Roger?"

"Livia?"

"Yes, Brick."

He took another breath. "Good-bye." He held the phone out for Roger.

While Roger carried on a monosyllabic conversation with Livia, Brick watched Ali Sabri in the garden. He had found a comfortable lawn chair and sat slapping idly at the leaves of a hedge and looking out over what of the heath he could see above the wall. Brick felt a rush of warmth for him, so damned out of place in that neat English garden, and yet he envied him, too. He had something to be here for that was, for him, as unequivocal as the clean shape of Ararat. Brick needed a chunk of that certainty.

Roger hung up and headed for the bar. "Tony's bad?" Brick said to him.

"Pretty bad. They say he'll come out of it."

Brick watched him pour himself another Scotch.

"You should talk to Ali Sabri."

"About what?"

"About whatever you wanted him here for."

"I didn't want him here, Brick."

"Whatever you were, Roger, you were never a bastard. Talk to him. He's come a long way."

Roger sighed. "I don't know what I can say to him before the others get here."

"The others?"

"Brenner's coming, too."

"Roger, look at me. Is it safe for Ali Sabri—hell, for me—to be here."

"Nobody's planning on hurting anybody else, Brick. Word of honor."

Brick stood, feeling very heavy. "Talk to the man. I'll be back by seven."

"Whither?"

"I don't know—the heath, somewhere. I can't sit here for two hours." He regarded Roger a moment. "You know what this is like, being here with you and talking to Livia? You ever have one of those dreams where you were with people you knew and all of a sudden they were somebody else?"

"Have a good walk, Brick."

Brick let himself out the front door. He should tell Ali Sabri he was going, he knew, but he wasn't up to explaining anything to him. Roger could handle him; they could tell each other tales of the Hodja. From himself, he needed to try something he hadn't had the chance to do in weeks: be alone. At the gate to the complex he looked back. Ali Sabri was still sitting by himself in the garden. Through the glass wall he could make out Roger, back on the telephone again. Brick felt a twinge of guilt at leaving Ali Sabri like that—and a twinge of doubt when he wondered who Roger could be calling so soon. To hell with it. He'd had enough wondering. In less than two hours he'd have some answers—about the past and about the future. He could wait that long.

* * *

The afternoon's mugginess had congealed into the
evening's chilly rain by the time Brick made his way
back up the heath. The walk had helped, and in an
odd sense the rain was helping, too. He was alert,
busy inside in a way he wouldn't have been if he had
spent the afternoon moping in Roger's town house.
And it could have been that alertness that made him
know something was wrong when he turned through
the gate. There should really be nothing strange
about all the draperies being drawn in a house so
full of glass on a wet, chilly evening. But it wasn't
like Roger to do that. He liked the grand style too
much. He wouldn't live in this place and then shut
it up like a topless bar while all the lights of London
were coming on outside—not with new people in the
house to impress.

"Mr. Rustin?" The gatekeeper stood in the doorway of his booth, blinking out at Brick through the
rainy dusk. The man's coat, hair, and face seemed
to be all dyed the same tone of gray.

"Yes."

"Thought I recognized you. Got this for you."

Brick crossed a few yards of cobbles and took the
key the man held out for him. "Said it was all right
for you to be here. Said you might be staying a few
days."

"Who said?"

"Well, Mrs. Lo Presti did. But they was all in the
car."

"All who?"

"Well, she was and the older gentleman driving
and that Indian chappie of yours in the back."

"But not Roger."

222

"Well, of course him, too. It's his house I'm giving out the key to."

When Brick swung the door open, the empty house hummed with unseen electrical things. Brick checked the upstairs bedrooms, the study, the deck, the bathrooms (her makeup case was gone) before he noticed the manila envelope on the dining-room table. It had his name on it, written in an elegant hand he recognized as Roger's.

A flurry of hundred-pound notes fell out first when he shook it open, and then the letter. It, too, was in Roger's hand.

"Dear Brick," it began. "I won't take your time apologizing. I know you'll understand how sorry I am. There are three thousand pounds here, enough to get you home and hold you for a while. They are what you're owed, plus some extra. You've earned them, so take them, damn you!

"You're welcome to stay in the house until you can get yourself together and arrange for a flight home—or wherever. In a few days a real-estate agent will come by to put it on the market. By then I imagine you'll have decided on where you're going.

"Ali Sabri is safe, and will continue to be as long as I have any say. I wish I could tell you more and could have answered your questions, but I think that in the long run you'll be better off this way.

"I'm a sentimental sort, as you know, and could easily get that way now. I won't see you again, I imagine. Take care of yourself, old brick."

Below Roger's signature was another note, this one in a woman's hand: "We all owe you a very great deal, Brick. I wish we could have lived up to you. And I wish other things about you and me, too. Please believe that. Livia."

Brick dropped the letter into the pile of banknotes. He walked to the draperies and pulled them. London glowed below him, lighting the low clouds with a pale gray light. Raindrops chased each other down the glass, distorting the hedges, the parking lot, the Jaguars and Mercedeses, the high stone walls.

Behind him, the desolate house continued to hum.

BOOK II

Seven

He knew he ought to have seen Claire, Roger's wife, in Washington first. But that would be painful; he needed time to grow some insulation. Claire could come later, when the most obvious thing, the Montreal trip, was done and he had to start putting together smaller pieces.

His father agreed to lend him his Buick for the trip, but not cheerfully. Gray had metastasized from his temples throughout his weekly trimmed red hair now, and he looked less distinguished than old, Brick thought. His Henry-the-Eighth, square face was sinking into jowliness, and the lope Brick remembered in his walk was slower, more measured, as he paced the living room and reasoned.

"Let it go, Brick. You're lucky to be out of it—and

227

alive. There are stories I know about those kinds of people that—"

"You could help, if you wanted."

"Me? NSA is a passive outfit, you know that. We just gather information. No cloak-and-dagger nonsense."

"But you know people. You could give me contacts."

His father dodged a macrame-dangling Boston fern and stared out the picture window toward the distant Blue Ridge. "I've got to go away this week. I was hoping you'd stay home with your mother. She hasn't seen you in years, to all intents."

"Where to?"

"Consulting work," his father said with the same finality he'd said "codes" when Brick was a boy. Brick glanced at the Aeromexico ticket envelope on the bookshelf full of *Reader's Digest* condensed books beside his father. There had always been foreign ticket envelopes waiting for his father. And the books he read were always condensed, like intelligence summaries. "You've only been home a week."

"I can rent a car if you'd rather." Brick felt as stubborn as a child. Even after all these years, his father could make him feel that. And as for seeing his mother—he knew he was an embarrassment to her, jobless and at home again. She always seemed to be running somewhere these days, eating up endless tanks of gas on her way to functions at the houses of people she simply couldn't conceive he didn't know. He knew she loved him still, but would be just as glad not to have to explain him.

"What do these people mean to you, son? I think there's a woman, a married woman, among them, isn't there?"

Brick's face flushed. "For the love of God, Dad. There's a man I've been close to since college among them, too. And another man who might change the whole mess in the Middle East." He caught himself and calmed. "Am I being kept track of, Dad? By your people, I mean."

"Benignly. And not precisely by *my* people. They've left you to me, in effect. The Turks have told us all they know, which is no more than you do. There's not much interest in the thing here."

"Jesus."

"The Kurds are unreliable. We're keeping our distance, that's all."

"You mean we can't control them."

"Frankly, I don't think we've ever understood the Middle East well enough to control it. The British did, in their day. Now, if the Turks and the Israelis do, and think they can make a deal with the Kurds, more power. I imagine we'll try to get on the bandwagon when the time comes." He turned from the window. The room smelled of lemon air-freshener. "You've got tŏ *do* something with yourself, Brick. You can't waste time with this thing anymore. You're thirty-three."

"Thirty-two, Dad." His father fiddled with the ticket envelope on the bookshelf and avoided his eyes. "I'll get an apartment as soon as I'm able."

"That's not it. Brick...no, never mind. Take the car. Just stay out of trouble and have the good sense to realize when you've gotten into something too deeply, that's all I ask. And don't tell your mother any of this, for God's sake."

He drove straight through to Montreal, the freeways and neat Howard Johnson'ses and Hot Shoppes as foreign to him as mosques and marketplaces once would have been. He was a stranger, uncomfortable and countryless. In Montreal, he tried the longest shot first. There was no Anthony Lo Presti in the phone book, but information had one. When a recording told him that the number had been temporarily disconnected, he drove out to the address information had given him. No, the French-accented housekeeper told him in the sprawling white Georgian house at the end of a tree-tunneled drive near the river, neither M. nor Mme. Lo Presti were in. M. Lo Presti had come home but was away again for his health. She forwarded his mail to his office. Did Brick know M. Lo Presti had been in an accident? If Brick was such a good friend of M. Lo Presti's, why did he know so little? She didn't think she should tell him anything more. And was he certain he wasn't selling something?

His next stop was a bookstore. Tony had been tired of "publishing cookbooks," he had said. Cookbooks? the clerk asked. The biggest publisher of books like that—cookbooks and self-help and psychoanalyze-your-dog and do-it-yourself battleship building, good sellers all—was Nova, the clerk told him with a conspiratorial leer. Brick called them. Ah, yes, the receptionist said. Mr. Lo Presti was associated with Nova, certainly, but for the present, not actively. All his calls were being taken by the editorial director, Mr. Perkins. Mr. Lo Presti was out of the country. No, no one was quite sure where. He was under doctor's orders not to be disturbed, she understood. Would Brick like to speak to Mr. Perkins, who was in a meeting at the moment, but if he would care to leave a number...

No, thank you.

On the long, muggy drive back, Brick constructed

things, lists of possibilities, options. He wasn't really disappointed that Montreal had turned up nothing. It had been the obvious place to begin, so he had begun there. His greatest surprise would have been if he *had* turned up something. So now where? A smart man would say *home,* to a sensible job. A smart man like his father. All right. Then take a slightly less smart man, like himself. He would say that Claire was the next most obvious place to go. Would Roger really just abandon her and the kids? He doted on the two boys. Even if he was out of touch with them temporarily, he couldn't stay away forever.

But there was the other problem: seeing Claire would be painful. He would have to lie to her about Roger—and, at last, have to *not* lie to himself about Roger. That one he would put off a little longer.

The Turks, his father had said, knew as little as he did. He would accept that for the moment. Only Major Özpamir would be likely to know anything the official channels didn't, and Major Özpamir might as well have fallen off the edge of the earth with Tony and Livia and the others.

Who, then?

The piece of this thing that was most mysterious so far was the Israelis. Most mysterious, and least likely to want to stop being that way. They had to have wanted Ali Sabri mighty badly, to have something mighty important in mind to have allowed Livia and Brenner to double-cross the Turks as they had. Brick wouldn't win any popularity contests by announcing himself at the Israeli embassy right now. If he got in, he bloody well might not get out again.

But no, the Israelis couldn't risk that, not with

his father a deputy director of NSA. Another kind of code, and one he was damn grateful for now.

Or thought he should be grateful for, until he decided that the Canadian Chevy two cars back was truly following him. He had first noticed it at the Canadian border, pulling off the highway so that it wouldn't be directly behind him at the customs check. Then again as he had stopped for gas, passing the gas station but waiting at a hot-dog stand a mile or so down the road. And then once more when he picked up the New York State Thruway at Albany, hanging back and choosing the toll booth farthest away from him. Behind the tinted glass of the dark-green sedan, he could see only that there were two people in the car: men, women, or androids he couldn't tell. They never got too close, never seemed to want anything from him. Just to follow.

Nonetheless he was nervous. That they didn't want anything now didn't mean they wouldn't want something later. He sped up to lose himself in traffic.

Twice he thought he had lost them, once in New Jersey and again on the Baltimore–Washington Expressway. But twice he was wrong. He stopped to test them just before he got to the Washington beltway. They passed him once more. They were waiting for him again at the next rest stop.

His nervousness turned to active worry as he left the beltway for the Shirley Highway, south toward the far Virginia suburbs where his parents' house was. His mother probably wouldn't be home. That meant he would have to fumble with a key before he could get inside to the bedroom and the drawer his father kept the revolver in. Used to keep the revolver in. What if it wasn't there? There were four acres of woods around the house—nobody would see or hear anything that went on.

But he would have to risk it. "Stay out of trouble," his father had said. Pig's ass! If he saw a cop on the highway, he'd try to flag him down. But if not, the last thing he would want to do was go through Manassas or one of the other small towns and try to locate a police station. Lost, on a side street, he would be a hell of a lot worse off than he was now, where he had running room. He pressed the accelerator and watched the turbo-indicator light come on and felt the extra push of power and was bleakly comforted.

From the many lanes of the Shirley Highway, he had nine miles of two-lane to go before he hit the dirt road that led to his parents' house, hidden with a dozen others like it in the woods of what had been a farm twenty years before. The Canadian Chevy hung back again, still giving him a head start as he left the freeway. Brick floored the Buick, slicing past hippopotamus Winnebagos and wallowing camper pickups on their way to the Bull Run battlefield. Any other time, he'd have had half the Virginia State Police on him by now. But all he got were geriatric glares from drivers of Good Sam Club–stickered campers and erect fingers from Caterpillar-capped farmers in hay trucks. The green Chevy took its time, passed safely, kept its distance—but didn't go away.

Brick fishtailed the Buick onto the dirt road, hoping to raise dust clouds to blind the Chevy. He figured a mile, not much more, to the house. He checked the rearview mirror. Plenty of dust, all right. So much he couldn't see how close the Chevy was.

He abandoned the Buick in the drive, snatched the keys and ran. At the door he cussed the new key his father had had made for him, still stiff in the lock. As the door slammed open he risked a quick glance behind him. He could see nearly the whole length of the dirt road. Dust drifted slowly away from it onto the bushes. It was empty.

Beyond it, part of the two-lane was visible through a break in the trees. The green Chevy moved at a leisurely pace along it, heading back north. Brick leaned against the doorjamb and flung the keys out onto the driveway. He was panting, angry and afraid at the same time. Goddamnit to hell! He had been escorted home, no more. All the way from Montreal!

The next morning, on his way in to the Israeli embassy, he stopped in Fairfax and bought a pistol.

The second time he went to the embassy, four days later, they took the pistol away from him. The first time he got no further than a receptionist, who let him leave a note for the military attaché (he would have left it for the Mossad intelligence officer but the receptionist would have denied there was one). Two days later he got a call from a serious-voiced, slightly urgent man who identified himself as a Mr. Landau in the political-affairs wing. Would Mr. Rustin care to come by at his earliest convenience? A Colonel Corden would like very much to see him. Mr. Rustin cared to.

The Santa Fe–style Israeli embassy was even more of a fortified bunker than most of the U. S. embassies Brick had been in. Iron gates, TV monitors, armed guards, metal detectors, searches—and then busy corridors with offices people darted in and out of like characters in a Marx Brothers routine, and then more barred doors into a quieter section with fewer offices, thicker carpeting, and more armed guards.

The man, younger than Brick, who had come down to the reception area to escort him was Mr. Landau. He wore rimless glasses and a three-piece suit and had a twitchy smile. He could, Brick decided, only work in the political-affairs section of a foreign embassy.

The room he led Brick into was unquestionably a government office, with its standard off-white walls and issue desk and plastic chairs, but it had been softened by a carpet and paintings—watercolors of deserty landscapes that Brick imagined were in Israel—and family portraits: a man in an officer's uniform, a young middle-aged woman, and two children in their teens—a handsome boy in a uniform and a pretty girl in a school dress. The man who stood to greet him from behind the desk was the man in the photographs. He was heavily tanned and sharp-featured, the kind of man you expected to see with his fatigue sleeves rolled up, standing beside a tank in the Sinai explaining troop movements to a newscaster.

"I apologize for the delay in getting back to you, Mr. Rustin," he said, taking Brick's hand and guiding him to a chair. "I'm Jacob Corden. I was in Israel. When the telex about your visit came, I delayed a day there for a briefing. I do indeed want to talk to you, very much." His accent was New York, not Tel Aviv.

"To tell me something, or to find out something?" Brick said. He spoke pleasantly, wanting to seem more at ease than he felt.

Corden smiled. "My job is to find out as much as I can and give away as little. Will I be able to do that?"

"Not if I can help it." Brick smiled back.

"Rustin. On an outside chance, is your father—"

"Yep, if that matters."

"Does he know you're here?"

"No, I don't think so."

"Do you mind if I ask why not?"

"He's away. And I'm not really here on his part anyway."

"Do you want him to know you were here?"

"Not particularly."

Corden raised his eyebrows in an implied question to Landau. "Daniel?"

"I don't know Mr. Rustin at all," Landau said.

Corden turned back to Brick. "Your note was cryptic, Mr. Rustin. You say you were actually with this—" He lifted the paper on his desk and scanned it. "This Brenner party. In the Soviet Union?"

"Yes. In Erevan."

"Where are they now?"

"You don't know?"

"Let me be honest. I knew nothing about this whole thing until I was briefed on it yesterday in Israel. I can tell you only what I was told. Fair enough?"

"Where did they go from London?"

"They were in London?"

"Oh, come on, Colonel."

"That was an honest question. The last we heard from the Turks, they reported that the Kurd—Sabri?—was out of the Soviet Union, and then that the whole bunch of them vanished, went back like genies into their lamps, as I understand it. There was no mention of you. Ever."

"Nobody said anything about Ali Sabri and myself being held in Istanbul by a Turkish major?"

"Nothing."

"About seven dead people?"

"Nothing. Why don't you tell me about it?"

Brick considered. He had nothing to gain by *not* telling this man what he knew—and as best as he could figure, Ali Sabri had nothing to lose. So he summarized the trip out of Kurdistan, the escape from Turkey, the town house in London. Landau made notes while Corden nodded and seemed to understand. When Brick was done, Corden asked him a few questions—the address of the house in London, the license number of the green Chevy, which he swore to Brick had not been connected with anything Israeli. "And you're here because you want to find these people," he said at length. "Why?"

"That's everybody's favorite question, Colonel. Does it really matter to you?"

"Yes. Don't do it."

"I *am* doing it."

"Then nobody, let me repeat, nobody can protect you. No government, that is."

"That sounds like a threat."

"Far from it. I'll tell you some things and if you don't agree with me—well, you decide." He picked up the paper in front of him again. "Livia Lo Presti lived in Israel for several years. She didn't do so well, the records show. She was in the army for a while, on a kibbutz for a while, worked in an orphanage for a while. Her parents were supporting her most of the time—even while she was on the kibbutz, which they weren't supposed to do. But she never stuck with anything. She apparently had enough idealism for any of the jobs—and she went for the jobs that demanded the most idealism—but none of the dedication. Nobody asked her to leave, of course; we couldn't do that even if we wanted to. She had a

Jewish mother; that gave her the right to become an Israeli citizen. But, well, when she went home for a summer vacation, apparently nobody was too upset when she married Tony Lo Presti and stayed in Montreal." He grinned. "Is there such a term as a Jewish Canadian princess?"

"There is now," Brick said and answered the smile.

"Brenner, now, is authentically Israeli. We know less about him than we should have known to agree to this deal of his."

"*His* deal?"

"His deal. He came to us with the idea. All we did was agree to furnish the arms and to cooperate with the Turks if by some chance it all were to work out. From what I was told, nobody had much confidence in the possibility. But we've learned to take chances. And Brenner had already sold the idea to somebody in the Turkish military. I have no idea how he made the contact with the Turks, but it was arranged through a third party—that much we know."

"I think I have an idea who."

"Your friend Roger? I doubt it. He was involved in the contact, but he didn't initiate it. He couldn't. He wasn't enough of an insider." Something caught Corden's eye and he leaned across his desk. "You can stop taking notes now, Daniel," he said to Landau. "We know all this already."

Landau stuffed his notebook into a folder as if it were something he had been caught lifting from a department store. Corden went on. "Brenner has lived everywhere—too many places for us to have kept up with him well. We lost him in Central America for three years once. We aren't even really sure how he makes his living. Teaching an occasional course in archaeology wouldn't do it. He has done some work for us before—nothing I want to go into—and it's turned out well enough. But we're as surprised as anybody at this Sabri thing."

"Surprised enough to want to do something about it?"

"If we can—but not to go out on a limb. The Turks think we're behind what happened; they've made that plain enough. We'd like to clear that up, but, well—as far as the arms deal is concerned, that's pretty dead. We'd like it to work, of course, but we'd have to start from scratch with the Turks again. If they'd let us."

"What do you mean, 'clear that up'?"

"What could we do? Nothing, so far as Brenner and the others are concerned. We'd have to give the Kurd to the Turks as a gesture of good faith, I suppose."

"That would shit, Colonel."

"So you shouldn't be so anxious for us to find them for you! And now do you see what I mean? No government is involved in whatever's happening. If you get your ass in a sling, who can you turn to?"

"What do you think *is* happening?"

"I haven't got the slightest goddamn notion."

Back outside, the pulpy heat of the Washington afternoon sidewalks surrounded Brick like the waters of a tropical aquarium. Every thread, every possible connection between what had been in Turkey and what now was seemed to be as neatly snipped and tied off as an umbilical cord. Whoever Brenner was, whoever Livia was, they were one hell of a surgical team.

He had heard what the Israeli colonel had said, and he hadn't heard it. He was in no fever now, as he had been in Turkey for those weeks. Instead a vague exhilaration, a subterranean expectation, buzzed around just below the surface of his consciousness. Nobody, repeat, nobody could protect him now. He had heard that, yes. A smart-enough man, like his father, would have heard and heeded. A slightly less smart man, like himself, took it to mean something else. This thing was his and his alone now. His enemy, his dragon to slay. When he had decided on Ararat that he was going to cross the river with Tony and Livia, he had taken on something that now only he could finish. Nobody, repeat, nobody would stop him now.

When he had last seen Roger and Claire's town house, it had been one of the first being "reclaimed." Most of the others around it on A Street, just behind the capitol, were still unregenerated, i.e., run down and inhabited by blacks. Roger had caught the trend early, had bought cheap, and now all the other town houses on the shady, quiet street were as fresh-painted and patched and white-tenanted as Roger's. Brick figured Roger's must have quadrupled in value in the past ten years. It was close to everything, fashionable, and a smarter buy than Georgetown. All you had to do was get hold of some paint, force a few niggers out, and *le voilà!*, as Roger would say.

It was a pity Roger wasn't still around to enjoy it, Brick thought as he rang the bell and tried to imagine what a few years had done to Claire. If he had to find a word for Claire, it would be *wispy*. Her fine, never-quite-contained blond hair was wispy; her clothes, the way she moved in them, were wispy. Even her voice was, though when he had called her just after he left the embassy, the years and enough

240

vodka tonics and Gauloises (the one thing about her that was far from wispy) had deepened it. Was she fat now? Had she let herself go to hell since Roger had left? Started to drink too much? What happened to women like Claire when their husbands ran off? Or they ran their husbands off? Turkish women simply didn't run their husbands off; Brick's experience was limited.

If Claire was an example, what happened to women like Claire when their husbands were gone was that they looked better than they ever had. As she stepped across the threshold to hug him, he saw that the adolescent gawkiness that had stayed with her for so long had finally worn away. Hers was a woman's body now, full breasted and at ease with itself in a flowing, half-sleeved white blouse and dark-blue jogging shorts. The sun caught all the errant wisps of her hair. What was that poem, Brick thought—delight in disorder? He delighted.

"The kids?" he asked as she led him into the bay-windowed living room.

"Camp. Till next week," she said. "Well. You don't look even vaguely Arabic."

"Turkish."

"They're not the same?"

"It's a common mistake. *You* look—hell, wonderful."

"It's a common mistake," she said. "When did you get in?"

"Last week."

"You waited a whole week! Is it senility?"

"No. Reverse culture shock." The room was as he would have imagined it: cool white, with green growing things and tastefully small paintings and draw-ings, except for a huge, bold abstract painting over the fireplace. Claire sat on the ivory burlap-textured couch and patted it for him to join her. He sat and she gave him a seriously appraising look.

"Being over thirty agrees with you," she said. "When was the last time—at the place in Vermont for Christmas, wasn't it? Four years ago?"

"Five."

She offered him a soft, silly smile and reached for his hand. "Holy cow. Lot of water under the dam."

"Not over the dam?"

"No, not when the dam's busted. Roger's gone, Brick."

"I know."

Claire let his hand go. "You know?"

All the way here Brick had tried to make up his mind what he was going to say to Claire, or what he wanted to hear from her. Now, seeing her, he knew that he was going to tell her whatever would hurt her least. And that was probably as little as possible. "He wrote me, but he didn't give me details. Where is he?" He made the question as offhanded as he could.

Claire shrugged. She started to give him her silly smile again, but the tears caught her halfway there. "I don't know, Brick. Shit, I don't know."

This time he reached for her hand. "He doesn't write? Call? Anything?"

"Nothing. Not for weeks. He was in London, then...nothing, just those goddamned checks from nowhere."

She tried to choke back the tears and looked around for something, a tissue, Brick supposed. Not finding one seemed to be a kind of final blow and she buried her face in the couch, letting the tears come

242

in great heaving sobs. Brick crossed the room and jerked a handful of tissues from a Lucite holder and sat beside her again, close enough this time to ease her against his shoulder. She took the tissues and held them in a wad against her eyes, hiding. On an end table, Brick saw Roger's picture still standing beside Claire's and the boys'. He looked yachty and at ease beside water somewhere—the old Roger. You son of a bitch, he thought.

"I'm sorry," Claire said into his shoulder. "I thought I was all done with this. It's just seeing you, Brick..."

"It's OK," he said. "You want to talk about it?"

They sat for a while until her breathing calmed. She turned her face from his shoulder but didn't move away from him. One of her sandals had come off, and the other dangled precariously. Brick let his eyes rest on her legs, which had a tan almost too perfect to be real. The slightest trace of perfume rose from her, really more an afterscent of bath powder than perfume. Something in him began to stir that he didn't want to stir, and he forced his eyes to move to a small pen-and-ink of a horse on a unicycle on the wall. It helped.

"I don't really know enough to talk about it," Claire said. "There were just those *people* around all of a sudden, then trips everywhere—Montreal, Texas, Mexico, London. And when I'd ask him what it was about, he'd just tell me something stupid like 'consulting work,' and flash one of those checks at me like that could justify anything in the world."

"Those checks from nowhere?"

"No, not really nowhere. Just nowhere I ever knew existed."

"Like?"

"The Cayman Islands. Is there such a place?"

"Somewhere. Do you remember the name of the bank?"

"Oh, boy. Do I. Banco de Todas las Americas. How's that for a stuck-up name? Bank of All the Americas."

"Did you know any of the people who came around?"

"Not beforehand. One of them was sort of nice, a Canadian who had something to do with books, I think. But the others—God!" She let the other sandal drop and curled her legs up beside her on the couch, settling in against Brick. Her blouse hung loose and open so that he could see almost all of both breasts. They were as tan as the rest of her. "There was that nervous Austrian who always reminded me of a spin-off from Walter Slezak that never quite made it. And I never could keep those Texans and those Mexicans in tacky suits straight. I tried to stay away from them."

Brick pulled his eyes away from her breasts, listening now with all of his mind. Consulting work. Mexicans in tacky suits. The Aeromexico ticket on his father's bookshelf. Dear God.

"You never did find out what they were here for?"

"No. All they talked about that I heard was *money*. Forever. Always whipping out pocket calculators and playing with them. Wouldn't you think people would get tired of nothing but numbers all the time? Numbers are always the same." She looked up at Brick suddenly.

"Always the same. Yep."

"And then when Roger bought a town house in London and I...oh, Brick, I didn't think he'd take me up on it when I told him to go. And I really didn't tell him to go. I just told him he'd have to choose. The boys never saw him anymore and he was a bastard to live with and something was going on I didn't want to be a part of. I *felt* it. Even in bed..." Tears started again, but she shook her head and they stopped. "I tried going to your father to see if he'd let Roger out of it. I thought if I explained what it was doing to Roger that he would—but it didn't help. Your father was kind but he told me the same thing that Roger did, that what they were doing was all right and that the secrecy was only normal for business nowadays and that I shouldn't worry. Roger threw a fit when he found out what I'd done and moved out afterward. I didn't *know* him anymore, Brick."

Brick concentrated on sitting very still and speaking very calmly. "My father and Roger were working on something together?"

"You didn't know about that? Oh, I thought surely your father would have...or at least Roger..." He felt her body tense. He slipped his hand from her shoulder and lightly stroked her hair, then eased her head down onto his shoulder again. She relaxed.

"I wouldn't make too much of it. Dad and I didn't write often. And I'm sure Roger was planning to tell me, if he'd been here." Lie, Rustin, lie.

"You don't know, Brick. You don't know what Roger would have done. *I* don't. Roger told me your father first came to him on whatever it was they were doing. But your father told me Roger got it all started. I think I believe your father. Roger was involved with that Austrian before he went to see your father, that much I do know." She pulled away from him and sat up, her eyes brightening. "*You* can ask your father about it, Brick. You'll do that, won't you?

Even if he wouldn't tell me what he knows about Roger, he'll tell you."

"Sure," Brick said, thinking fat chance, fat chance. "He's out of town. As soon as he gets home."

"God, I'm glad you're here," Claire said, settling again. They sat, Claire drawing little imaginary circles on her leg with a finger, lost somewhere in a silence that would have been awkward had she not been so far away. Brick watched her finger draw the little circles, refusing to think, knowing that he would have to be by himself when he did. At length she said, "Do you remember how I met Roger?"

"It always seemed to me you two had been together forever."

"I don't believe you. I was your date that night. Roger was with that awful Sartain girl whose father owned Costa Rica or something, and we drove up to that inn at Sugarbush. Sugarbush wasn't such a big deal then."

"OK, I lied. I remember. You were in my English class. I was scared shitless to ask you out."

She drew some more circles, then stopped. "Maybe I should have stuck with you, Brick. Maybe we should never have gone out with Roger and whositz."

"You two would have found each other anyway."

She sighed. "Probably, goddamnit." She went back to drawing her little circles. Brick covered her hand with his, and let his fingertips trail across the down on her leg. "Brick?" she said.

"Uh huh."

"I caught you ogling my breasts, you know."

"They're pretty oglable."

She laughed. "If we did it, it wouldn't really be like messing around on Roger, would it? Not with you, I mean."

"Not with good old Brick, no."

She turned her hand over and squeezed his. "I didn't mean it that way, Brick. I'm sorry."

"I know."

He bent his head toward her, and she raised hers simultaneously. When he kissed her, the kiss she gave back was anything but wispy. She moved his hand to the inside of her thigh and left it there. Brick drew it up further, to her jogging shorts, and cupped it over her. She opened her legs.

When he stood to lead her toward the stairs, his glance caught the picture of Roger again. I owe you this, you son of a bitch, he thought. We both owe you this. And then as Claire pressed against him at the foot of the stairs, owing didn't matter.

To catch the banks before they closed, he stopped at a pay phone to call his father's banker. Oh, yes! the man told him. Cayman Islands. In the Caribbean. That place and Panama were laundries for any kind of funds you wanted to slip out of Latin America—or anywhere else, for that matter. Looser than Switzerland and a hell of a lot closer. And the Banco de Todas las Americas? He checked. Classic case, he told Brick. A post-office box. You were a politician in trouble and wanted to empty your country's treasury before you hit the road? A banker or a businessman who had to get around your country's restrictions against sending currency out? You used a shadow bank, like the infamous Banco de Todas las Americas. Set up a branch of it in your country, started making loans back and forth, transferring funds, making deposits—and *presto*, before anybody else could figure out what was up, you were home free. Handy things, shadow banks. Some of his best accounts had come through them.

But what in the hell, Brick wondered as he dodged buses across the Arlington Memorial Bridge toward the beltway, what in the hell did Mexicans and Texans and Israelis and Canadians and Turks and shadow banks have to do with the man he had slipped out of the house on that quiet street in Erevan?

And his father. What did his father have to do with any of it? Damn! From the first mention of him in Roger's letter, Brick should have guessed he was involved. Lesson: never underestimate your old man just because he's your old man, Brick thought, never forget how little you really know about who he is. But why had his father gotten *him* mixed up in the thing? At least in that, Brick felt reasonably sure he could see the man's mind working: still trying to "straighten Brick out." Find a way to get him out of Trabzon and slip a few thousand dollars to him, so he would come home. Only Brick had gone much further with it than his father ever suspected he would. Lesson, Dad: never underestimate your son just because he's your son.

That's why his old man was so anxious to talk him out of digging anything up on Ali Sabri. Anything he might find could well lead to him, too. And while his father might not be ravingly proud of him, Brick credited him with at least the standard allowance of fatherly feeling! A decent protectiveness, enough pride not to want his son to discover he was involved in something rotten. Ah, Dad, Brick thought. How you must have coveted being a *real* spy these many years.

He must have known Brick wouldn't discover anything in Montreal. That's why he had given in so easily on that part. And he must have given Roger credit for more foresight than he had shown about Claire. He hadn't figured Roger would just disappear so totally without at least coming up with some cock-and-bull story to convince Claire to keep her mouth shut.

And his father's involvement explained one thing that had puzzled the Israeli colonel: who had made the Turkish contact. His father had worked with the Turkish military for years. Of course Roger would have come to him for the contact.

But damn it, why?

When one set of pieces began to fit, he turned over a box and a dozen new pieces he hadn't even known existed fell out.

If there was a real victim in this so far, it was Claire. He felt slightly sleazy not telling her what he knew. But there would have been no good in it. Any good he could have given her, he had given her in that bedroom where Roger's hairbrushes and shaving lotion still sat on the dresser. He had let her know that somebody she trusted still wanted her. And damn it, he *had* wanted her! Had wanted her for years, without admitting it to himself. But he knew that he could never step into Roger's life like that for more than a moment. He would get Roger back to Claire if he could. But he could never *be* Roger for her.

It was dusk by the time he pulled into the driveway. His mother's car was in the carport. He had hoped it would be, had wanted the company. But there was another car, too, which annoyed him. He didn't want to try to make conversation with his mother's friends tonight.

But as he pulled up behind the car, he doubted it belonged to any friend of his mother's. Not that scruffy Pinto with peeling bumper stickers on the trunk that said things like *No Nukes* and *Help, The Paranoids Are After Me,* and a missing back bumper, and a pair of foam-rubber dice hanging from the rearview mirror, and a row of outdated Georgetown University parking stickers in the back window. He sat for a minute scanning the house to see if he could spot anything wrong. Then, as he got out of the Buick, he took the revolver from the glove compartment and slipped it into the waistband of his jeans, under his shirt. Not much concealment, but at least his mother wouldn't be freaked if she saw him approaching the house.

The door from the carport wasn't locked. In the kitchen, he paused to listen. Quiet music, his mother's "easy-listening" station on the stereo, seeped in from the living room. There were no voices.

Then, from the doorway to the hall, his mother charged into the kitchen. She had gotten chubby since Brick had been away, but her energy level was still as high as ever. She was no taller than Brick's shoulder, and she kept her auburn hair—probably dyed now—cut close so she could be up and moving in the morning while other women would still be standing in front of mirrors with curling irons. "Brick," she accused in a stage whisper. "You simply have to do something."

"Sure," Brick said. "What something?"

"Those two friends of yours on the sun deck. They actually wanted to come in*side* and wait! They've been here for two hours. Two hours! I tried conversation but the man doesn't speak enough English to make sense and the girl—well, the girl hasn't the

250

slightest notion of what polite conversation even *is*. She laughs at all the wrong things and...oh, just go *deal* with them. And I wish you'd let me know when you're expecting someone and at least be here to meet them. Your father would pitch a hissy."

"Pitch a what?"

"That's what the local people say. It's perfectly sensible, if you think about it." She pivoted and charged back into the hallway. Brick stared after her in wonder for a moment, then slipped the revolver out of his waistband and into a drawer. Whoever was out there had had two hours to be dangerous in if they had wanted.

They were both younger than Brick, mid-twenties he guessed. The man was unmistakable: Middle East. His thin nose and sharp cheekbones would have given him away immediately, even if the baggy trousers and too-short hair and nondescript black lace-up shoes hadn't completed the picture. When Brick stepped onto the sun deck he sprang up from a folding chair as if he half expected to protect the girl.

The girl was less placeable. Her features were not as sharp as the man's, her face rounder, with the slightest hint of something Oriental in the eyes. But her hair was as black as her friend's, her skin as olive. When she got to her feet, she was nearly as tall as the man was, which brought her to within three or four inches of Brick's height. She watched Brick coolly as he took her in.

"Hello," Brick said tentatively. The way she was dressed was as contrary to the man's clothing as Brick could have conceived: tight jeans with a hole in the knee; a plaid blouse tied off at the waist, which showed a few inches of stomach; old sandals; and three or four thin gold bracelets on each arm. Her long hair was tied back over her ears, which made her look a little severe, though there was nothing severe about the way she filled out her jeans and blouse.

"Brick?" she said. Only a slight trill on the *r* indicated she might once have had an accent.

"Brick."

"I'm Sevda. This is Hassan."

Hassan crossed to Brick and offered his hand limply, Middle Eastern style. He spewed something that might have been, "Very pleased to meet you."

"Well," Brick said. "Now we know one another."

The girl pulled a rumpled envelope from the back pocket of her jeans. "Here," she said and poked it at Brick. "When you're done, we can all go in my car, but if we take two I won't have to bring you all the way back out here."

"Great," Brick said. "Where we heading?"

"It's in the note," she said.

Brick tore open the envelope and checked the signature first. When the scrawl came together into words for him, he felt a surge of excitement. Look for something hard enough and it found you! He sat down on a deck railing. Tony Lo Presti.

"Dear Brick," it began. "I know it's a lot to ask, but could you see me? I think you are still interested or you wouldn't have come to Montreal. Maybe we can clear up some things.

"It would be better if you were to come to me. If your father is home, please don't let him know where you're going. Sevda and Hassan will bring you. They're OK."

Brick looked up from the note. Sevda and Hassan were still standing. "Why didn't he just call?"

"You're unlisted," Sevda said. Hassan nodded as if he might have understood what she said.

"You want to sit down?"

"My rump's tired. I've been sitting for hours. You coming?"

Brick stood. "Where is he?"

"Not too far."

"On a scale of one to ten, how far's that?"

Sevda sighed impatiently. "Near Washington."

If he rode with them, he could ask some questions—but he judged his chances of getting any answers to be less than magnificent. Even if he knew what questions to ask. He decided he'd rather have the mobility the Buick gave him—just in case.

He stopped in his bedroom for a Windbreaker to conceal the pistol beneath, even though he knew he would look silly in it on such a hot night. He thought he could trust Tony, that Tony had come up with the short end of something just as he had. But he had learned something in Turkey and the Soviet Union. He had rediscovered what it was like to be afraid, to be like a child in a world that tricked you into believing that it was safe just enough of the time to be dangerous. When he was a kid he had loved dogs, but one day he had come across a wild dog in the woods near this house. The dog had chased him, terrified, right to the door. He didn't stop caring about dogs, but forever after when he met a strange one he found himself looking for running room, or for a stick to pick up, just in case.

He would take the pistol.

As he passed his mother's room she called to him. "Yes, Mother."

"Are they gone?"

"Leaving. Me, too. I won't be late."

"If anything happens to your father's Buick—"

"He'll pitch a hissy. I know."

"Are they Turks?"

"More or less."

"Brick?"

"Yes, Mother."

"This doesn't have anything to do with dope, does it? I've read about Turks."

"No, Mother. Not dope."

Dear God, he thought. I wish it were that simple.

He followed the smoking, bouncing Pinto into an older section of Arlington, once a good suburb of Washington, now turning into the kind of slum the people who first moved there had left Washington to avoid. It was working people and welfare people: torn screens on the porches of the narrow houses, busted steps, peeling paint. Before long, buyers like Roger would rediscover it and the working people and welfare people would have to find a new slum. It would be easier if the government would just build slums to begin with and avoid the damned constant movement, Brick decided.

It was after nine when they stopped, soundly dark even for a late-summer, daylight-savings-time Washington night. The building they stopped in front of was unmistakably a firehouse—or had been. It too was dark now, its ornate but grimy facade lit only by the long pale streaks of light from a street-lamp on the corner. The Pinto pulled up in the drive-way, and Hassan hopped out to motion Brick to pull in beside it. Half-a-dozen other cars were already there, in the drive and along the curb. There would be no fire trucks leaving tonight. But it *was* a firehouse, for God's sake!

The night was loud with cicadas and radios and voices from front porches, and spiced with cooking odors. An unairconditioned world, like Trabzon. Brick had his first flash of real nostalgia as he stepped from the Buick and felt the warm, damp air bathe him. He turned his back to the Pinto and looked along the porchlight-puddled street, breathing it in.

And then he was reminded of other things about Turkey. Hassan caught him in mid-turn, off balance. Brick flung his weight against Hassan's lesser size, but the balance was crucial. Hassan had him in an arm lock and flattened against the Buick before his hands had a chance to grab anything but air. Hassan growled something vaguely like English at him. Brick picked out the word *gun* as Hassan's hand fumbled beneath his Windbreaker for the revolver.

"Damn it, ask!" Brick said, too surprised and angry to give a damn that Hassan might be planning something with the revolver once he had it.

"Hassan!" Sevda ordered, coming around the Buick and pulling Hassan away. The Kurdish that she fired at him was too rapid and colloquial for Brick to make much of, but Hassan let him go and stepped back. When Brick turned, Hassan was stuffing the revolver in his pocket and looking sheepishly defensive.

"Look," Sevda said. "I'm sorry. But you shouldn't have had a gun, all right?"

"Do you blame me? Especially after this crap?"

"Cool off. I just told him to see if you had one. He didn't understand. He's just out of Kurdistan. He freaks."

"Shit, so do I. Is Tony Lo Presti really here?"

Sevda nodded toward the upstairs windows of the

firehouse. In the streetlight, Brick saw the folds of blackout curtains through the dust-painted panes. "Up there."

Hassan patted Brick's shoulder and smiled, apologizing. Brick scowled back warily, and let Hassan lead toward a side door just around the corner of the building from the huge old wooden doors, nailed shut now, that once had swung open to let the screeching fire trucks out. Above the side door was a small wooden sign that said Kurdish People's Hall in English and Kurdish.

"That Kurdish you spoke," Brick said to Sevda as Hassan unlocked the door. "It sounded native."

"It's native," she said, and motioned him inside. "But rusty."

The one large room of the downstairs was half-filled with boxes—canned goods, tins of cooking oil, jars of olives—and with a half-dozen long racks of clothing, mostly used but some still bearing price tags. Gathering dust in a corner sprawled a pile of appliances: old toasters and electric fans and hotplates. In another corner a stack of ominously unmarked crates poked out from beneath yellowed sheets. A single bare bulb lit it all. Guns and butter, Brick thought.

Hassan started up a long flight of wooden stairs. Sevda saw Brick studying the room. "When people first come over," she said, "they need things. To get started. They don't like welfare."

"And those?" Brick pointed to the unmarked crates.

"They need things," Sevda said.

At the door at the top of the stairs, Hassan identified himself. A couple of bolts clicked, the door opened a few inches, and light spilled onto the stairs from behind a face. Then the door opened only wide enough for them to enter single file.

Two guards in quasi-military uniforms—khaki jumpsuits, sashes, turbans and automatic pistols—shoved their fists into the air and shouted a sharp single syllable, something like "Hai!" when Sevda came into the room behind Brick. Brick started uncomfortably. The salute, the shouting were too reminiscent of other salutes from a hundred World War II movies he had seen. Sevda acknowledged them without much interest. No ordinary graduate student, Brick thought.

The room was haphazard: a few old couches, a couple of long tables with mimeo machines and leaflets waiting to be collated on them, folding metal chairs. A red banner that said Long Live Free Kurdistan hung from wall to wall above one of the long tables. Cigarette butts littered the oiled wood floor, and the rich, thick smell of black tobacco soaked the air. A dozen men and a couple of women sat on chairs around a couch. They had evidently been interrupted in an argument, from the fierce look on some of their faces. Most of them were dressed in the same baggy street clothes as Hassan. A few wore Kurdish turbans, one (who didn't bother to turn around) a suit. The women were frumpy in housedresses.

From the couch, rising like an Italian Poseidon from the sea of Kurdish faces, Tony Lo Presti struggled up on crutches, his brows touching in familiar Mephistophelian concentration. Thinner, with a sickroom grayness to his face, he made his unsteady way across the room toward Brick. Sevda hurried to help him. Once his brows unfolded, his smile seemed genuine. Brick relaxed a little—but not wholly. The last time he had seen Tony, Tony had just killed two men and had left knowing that Brick was going to sleep with his wife. And now, he showed up from nowhere among these back-street revolutionaries. Brick looked for running room. There was none.

"Brick! No *raki?*" Tony said, balancing himself and holding out his hand.

"Yok, efendi. Not this time. Could you handle it?"

Tony looked down at his hip. "You mean this nonsense? Couple of steel pins and six weeks more of hopping around on these damn crutches and I'll be a new man. Come sit." He pivoted on a crutch and hobbled back toward the couch.

"What happened to you, Tony?"

"Caught a couple of bullets. I thought you knew that."

"That's not what I meant."

"All in good time. Want you to meet some people. You know Sevda and Hassan."

"In a way."

"Then by all means, allow me." He stooped. "Sevda Sabri, Hassan Kutlur—Brick Rustin."

Hassan grinned, guessing a joke but not understanding it. Sevda, who walked beside Tony protectively, gave her impatient sigh again.

"Sabri?"

"He's my uncle," Sevda said. "My favorite uncle— or he was last time I saw him ten years ago."

"You're a hell of a long way from Kurdistan." In many ways, Brick thought.

Tony hobbled forward. "Sevda's a graduate student. Poli Sci, isn't it?"

"International relations."

"One of those things, anyway. At Georgetown.

She's also political coordinator for this outfit. I think that means she issues proclamations."

Without Livia, Brick thought, Tony was much less on edge, more assured, as if he had a separate personality that existed only when he was on his own. Like the night he and Brick had flung their empty *raki* bottle off into the Black Sea. Brick still liked him, and was glad.

"The man with the gray moustache and the head scarf," Tony said, indicating a man who had been sitting beside him on the couch, "is Muhamed Rashid. He's something like the elder headman, at least among the Iranian Kurds here. And this gentleman"—he stopped beside the man in a suit, who still kept his back to Brick—"I think you know."

"I've been afraid he wouldn't be so glad to see me," the man said as he rose and offered his hand. Brick stood for what seemed a good half minute before he remembered he should take the hand. Major Özpamir's hand.

"It all started to come together a couple of weeks ago," Tony said. They sipped tea out of the familiar little glasses, the torturous formalities of Middle Eastern introductions and small talk out of the way at last. "A case of Scotch and I were recuperating at home and a cable comes from the major. Must have been just after you and Ali Sabri were in London. He said he was coming to Washington and wanted to know if he could see me. I hadn't heard a word from Livia since they wheeled me onto the plane in Erzurum. So hell, *yes,* I told him. He was a godsend. At least until I found out that *he* wanted information from *me.*"

"Namely?" Brick said.

"Where Ali Sabri was, of course."

"And you don't have any idea."

"No! Well, not precisely. Listen, Brick. About Ararat—I want to clear that up. Livia got back to the camp before you did—you know that. Ali Sabri and I were already there. I tried to get her to sleep while I went to look for you, but she...well, she gets nervous. You saw that in Erevan. She kept saying things about starting back right that minute, that she had seen you make it out of the river and you would be all right. I believed that—still do—but none of us was in any shape to start back just then. I do things for Livia that nobody in his right mind would, but that was something I just couldn't—even Ali Sabri couldn't go on without some rest. She seemed to calm down a little and told me to go back into the tent and rest, that she'd come inside in a minute. Well, I drifted off and when I woke up she was gone. It was still darker than squid piss, but I took off after her."

"Ali Sabri heard you. You left less than an hour before I got there," Brick said.

"Be grateful you didn't make it. You might have been with me. Like that Iranian, that Colonel whoever."

"Rize," Major Özpamir said. He was listening with only polite interest. Brick imagined he'd heard this part before.

"That one. He woke up as I was leaving and insisted on coming along—afraid of losing his commission, I suppose. We found Livia a couple of miles away already. With Brenner, that ass. Brenner pulled a gun on us when we came up. He was there with some pack mules—I guess he left the hotel in plenty of time to catch up to us, but had hidden out.

He had a couple of big Turks with him, and the plan was to surprise us on the way back and make off with Ali Sabri. Don't ask me why. I hope to hell *you* know that."

Brick shook his head.

"Shit," Tony said. "Square one." He looked to Major Özpamir, who unclasped his hands and made a gesture as if he were holding an open book. *Kismet,* he was saying. Fate, luck. The Kurd Tony had pointed out as the Iranian elder nodded appreciatively.

Tony lost himself in thought for a few seconds, then went on. "Well, we blew Brenner's plan for him. When they saw us, the two big Turks with guns started blasting away. Hell, I'd had enough of that sort of stuff, so I ducked and went for Livia—wanted to knock her down out of the way, *some*thing. Rize went down, too, but he started blasting back. Brenner got him. But he'd gotten one of the Turks, and once I jerked Livia behind a rock, I got the other one. And then Brenner got me. He'd have finished his job if Livia hadn't drawn down on him. Picture that— cookbook publisher and wife in a shootout at the OK Corral. Christ almighty, Brick."

"I can picture it. I saw you in Erevan."

"I'm not proud of it. Any of it. Anyway, I don't know what Livia said to Brenner, but she calmed him and I guess convinced him she had a better plan. Hell, he wanted to go back to camp himself for Ali Sabri! And then next thing I knew, they had me slung on the back of a mule and Livia was telling me that I had to keep my mouth shut or we were all in a Turkish jail for the rest of our lives. Brenner made up some horsepiss about you and Ali Sabri shooting everybody up and taking off to Iran, and

I was enough out of it not to care one way or the other. Until Livia didn't show up in Montreal."

"Before it all happened—you didn't have any notion?"

"No. Hell, no. I knew that half the Middle East would want to stop us if they found out, but not a crummy thing else."

"And you bought the whole story, too?" Brick asked Özpamir.

Özpamir looked patient and professorial. "I had nothing else to go on, Brick. Not until the purser on the *Ege* reported that you were on board. Then it was too late. Dr. Brenner and Mrs. Lo Presti were out of the country."

"You're certain of that."

"Positive."

"So Ibrahim and that woman in my bedroom— they self-destructed."

"No, Brick. You recall there was another member of the group. But he didn't go on the expedition. He stayed behind in Ankara—and then remained in Turkey a few days longer than the others did."

The taste of the tea turned metallic in Brick's mouth and the honey-sweet pastries one of the women had served stuck at the back of his throat. "No," he said. "Roger's not capable of it. He's just flat not."

Özpamir fixed him with his sad, hollow eyes. "He was capable of it. He was afraid and surprised. He expected you to be in the bed."

"That's the trouble."

Özpamir made his book-holding gesture again. "If it had been you, Brick, he wouldn't have been afraid and surprised."

Brick stood and took a few aimless steps toward

262

the door. He thought of Claire, of Roger's picture, of the two kids coming home from camp. Of them waiting, thinking Roger was still or could ever again be a presence in their lives. The son of a bitch. He was dead to them now. Dead as the gold-toothed, peroxided, harmless man and the faceless woman he left for Brick to find. The son of a bitch.

The two ersatz storm troopers by the door stood as Brick approached. He didn't want to look at them. He turned back to the couch but didn't sit. "All right," he said to Özpamir. "Finish. Why did you let Ali Sabri and me out of the country? Why are you here?"

"I'm very sorry," Özpamir said in Turkish, as if he were afraid of losing face with the Kurds.

"Finish."

"The last night I had dinner with you and Ali Sabri at the Pera Palas, I had just come from a staff meeting. The Israelis had informed us that they were pulling out of the arrangement. It had gone too wrong for them. My headquarters in Ankara had decided that the only solution was to bring Ali Sabri there and put him under arrest—Ali Sabri and yourself. I couldn't let that happen."

"That's not enough."

"No, it wasn't. I still believe in the arrangement. I decided that only by letting Ali Sabri go free and beginning all over again with the Israelis could it ever have a chance. I simply didn't count on Ali Sabri disappearing so quickly."

"I didn't either. Why aren't you in London, then?"

"Patience," Özpamir said patiently. "I still believe in the arrangement. I came to find Ali Sabri. I had had contact with Sevda while the whole thing was being planned. So I'm here and Tony's here."

"And you haven't found Ali Sabri."

"No. He's not in this country."

Tony broke in. "We don't *think* he's in this country, anyway."

"He never got out of England?" Brick said.

"My money says he's in Mexico," Tony said.

"You might not believe this, but I don't find that so strange."

"So you *have* heard something."

"No. Why do you think he's in Mexico?"

"I don't think Livia's as good at this as she ought to be. She sent me a postcard."

"With no return address."

"With no return address. But with a Mexico City postmark. She didn't want me to worry, she said."

Sevda snorted. Tony glared at her.

"There are fifteen million people in Mexico City," Brick said.

"Roger said you used to live there. Right?"

"For a few months a long time ago."

"Spanish?"

"Restaurant Spanish. It was better ten years ago."

"*I* can't go to Mexico City. Not like this. Özpamir can't go. His assignment doesn't cover that. They'd hang him. That only leaves one of us, Brick."

"Oh, no," Brick said. "Oh, no."

"I'll beg you if I have to. I'll pay you whether I have to or not. Your father surely has contacts you can use."

Brick laughed. "Yeah."

"But he can't be told details. Your government's not involved in this—and shouldn't be."

"Don't worry. I won't tell him."

"Then you'll go?"

"In a pig's ass I'll go."

"Brick, I want Livia back. I don't care how. I want these people to have a decent chance. I want Ali Sabri to have a decent chance; I didn't mean to, but I helped fuck up the best chance they've had in years. Please. Look, I *am* begging you."

"Don't!" Brick said and looked away, embarrassed for Tony.

"What do you want done with Ali Sabri? Sent back to a jail in Ankara?"

Özpamir broke in. "No. We want him here, safe, while I try to work out the arrangement with the Israelis again. I think it can be done."

"If not?"

"Then he stays here—or wherever he wants to go. Except Turkey."

"What do *you* want, Brick?" Tony said.

Brick leaned back in the hard metal chair. What the hell did he want? He had thought he knew. But Mexico...? "Tony—after you left Livia and me, we..."

"I don't give a damn. Bring her back. What else do you want, Brick?"

Brick sighed and sat forward in the chair again. "The same things you do, I guess. I'm an asshole romantic—isn't that why each one of us is here tonight?—and I don't want to go into it. Leave it at that."

He looked at Sevda, expecting the impatient shrug again, uncertain as to why he cared what her reaction was. This time her eyes remained steadily on his; she was giving him no clue to what was behind them. They were a clear chocolate, he noticed, like Ali Sabri's. He looked for Ali Sabri's humor in them, the good nature that tempered his purposefulness. Maybe it was there—buried. But they were good eyes nonetheless, strong, sure eyes. He found himself not wanting to let them go until he got behind them.

"No more than that?" Tony asked.

"Yes, more." He stayed locked onto her eyes. "Something is at stake that a reasonable man can give a shit about. That's rare, romantic or not." Her eyes didn't change as they moved from Brick to Tony, who sat forward anxiously on the couch. "If you can only make a country without those SS types at doors."

Her eyes slapped him, then went back to Tony.

"Does that mean you'll go?" Tony pressed.

Fifteen million people in Mexico City. But no, not really fifteen million, not if you were looking for a foreigner, and a foreigner of a certain class. Brick knew you were searching in a small town then. A colonial town, one he had been part of for a while. Its unofficial citizens went to the same restaurants, drank at the same bars, bought their clothes in the same stores, belonged to the same clubs, sent their kids to the American school or the British or the French or the German schools, went together to ballets at Bellas Artes, lived in the same colonial compounds, got sick together in the same American–British hospital. If you had ever lived in Mexico City, and had ever been a member of that class, you were known. You could become invisible a damn sight easier in Haymarket, Virginia.

And Jack Callahan was in Mexico City. Uncle Jack, Brick had called him when he was a kid—Jackrabbit. As far back as he could remember his parents, he could remember Jack Callahan. First working with his father when NSA was just being formed after the war, then off into something in the Foreign Service, some kind of international business consultant. Jack had been too much a genuine, gentle good ol' boy to make a good conspirator, Brick had always figured. He'd been in the embassy in Mexico for years, far longer than the normal tour. So far as Brick knew, he had kept only in Christmas-card contact with the family since he had been there. Whatever his father was up to now, Jack wasn't likely to be privy to—and so his father would avoid making contact with him or letting him know when he made his trips to Mexico City. Brick hoped.

In that small colonial gringo town, who would Jack Callahan know—no, who *wouldn't* Jack Callahan know?

The colonel in the Israeli embassy had said they had "lost" Wolf Brenner in Central America for three years. The flow of people and money between Mexico and Central America was constant. Brenner had sent Mexicans to Roger. Maybe, just maybe...

"Did Wolf Brenner ever talk about Mexico?"

"Every chance he got," Tony said. "He loved it."

"What part of Mexico?"

Tony's eyebrows slid together in thought. "Mexico City. I got the impression he spent a lot of time there once. Business, he said."

Brick felt the exhilaration that had chased him all the way to Ararat sneaking up on him again. Go away, he told it. But it was as persistent as the loneliness he had felt that hot day among the roses of the abandoned village in Armenia. The loneliness that he had lost for a time with Livia, with Ali Sabri, with this book he had let himself pick up when he got Roger's letter in Trabzon. The loneliness that waited for him in Washington if he put it down.

God, God, God.

"If life is no more than merely real..." Ali Sabri had told him.

God.

"Sure," Brick told Tony. "Why not?"

Relief and disbelief fought it out on Tony's face. "You mean why not *go?*"

"Sure." He tried to sound nonchalant.

"It's crazy to go."

"You trying to talk me out of it?"

"No, no. Hell, no."

"It may not be all that crazy."

"Hey, I'll take your word for it. When?"

"In the morning."

Özpamir touched Sevda's arm. "Is that possible for you?"

Sevda looked down at an imaginary bug she brushed off her jeans. "Not so convenient. But possible."

Brick looked from one to the other of them, waiting. He was about to learn something he wasn't certain he wanted to.

"Brick," Özpamir said. "There is one thing more."

"Always."

"Sevda will be going with you. It's their decision." He opened his hands to take in the moustached, serious faces that surrounded them. The elder headman nodded. The tips of his gray moustache jiggled. Somebody blew a puff of black tobacco at Brick. The room grew quiet as frost.

"I thought this was between Tony and myself," Brick said.

"No," Sevda said with a surprising softness. "My uncle is involved."

"You can't bring one back and leave the other," Özpamir said.

"All I planned to do is find them."

"If the occasion arose, could you stop there?" Özpamir said.

Brick hesitated. "No."

"Then I'm going," Sevda said with finality.

"Bak." Özpamir's rapid Turkish caught the Kurds off guard. "If we don't cooperate with them, what happens when Ali Sabri gets back here? We need them if we're going to put together the arrangement between them and the Israelis again. And you need *her;* if you find Ali Sabri, you're going to want somebody with you he trusts explicitly. Do you think he's going to trust any of us now?"

"English!" the elder headman bellowed.

"All right," Brick said. "All right. We go together."

"Do you object?" Sevda said. She gave the imaginary bug a last flick and raised her chocolate eyes to him.

"Should I?"

She flashed him her shrug again. "We'll see."

The radios and voices were quieter now, the smell of food given over to the subtler smell of the last of the summer's flowers. Hassan handed him back his pistol as Brick unlocked the Buick. Özpamir, Tony, and the Kurds had stayed upstairs to argue some more, probably about him, Brick imagined. The ersatz SS men had seen them to the downstairs door. He pitched the envelope of bills Tony had given him onto the seat. Their plane would leave at eleven. Aeromexico.

"Your remark about the guards wasn't called for," Sevda said as he lowered the windows of the Buick.

He wanted the night air, not stale "conditioned" air. "We need them here. But we won't in Kurdistan."

"They get to be a habit."

"Are you a cynic—a real one?"

Brick smiled at her, and she gave the smile a hint of an answer. "I'm an asshole romantic, remember?"

Her seriousness returned. "I'll pick you up at eight."

"That's early."

"We'll have breakfast. We'll need to talk."

"Not tonight? A drink, maybe?"

"Breakfast."

Brick let it drop. In truth, a drink was the last thing he wanted. "One thing I forgot to ask. How did you find me?"

"Tony had you followed from his house in Montreal. Of course."

"Of course."

Unexpectedly, she reached for his hand and squeezed it. "Thanks," she said. "It means a lot." She pulled her hand away and bounced behind the wheel of the Pinto before he had a chance to answer. "Eight," she called. "Packed and ready!"

The Pinto stuttered away. Eight. Aeromexico. He closed the door and sat very still and stared at the dark-and-light streaked facade of the firehouse for a long time before he started his father's Buick.

Eight

The marine with eyes like a computer display who
sat behind the bulletproof glass glanced from Brick's
face to his passport photo and back to his face again.
"I'll call upstairs for you, sir. Mr. Callahan will have
to come to escort you." He held out his hand for
Sevda's passport.

"Her passport's Iraqi," Brick said.

The marine dropped his hand. "I'm sorry. She'll
need a pass."

"From Jack Callahan?"

"No, sir. Mr. Callahan's not authorized. If you'll
have a seat..." He pointed to a row of plastic chairs
along the wall populated by patient, blank-faced
Mexicans, and picked up an intercom phone.

"But she's with me."

"I'm sorry, sir." He turned his back and dialed.

"Oh, to hell with it." Sevda spun and, clacking her platform heels on the tiles of the embassy lobby much louder than she needed to, strode to the street door. The waiting Mexicans looked up at her with minor interest, except for those whose eyes licked from her feet to her bare shoulders. Brick agreed with the gesture. The torn jeans had given place to a low-cut white voile dress and stockings, and her hair now bounced loosely about her shoulders. Brick figured she must have been up half the night before they left, remaking herself for the trip. The effort had been worth it.

He caught up with her just outside the double glass doors, at the head of the broad stairs that led down to the swirling, honking traffic of the Reforma Boulevard. "Terrific start," he said.

"What a waste of time!" she said. "People who are hiding don't register their passports with their embassies. This is the last place we should be."

"You thought it was a good idea at breakfast yesterday." Brick knew that was unfair. She would have accepted any suggestion in the coffee shop of National Airport; nervous, probably operating on no more than a couple of hours' sleep, on her way to a country she knew nothing about. But it was the obvious place to start, and in addition to Brick's weakness for beginning with the obvious, it would give them an excuse to make contact with Jack Callahan. Callahan's status as Old Family Friend went further than that: family rumor had it that he had been the man his mother was supposed to marry back during the war, before he brought his shipmate home to meet her—a shipmate whose name was Frank Rustin.

"It was a good idea before I knew I would be treated like a spy," Sevda said.

"Do you know how many plots there probably have been to blow up this place?"

"Not by Kurds. What about all those *useful* places you said we were going to check?"

"Patience, as your uncle would say."

"That's the trouble. Oh, just go do your business. I'll wait for you somewhere." She scanned the Reforma for the few blocks you could see through the yellow, eye-searing smog that choked the streets. She pointed to the Cinzano umbrellas of an outdoor crêpes restaurant squeezed in among the travel agencies and boutiques and galleries across the boulevard. "There. I'll have breakfast."

"Nowhere else," Brick said. "I won't be long."

She flashed him a quick, withering look. "We'll see."

She was busy refusing to acknowledge the marine guard at the gate at the foot of the stairs when the hand dropped on Brick's shoulder, heavy and squeezing, and the Arkansas voice rumbled at his ear, "Well, well. El kid in person."

Brick reached for the hand and squeezed it back. "Jackrabbit!" he said.

"Call me that in public and I'll whack your bottom." Callahan stepped beside him. Brick recognized the outline of him, the potbelly and straggling hair and sharp, small nose chopping its way out of pudgy cheeks. But, too, he didn't recognize him: hair gray, not black, and cheeks, once pink as a rabbit's ears, now whiskey-blossomed and open-pored. Callahan stared after Sevda through unfamiliar bifocals, plain and government issue. "Friend of yours?"

"I'm not sure," Brick said.

"Mexican? You move fast."

"Nope. Kurd."

Callahan smiled—covering, it seemed to Brick, a hesitation before he answered. "Hell, that's exotic. She could be a friend of mine if she wanted." He threw his arm around Brick's shoulders and wheeled him around toward the doors. "Hey, damn, you haven't come to see me at work since your old man brought you by in Havana. I don't reckon you're responsible for what happened after you left there, are you?"

"Sure was. Eight-year-old *Fidelista*. I didn't think you'd remember that."

They passed the envious waiting Mexicans and the computer-eyed guard and crossed into an open courtyard. The embassy hadn't changed much from the way he remembered it in his student days: monolithic from the outside, arranged like a vast motel around a patio on the inside. "Tell you the truth, I might not have remembered if the old fart hadn't mentioned it yesterday. How come he didn't tell me you were here?"

Brick didn't break stride, and hoped the tension that snapped into his shoulders didn't make its way to Callahan's arm. Great God, he thought, feeling a familiar dread again. Not you, too, Jack. Not you. "I wasn't. Just got down."

"You been in Turkey, right? Don't you like staying at home?"

"Last of my wild oats, Jack. Looking up some old friends."

"Well, you found one. We gonna be able to feed you while you're here? We got to give your old man his farewell meal last night. Your turn now."

"I missed him, then?"

"Leaving today, he said. Hey, you knew he was here, didn't you?"

"Do we ever know where he is?"

"Still pulling that crap, is he?" Callahan led through a door that said Agency for Economic Development, then just inside the hallway, held another door for Brick that read John Callahan, Private Sector Liaison. A pleasantly dumpy secretary smiled up at them briefly as they passed through an outer office and into a thickly carpeted inner one. Callahan motioned Brick toward a leather easy chair.

"Doing pretty well for a bureaucrat, Jack," Brick said.

"Impresses the businessmen. That's my job these days, impressing businessmen and making sure the money keeps flowing back and forth across the border. You got some money you need to flow?"

Brick laughed. "Was that what Dad was down for?"

Callahan swayed around his desk, and for a moment his back was to Brick. He used that moment to ask, "You know about that stuff, do you?"

"The consulting stuff? More or less." Brick let his laugh trail away into a fixed smile. Hold it steady, Rustin. Don't think about it, just do it.

Callahan dropped himself into his chair. He studied Brick's face for a time, as if he were deciding something. "That why you were in Turkey?"

"Partly."

"Well, well. The old man's getting more close-mouthed than ever. I'd have thought he'd tell you he was here, then."

"I didn't get to see him, Jack. He was gone before I got back from Turkey." Brick knew it was a bad lie. He was off balance, flailing, wildly hoping his father would have wanted to keep him out of the conversation with Callahan as much as possible.

"Oh?" Callahan spun an ashtray on his desk. His voice got deeper and more Arkansan. "'Tain't what he told me, Brick."

Their eyes met. Brick crossed his hands over his stomach to keep the quick panic there, away from his voice. "Jack..."

"What you up to, Brick? You gone over?"

Brick stood.

"The man's your daddy, boy. You can't go over on him. And what about your mama—what'll it do to her?"

"I'm leaving, Jack."

"Sit down, Brick."

Brick took a step toward the door. Callahan made no move to stop him. "Hey, this is Jackrabbit, Brick. Talk to me a minute. I'm asking you."

"Then tell me what's going on."

"I thought you said you knew."

"Tell me, Jack. Please."

"Your mama's the one going to be hurt by this, Brick. It's just business. Go on home."

"Christ, Jack. Who's *not* involved in this? For God's sake, tell me what's going on!"

"Go on home. I can't let your mama be hurt. Your daddy can take care of himself, but..."

"I want to know where Wolf Brenner is, Jack. Tell me and save me some trouble."

"Swear to God, Brick. I don't know. That's not my part of it. I just handle the stuff with the Texans for your daddy."

"Then tell me about the Texans."

"I can't do that."

Brick moved the rest of the way to the door across
the spongy carpet. He couldn't bear any more, not
with Jack Callahan mixed up in it, too—aging, probably afraid, trying to be gallant about his mother,
who hadn't thought seriously about him since 1944.
"Don't tell Dad, Jack. If you don't want any of us
hurt, don't tell him. It's the only way, and you know
it."

"Goddamnit, Brick..."

The closing door squeezed his words off. "Sir!" the
dumpy secretary said as Brick passed her. "You'll
have to be escorted, sir."

Brick was out of the office and into the patio before
she reached the hall door. "Young man!" she shrieked.
Brick ignored her, ignored all the stares her shriek
brought from all the walkways around the inside of
the patio—ignored all but the readout in the marine's eyes that said *target sighted*. He swung out of
his glass booth just as Brick reached it. His .45 automatic was drawn.

"Where's your escort, sir?" The "sir" was surly,
insulting.

"Fuck you," Brick told him, stupidly, blindly
pissed at the people with guns and lies who had stood
in front of him for weeks. He kept going.

"Halt!" the marine ordered as Brick passed him.

Brick heard a bolt cock, a bullet chamber. He saw
the Mexicans sitting around the walls of the lobby
in front of him dive for the floor, make for the double
glass doors, or—in the case of the timid—freeze,
their eyes darting.

He stopped. Above the scramble of people he heard
the intercom buzzing, frantic and staccato. He waited
without turning around, not afraid but peacefully,

happily angry that he had something as tangible and available as a smart-ass marine to hate.

The buzzing of the intercom stopped. From the corner of his eye Brick saw the marine with the receiver to his ear, leaning from the booth with the .45 aimed steadily toward his back. Then the receiver slammed down and the marine reluctantly holstered the automatic. He stepped close to Brick so that no one else could hear him. "Mr. Callahan says he takes responsibility," the marine said, still surly. "I'm gonna report him. Get out of here."

"Kiss off," Brick said.

"Catch me off duty, motherfuck."

Sevda watched him calmly as he suicidally dodged the *pesero* jitneys and buses and taxis and sputtering Volkswagens that charged toward him from the Reforma's monstrous roundabouts like artillery shells. As he trotted across the relative safety of the access street, she finished the last sip of her *café con leche* and touched her lips lightly with her napkin. Brick flopped in the wrought-iron chair beside her to catch his breath.

"You look as if you need a coffee," she said and motioned for the waiter.

Brick waved him away. "Have you paid yet?"

"No." She looked puzzled.

Brick fished a fifty-peso note from his pocket and dropped it on the table. "Let's go."

"Did you find *that* much out?"

"I found out a hell of a lot more than I wanted to." He stood and took her hand to pull her to her feet. "We won't be the only ones out hunting now. With luck, we'll have a couple of days before they can locate us. I want to make good use of those."

* * *

Mexico City was a wheel, a vast, slow-turning wheel that each year creaked louder and turned more slowly on its splintering axle. From their hotel behind the old Lotería Nacional building, at the hub of the wheel, they crept along its spokes in the rented Volkswagen through smog-bound, overheating traffic toward the outposts of the colonial world they were sifting. A trip out Insurgentes Sur to the rambling San Angel Inn for lunch and a bribe to the head-waiter to dig around for a Sr. Brenner cost them a morning. A check of the patio cafés and bars of the Pink Zone devoured the afternoon. Pieces of dinners and more bribes at half-a-dozen other restaurants, from the soft elegance of the old Hacienda de los Morales to the *jarocha* marimbas of the Fonda del Recuerdo, chewed up the evening. The night was swallowed by the mariachi-band bars of the Plaza Garibaldi, and then by a swing in and out of the late-night cabarets that the tourists didn't know about.

They left the last one near dawn. It had been only a suite of collapsing rooms over a taco restaurant on narrow Dolores, the street of sorrows, in Chinatown. An old woman had sung Piaf songs, a professor of something at the National University had played his Cosmic Suite on an upright piano, joints and brandy had gone around, and nobody had heard of Wolf Brenner. Weary, a little stoned, they walked the few blocks to Boulevard Juarez and the Volkswagen. The last of the Mexico City night people were going home—the pimps, the strip-joint hustlers, the bartenders; and the first of the morning people were coming out—the early-shift desk clerks, the window washers, the bus drivers and cops. Brick and Sevda collapsed on a bench in the Alameda Park to watch them cross paths in the early-morning, gray damp.

Sevda absently studied a whiskered man fishing debris out of a fountain with a net, poking the occasional wet coins he found into a bag tied to his belt. She sighed, this time not impatiently. "I know how he feels," she said. "Maybe we should buy a net."

"Ready to give up already?" Brick asked.

"Could you keep it up like this?"

"Not for the rest of my life."

"You could go home."

Brick dredged up enough energy to laugh. "Where's that? You know, they say that there are only two kinds of gringos who wind up in Mexico: those who aren't wanted back home—and those who are. I may stay here for good."

"You don't stay anywhere until you find my uncle for me. Where to today?"

"Couple of hours' sleep, then the University Club, Jewish Community Center, Israeli embassy—places like that. Be civilized and we may even slow down enough to have an uninterrupted dinner someplace tonight."

Sevda stood and stretched. Even rumpled, the thin white dress looked fresh on her. "We'll see," she said.

In the hotel, Brick's sleep came hard to him. He was overtired, yes. He was half expecting the door to come smashing down and a squad of Jack Callahan's mysterious Texans and Mexicans to drag him out somewhere (his pistol had made it through customs in his suitcase, but he had no faith that he would use it). But more than that, his mind wouldn't shut off. The meeting with Jack Callahan had changed something, though he couldn't name just what yet. But it had to do with an edge this business once had had, an apparent rightness like an edge on a sword, say, that looked clean and sharp until you got too close to it and saw that it was really pitted and rusting. The news he'd gotten about his father, then about Roger's trip to Trabzon, and now Jack Callahan—it had all come about so quickly, so goddamn quickly. And had shoved him so goddamn close to the edge of the blade...

He had felt good yesterday morning, when he had had the moment of clean anger against the marine. That had drained away damn quickly, too. He wanted it, or something like it, back.

And he wondered that he hadn't felt the excitement he'd expected at being close to Livia again. She had been—was—so much a part of the reason he'd begun this trip, part of the salvation it offered him (the visible part, like an ark to grab hold of) that without her he couldn't imagine going ahead. He needed that back, too.

To hell with it. He was overtired, that was all. He listened to water running in Sevda's bathroom next door and told himself how tired he was. What was she doing now? He imagined her stepping into the shower. Damn her; it ought to be Livia he was imagining.

Pity, Ali Sabri would have said. No chance with that one, chocolate eyes or not. She and he were eggs and apples. Nevertheless, he concentrated on the sound of the water and drifted toward sleep.

The short, insistent rings, spleen of a bored switchboard operator, came as relief from dreams he didn't remember and didn't want to. The old-fashioned, heavy receiver was lead in his hands, his fingers swollen from Mexico City's 7200-foot altitude. He held it and breathed into it, listening to the silence on the other end until he was sure enough of where he was to answer it. Midmorning light pushed against the imperfectly closed curtains. His voice cracked when he spoke.

"Hello?"

"Señor Rustin?" The voice was a man's, the sort of confident god-voice used by Mexicans who are accustomed to being listened to.

Brick cleared his throat. "I think so."

"Habla español, señor?"

Brick considered answering in Spanish, but decided he wasn't up to it. "Not right now."

"Ah, *bueno*. I hope I didn't wake you." The voice's English was accented but fluent.

"Who is this?"

"My name is Armando Soto, Mr. Rustin. I am calling you to be of service."

"Wait a minute." Brick put the receiver down and went into the bathroom to splash water on his face. He took his time. A tour guide? Surely no more than that. Nobody should have had time to locate him yet, not unless they had resources a hell of a lot bigger than he could have imagined. Or would want to imagine. He picked up the receiver again hoping that it was dead, that the tour guide had given up. "OK. Service."

"Jack Callahan is a mutual friend of ours, I think."

Brick eased himself down onto the edge of the bed. No tour guide. "I know Jack Callahan."

"Jack suggested that we talk."

"Do you know why I'm here?"

"Not precisely."

"Then how do you know you can be of—service?"

"I think we may have some mutual interests."

"Can you tell me how to find a man named Wolf

282

Brenner?" Damn it, he wanted a cup of coffee. That was a question that gave away more than it asked.

There was a pause on the line. "At the moment, I'm not prepared to answer that, Señor Rustin. We should talk first. May I send someone for you?"

"No," Brick said too quickly. "Send someone for you." Christ, that sounded much too much like a line from *The Godfather*. "I'll meet you."

"Bueno. May I give you an address?"

"No. You come here. To the restaurant."

There was another pause. "Señor Rustin, if I were planning on harming you, would I call for an appointment first?"

Now it was Brick's pause. "OK."

"On Ejército Nacional, the Grupo Primero building. Suite 506. For lunch?"

"Not today." Stall, use the time. Now that they'd located him, they would give him a little rope.

"As soon as possible would be best, I think."

"Sure. In a couple of days."

"Tomorrow perhaps, *señor?*"

"I'll try."

"At one, perhaps. And feel free to bring your companion. La señorita Sabri, is it?"

"I'll try." He could have gotten her name from the desk clerk, Brick thought. He'd feel easier knowing it had been something that simple.

"Hasta mañana, then."

It should have all been simple, Brick thought as he sat on the bed and waited for his head to finish unfuzzing. He was going to ask around in the right places, get a little help from an old friend, Jack Callahan, then finish some business he'd started up on a mountain in Kurdistan. Never mind just how he was going to finish it: he had no way of knowing that till the time came. But things kept getting in the way. Jack Callahan did. Brenner's damned stubborn invisibility was. And now, for God's sweet sake, Grupo Primero was. Whatever a Grupo Primero was.

At breakfast, he found out from his waiter that what a Grupo Primero was, was everything. It hadn't even existed when Brick was a student in Mexico, but now, the waiter said, everybody knew what Grupo Primero was, señor. Grupo Primero manufactures things, señor. It builds things. It buys and sells things. It imports and exports things. It owns banks, boats, apartment buildings, resorts, señor. What happened, señor, was that the big manufacturers decided that they shouldn't be competing this way, the newspapers say, so they just got together and made a company bigger than anybody else's, señor. And now they don't compete with each other but with the Germans and the Japanese and the gringos, begging your pardon, señor, so that it's not Mexicans against Mexicans, but Mexicans against those other people, and that's better for us all because we have more jobs and respect and we're better organized, the newspapers say, señor.

"I don't want to see them," Sevda said. "I don't want to know how they're involved. You know about Krupp and those people in Germany before the war? What's the difference?"

She had been bathed and dressed and ready when Brick knocked on her door. Could she have done all that, have had her hair as much in place and her makeup as fresh, and have slept at all? He watched the ruffles on her light-blue dress flounce as she attacked an omelette with an appetite he couldn't imagine having, and he was in awe.

"Don't be such a graduate student," he said. "If

we don't go see them, they'll come see us. Unless we find what we're looking for before lunchtime tomorrow."

"I'm better off being a graduate student than an asshole romantic. At least I'm learning to *do* something." She speared a hunk of ham. No danger of a Moslem fundamentalist rebellion from this one, Brick thought. "It's just that I can't imagine these people having any possible connection with Kurdistan. I don't trust any of this. And it's a waste of time."

"Could you have imagined Israel's having anything to do with Kurdistan?"

"That's different." She signaled the waiter for another cup of tea, gold bracelets ringing and flashing. "OK, you're right. It's not that different. What do you think they want?"

"Something we've got. They won't be just giving away free samples."

"No deals with them about anything. Whatever they want. Agreed?"

"You're the political coordinator," Brick said. "I'm the asshole romantic."

Sevda speared another piece of ham, smiled, but didn't answer.

The day sweltered by until the obligatory rainy-season afternoon thundershower. By then the University Club, the Jewish Community Center, and the Israeli embassy had all not heard of Brenner. During the cool of the rain, the *Mexico City News,* the American Chamber of Commerce, the Anglo-American Directory, the North American Institute, and the synagogues had their chance to not know him. Yesterday, Brick had been frustrated. Today, since the phone call, he was fatalistic. Whoever had found him in his side-street hotel as quickly as they had, could make sure anybody they didn't want found would stay well out of sight. He was much more interested in trying to figure out where to fit the most misshapen piece of this thing yet: Grupo Primero. The thread that connected the dead volcano of Ararat to the almost dead volcano of Popocatepetl outside this city just wouldn't weave itself for him, even speculatively. Oil? Hell, Mexico had all the oil it needed, and the government controlled that, besides. What else did the Kurds have that a huge Mexican corporation might possibly want? Sheep dung? Mountains? People? Plenty of all those in Mexico.

Whatever they wanted, *he* wanted desperately to know before he met them whether he was going to be able to dig up any lead at all on Brenner and the others. That was one card he wanted to hold. No matter how futile it was, he would keep looking.

Maybe Sevda had a built-in fatalism, or maybe it was just good sense and single-mindedness. But she refused to speculate. They had business to do, and they did it, period. By dinnertime, Brick had exhausted both his body and his ability to speculate. He admitted her wisdom.

"I intend to eat," he told her as he swung off the circus of the *periferico* beltway and into the more subtly demonic city traffic toward the Forest of Chapultepec. "I intend to sit in one place, drink wine, and finish a meal. I intend to do my duty first by bribing the headwaiter with Tony's money at a decadently spectacular place called Del Lago—if it's still there—then to eat decadently well on Tony's money. Want to come?"

"Do you really want to find Wolf Brenner? I have my doubts."

"I do. But I don't think we're going to. Know why?"

"No."

"Because he's a man no one would have noticed. He's a cipher." He slowed, trying to remember the turn to Del Lago. "Last chance. Want to eat?"

She kept her eyes front. "We have to eat."

The smog went into hiding at night, like the heat. Outside the soaring glass wall of Del Lago, the clarity of the changing patterns and colors of the huge fountain in the lake let you believe a good lie, Brick thought. You could believe that you'd get up in the morning and see the white cloth of snow on the volcanoes, the way you had been able to years ago before the smog blotted them out forever. It was a good lie like the two huge palms that grew in the center of the restaurant, aliens here at this cold altitude, and like the soft Latin music from the dinner-jacketed band, and like the silver wine buckets, and the restaurant itself, its many levels rising away on a sea of blue carpeting until faces on the highest balconies became only ovals above expensive suits and elegant dresses. Here beside this lake, with the second bottle of chilled Mexican Ocala wine just opened, surrounded by the shadowy trees of vast Chapultepec Park, Brick could believe for a while that this was the way Mexico really was. Could pretend that they weren't in the middle of a city sinking under smog and people and poverty and cruelty, that out there beyond the lake and trees in the dark there weren't endless hungry shanty towns springing up faster than the army could bulldoze them under. He poured the wine and pretended.

"Nouveau riche," he said, sweeping his hand around at the tables nearby.

"We're underdressed," Sevda said, and accepted the wine. "No matter what they are."

"Piffle. Did you like the *ceviche?*"

"Yes." She sipped the wine and leaned back into her chair, relaxing. "I'm not sure what it was, and I feel guilty about being here, but it was good." Her eyes wandered among the tables, lingered on the dance floor, and came back to Brick. "Did you come here often—when you were here before?"

"A few times. That was a long time ago; it was cheaper then."

"By yourself?"

"No. I usually brought somebody."

"You mean a woman."

"I mean women."

"I see." Her eyes left Brick and followed a waiter. "Have you ever been married?" she said with studied casualness.

"Not that I know of. Why?"

"Oh—most men your age have, I suppose. Just curious."

"That surprises me."

"That most men your age have been married?"

"No. That you'd be curious."

She flushed and began to sweep bread crumbs into a little pile on the tablecloth. "Does it?"

"I didn't mean to embarrass you."

"I was just—curious. That's all."

"How about yourself?"

"Married?" She laughed nervously and scattered the bread crumbs. "Never."

"Any men around?"

"Not now."

He watched her sweep the bread crumbs into little swirls. "No time for them?"

"I care about what I'm doing, if that's what you mean."

"And only for that?"

"This is a silly conversation." She finished her wine. "You say everything was 'a long time ago' a great deal, you know."

"It was."

"Everything's all over, then?"

"It was."

"That's a tricky thing to say."

"I'm tricky, all right." He reached for the wine bottle, but she put her hand over her glass.

"Why were you in school here?"

"I'm not sure. There was an American university here then. I wasn't doing so well back home. My father thought a semester among the *real* misfits might do me some good, I suppose."

"Did it?"

"No, ma'am. I think I learned something from them."

"Antiheroes are out of fashion, Brick. It doesn't suit you very well to be one, either."

He poured himself a glass of wine from the bottle he still held and downed it. "Second surprise," he said.

"What is?"

"That I care you said that."

Her eyes met his, as if she were checking to see if he was making fun of her. She started to say something, then shook her head.

"Dance?" Brick said.

She glanced at the dance floor. The song was a

slow, sentimental Augustin Lara one that had filled the floor with dancers. She nodded. "OK."

She danced well, nothing fancy, but smoothly and naturally—which was something else she hadn't learned in Kurdistan. Not this kind of dancing. The song ended and they stayed on the floor for another. At first they had danced at a distance, like blind dates on prom night. But sometime into the second song, she let herself ease closer to him, then rest her head on his shoulder. A third song began. They stayed on the floor.

"I think I wish it weren't this way," she said quietly, after a time.

"What way?"

"I think I wish that I were one of them, one of these other people here. I wish we were just tourists from Syracuse, or somebody who came here because they didn't have anything better to do."

"Always?"

"No. But for tonight I wish it."

They maneuvered toward the edge of the floor, away from the crowd. As they moved, Brick could feel the ripple of her body beneath the blue dress. He wondered if she was as conscious of his body as he was of hers, and in his self-consciousness he missed a step. For tonight, pretend. It should be this way. It *is* this way.

"What would we do in Mexico City, if we were just people?" she said.

"Oh, we'd come to this place, I suppose. We'd spend a lot of our time in the Pink Zone buying things. We'd walk along the Reforma until our feet hurt and we found a café to have a *capuchino* in. We'd meet somebody for drinks at the Marie Isabel in the evening. We'd make love at night." She tensed. He went

290

on, talking too fast now. "We'd see the *zócalo* and the cathedral, and we'd take a couple of day trips to buy silver in Taxco and have lunch in Cuernavaca. We'd drive up into the mountains and eat some *carnitas* at Rio Frio. We'd ruin our shoes at the pyramids. We'd watch the kids play soccer in Chapultepec Park, then go to the Museum of Modern Art and to the Anthropological Museum—"

Brick stopped abruptly and stepped off the dance floor onto the carpet. Idiot, he told himself. *Idiota!*

"What's wrong?" she asked.

"The Anthropological Museum. Christ, where else?"

"Where else what?"

"Brenner, where else Brenner! What's his passion? He's been on digs everywhere, Tony told me. If he's known anywhere in Mexico..."

He watched her face slip from puzzlement to understanding to disappointment, and she turned away to weave among the tables toward theirs. He caught up with her. "I'm sorry," he said. "I should have waited with that."

"No," she said. "I'm glad you remembered it. It was just a...stupid mood." They reached the table. A smiling waiter stood by it with the check. Brick wanted to hit him. "We're not just people after all, are we? Not for now." She took his hand and forced a smile. "Come on. Tell me about the museum."

A good lie, Brick thought when they stepped out of the restaurant into the high, cold night and the door closing behind them cut the band off in midchord. The smog bit at his eyes. A lovely lie, for a while.

* * *

Yes, *señor y señorita,* the subdirector was certainly in, though *el director* himself wouldn't be in until later and maybe not at all and even if he were they would need an appointment to see him and who knew when they could get an appointment; being *el director,* he was a busy man, the guard told them as he led them through rivers of schoolchildren up the staircase to the second level of the museum. Outside in the courtyard the great circular waterfall splashed, and a recording of a conch-shell trumpet announced the hour: ten o'clock, opening time. *El subdirector* was a busy man also but if the *señor* and *señorita* had a few minutes to wait, no doubt just a little while, *un ratito,* perhaps they could have an audience with him, since their business was urgent—and surely it was urgent, because he had noticed that the business of *norteamericanos* was always urgent.

Ten o'clock. Three hours until lunch with Grupo Primero. A minimum of an hour's waiting time in the office of the subdirector, then at least three quarters of an hour to the Grupo Primero building on Ejército Nacional. That would leave them an hour and a quarter to follow up any leads they might get. Not much, not in Mexico City.

It was even less by the time they finished their hour-and-a-half wait. *El subdirector,* no older than Brick, with styled hair and a pencil moustache and a walk that defied gravity because he leaned at least twenty degrees backward while his feet leapt out in front of him as if he were smashing roaches, passed with great leisure through his outer office half-a-dozen times while they waited, smiling each time. No one went in to see him. No phone calls came. When they at last were sent in to him, he was reading a book, all courtesy and apologies. But Brenner?

Brenner, Brenner, Brenner. Oh, *Brenner!* Could that
have been the strange man with the hair that always
went—this way, and the eyes that were always
going—like this? He had come in about a year and
a half ago to see *el señor director* with some odd
notion about finding ancient Jewish trading posts
on the coast of Veracruz from the classic Olmec period. That man? If it was, they sent him to Ursula
Braun, over at the National Institute of Anthropol-
ogy and History, who had worked once with some
German baron with the same wild fixation. Ursula
had actually listened to him—even gotten friendly
with him. She took in waifs, Ursula did. They should
see Ursula. He believed Ursula was in the field these
days, out at the pyramids of Teotihuacán. They
should run out there. And be sure to give Ursula his
best.

"That kills that," Brick told Sevda as they swam
through the schoolchildren again. "Couple of hours
just out there and back, at least."

"You're not excited? That's the first positive thing
we've gotten!"

"You're sure it's positive."

"Of course it is. It means Brenner was here, and
he wasn't invisible. He *can* be found."

"Not before lunch."

"Look, you wanted at least a lead before you saw
these people. You've got it, *inshallah.*"

"Inshallah? First time I've heard you use that."

"First time I've needed it." Without warning she
slapped Brick's butt and skipped away a step, surprising him and scandalizing schoolteachers. "Let's
go see a Grupo Primero. I feel good."

Brick laughed and grabbed for her. She skipped

away, her eyes and bracelets flashing. "Never quicker than a Kurd," she said.

The only thing about the lobby of the Grupo Primero building that told you you weren't in Chicago or Milan or Tokyo was the mosaic of cast-concrete Aztec calendars. From the outside it was as faceless and "modern" as the corporation that built it. That was deliberate, Brick knew: like Holiday Inns, no surprises, so a corporado would feel as much at home in it as he would in Chicago or Milan or Tokyo.

No surprises in the automatic elevator, either, or the faceless walls of the fifth-floor corridor, or the door that merely said 506 on it. No surprises at all until they opened the door to a waiting room with Jack Callahan in it.

Callahan lowered his head like a bull to see above his bifocals as he stood. A pretty receptionist, as overdressed as all Mexican receptionists, looked up expectantly. Brick ignored Callahan and said to her, "Brick Rustin to see Armando Soto."

"Momento, señor." She buzzed an intercom.

"Aw, come on now, Brick," Callahan said. "Hell, I changed your diapers, boy."

"Thought you'd keep a lower profile, Jack. Don't your guys put it that way?"

"Just business, Brick. And I'm keeping a lookout for you. Your mama would want me to."

"Is that why I'm here, Jack? Just business?"

"Believe it or not, it is. Look here. These people told me I could talk to you a minute first. They're respectable business people, Brick. They don't intend you any harm—they got to make a profit like everybody else, and they got to be a little aggressive to make it. But the less fuss they make, the better for them. They think a lot of your daddy and they don't want to see you get into anything. Just listen to them, son, that's all I ask. They won't do you wrong if you don't make 'em."

"What are they going to tell me, Jack?"

Callahan clapped his hands together like a TV preacher. "I don't know, Brick, swear before God. I told you the truth—I'm just here because of you. They didn't even take to the idea that I came at all."

"I appreciate it, Jack."

Callahan's nose nearly disappeared between his cheeks as he smiled. "That's my boy talking! Reckon this is Miss Sabri?"

Sevda nodded at him as if he were a restroom attendant.

"Well, you make a nice couple," Callahan went on. Sevda made a noise. The intercom buzzed and the receptionist stood. Callahan winked and poked Brick with his elbow. "Just remember, don't do yourself wrong in there. I'll wait for you out here."

"Your mother almost married that?" Sevda whispered as the receptionist opened the door to the inner suite.

"He was good to me," Brick said. "Even good people can do stupid things." Maybe righteousness could help his nerves, Brick hoped as he followed the receptionist into the suite.

A buffet was spread beneath the window of the suite—white linen, wine buckets, soup, roast beef, chilaquiles, Spanish ham, rice, fresh vegetables—and a white-jacketed waiter was just vanishing through a side door. From behind a long mahogany desk, as featureless as the building, a man rose to greet them. Two other men followed him to their feet from armchairs in front of the desk.

The man behind the desk was as bland and faceless as the desk and the building. Middling height, gray tailored suit, fortyish, hair with no particular style, moustache, and the vaguely Indian features of a mestizo. His only distinction was a large diamond ring on his right hand, the hand he extended to Brick, and then to Sevda in turn. As Brick took the hand, he recognized it as the hand of every hot-dog businessman and bureaucrat he'd ever known: a little pudgy, nails manicured and lacquered, downy hairs on the back. He wondered if they ordered their hands from the same places they did their suits.

"Armando Soto, your servant," the man said. Brick recognized the telephone voice. "I appreciate your coming." He introduced the other two men, attaching endless Spanish names to them that he said so quickly you knew they weren't important. The two were distinguishable to Brick only in that one was short and fat and the other wasn't. They ordered their suits and hands from the same place Soto did. "May I offer you a drink?"

"Scotch," Brick said. Sevda shook her head.

"Please," Soto said, indicating the buffet table while he opened doors to a bookcase wet bar and fussed with drinks. Sevda looked at Brick, shrugged, and picked up a plate. The two other men, Short and Not Short, stood back and nodded and beamed. They took their wives on shopping vacations to Dallas, Brick decided as he joined Sevda, and were members of the Mexican Lions Club. It would be impossible to dislike them; they would smother you in hospitality if you tried.

They all sat around a round conference table and ate, making small talk and saying how good the wine was until Sevda clearly couldn't stand it any longer, even as used to Middle Eastern protocol as she was. She plunked an olive pit on her plate and said abruptly, "Why are we here?"

"To enjoy your lunch," Soto said without hesitation.

"I've enjoyed it," Sevda said.

"More wine?" Soto asked Brick.

"No. But that was a good question my friend asked."

Soto sighed. There was something lizardish about the sigh, more a hiss than a sigh, Brick thought. "I'd hoped we could finish dessert first."

Brick waited. Sevda plunked another olive pit.

"I suggested lunch," Soto began, "because I would like this relationship to be as much friendship as business. It could be very fruitful either way. Do you know what Grupo Primero is, Mr. Rustin?"

"Generally. Enough, I think."

"Miss Sabri?"

Sevda nodded.

"I am only a functionary, let me make that clear. My job is coordinator of just one part of Grupo Primero—no, just one division of one part, our overseas construction division. It's new to us, and we work closely with those we can learn from. You both are aware that this country has suddenly become one of the most oil-rich nations on earth, are you not?"

"Who's not?" Brick said.

"Unfortunately, the government controls all of our oil. But the technology to develop it does not come from the government. Most of it does not even come from Mexico. It comes from your country. We want to learn as much as we can of that technology. We want to become capable of building the very large complexes that are needed to support refineries and

297

oil fields and the new cities that go with them. But we also want to make a profit while we learn. Have you heard of a company in your country, in Texas, called Daltexco?"

"Heard of it," Brick said. "No more than that."

"Allah, Allah," Sevda said. "Daltexco."

"You know it, then, Miss Sabri?" Soto said.

"Never mind," Sevda said. "Go on."

"Pues, bien. My division of Grupo Primero is affiliated with Daltexco. Daltexco is the largest overseas construction company in the world, you understand. They built many of your airfields in Viet Nam once, and have worked for many years in the Philippine Islands, India, South America, Taiwan—and even China now. And in the Middle East, Miss Sabri. Very heavily in the Middle East."

"I know," Sevda said.

"I supposed you would. What you perhaps don't know is that Daltexco has invested very heavily in Grupo Primero. It is, oh, politically more convenient—*digamos*—for Grupo Primero to win certain construction contracts in many parts of the world than for Daltexco these days. Mexico, after all, is a third-world country, *no?* We are underdeveloped."

Short and Not Short beamed and nodded again.

"Are you following me, Miss Sabri?" Soto said.

"I think I'm ahead of you," Sevda said.

"Then you know how greatly Daltexco depended on the Shah in Iran."

"Oh, yes."

"And how heavy their losses were there."

"Yes."

"And you can imagine how large the rebuilding program is going to be there because of the war with Iraq, and the revolution."

298

"Let me imagine for you, Señor Soto," Sevda said. Her voice was sharp, with an edge of sarcasm to it. "Let me imagine how useful a Kurdish rebellion is to you—especially since most of the oil fields in Iraq are in Kurdistan, too. Billions of dollars worth of construction projects useful, would you say? If only there could be some sort of arrangement beforehand? That's a very long chance, Señor Soto. We would have to succeed first and then keep our word afterward."

Soto stood and poured a round of coffee. "Bluntly, yes. But our investment—ours and Daltexco's together—would be relatively small. You need arms. Fine. The Israelis would see to those, as Wolf Brenner explained it to us. But you also need political support outside the Middle East. You need money for supplies—medicine and food and uniforms and such. We can supply all that to you. You can pay us back in kind or otherwise when the time comes. It's a business proposition, *señorita*. Your uncle would have understood it perfectly."

"What the hell do you mean, would have?" Brick said.

"Cream and sugar?" Soto said. "Brandy?"

"Screw brandy," Brick said. "What's happened to Ali Sabri?"

"Nothing's happened to him, as far as I know. Or perhaps better, I don't quite know what's happened to him. Mr. Brenner has turned out to be...unstable. You see, we contracted with Mr. Brenner to bring Mr. Sabri here for a talk before he went back into Iran. We wanted to give him certain assurances of help and to get—certain assurances from him. We had worked with Mr. Brenner before in our banking operations, and—"

"In the Cayman Islands," Brick said. "Banco de Todas las Americas." Pieces, he thought. All there, waiting, clicking into place.

Soto smiled. "These *señores* know more about that than I do." He gestured toward Short and Not Short. "I asked them here today because they're in a position to discuss financial transactions, if Miss Sabri wants. It's a very useful bank, I understand, for certain of our operations. Sadly, it had proved very useful to Mr. Brenner in other ways before this particular operation, ways which ultimately made him unfit for us. And before you ask, please, I'm not prepared to go into them. Just accept that he muddled the operation from the beginning—shootings, even killings, I understand. Then thanks only to you, Mr. Sabri made it to London, Mr. Rustin."

"That wasn't Brick's fault," Sevda broke in. Atta girl, Brick thought, surprised and pleased.

"Nonetheless, we're grateful to him. But, *enfin*, the short of it is that Mr. Sabri is no longer in our hands, and Mr. Brenner is no longer one of our subcontractors. I'm sorry."

Sevda leaned forward over the table toward Soto, her eyes angry and hard. "Then whose hands *is* he in?"

"We're doing our best to bring him back safely, Miss Sabri," Soto said, his god-voice oozing assurance. "I'll ask you to trust me about that. And I'll suggest you and Mr. Rustin return home for the time being. No, I'll beg you to, for the good of all of us. Something very delicate is happening that you might well upset..."

"Something very delicate is happening right now," Sevda said. "You want us to trust *you*, when you're responsible for this whole...this whole...oh!" She shoved back from the table and stormed to the window.

"Think, Miss Sabri. It is far in our best interests to maintain a friendly relation with you. We want to help your people, and so we *must* have your trust. Why should we willingly violate it?"

"What about the others?" Brick said. "Where are they?"

"We are no longer in contact with them, Mr. Rustin."

"But you know where they are, at least. Or where they *were*."

"They were in a guest house of Grupo Primero, near Puebla. But I give you my word they aren't now. From there, I don't know."

Sevda turned from the window, very controlled. "And if we do go home, will you locate them for us?"

"Go home, Miss Sabri—just please do that for me. Take a message to your people that they have a friend here. Those other three, they're not useful to you. They're only a complication now."

"Are they alive?"

Soto spread his hands on the table as if he were going to hold hands with Short and Not Short, and looked from one to the other. "Miss Sabri, we are a respectable business. We want to offer you a mutually beneficial arrangement. We are not in the business of killing people. Please, you and Mr. Rustin leave this to us."

Sevda scooped her purse off an end table. "We'll see," she said.

"Whoa..." Brick said.

"Brick, you agreed. This part of things is mine."

"Would you like us to arrange a flight for you, Miss Sabri?" Soto said.

301

"I can take care of that," Sevda said.

"Will you contact us? We'll be glad to make financial arrangements with you if—"

Sevda started for the door. "No, thank you. That's taken care of. Brick?"

Brick wondered if the Mexicans were as confused as he was—or he hoped they were. Had she promised them anything? Hell, who knew? No matter what she looked and talked like, she was a Kurd, Ali Sabri's niece all right. Wherever she was, she was in the Middle East. He followed her to the door, all admiration.

Jack Callahan wallowed to his feet in the outer office. "Hey, kid!" he said. "How'd it go?"

"No problem," Brick said.

"Lord, I'm happy to hear that. You don't know how much easier that makes my mind." He reached for Brick's hand. Brick stopped to let him take it. Sevda kept going. "When can we feed you?"

"I'll be in touch," Brick said, pulling away.

"Love to your mama and daddy," Callahan called after him. As the door shut behind him, Brick caught a last glimpse of Callahan: he was looking to Soto, who stood beside the assembly-line receptionist. Soto was frowning and shaking his head at him.

"Just what do they think they *can't* buy!" Sevda raged as the Volkswagen sliced in and out of the traffic of Insurgentes Norte toward the pyramids. "How stupid do they think we are?"

"Well, he's got something you need," Brick said abstractedly, trying to avoid a killer bus. People and pigs grinned at him from the luggage rack on top of the bus, and passengers inside it cheered the driver on.

"And he's the only one? Dangle enough dollars or pesos in front of the poor simple Kurds and they'll be yours forever? Do your killing and settle your scores for you? What does he know about deals? We've been making deals since before his people quit eating each other."

"So he can go to hell."

"No. That would be stupid. Let him deal—but on our terms, when the time comes."

"What about your uncle—what will he say?"

"Unless the Soviets scrambled his brains, he'll say the same thing."

"They didn't."

"Then he'll do what we've always done: deal with the devil if we have to to survive."

The killer bus swerved to avoid a family on a bicycle, and boxes tumbled off the roof into the traffic. The bus slowed; the driver's face, framed by tassels and dangling Virgins of Guadalupe, was frustrated and furious. Brick beeped and escaped.

But there was no sport in the escape. The feeling he'd had yesterday morning in the hotel, trying to sleep, wouldn't leave him be. His edge was dull—even duller since the meeting with Soto. How could you hate Soto, or hate Jack Callahan? Or even hate your own father? You could hate villains with waxed moustaches. But you couldn't hate something that didn't exist, that was only a legal term, like "corporation" or "government." And the people who kept those organizations going weren't evil, for the most part; they were loyal, they slept well at night when they'd done a good job. Their companies got things done that needed doing. They were decent to kids and dogs. They took care of their parents. How could you hate them, any more than you could have hated

the gray men in the dock at the Nuremberg trials
if you'd met them on the train?

But there was no sport in slaying a dragon that
had no face, either. Daltexco and Grupo Primero
were no world for an asshole romantic. They had
developed the ultimate defense: anonymity. You
couldn't hate that either, but still, still there was
something so goddamned hateful about it.

What had been clear on Ararat was too goddamn
much like the yellow smog now. You looked a little
distance into it and everything got fuzzy, then disappeared altogether. He wanted out of it, wanted to
get back to someplace he could see from again.

But he couldn't get out of it, not yet. There was
Livia, and something left to settle with in that. There
was Ali Sabri. There was Sevda now, lost in thought
beside him. He looked at her and felt his throat
tighten. That won't do, Rustin, he told himself. Won't
do at all.

They passed the old Cathedral of Guadalupe, then
left the city for the open highway. Nobody from
Grupo Primero would try to stop them if they found
out anything at the pyramids. Soto had pleaded his
intent to handle the Kurds gently for now, and Brick
believed him. Yet still, he was uneasy. Suddenly too
many pieces had fallen into place too simply. And
now there were new parts of the picture he hadn't
even known existed: Ali Sabri was "in somebody
else's hands." Brenner and Livia and Roger were on
their own now. And that could be dangerous. He
wanted it all to be over, settled.

"If this doesn't turn up anything, you ready to
quit?" he asked Sevda.

"Of course not," she said, swimming out of her

brown study. "If nothing else, we promised Tony. We're spending his money."

"Just asking," Brick said. "Tell me something."

"If I can."

"Was there anything between you and Tony?"

"Now it's my turn to be surprised. No, there wasn't anything, but I'm flattered."

"OK, then tell me something else. Who are we looking for?"

"All of them—Livia Lo Presti to my uncle."

"And you think we can get to Ali Sabri before Grupo Primero does?"

She shrugged her impatient shrug. "It's not impossible."

"Christ, that kind of thinking runs in your family, you know."

"Probably. Now it's my turn. What was between you and Tony's wife?"

Brick hesitated. "Not much."

"Oh?"

"Well—it depends on which side you're looking from. Does that matter to you?"

She turned her head away. "Why would it matter to me? It just explains some things, that's all."

"Then why don't you look at me?"

"Shut up."

Ursula Braun wasn't in the field shack. But she would be; she was out checking the excavation of a new preclassic level of the priests' quarters and would be back most surely in a few minutes, the famous "ratito." It was a little after three. Brick decided four-thirty would be a good enough time to come back for her; by then, chances might be at least fifty-fifty she'd be in.

· How many years had it been since Brick had seen this vast temple city of Teotihuacán—ten, eleven? It had stuck in his mind well: the huge Pyramid of the Sun dominating everything like a barren, terraced mountain; the lesser Pyramid of the Moon, more intricately built, watching like a grim kind of mother at the end of the great oblong plaza that ran the length of the many temple platforms. He had liked to come out here on weekdays then, as now, when the mob of tourists was smaller and he could occasionally find a quiet corner where he could let his imagination go. The place had been abandoned even before the Spaniards came, had been only mounds and heaps of stones for hundreds of years after the Aztecs had been overthrown, till the dictator Diaz had had it rebuilt in a burst of national glory-hunting. But Brick repopulated it—or had, when he was a student. And even now, as he and Sevda wandered among the tour guides blathering in half-a-dozen languages to groups of hot and hungover tourists, he could bring some of it back. He told her about the drums and flutes that led the processions of plumed nobility, the priests with blood-matted hair, the wails of the captured warriors who were sacrificed each dawn to feed the hungry sun and give it strength to rise.

"From up there," he said, and pointed to the top of the Pyramid of the Sun. "For festivals sometimes they would throw them down those steps after they cut their hearts out, and priests at the bottom would skin them and dance in their skins."

Sevda shuddered. A group of kids, urchins from one of the shantytowns outside the grounds, swirled around them after a soccer ball. Sevda covered her nose against the cloud of dust they raised. They were lean and tough, pants too short below faded, frayed shirts. Brick glowered at them.

"I don't like this place," Sevda said. "Too much death everywhere."

"That's what Mexico was all about," Brick said. "Was, hell—is. You want to get out of the dust?"

"*Is* there a place out of it?"

Brick pointed to the top of the Pyramid of the Sun again. "Yep."

"You want to *climb* that?"

"Burn some stuff out—I think we could both stand that."

Sevda scowled at the long, steep flight of steps that cut straight up the face of the pyramid, like a macabre Jacob's ladder. "I could stand some burning. Let's go."

They stopped to rest on one of the terraces halfway up; even with the sky overcast from the approaching afternoon rain, and a good breeze, they were both sweating.

And Sevda found Jack Callahan.

"Brick," she said, her breath coming short in the high altitude. "Down there, with those kids."

Brick followed her eyes down to the pack of urchins that had surrounded them in the pickup soccer game. Jack Callahan knelt among them. He was pointing up toward Brick and Sevda on the pyramid and passing something out among the kids, something that looked like peso notes. A couple of the older kids, who seemed to be fourteen or so, were nodding. Then they motioned to the others, a dozen or more, to come with them, and broke into a trot toward the pyramid.

Jack Callahan levered himself to his feet, belly swaying, and followed.

"Jack, Jack, Jack," Brick said, more to himself than Sevda. "What the hell, Jack?"

The kids reached the bottom of the pyramid and waited for Callahan. When he had nearly reached them, he flipped his hand for them to start climbing. There were no more than a score of tourists braving the pyramid now, most of them resting on the long terrace below Brick and Sevda. The few who were on the stairs stepped off onto a terrace when they saw the phalanx of kids clambering toward them. Only one other couple was higher than Brick and Sevda—a black couple who were on their way down. They passed, helloing and smiling. They made it only to the third terrace down before they were forced off the stairs.

Below, on the dusty grand plaza, the groups of tourists who packed it still clustered around their guides, or strolled with cameras growing from their faces. Here and there a uniformed guard lounged, or tweeted his whistle at a tourist who looked as if he might be tempted to carve his initials on something. Even at this height, halfway up, they were all thumb-sized. Beyond the plaza Brick could see the matchbook cars in the parking lot, and beyond them the straggling villages that surrounded the dead city, and beyond those the eucalyptus trees and empty fields that stretched out of sight onto this vast high plain. No help. No help anywhere. He swallowed fear. Like all those poor bastards who had to keep climbing a thousand years ago.

He took Sevda's hand. "Come on," he said, and moved onto the steps.

"Up?" she said.

"You want to try going down?" He tugged at her gently. "The top's flat and fairly wide. I'd rather deal with this there than here." Sevda glanced at the narrow terrace she was on, then stepped onto the stairs beside him.

The kids came to within a couple of terraces of them, then slowed. Even without a rest, they didn't seem nearly as winded as Brick knew *he* was. They could catch up easily, could surround them in seconds if they wanted. But they were hanging back, as if they had been instructed to. Below them, Jack Callahan followed step by painful step.

Brick made out individual faces now. The two older boys, the leaders, were closest. One of them kept checking behind him for the younger boys, motioning them to speed up, slow down, stay in some sort of order. But the other, the taller of the two, kept his attention fixed firmly on Sevda. The wind flattened her skirt to her, outlining her buttocks and legs as if the skirt were wet and molded to her. She looked behind her once and he caught her eye. He smiled, then puckered up his lips into a kiss. She turned around again, quickly, and held Brick's hand more tightly. The boy's coarse hair was uncut and matted, and streaks of sweat cut the dust on his dark face like scars, or paint. His features were sharp and heavy, his eyes obsidian and Oriental—no mestizo, but pure Indian. He caught Brick looking at him and spat, and Brick saw that he was walleyed—one eye focused relentlessly ahead of him, the other watching nothing but the sky. Brick turned his attention back to the stairs and sped up.

At the top, which was the size of a large living room, he and Sevda dropped down onto the dirt and sparse grass, panting and weak. "Rest a minute," he told her. "We've got some time."

"Time before what?" she said. She tried fruitlessly to sweep away the hair that clung to the sweat on her neck.

"Jack wants to talk."

"How do you know?"

"Look," he said. She sat up so that she could see over the edge. The kids were spreading out around the last terrace before the top, surrounding it. But none of them was making any move to come onto the top itself. Only the walleyed kid stayed on the steps, his head just above the edge so that he could keep his one focused eye on her. Sevda tucked her skirt more tightly around her and made fidgety efforts at closing her blouse more than it would close.

The breeze had turned into a wind now, and thunder rolled in the distance. The overcast was gathering itself into rain clouds, and dust devils skittered among the tourists in the grand plaza. Behind the boy on the stairs, Jack Callahan stepped, puffed, rested; stepped, puffed, rested. The other boys squatted, watching and occasionally whistling a signal among themselves. Every now and then one of them would giggle, or make a half comment in *caló*, street slang that was as alien to Brick as Swahili. Some examined their new fifty-peso notes—barely a buck. Jack had bought strength cheap.

Jack made the last of the steps on hands and knees, wheezing and red-faced. The boy stepped aside for him, but made no effort to help. Nor did Brick.

"God a-mighty," Jack gasped, collapsing beside Brick. "Lemme rest."

"Take your time," Brick said. Callahan nodded

310

and pounded his chest and tried out a weak smile on Sevda. She glared her restroom-attendant look at him again.

When he had some of his breath back, Callahan said, "Never been up here before. Never come up here again, by God."

"I think I'd rather you weren't here now, Jack," Brick said.

"Look here, Brick. You going home or not?"

"Sooner or later."

"Naw, that won't do it, son."

"They send you up here, Jack?"

"Nobody *sends* me anywhere. I do what I think's right."

"Then tell me what's right."

"You about to mess up something if you stay around here, son. Your mama's got two things for her in this world now, your daddy and you. Reckon she could do better without you than him, don't you think? You not around much."

"Probably."

"Now, I don't know just what's going on, but I do know that the folks at Grupo Primero are counting on your daddy to get some irons out of the fire for them. And I know that your daddy could get hurt if it goes funny. So Brick, Lord, as sorry as I am about it, I just can't let you and this lady get in the way. You understand that, don't you?"

"What does that mean, Jack?"

"Just promise me, swear to me right here that you'll go on home first thing. I'll take your word for it."

"Sure, first thing."

Callahan looked at Sevda. She bored her chocolate eyes into him. "We'll see," she said.

"Lord a-mercy, lady!" Jack said. "Don't do that."

Brick maneuvered himself into a squat. "Jack, I think we'll start down now. We've got to see somebody."

Callahan's splotched face sank, and he looked sadly over his bifocals. "You ain't going to do it for me, are you, son?" As in his office, his voice grew deeper, more full of Arkansas, as if he were working himself up to something.

Brick couldn't lie to that face again. "No, Jackrabbit. I'm not."

There were tears in Callahan's eyes. "I got drunk with your daddy the night you were born. I used to wipe your little ass for you. *Lord,* I hate this, Brick!"

Brick stood and helped Sevda to her feet. Callahan rolled and grunted to his. A gust of wind full of the smell of rain lashed at him and he turned his face away from it. As he did, the wind and the motion allied themselves, and his glasses tumbled into the dirt beside him. He didn't stop to pick them up. *"Oye muchacho!"* he shouted in the general direction of the boy on the steps. "Now, *ya!*"

The boy took another three or four steps up. Then he whistled lightly, almost a birdcall. The other older boy echoed him, and the whistle went around the terrace, like trills on a flute. The rest of the boys stood now and moved toward the stairs behind the walleyed leader. Callahan stepped out of the way. The walleyed boy reached in his pocket; in one swift movement he pulled out a black, hawk-billed knife and flicked it open.

The pistol, goddamnit, why hadn't he brought the pistol, Brick thought as he backed away, pulling Sevda with him. Sevda's eyes didn't—or couldn't—leave the knife. The boy held it at waist height, switching it back and forth like a cat's tail, advancing. He rose steadily and slowly up the last few steps, as if he were growing out of the pyramid. The other boys streamed over the top behind him and spread out.

"Lord, I hate it, Brick. I hate it," Callahan said. Without his glasses, his eyes seemed only half the size they had been before. As he talked he moved his foot gingerly across the ground around him in the direction his glasses had fallen.

The boys kept making their low whistles and trills as they approached, though the sounds were half swept away by the lashing wind now. A couple of them beat out a steady, slow rhythm on their thighs with the flat of their hands. But the walleyed one was silent, aiming himself not at Brick but at Sevda. He was leaving Brick to his lieutenant, and to the others.

That concentration gave Brick the chance he needed. Hardly any chance, really, but all he had. He and Sevda had backed as far as they could: behind them the stone terraces leapt away to scrub grass at the rear of the pyramid, far below and inhabited only by wandering dogs. If they fell from here, no one would see it happen. An accident, two tourists not being careful. Crap! The stupidity of that, the notion that it could be gotten away with so damned easily gave Brick the anger he needed, like the marine guard in the embassy had given him. He crouched, pretending to keep his attention on the second-in-command. The leader came closer to Sevda, matted hair lashing at his face in the wind. He was a yard away when Brick sprang.

He caught the boy with a body block; he heard the wind *oof* out of him, and lifted, kept driving across the uneven surface of the pyramid. Just before the edge, he slammed him to the ground and twisted the knife out of his hand. The boy fought for breath, his askew eyes rolling. Brick spun to face the others. He had the knife now, but, Christ, what was he supposed to do with it! Slash up twelve-year-olds? Sevda ducked past the boys nearest her and ran to his side.

"Hey, what the hell?" Jack Callahan was saying, blindly stumbling toward Brick. "Hey, *que pasa, muchachos?* Where the hell are they?"

The second-in-command móved now. He motioned for some of the boys to slip into place behind Brick and Sevda. A couple of them hopped down to the first terrace to cut off any retreat toward the stairs that way. And Jack Callahan kept coming.

"Back off, Jack," Brick yelled at him. "Goddamnit, back off."

"Brick? Hell, boy, where you at? You change your mind? Lord, that makes me—"

Brick caught movement from the corner of his eye, as he looked for room to get away from Callahan, who bumbled on toward him. The leader had gotten enough of his breath back to get to his feet, still groggy, but in motion. He dove for Brick. Brick side-stepped him easily. The boy glanced off Sevda, tottered, grabbed, and found Jack Callahan. Callahan went down with him like a heavy bag of something on a rotten rope—went down, and over the edge with him.

The two of them gained momentum on the steps, then rolled off them. Still clasping one another, they hit the first terrace, bounded out into the wind, broke apart like a rock shattering, and raced each other toward the roiling dust of the grand plaza, tumbling, leaping, flaying themselves on the sharp ledges.

314

The boy stopped one terrace up from the ground. Jack Callahan, heavier and rounder, hit the dust and rolled half-a-dozen times. There was nothing to stop him; his arms dangled from threads of muscle and skin, nothing more.

"Vámonos," the second-in-command shouted to the other boys. *"Ándele ya!"* He hit the stairs running, awkward and flat-footed to keep his balance. The smaller boys tumbled after him, passing him in steps so short and graceful they were almost a dance.

At the bottom of the steps guards tried to catch them, but they slipped through their hands like minnows. Tourists clustered, holding on to their gaudy sombreros and straw beach hats against the whirling dust and the first heavy drops of rain.

Brick watched them awhile, then went over and picked up Callahan's unbroken, ugly glasses.

The *señor* had no doubt been up to something with those boys, but *quién sabe,* who knew what, the *federal* cop told Brick when he finished taking their statements. They were no doubt teasing him and took his glasses—no doubt after his wallet, too. What misfortune! Bad ones, those. The fault of overpopulation. The cop was a good Catholic—of course, *señor*—but people bred like cats these days and was it any wonder their children were... Would the *señor* be available for more questions later? Ah, the Hotel Frimont. The cop hoped that this wouldn't spoil *las vacaciones* for the *señor* and the *señorita.*

Brick had given his statement mechanically, leaving out everything but the fact he saw Jack Callahan and the kid fall and that yes, it was an accident. He was trying to leave other things out, too, in his own head. If only he could, he would blot Mexico out, every-

thing that had happened since he had been here. He
tried to reconstruct Jack Callahan, put him back together as he had been on Christmases and Thanks-
givings in Washington, a drink in his hand, singing
boozy songs with his father and mother. Something
intact—he wanted to come out of this nightmare he'd
volunteered for with *some*thing still intact. Not in
pieces, held together by threads and tags of things as
Jack Callahan had been. As he damn well wouldn't
let himself remember Jack Callahan being.

Sevda stayed close to him. The *federales*—macho
and gentlemanly—left her pretty much alone. She
told Brick that it was all right if they went back to the
hotel. Get drunk, if he wanted. Wait awhile.

But he knew he didn't have a while to wait. There
was urgency in this now, the need to have done with
it fast, before whatever had kept him going so far gave
out altogether.

They caught Ursula Braun just as she was finish-
ing her reports for the day, rain clattering on the tin-
roofed field shack loud as hail. Ursula Braun, just past
middle age, with a classic German accent and a comfortable padding of fat, remembered Wolf Brenner
well. An amateur, of course. Self-taught. But dedi-
cated, from time to time; she could never tell when he
was going to be running off somewhere in the middle
of a dig. Unreliable, and those eyes of his would never
be still! But they could speak German together, read
from German texts—and so she enjoyed him. He had
been to her house, and she to his—which was in Po-
lanco, she believed. Calle Goethe. Just let her check
her files a moment—*Ja!* Calle Goethe, 1233. Three
years ago that was, but still . . .

The architect who occupied the lower floor of 1233
Calle Goethe rented the building from Mr. Brenner,

316

yes, but he hadn't seen him for at least two years. All he knew of him was the address of a bank in the Cayman Islands where he sent his rent payments. Or, no...there *was* an address that he'd forwarded a package to once, somewhere up in that new section of Lomas on the Toluca highway, almost to the Desert of Lions. Would they mind terribly coming back in the morning and he would dig around for it? *Pues*, if it was urgent...

If you *were* anybody—a foreigner or a millionaire who lived like a foreigner—you lived in Lomas. And Lomas was growing, Brick saw as the Volkswagen climbed into country that had been no more than shacks and two-shelf grocery stores when he had last been here. The older white, walled houses gave way to angled, decked, landscaped, glass-heavy ones as they wound through the new section on rain-slick roads. New people who wanted to show their money, not keep it hidden behind walls in the old way. Foolish people, in a country of the poor like Mexico.

The address the architect had given them was one of the new houses. It was after dark by the time they found it. Brick drove past it twice. The garage was shut, so he couldn't tell if there were cars in it or not. And there were few lights on, few enough that they could have been left on only to trick burglars. Damn it, he had wanted some sign, something that would keep him from having to go in blind.

He pulled off the road at last on a lot where a new house was going up, a couple of hundred yards down the mountain. As he did, Sevda touched his arm and said, "Are you OK? Want to come back in the daylight?"

"I think daylight's the last thing I want now."

"It's almost over."

317

"Yeah."

She leaned over and kissed him. "It is, I know it."

He kissed her back and thought, Two lovers parked on a dark road. And then, Another good lie. He pulled away and opened the door. Don't think. Keep going, keep going. Turn the page. "You can stay here, if you want to."

"Now?"

They walked the distance to the house on the opposite side of the road, keeping as much as they could to the shadows of the eucalyptus trees. Beside them the land fell away into a deep *barranca,* and on the far side of it, shacks clung to the hillside. The yellow light of kerosene lanterns spilled from them. A hell of a lot more than a *barranca* separated them from these new houses, Brick thought as they stopped in front of the one that might be Brenner's. On the edge of a cliff, Brenner, on the edge of a cliff.

They waited for a truck to whine down past them from the mountain, then dashed. At the house, they crouched in the shadows beside the garage and listened. From somewhere, very faintly, music came. Subdued and moody music. Debussy, Brick guessed, maybe *La Mer.* It seemed to come from the walls of the house itself; there was no locating the listener by the sound alone. Cautiously, they moved around the house, Brick expecting at each step that some sort of radar burglar alarm would blast at them.

There were no lights at all upstairs and none in the front of the house. At the back corner, off a small concrete patio, a bare bulb lit up an empty maid's room. Then farther, a dim counter light glowed in a kitchen, where clean dishes in a drying rack waited to be put away. The maid was already done for the evening, then, was off in the shadows of another backyard with a gardener or a houseboy. They rounded another corner. Only one other room was lit, a room with wooden shutters partially closed. Now they could tell: this was the room the music came from. In it, a color television with the volume turned off flickered—people were trying to climb a greased pole while a pudgy MC cheered them on. A record spun on a turntable beside the TV. Books lined the wall, and a desk sat just below the window. The shutters hid the rest of the room— except for a pair of feet in men's house slippers and a table with a decanter of brandy on it.

"It could be anybody," Sevda whispered. "Somebody we've never heard of."

"You want to ring the doorbell and find out?"

"You're not serious, are you?"

"No. Come on."

They made their way back across the wet grass to the concrete patio by the maid's room. The wrought-iron gate was unlocked, but closed with a bolt that made a painful, long screech as Brick reached through and pulled it. They ducked and waited. Another truck whined by, then silence returned. In it, Brick heard Sevda let out a long breath.

The maid had slipped out of the kitchen in a hurry after the last dish was done, Brick figured. The door was closed, but not locked. It opened with a soft click. Inside the kitchen, they stopped to listen. The music ended, there was the sound of an automatic turntable, and now a Vivaldi succeeded the Debussy—probably not Wolf Brenner's taste, either one. Brick's stomach sank as he realized whose taste they were.

They followed a slant of light from a half-closed door. Brick held out his arm for Sevda to get behind him, flush against the wall, before he stepped to the door.

319

"Roger," he said. "It's Brick."

The music metronomed on monotonously for a moment. "Well, hell, old Brick." The words that came from the room were slurred. "Come on in and have a drink with Unca Roger."

"I don't have a gun, Roger," Brick said.

"Mercy. Neither do I. Hate guns."

Brick eased the door open and stepped in. Roger sprawled in an easy chair. He raised a snifter of brandy to Brick. "Cheers," he said.

Brick motioned for Sevda to come in. When Roger saw her, he shoved himself to his feet and made an unsteady bow. "Why, Miss Sabri. Absolutely charmed. We can have us a real little fiesta now!"

"Hello, Roger," Sevda said. Her voice was flat, but gentle.

"One of my most trusted advisers, was Miss Sevda Sabri, Brick. Read everything on the Kurds that came across my desk. Even your stuff. Graduate students—they work cheap and they're smart. Brandy? Something else?"

"You by yourself?" Brick asked. He wasn't shocked that Roger knew Sevda; it was logical that he would. But he was disappointed. Roger had beat him even to her.

"All alone."

Brick poured himself and Sevda snifters of brandy. Roger offered Sevda his chair. She refused it and spread herself out on a Spanish-colonial bench beneath a bookcase. Brick took the desk chair, and Roger sank back into his easy chair. "Just get in?" he asked.

"Couple of days ago," Brick said.

"You work quick, old friend. How'd you find me? El old Grupo? Jack Callahan?"

"Jack's dead, Roger."

"Old Jack? Did you do it?"

"No."

"Then I don't think I want to know. Never mind how you found me. Have you seen Claire?"

"Yes."

"Does she miss me? How about the boys?"

"She misses you. She says the boys are fine."

"I think you always had a crush on Claire, old Brick. Anything come of that?"

Brick glanced at Sevda, who sloshed her brandy and studied it. "She wants you home, Roger."

"Question answered. I deserved it, I suppose. Ali Sabri's not here, you know. And you're a bastard."

"Did you think that when you were in my room in Trabzon?"

Roger stopped his brandy snifter in mid-sip, looked at Brick through it, then finished it. "I didn't think anything. I saw somebody who wasn't you, and I just didn't think anything. If it had been you... well, you know better than that. If you don't, there's a pistol in that desk drawer. You're welcome to it." He poured himself another drink. "I'm drunker than owlshit, Brick."

"Where *is* my uncle?" Sevda said.

"I'm out of that, you know. I am, Brenner is, Livia is. All got fired. I *know* I'm out, but Brenner and Livia just won't give it up. Watch out for that little wimp, Brick. Waaaay on the other side of the river, that one is. Me, I'm going to buy me a planter's hat and sit on a verandah somewhere down here and drink rum and rot."

"How'd you get involved with him, Roger?" Brick asked.

"Like I told you, sort of. Scout's honor. Livia just

walked into my office one day. Blap! She was Brenner's student, you know. Her parents went bankrupt—though I suppose she gave you that song and dance about them being millionaires still. She just couldn't stand the notion of being dependent on old Tony forever, I guess. Or something. See how simple it all is? Old greed. Got me, got Livia, always has had Brenner. And to answer your question, Sevda—your uncle is somewhere you don't have a snowball's chance of getting him out of. Truly sorry, but he is. More brandy?"

"But where, Roger, *where?*" Sevda said.

"Do you more harm than good to know." His head lolled back on the chair. Brick reached to the table and eased the brandy bottle off it. "In the kitchen," he said softly to Sevda. "Find some coffee."

"Coffee ruins good brandy," Roger said. He sat up. "Just not sleeping, old Brick. Not for days and days and days."

Brick looked for a clear space on the cluttered desk to put the brandy bottle down in. There wasn't one. He shifted the least important looking of the loose papers to the side. The empty Aeromexico ticket envelope that slipped from under the utility bills and advertisements normally wouldn't have stopped him. But when it fell off the desk, he picked it up and saw the name penciled on it. Rustin. He held it a minute, then dropped it into a wastebasket.

"How long ago was my old man here, Roger?" he asked casually.

"This afternoon," Roger answered as casually. "Sorry about him, too. You know, I really, truly had no idea it would get this—complicated when I got him involved. Just a little consultant's work, put us in touch with a couple of people, pay off his mortgage...keep it in the family. I had no idea at all. Especially about the whole ridiculous Nicaraguan affair."

Brick reached for Roger's glass and poured him another drink, waiting. To hell with it; this wouldn't be the first time Roger had gotten stinking drunk. Just stay awake a little longer, a couple of more pieces longer...

Sevda was alert, her back straight on the hard bench. "Nicaragua?" she said when Roger didn't go on.

"Well, whoops," Roger said. "Seems I said the magic word. OK. Yes siree, here we go. Nicaragua. Your Agèd Parent is heading for Nicaragua, Brick. Your uncle is already *in* Nicaragua. Mrs. Lo Presti, née Livia, is *in* Nicaragua. There. Where's my duck, Groucho?"

"Roger, sit up, damn it." Brick leaned over and took Roger's arm. "Talk to me."

Roger's heavy eyes met Brick's and strained to focus on them. After a time, he gave up the effort and reached for Brick. "Hug my neck, you bastard," he said.

Brick knelt beside him, and Roger buried his head in Brick's shoulder. "It's all fucked up, old Brick."

"I know, Roger. I know." There was no anger in Brick now. Pity, yes. And the knowledge of one more goddamn thing he wanted intact again. But all the king's horses, and all the king's men..."Tell me about it."

Roger pushed away. He tried to compose himself, reached for his drink, and knocked it onto the floor. He stared at it sadly a moment. "They came in here one night, you know. Two weeks, fifteen days ago. Just Ali Sabri and Livia and myself at home. We hadn't even been here long enough for el old Grupo to talk to Ali Sabri yet. 'Bout six of them came in, little dusky devils with guns. Then they just walked out with Ali Sabri—bye, all gone! Oh, was Brenner unhappy. But it was his fault, no bout adout it. Right? Where's my drink?"

Brick handed him his own. "I want to see it all come out all right, Brick. I really do. Maybe after a while we can go to Costa Rica or somewhere, huh? Claire and the boys come down, you move down. Old days?"

"Old days," Brick said.

"It was that bank of Brenner's that did it all. Listen to me. Just before Somoza went under in Nicaragua, the whole national bank of Nicaragua went out of the country through Brenner's phony bank. Seven, eight hundred million. When the Sandinista people got hold of it, there wasn't even enough left to pay their postage with. Real down for 'em. Well, they want it back, of course, so they've got lawsuits filed against everybody and his brother in half-a-dozen countries. But that's slow. Aaaand, they've got a bona fide revolution to make work down there, and people to feed and such, so some of them just don't seem in the mood to wait. Logical?"

"Logical," Sevda said.

"So they keep close tabs on Herr Doktor Wolf Brenner. They know what's up, so when he hits quaint old Mexico with Ali Sabri—snatch! Now they've got something he needs back. Hell, they've got something el hot-shot Grupo Primero needs back, more to the point, methinks. So comes the message: we've got him, you pay. El Grupo gets upset and has somebody in the Mexican government yell at the Nicaraguans, and comes back el message that the Nicaraguan government doesn't know anything about it. The people

who have Ali Sabri are some bunch down there—
some 'faction' we'd have called it in the good old *Middle Eastern Desk*—that they don't control. Meaning,
I do reckon, that yeah, they know he's there and they
sure as hell would like a few hundred million but they
can't *officially* condone anything like that, so they're
going to sit on their hands. Do you blame them?"

"Not at all," Sevda said. There was admiration in
her voice.

"So Brenner starts negotiating. Livia flies off to
Managua with all sorts of Brenner's ideas for stalling.
But el Grupo has decided we're all a bad investment,
so they can us. And *they* start wanting to negotiate.
Well, they need an honest broker. And I'm most righteously unhappy about the way things have turned
out, so I find them one—somebody officially connected with the United States of America government, which bunches of people still more or less trust
for some mad reason. I figure that way everybody's
more likely to come out of this in one piece than if
Brenner's handling it. And *le violà!*"

"Has the old man left for Nicaragua yet?" Brick
said.

"This evening, I think."

"Does Brenner know about it?"

"Gracious, no. Not yet. El Grupo should be telling
him about it just about now."

"Then what in hell are you still doing here?"

"Well, I really don't know. Not to worry. Got my
pistol—I *do* hate them, truly." He struggled to his feet
and fumbled with the desk drawer. "Good old pistol,
all right. Right here?"

Brick eased him back into his chair.

"Where can we take him?" Sevda said. She put her
brandy down and came to help Brick with him.

"The hotel for now."

"No, no. Unca Roger's going to unmess his own mess this time." He batted Sevda's and Brick's hands away.

"Roger," Sevda said, easing his hand down and holding it. "How is Brick's father going to find my uncle?" She was gentling him, the way you would a skittish horse.

"Why, through old Hoover Blue, of course. There's a name for you, Brick!"

"Who's Hoover Blue?" Sevda said in the same gentle voice. She was good at this, Brick thought. She'd read Roger from the time they came in.

"Right there's Hoover Blue." Roger pointed to the desk drawer. Brick opened it and beneath the revolver found an address in Roger's neat handwriting: "In front of Texaco Station, kilometer 46, Old Leon Highway."

"This one?" Brick said.

"The very one. Hoover Blue's. I don't think they have proper addresses down there. Primitive, primitive."

"Who *is* Hoover Blue?"

"Haven't the slightest. Just the man we're supposed to contact." His head slipped to the side again. Brick caught Sevda's eye. She nodded. Brick stood and put his hands beneath Roger's arms.

"OK, cowboy," he said. "Can you walk?"

"No place I want to walk," Roger mumbled, and slapped weakly at the chair.

Brick heaved him to his feet. Roger tottered, and Brick ducked under his arm to hold him. "Get the other one," he said to Sevda.

They started for the door, Roger hanging between them like a thief on the cross. He mumbled something but didn't protest. Then at the door, he found his footing and shoved back into the room. Sevda lost his arm and he tumbled back away from Brick. He bounced off a bookcase and the needle shrownked across Vivaldi. Brick grabbed for him but Roger lurched past him to the door. "Going home," he said. "Don't like bloody cheap hotels."

The hallway exploded just as Roger staggered into it. Exploded three quick times, and with each explosion Roger jerked. On the last one, his ear vanished. Sevda took a half step toward him, but Brick flung her back into the room. "Behind the chair—shit, *somewhere!*" he yelled at her. He fumbled in the open desk drawer for the pistol, grasped it, dropped it, found it again. He couldn't see Roger in the door anymore. He fired twice at nothing, for the noise, and dove for the floor. Sevda screamed, her voice buried under the shots. Brick dragged himself to the door and fired blindly into the hallway. Nothing answered him. He inched forward again and took a chance—his head rapidly into the hallway and back before whoever was there could aim. He hoped.

The hallway was empty. Brick heard the sound of a door slamming toward the front of the house. He scrambled up, into the hallway and through a dark living room. A mirror on the wall rocked in reflected light. Brick jerked the door open. For the barest moment, he met Wolf Brenner's darting eyes in the streetlight, and then Brenner was in the car, wheels spinning on the wet grass, slaloming onto the highway. Brick closed the door slowly.

He found Sevda kneeling beside Roger. Roger smelled like a broken bottle of brandy. He lay with his head turned toward the wall and a leg tucked up underneath him as if he had been wanting to crawl away, to hide. Sevda was trembling, and crying softly. Brick sat next to her on the carpet. After a time, he let his hand trail over Roger's shoulders. It bothered him that Roger looked so uncomfortable. With luck, Claire would never know how it happened. Burglars, she would probably be told.

He took Sevda's hand. "We have to go," he said, forming words a burden. "Before anybody comes."

She nodded and closed her eyes a moment, squeezing the tears out of them. Then she wiped her cheeks with her fingers, a scrubbing motion as if she were trying to brush away spider webs. "We can't stop, Brick," she said.

"There's nothing else we *can* do," he said.

"We can get to my uncle and to Tony's wife before the others do."

"For God's sake, why?"

"To get them out of there—wherever *there* is."

"Aren't there enough people doing that already?"

"For what—so that this can all start over again? So that they can be brought back to Mexico? Or what if the price is too high for Grupo Primero? What if my uncle isn't 'cost effective' enough?"

Nothing in Brick wanted to go on, no part of him wanted to learn more. He was as certain of that now as he had been certain once that he had wanted to. There was no edge at all now; he looked at Roger's body in the dim light and he knew he was scraped dull and flat as the head of a hammer. But he realized, too, that he *had* to want to go on—no, that he had to *do* it. It was because he didn't want it anymore that he had to see it through, precisely because of that. It wasn't the other people anymore that he needed, nor this puzzle, but something in himself. If he was to salvage anything intact, to make sense for himself, it would have to all be based on this: so many goddamned unfinished books opened in his life. There couldn't be another one. He was thirty-two. This one had to be finished, to the impossible last page.

They stepped around Roger's still body. At the end of the hallway, Brick hesitated, but didn't look back.

Nine

Empty lots, weeds, a few cracked buildings, smatterings of rubble. Here and there a raw new fountain in the beginnings of a park, or a bulldozer crawling across a heap of dirt like a dung beetle, trailed by a ragtag crowd salvaging the scrap metal it scratched up. In the near distance beside Lake Managua the lonely cathedral and government palace and national theater, unlikely survivors. Downtown Managua once, the taxi driver had told him, before the great earthquake a decade ago. Maybe downtown Managua again, since the revolution. Someday.

Frank Rustin. The name had been in the register, all right. A room in the same wing of the hotel as Brick's, a couple of floors down. Brick would have to go to it soon, knock and wait the agonizing seconds as his father's footsteps approached the door, then

face his father's face. His father wouldn't be angry.
It wouldn't be that easy. He would try to overwhelm
Brick with reason, with fatherliness. And what
would the son answer, Brick wondered. How would
he explain the reason he was here, tracing his father
to this strange, pyramid-shaped Hotel Intercontinental that looked out over the desolation of a ruined
city? What would he "propose" to his father? What
would he *demand* of him? Christ, Christ, Christ.

He paced impatiently onto his balcony and leaned
through the flower pots that lined the low wall.
Where the hell was Sevda? She had been unpacking
for what seemed an hour. They were safe enough
from Brenner for the moment—he hadn't been foolish enough to risk taking the same flight down that
they'd taken—and Brick's father was no problem as
long as he was still here in the hotel. But damn it,
now of all times he had to move, to not allow himself
to take anything apart.

On the street below, toward the grounds of Somoza's grim former command bunker, a Cuban officer, arrogant in a tailored uniform, lectured his
driver beside a Land Rover. Here and there kids in
pieces of fatigue uniforms—some with M-16s, some
with Uzi machine guns, some with old shotguns—
hung around guarding nothing in particular. Beyond
them, a row of battered taxis waited under magnolia
trees, their drivers alert to any chance to change
Nicaraguan cordobas for black-market dollars or ru-
bles or marks with the hotel's guests. No hurry, nothing in a hurry but Brick himself. Brick half hoped
he would see the familiar lope of his father getting
into one of the taxis, done somehow with his nego-
tiations and on his way out of his son's life again.
Then it would be too late to stop him, too late to keep

this Turkish puzzle-ring of events from locking into
place forever as some fate, some *kismet,* surely had
wanted it to do all along. Then he could go down to
the pool, order a drink with Sevda, and let all these
other people's lives slip away from him. Maybe Roger
had been right, he thought as he felt the soft air lull
him and watched the thunderheads build lazily out
over the great blue lake. A planter's hat and endless
rum and a shady porch, and to hell with the rest.
Roger, the poor bastard: he hadn't even been able to
save *him,* who had been his best friend once.

Brick hadn't written Claire—wouldn't write her.
It wasn't cowardice. Hard as getting the news in a
phone call from somebody in the State Department
would be, it would be less brutal than the answers
he would have to give her if she got it from him. He
would see her when he got home—if he got home.

He shoved away from the wall. He was doing it,
was taking things apart, damn it. In his room, the
wall clock showed that the hour he thought he'd been
waiting for Sevda was more like twenty minutes.
He'd give her ten more minutes, time for him to at
least check on the next flight Brenner could be on—
and to have a drink before they went to see his father.
Patience, he heard Ali Sabri's voice saying, patience.

The lobby that Brick shouldered his way through
to the bar was an isthmian Casablanca. A party of
baggy, bearish Russians trooped through counting
their fresh, black-market cordobas, comparing rates.
On a couch along the wall, a conversation in German
stopped in mid-guttural while the Russians lumbered by. A Japanese businessman complained about
something to the desk clerk in an utterly incompre-
hensible English and the desk clerk nodded as if he
comprehended; next to him, a tall American shouted

something about an editor into a telephone. Latins clustered and cast suspicious eyes at one another as they apparently tried to figure out each other's accent: Mexican, Cuban, Argentinian, and a handful of others that Brick didn't pretend to have enough Spanish to recognize. And beneath it all, the sultry, slurred Spanish of Nicaragua beat like a rhythm section from bellhops, doormen, maids, high-class hawkers.

The bar came almost as a relief, a plush, plastic cave where nothing seemed to move. A gray, military-looking Englishman droned to a bored couple about something in Egypt once; a pair of local lounge lizards with gold crosses around their necks stalked a stewardess; a pianist, his face incapable of irony, sang a bad English version of "Mañana is Good Enough for Me"—a school for patience he didn't have time to learn from, Brick thought as he threw down a shot of dark, thick Nicaraguan rum and plunged back into the noisy lobby.

"One Lanica flight a day from Mexico City, sir," the clerk told him without checking. "You were on it." Brick thanked him, relieved, and turned away. "Oh, Mr. Rustin!" the clerk called after him. "Are you and the *señorita* still going to keep your rooms for the night?"

"Why shouldn't we?"

"Well, since the other Mr. Rustin checked out, I thought maybe..."

"He checked out? When?"

"Just before you checked in, I believe."

"Damn it, you told me you had him in the register."

"I did, yes, sir. But, you see, the cashier has to make out a report, and it has to be posted, and..."

334

The elevator was too slow, clogged with bellhops propping the door open to load and unload bags. Brick took the stairs three at a time, gulping the heavy tropical air, lunging past a cringing family of Jamaicans. The "corridor guard," another kid in a piecemeal uniform, stood up in alarm as he pounded on Sevda's door.

The papers for the rental car took forever. Rain marched in great sheets across the devastated city in front of the Intercontinental like some kind of Biblical plague, and windowpanes rattled with thunder. The revolver nested well beneath the loose *guayabera* wedding shirt Brick had bought to hide it. If his father got to somebody named Hoover Blue before they did, they would lose the one thing they had on their side: surprise. There would be no walking up to whoever had Ali Sabri and bluffing until they had a chance to slip him away. Where Brick went now, the revolver went.

"Visa or Master Charge?" the bright-faced girl at the Avis desk asked.

"Some revolution," Sevda muttered.

Hoover Blue was everybody's only key to finding Ali Sabri. So it was a race now: Brick's father had a head start, and Brenner wasn't here yet. But they were all in it, and they would all finish it, no matter how different their reasons. Brick wondered about his father's reasons—money, yes, but maybe stubbornness, fear, the need to prove something to himself, too. Probably as tangled as his own reasons had been, though those were each day, each hour, less tangled.

The five-year-old Plymouth grunted and moaned for a good ten minutes before it cranked in the rain, the attendant all the while whispering to it as if it were an ailing mule. But, musty-smelling, ashtrays full, gas tank nearly empty, seat covers ripped, it ran.

They crawled through flowing streets north, toward where the Avis girl had told them the old highway to Leon ought to be. Within a mile or so from the hotel, the empty lots began to fill. More and more buildings that the earthquake had missed appeared, and squatters' shacks filled vacant land around improvised marketplaces. Signs painted in the red and black colors of the Sandinista revolutionary movement, peeling now, announced every few street corners the new names of neighborhoods, each one named for a dead hero of the revolution. At an occasional roundabout in the road, statueless pedestals cowered among the weeds. There had been Somozas on them once, dictators whose stone images had fallen, Brick thought, a hell of a lot more quickly than Ozymandias's. It was the century: everything was disposable, even history.

"What will you do if he's there, Brick?" Sevda asked. She strained to see through the rain ahead. She had said little since they left the hotel, but her face was drawn, her eyes avoiding his.

"My father? It's worse if he's *not* there. Then Hoover Blue probably won't be either."

"When do you expect Brenner?"

"Tomorrow."

"Then at the most we have just tonight for a head start."

"Just tonight."

She stared at a scrawny dog Brick steered around. "Your father will be there." The attempt at confidence in her voice failed badly. Brick reached out for her hand, but she was huddled against the door, too far away.

At the edge of the city, where a drenched high-school girl in fatigues (that a red lace bra peeked from) made a futile effort at directing traffic, Brick followed a leaning sign that pointed toward Leon, Old Highway. And history, disposable or not, backed up.

The buckling pavement was washed away altogether in places, as it cut past huge ceiba trees, whose trunks rose white and straight almost to the low thunderclouds before they branched out into an umbrella of leaves. Among orchards and banana patches and fallow cotton fields, potbellied kids stared out at them from the shelter of sparse cane lean-tos. Around the huts grew spreading, nameless trees that bore great red or yellow flowers bigger than the children's heads. The road climbed beside empty beaches along the lake, and in the rare moments when the rain slacked, the outline of a volcano showed jutting into the waters in the distance. They met no other cars. Now and again bedraggled cows sloshed across the road in front of them, herded by mounted men in rain ponchos, their faces hidden beneath hats pulled low against the slashing water.

And at kilometer 46, there *was* a Texaco station — of sorts. A wooden building with a rusted tin roof leaned away from a couple of forlorn gas pumps toward the forest, as if it were trying to escape from them. Next to it, a dozen rotting tables in the mud marked the site of a vanishing open-air restaurant. The only customer was the frame of a gutted tractor that sat upside down among the tables. And across the road from the station, whose Closed sign had been half chewed away by goats, spread the outbuildings and house of what once might have been a small farm or plantation.

Only the house was in half-decent repair now. It was a long tin-roofed wooden building with rough gingerbread along the broad porch and with pots and cans of flowers hung from every hangable spot the length of the porch. If it had been painted once, that had been long enough ago for the rains to have washed the last smudge away. Everything was a uniform gray except the hundreds of bright flowers—the flowers and the dress of the bony mulatto woman who sat among them in a rocking chair watching the old Plymouth slow.

There was no other car in sight. Sevda swore beneath her breath in Kurdish.

Brick stopped in front of the house and rolled his window down. *"Aqui vive Hoover Blue?"* he shouted over the heavy clatter of the rain.

"Hoover Blue's house, yes," the woman answered in English. The accent sounded loosely Caribbean.

"I'm looking for a man named Rustin. Has he been here?"

The woman rocked and regarded him a moment. Then, abruptly, she got up and disappeared into the house, screen door twanging behind her.

"Wrong question," Brick told Sevda.

After a time, the screen opened again. A man in his fifties, like the woman a mulatto, stepped out onto the porch. He was thickset, dressed in overalls and a torn T-shirt, and wore a baseball cap with CATERPILLAR on it. His face was guarded, but intelligent. Curls of graying hair straggled out from under the cap. His skin was lighter than the woman's, and his features were sharp, his cheekbones high

and prominent. He stooped at the edge of the porch
and peered through the window at Brick and Sevda.

"You asking for Hoover Blue, sir?" he asked in
the same Caribbean lilt as the woman.

"Yes. My name's Rustin."

"Oh, no, sir. Mr. Rustin been here and gone. That
won't do, sir."

"He's my father. I'm Rustin, too."

"Well, well. You sure will be if you don't come up
here out of the rain, sir. *I'm* Hoover Blue. If you
looking for me, we best talk."

"Mashallah," Sevda said with the sound of a
spring uncoiling.

They were Mosquito Indians, Hoover Blue and his
wife—a mix of Carib Indian and runaway Jamaican
slave—from the swampy Caribbean east coast of
Nicaragua called the Mosquito Shore. They spoke
English first, Mosquito dialect second, and Spanish
last, Blue told Brick while they ate. And so far as
Brick could gather from him, the Mosquitos and the
Nicaraguans did a pretty successful job of ignoring
each other—or had, until the revolution. Blue
seemed to like it best the old way—more money in
smuggling than in revolution. Or than in the Texaco
gas station business after the tourists got scared
away by the revolution.

"So what I have with this man, this Comandante
O'Brien—he got the name from a book, sir—is
purely a business arrangement." He said the phrase
lovingly, as if the notion of it pleased him greatly.
His wife boiled water for coffee at a wood stove, and
a kerosene lamp on the table they sat around spilled
yellow light on the remains of the fried plantains
and beans and stringy broiled beef she had stretched

to feed them all. "My home was near where his camp is now—it's in the jungle and plenty hard to find, I assure you. My mother has a little farm, a *finca,* near there still. So I take people to Comandante O'Brien, and he knows I will be careful who I bring because my mother lives so close to him."

The "careful" part had been the hardest to deal with. Blue had cocked his head and paced and fretted when they told him what they wanted; he had already sent his youngest boy along with one Mr. Rustin. What to do about a second one? Sevda had paced, too, and bribed and wept. Brick had reasoned and pleaded—and bribed. At fifteen hundred dollars, Blue had bent. At two thousand, he had crumpled. Except on one thing: it was too late to go today. Nothing could move him. Long way, sir, he said. Long way in the car, long way in a boat. First thing in the morning. Maybe still catch the first Mr. Rustin if he had had trouble finding a boat. Brick and Sevda could stay with him tonight, no charge. Supper included. Sevda had spent the rest of the afternoon in a funk on the porch, watching the rain. Supper had revived her somewhat—but not much.

"Ah, well," Blue went on. "I was told to bring a Mr. Rustin. Now there are two Mr. Rustins. How do I know which Mr. Rustin Comandante O'Brien wants to see?" He winked and patted his wife's almost nonexistent bottom as she plunked a cracked cup of coffee in front of him. The rain had settled into a steady drumroll on the tin roof, and a half dozen night moths dove in and out of the lamplight.

"On the Mosquito Shore, sir," Blue said. "We say about revolutions that they don't change the horses, they just change the riders. Maybe this one in Nicaragua is a different kind. They say it is. But Comandante O'Brien—I don't think anybody in the government likes him too much. The government wants to do things one way, to go slow for a while, and O'Brien wants to do them another way, to go quick time. So he says he's going off into the jungle to train guerrillas to fight in other countries. And the government is a deal afraid of him—he was a *comandante* in the revolution, so he's plenty popular, you know…so there he is, sir. There he is."

"Have you been in his camp?" Brick said.

"Oh, yes, sir. I took the lady there, didn't I?"

"Livia."

"That lady, sir. She was a friend of yours?"

Sevda made a noise with her coffee. Brick caught her eye and she gave him a saccharine smile. "Well, was she?" she said. Hoover Blue's wife sat down at the table and looked from Sevda to Brick and back and cackled softly to herself.

"I knew her," Brick said.

"Sure," Sevda said, and turned her smile on Blue's wife.

"A very nervous lady, Mrs. Lo Presti was," Blue went on.

"Was there a man there—somebody she might have been looking for? A foreigner?" Brick said.

"I don't know, sir. I don't stay long, you see."

"Does O'Brien have many men?"

"Quite a few, yes. Plenty, I believe."

"Plenty for what?"

"For whatever he needs." Blue took a bottle of *aguardiente* from a homemade cabinet beside the table and poured some into his coffee. "He is not a man I could be friends with, Mr. Rustin. I don't think I know *what* kind of horse he's riding." As he put the *aguardiente* back, an old kitchen clock on the cabinet

341

bonged mournfully. Blue stared at it until it stopped bonging, then heaved a great weary sigh. "Well. Early day coming, sir."

His wife popped up from her seat and scurried around the table toward a pink curtain that hung in a doorway off the kitchen, still cackling softly to herself. "Only got one extra bedroom," she said to the door as she went through it.

Blue sipped his coffee. Sevda said, "What did she say?"

"Only got one more bedroom," Blue said. "That going to do?"

A match flared behind the thin curtain of the room Blue's wife had gone into, then the light from a kerosene lantern glowed. "We'll see," Sevda said.

Brick lay listening to the diminishing sound of the rain, to the soft clucking of a hen beneath the wide floorboards, to the rustling of the straw-filled mattress beneath him as he tried to get comfortable on it. The warm smell of kerosene filled the room. The walls were bare wood, and empty except for a couple of old calendars, a yellowed newspaper photo of Herbert Hoover, and a framed color print of Queen Victoria. Somehow he felt at ease here, back in a place where things could go slowly enough to be looked at one by one as they passed—not always jumbling by as on some gigantic, confused modernist mural which you could make out only a few abstract pieces of at a time. Not that the sense of urgency, of hurry, was gone. Sevda's presence reminded him of that, as she busied herself laying out her jeans and tightly tailored shirt—her graduate student uniform—for the morning.

He didn't imagine she looked forward to the morn-

Robert Houston

ing any more than he did, or had any more idea of
what it would bring. He let his eyes wander down
her back, linger on her tight, half-teardrop-shaped
butt, then moved down her dress to the strong curve
of her legs. He liked her back; Christ, he liked *her,*
in a way he hadn't been able to like a woman in a
long time. He liked her toughness and wiliness,
didn't really mind her defensiveness, admired her
certainty of purpose as he had Ali Sabri's—even
softened around the edges as it was by a kind of
naiveté that he understood. He remembered the
Kurdish woman who had given them ice on Ararat,
as he watched Sevda's gold bracelets flash in the
lamplight. What would she think of Sevda? She
would approve, he thought.

Approve in a way she could never approve of
Livia's sophistication, no matter how much in awe
of it she had been.

The thought of Livia stirred something in the pit
of his stomach, in his groin, that he wished hadn't
followed him here to this room, with Sevda in it. He
would see Livia tomorrow, at last. There were no
telephones left for her to hide behind, no London
streets for her to vanish into. The last piece of all
was ready to fall into place. And he wished that it
weren't.

"Brick." Sevda's voice surprised him with its softness, as it had in the firehouse in Virginia. "Are you
afraid?"

"A little," he said, knowing that they weren't talking about the same thing at all.

She gave her jeans a last pat and came and sat
on the straw mattress next to his. "About Tony's
wife, Brick—you haven't talked much about her."

"No, I haven't."

343

Her chocolate eyes ran quickly over his face. "Would you like to?"

"She's Tony's wife, that's all."

"Were you in love with her?"

Brick turned onto his back. The sound of the straw filled the room like a rush of wind. He watched shadows from the lamp play on the rough beams of the ceiling. "Yes."

"Did you know her very well?"

"Hardly at all."

Sevda made a clicking noise with her tongue. "Well," she said. "I suppose that can be the roughest kind."

"Can be."

"Do you still love her?"

"I'll find out tomorrow, I imagine."

"And you have to know that, don't you?"

"Yes."

The room sank back into the near-silence of the rain again. Brick heard the rustling of Sevda's mattress, and after a moment she blew the lantern out. In the darkness he heard her dress unzip, then slide off. And then he felt, not heard, her next to him. Her hair brushed his temples as she leaned and kissed him gently. "Good night," she said. "Good luck tomorrow."

When she had settled on her mattress, he reached across the dark space between them and found her hand. She let him take it, and held on. "Good night," he said. After a few minutes, her hand relaxed, and he heard the even breathing of sleep and realized the rain had stopped. The morning would be dry. He dreaded it.

They were leaving the lake and climbing by the time the sun caught them. A low, smoking volcano

rose at an easy slope from the cornfields beside them
on their left, close enough to sprint to. And in the
near distance on their right, the larger volcano Brick
had seen jutting out of the lake yesterday hid the
sun long enough to allow it to burst before them
across the lake fully risen. When it did, the world
was green, everywhere a dozen shades of green. A
mist seemed to breathe out from the earth itself, to
glow in the early sunlight and veil the ceiba trees
and cows and the morning glories that covered the
rail fences and the orchids that hung in tree branches
and the rounded mountains that stood before them
like the first mountains in creation. Everything was
just enough out of focus, softened just enough by the
mist to cause doubt that it was really there, the way
you might doubt the shape of a memory too far in
the past.

And then they were in the mountains themselves,
with a string of newborn volcanoes like a picket fence
behind them and sleepy, barefoot people watching
them pass from lean-to kitchens tacked onto reed
houses. The air was cool; the sharp smell of woodsmoke and the clean, rich smell of tortillas baking
on *comales* followed them through green valleys the
sun hadn't yet reached, and horses hardly bigger
than ponies bounded away from the road ahead of
them. In a ramshackle mountain town called Al-
varado they stopped at a truckers' cafe for a breakfast of eggs and slabs of pork roasted over an open
fire. A picture of Che Guevara hung over the cash
register, and the cashier took them outside to show
them the houses that Somoza had bombed in his last
fit of fury before he flew away to Miami. She wept;
Sevda hugged her; Brick was embarrassed.

By midmorning the land had flattened to a series

of low hills into which rivers cut deep, raw gorges. The towns became settlements of wooden shacks with names like Monkey Face and Fishnet Wharf that clustered in muddy disorder beside bridges or along vegetation-clogged riverbanks. There were fewer fields now, and more stretches of forest; fewer people, and more wasteland of swamp and abandoned banana plantation. And then when they came to the town called El Rama, the road stopped entirely. And with it, Brick thought, stopped the illusion that something called the twentieth century really existed. The mud that clogged the few streets of El Rama could have been the thick primeval mud of the morning of time itself, trying to suck them back into itself.

"No more car, sir," Hoover Blue said as they slogged out into the mud in front of a long, two-storey wooden building with sagging galleries running the length of the upper storey like something from a nineteenth-century tintype of an end-of-the-earth colonial outpost. "Only boats now."

Brick scanned the cluster of wooden buildings, the trails that led off into the jungle, the rutted street that fell away into the olive water of a broad, slow river. Next to the building they stood in front of, from which dangled a faded sign that read Hotel Wong, a wire enclosure surrounded a generator, a family of pigs, a dozen monkeys in cages, and a tribe of bright macaws. Three or four dogs lay on the wooden porch, and half-a-score more slunk in Brownian patterns through the mud. Across the street a scarred wooden bus, its nose pointed back toward Managua, idled alongside the cracked and dusty windows of a general store. A dugout canoe left a long silver wake as it paddled toward the vine-choked ruins of an old hacienda manor house across the river.

"Yep," Brick said. "No more car. Did my father come this way?"

"It's the only way, sir," Blue said.

"If he's still here, where would he be?"

They made a futile attempt to scrape mud off their shoes on the hotel steps. "Right here," Blue said. "It's the only place."

"OK, then," Brick said. "Give me a minute."

The inside of the building was dim, a high-ceilinged cavern of a room where a dozen tables sprawled in the semblance of a restaurant. As his eyes adjusted, Brick made out a few dusty game fish on the walls, some flyblown beer advertisements tacked here and there, and a Chinaman. The Chinaman sat behind a counter at the end of the room, as dusty and still and dry as the stuffed swordfish above his head. A score of keys hung from a plywood board behind him. He gave no sign that he noticed Brick—or noticed anything, even the ancient jukebox that blinked in the corner and blared a Freddy Fender hillbilly song so loud the floor shook.

Only the Chinaman, a couple of the kids with ragtag uniforms who sipped Cokes by the jukebox, and a barefoot man passed out at a table occupied the room. Brick crossed to a window. An empty patio, once a dance floor, crumbled into the river. There was no one else in sight.

"Tiene habitaciones?" he asked the Chinaman. "Do you have rooms?"

The Chinaman nodded.

"Is there a man named Rustin in one of them?"

The Chinaman shook his head.

"Was there last night?"

Another head shake.

"Any gringos at all?"

"Last night," the Chinaman said. His voice barked like a Chihuahua's above the noise of the jukebox. "He left on a boat this morning."

"What did he look like?"

The Chinaman shrugged. "A little like you. Older." He broke out into a gap-toothed grin. "You want a room?"

Sevda waited in the door, her body a dark outline in the watery light. She followed Brick back out onto the porch. "He's gone, isn't he?" she said.

"Yep."

"When?"

"This morning."

"Would he have had time to get to the camp?" she asked Hoover Blue.

"Oh, yes, ma'am."

"Well." She slumped into a one-armed rocking chair. "That's it. Right?"

"Is it?" Brick said.

"You tell *me*," Sevda said. "He's had time to make his deal—if it goes through. What could we possibly say now? Before, maybe we could have pretended to be from Grupo Primero—something!—long enough to get into the camp and figure a way out again. What do you want to do now? Make a commando raid? Allah!"

"Maybe." Motion, Brick thought. Stop the motion now, Rustin, and it's all over. Keep going. You're too close.

"Allah, Allah!"

"Look," Brick said to Blue. "Is there a way to get into that camp without being seen?"

"Not likely, sir."

"I don't care about likely. Is it *possible?*"

"Oh, maybe at night someway. I don't want to try it, sir."

"I don't want you to. But could you get us *close* to the place at night? And back out again?"

"Well..."

Sevda broke in. "That's foolish, Brick."

"Damn foolish," he told her. Then, to Blue again, "Can you do it?"

"Oh, the lady is right, sir. I don't like to make Comandante O'Brien angry. It's a plenty big risk, all around, sir."

"How much money do we have left?" Brick asked Sevda.

"How much will it take?" She looked to Blue.

Blue studied the slow approach of a mule across the road. "Five hundred more dollars."

"We've got it," Sevda said to Brick. *"After* he gets us out of there."

"Well?" Brick said. "Done?"

Hoover Blue edged a wet lizard off the porch with his toe. "Got to find a boat."

"How long will you need?" Brick looked at his watch. Its face was blank, the digits short-circuited by the humidity that steamed off the river and leaked out of the mud. "Can we make it by to-night?"

"Depends who's got a boat to rent, sir."

Brick took his watch off. "First man that volunteers a boat, give him this. Promise him that it works every place but here."

The boat was a *bungo,* a long dugout with an electric trolling motor rigged onto its flat stern. All there was, sir, Hoover Blue claimed. The other Mr. Rustin

had already rented the only launch in El Rama.
Nothing else but the big passenger boat that ran
downriver to the old British colonial port of Bluefields, on the Caribbean. And it wouldn't do for them
to take that one, would it, sir? Oh, no, sir. Full of
people.

A cloud of mosquitos followed them onto the river;
they lost them just about the time they lost El Rama,
a half mile down the river at the first bend. And
when they lost El Rama, they lost all sense of the
shape of things. The river—the Rio Escondido—
wandered past one last small hill, then stretched
itself out for a flat, winding course through a land
for which it was the only road. Now and again they
passed a canoe paddling slowly along the shore, fishing or filled with a peasant family heading upriver
toward El Rama for supplies. Most of the houses were
stilted huts on the riverbank with cane frames in
front of them from which small *bungos* were hung
high enough to avoid rising flood waters. Once they
passed a young mother and child swimming naked
in front of a hut; they flashed smiles from broad
Indian faces and made no attempt to cover themselves. As they moved further away from El Rama,
even the huts thinned. Cleared land left from the
banana-plantation days showed up occasionally,
steadily turning itself back over to the jungle, but
now trees and lianas and scrub undergrowth ruled
the long, unbroken stretches. The only things they
saw swimming here were the snakes, whose heads
sliced the water like periscopes, and crocodiles, who
watched them with lazy, heavy eyes beside great
floating islands of lily pads. The sky was clouding
again; in patches of sun the river shone silver, in
shadow it turned a dull green that mirrored darkly

the hanging trees and vines. Even El Rama seemed
civilized from here. They had come to a place not
only beyond even the basic shapes of civilization, but
beyond people themselves.

The sun had vanished by the time Blue aimed the
boat up a small stream that cut into the river from
the north. It might have been evening. The clouds
were so thick now that Brick couldn't tell whether
they or the turning of the earth was responsible for
the sun's disappearance. Sheet lightning flashed in
the eastern sky, toward the sea, and faint thunder
rolled in from the distance. The air was as still as
the drab water beneath them.

No one had spoken much. Hoover Blue gave Brick
a series of meaningless, uneasy nods whenever they
caught each other's eye. They spoke even less after
they dragged the boat onto the slick yellow mud of
a rough landing beside half-a-dozen other canoes and
headed up a trail into the forest.

At first the trail was broad and traveled, with
smaller trails leading off it into the undergrowth.
But as true darkness settled, it narrowed into no
more than a path. Brick took the revolver from the
waistband of his jeans and dropped it into the side-
pocket of his *guayabera* shirt, his hand resting on it,
ready. Every few minutes, Blue ran the beam of a
pocket flashlight ahead of them to get a sense of the
direction of the path. But mostly they walked in
darkness, Blue leading, Brick and Sevda following
and slapping away branches that raked at them or
spider webs that clung to them like wet threads. Now
and again things crashed away from them in the
dark forest; and Brick felt Sevda's hand touch him.

When they left the path, it was for an even smaller

one that Blue seemed to have found by touch. And then all paths stopped.

"There, sir," Blue whispered. Through the growth to the left Brick made out a faint glow, like the lights of a distant town. "I stay here."

"Where the hell are we?" Brick said.

"We come around to the side, sir. Through the bushes a way yonder, then across a little yucca patch that belong my mother, then some more bushes— you going to see the camp then, where the lights are. Go quiet."

"And you?"

"I'm going to be watching for you. Right here. But not watching till daylight, sir—I got to go before daylight. You too, sir."

With Blue's flashlight, they made their way through the first patch of growth. It had been cleared land once, and the vegetation hadn't yet had time to thicken. Nonetheless, briars ripped at their jeans and twigs crunched beneath their feet loud as firecrackers. Their best cover was the rising and falling roar of the insects, a shouting match of clicks and screeches above a steady undertone of wings. By the time they dashed through the waist-high yucca plants, Brick's pants were soaked with the dew and his face stung with sweat. The last twenty feet of bushes and vines they crossed on hands and knees. The glow of lights was bright enough to let them see outlines of the trees around them by now, but not bright enough for them to avoid the soft things that wriggled beneath their palms in the loam. When Brick stopped and Sevda moved up beside him, she shuddered and raked her hands against her wet blouse. They lay on their stomachs, hidden by the brush.

Robert Houston

"I've got one pistol. It's got six bullets in it." Brick whispered. "You understand what I'm saying?"

Sevda scanned the encampment. "Then throw it away. You might as well use it on *us*."

"Not yet. Not damn yet."

Before them, in the artificial brightness of floodlights mounted on trees, a dozen or more cane huts ringed a large clearing. Half of them were big enough to serve as small barracks or arsenals. The rest were no larger than the Indians' huts they had passed on the river. Men (and a few women) dressed in parts of fatigue uniforms or in jeans and undershirts sat on rough wooden steps in front of the barrack huts, talking quietly. Guns—rifles or machine pistols—rested beside most of them. The pulse of a generator sounded somewhere nearby in the forest, and the smell of roasting meat rose from cooking fires that burned near most of the huts. The smell reminded Brick how hungry he was, how long it would be before he could eat again, how he would gag if he tried.

"And now what?" Sevda said.

"Trust simple solutions, your uncle used to say. And wait."

After a time, one of the men on the steps got to his feet and pulled a skewer of meat from the fire. He put it on a tin plate along with something he slopped from a mess pot and took it to the door of one of the smaller huts. He stood at the foot of the steps and rapped on the wall. The man who came to the door to take the plate wasn't dressed like the others. He had on a white dress shirt with the sleeves rolled up and wore dark tailored slacks. He was tall, heavy-jowled, and even in the shadows the floodlights cast, his lined face and graying hair were unmistakable.

353

"Hello, Dad," Brick whispered.

The man who had brought the plate crossed the clearing and settled among his friends again. "That's a start," Brick told Sevda, forcing lightness into his voice. "We know where *somebody* is, at least."

"Brick, understand what I'm saying. Your father isn't important now. It's better if he doesn't know we're here. He's in no danger. We should go straight to my uncle."

"OK. Where is he?"

"We'll see him. You said to wait, didn't you?"

"Look, I'll be back for you. If something happens, get to Blue. Right away."

"Are you thinking, Brick? Do you remember why we're here?"

"Get to Blue if you have to. Right away." He slid away from her. Before she could answer, he had scrambled to his hands and knees again and was moving through the underbrush. Hell, no, he wasn't thinking. Shit and frogs. He wasn't that big a fool.

The hut was the third one away from where he and Sevda had been hiding. There was only one door, but a window—no glass or screen in it—faced the forest in the rear. Brick crouched by it, held his breath, and listened. Only one plate had been brought to the door. Would they bother to have a guard on his father? Barely audible above the sound of the generator, he heard the sound of a single spoon scraping against metal. He stood up.

His father sat at an unpainted table with his back to him. Besides the table and a single chair, an army cot was the only other piece of furniture in the room. From one wall, a huge poster of Che Guevara watched him eat; from the other, an even larger poster of Sandino, the founder of the Nicaraguan revolution. He ignored them and stared straight ahead through the open door into the clearing. Everything about him was out of place in the room, and the way he slumped over his food said that he knew it.

"Don't turn around, Dad," Brick spoke with a calm he didn't feel. The last thing he needed was for his father to make some move quick enough to attract notice from the clearing.

Involuntarily, his father's head jerked and started to turn. He caught himself. Slowly, he laid his spoon down and gripped the table. "I didn't think I'd raised quite such a fool, son," he said.

"Where's Ali Sabri, Dad?"

"Get out of here, Brick. As quick as you can."

"I can't do that."

His father sat in silence a moment. "Back up. Get into the woods. I'm coming out."

Brick dropped away from the window and eased back into the bush. He watched his father stand beside the hut and mime taking a piss, asking permission from somebody in the clearing. In a moment, he was crouching beside Brick.

"I don't care how you got here, Brick," he said. "I've got some guesses, but they don't matter. You want Ali Sabri out of here alive? Then however you got here, go back that way. If I can't get him out, nobody can."

"Can you?"

"I'm trying."

"That's not much of an answer, Dad." The familiar stubbornness Brick felt was as thick as the rain-heavy air.

His father picked up a twig and carefully broke it. "All right. No, I don't think I can. But I *know* you can't."

"What's gone wrong?"

"What always goes wrong? Money. This O'Brien has got no more notion of what goes on in the real world than a tree stump."

"He want's *all* the money?"

"All seven hundred million. He was a bulldozer operator before the revolution. What would you expect? From what he says, he thinks the politicians have stolen his revolution and he's got it in his head that if he can come up with that much money they'll think he's a hero and have to let him back in on it. The damnable thing is that he may be right. *I* can't argue with him."

"And he won't negotiate?"

His father gave a short, tight laugh. "Sure. He'll come down ten or fifteen million. That leaves him only about six hundred and eighty million away from what Grupo Primero's offering."

"So what will you do?"

"Go home."

"Go *home?* Just like that? Walk away?"

"Look, son. This is a business proposition, nothing more. There's some risk capital available, but it's not enough. Period. I've done my job. I wish to hell it had worked out, but it hasn't—I wish to hell I'd never let Roger talk me into this to begin with. Please believe me."

"He's dead."

"Who's dead?"

"Roger is. Uncle Jack is."

His father closed his eyes. "Jesus God. Both of them?"

"Both of them. Yesterday."

"Was it Grupo Primero?"

"No. Jack was—an accident. Brenner killed Roger."

Robert Houston

"Brenner! I thought he was out of this. They promised me..."

"Everybody agreed but Brenner, Dad. My bet's that he's on his way here."

"No wonder that damn woman wasn't upset! I'd expected her to pitch a hissy when I got here." He flung the pieces of the twig into the bushes.

Brick spoke carefully. "Livia's still here, then."

"Still very damned much here. I might have been able to talk some sense to that...latter-day Castro if she hadn't been." He was looking beyond Brick as he spoke now, following something in the clearing with his eyes.

"What does that mean, Dad?"

His father nodded toward the clearing. "That." Brick turned. From a hut across the clearing that was draped with the red and black flag of the revolution, a man in a tightly tailored fatigue uniform stepped down onto the muddy ground. He had a build of a boxer and a clipped Errol Flynn moustache. But he was too stocky for his part, Brick thought, his features too coarse. A bulldozer operator's body and face, a peasant's walk, no matter how much he tried to step into the clearing as if he were coming onto a stage. One hand rested on a pistol holster. The other he held out to the woman who followed him from the hut.

Brick remembered the first time he had seen her. She had been coming downstairs then, too, holding on to the swaying steel steps of a white ship on the Black Sea, trying to keep her glistening dark hair away from her eyes. The long hair was gone, sheared away in the foothills of Ararat before he had crossed a river with her, a crossing that had changed his life forever. But her heavy breasts still swung loose be-

357

neath the man's shirt, her motion was still the fluid
dance of a swimmer, the effect of her still breathtaking. He had to force himself to stay crouched in
these wet bushes, to not stand and call to her. To not
want to touch her.

She took O'Brien's hand. He helped her from the
last step, then wrapped his arm around her shoulder
and let his eyes travel around the clearing. The gesture was clear. This woman is mine, *cabrones,* it said;
anybody want to doubt that? Brick's stomach clenched.
Livia stood very still, her eyes fixed in space.

"I think she's got him convinced that Brenner can
come through for him," Brick's father said. "What
Brenner's got in mind, I don't know. But she's stalling for something. And as long as the man keeps
thinking with his cock, it's working."

Brick forced his eyes away from the clearing and
his mind back to his father. "Brenner has no way to
get here. I've got Hoover Blue."

"Do you? And do you have his son? The one who
brought me here."

"He's not still here?"

"Why should he be? These people can make sure
that I get back to Managua."

Brick reached for his father's hand. "Listen to me,
Dad. I think Brenner got to Managua today. That
means that he could be here by tomorrow night, easily. When he gets here, nothing's just a business
proposition anymore. It's not a question of your
'doing your job' and going home—if it ever was. If
anybody gets out of here, it's got to be tonight. Do
you understand me?"

"I understand *you've* got to get out of here. They
won't do anything to me. They can't afford to. Grupo

Primero wouldn't possibly deal with Brenner under those circumstances."

"Great God in heaven, Dad! Roger's dead, Jackrabbit's dead—and back there behind me seven other people are dead. That's part of the 'business proposition.' Please, Dad. Listen to me. Talk to me!"

"I won't be interfered with by my own son, Brick."

Brick smashed his fist into the wet loam. "Damn it, let me get through to you—let me break that goddamn code for once in my life. Let me help you. Help *me!*"

Brick's father's eyes leapt away from Brick again. Brick followed them back to the clearing. O'Brien and Livia were moving now, making a kind of grand progress around the clearing from hut to hut, stopping to chat for a moment at each. They were three huts away from Brick's father's.

"Dad. Now. It's got to be *now.*"

"What do you want, Brick?" His father's voice was distant, cautious.

"All of you—Ali Sabri, Livia, yourself. It's got to be that."

"I can help you with Ali Sabri. Not with the woman. There's no way in hell to get to her. Let her go."

"What about Ali Sabri?"

"They give me the run of the camp. Nobody will try to stop me if I move around. But there's a guard on Sabri."

Brick slipped the pistol out of his *guayabera.* "Take it. And tell him his niece is here. Her name is Sevda. I'll explain that later."

His father stared at the pistol. It was the look Brick remembered him using when Brick had brought home petrified frogs. "If I use it, we're all dead."

359

"Bluff, Deputy Director." Brick smiled. "You ought to be good at it."

His father took the pistol. "There are sentries along the path out of here, but nowhere else so far as I can tell. Where's Blue?"

"Not far. Away from the path. He can get us around it."

O'Brien and Livia moved another hut closer. "Let this place get bedded down," Brick's father said. "Where will I meet you?"

"Which is Ali Sabri's hut?"

"Next to this one—there." He pointed toward the hut that stood between his own and the one O'Brien and Livia were in front of.

"Behind it in the brush, then."

"Watch for us. And Brick—let the woman go. It's hopeless."

"I'll watch for you." He took his father's hand, squeezed, and crawled away into the scratching, wet underbrush. Thunder rolled, much closer now than before.

Brick was shaken. Seeing Livia with O'Brien was one of those things he knew he should have expected, but could never have brought himself to. Of course she was with O'Brien! She had been with himself on Ararat, with Roger in London, and now with O'Brien in Nicaragua. But it would be too easy for him to think of her as a bitch, a whore, the way his gut told him to. No. He and the others—with a twisted sort of honesty, Livia had chosen to make them part of her contribution to the "business proposition." Probably no more than that. To her.

Then he should walk away as his father wanted him to do. But he had carried her with him too long to just do that—her, or the idea of her. And he had

promises to keep—to himself, to other people. He
owed and was owed. He hurt. He was going to collect.
And that was *his* business proposition.

When he found Sevda, he had to stop her from
going to Ali Sabri right away. She didn't trust his
father, he knew that. Nor did she really believe Brick
ought to. Brick didn't care whether he ought to or
not. They had no choice but to trust him now.

The rain held off longer than it should have: thunder seemed to be all around them now, shaking the
ground like a dozen locomotives, but the air was still
dry by the time the last of the camp drifted into the
huts. Brick didn't imagine it could be very late—the
camp would surely be up just after daylight—but he
had no sense of the hour at all. Dawn was what
mattered now. Blue would be gone before dawn. The
jungle at dawn would be full of those people with
guns from the camp. Brick lay lucid and awake beside Sevda, trying to count minutes, trying to plan.
Livia. He had only till dawn to find a way to get the
few hundred yards to Livia. After so many weeks,
so many miles, now only hours, and yards. And with
feelings about her as tangled as they always had
been, like the wild roses in a village in Armenia. In
the breaks between thunderclaps, he listened to the
steady pulse of the generator, to things moving in
the jungle around him, to trees clashing in the wind.
And he listened to his plan form in his mind, building
itself as surely as the storm was.

And when it had a shape, he thought only about
dawn to keep from thinking about Livia in O'Brien's
hut, to keep from imagining. He reached for Sevda's
hand. She let him take it, as she had last night, and
gave back the pressure, without demanding more.

In the clearing, only a single sentry stood beside a wind-whipped campfire. What could have been an hour passed after the last light went out in the huts—including Brick's father's. The sentry paced and smoked and spat, the sole man left awake in the world.

"Soon," Sevda whispered. "It's got to happen soon. I can't stand it."

Brick's father left his hut just as the first heavy drops of rain thudded on the leaves. He nodded to the sentry and stepped to the side of his hut, as if he were going to the bathroom again. Brick lost him in the shadows. The sentry watched him for a few moments, hunching his shoulders against the rain. Then the sky fell apart. The wind came with a rush that made the floodlights bounce crazily, and the rain sounded loud as a forest fire in the trees. The sentry looked confused, started for Brick's father's hut, changed his mind, then ran for the shelter of one of the barrack huts.

In the brief seconds that it took him to reach the hut, Brick saw his father round the corner of the hut next to his own—Ali Sabri's.

"Now!" Brick took Sevda's hand and plunged through the brush, half blind from the rain, knowing that the limbs were tearing at his hands and face but not feeling them yet. Behind Ali Sabri's hut, they broke from the bushes, safe still in the shadows. Lightning smashed into the jungle no more than a hundred yards away. The floodlights faltered. Good, Brick thought. No generator could withstand rains like this. It must go out often. Just not yet, he prayed. Not quite yet.

Ali Sabri was the first one through the window in the back of the hut. He hung in it a moment, scanning the dark forest, then levered himself up and dropped. Brick and Sevda reached him just as he turned to help pull Brick's father through the window behind him.

"Ohhhh, my friend Brick!" He slid Brick's father to the ground and wrapped Brick in a wet, smothering hug. "And Sevda? That's really Sevda here in this place?" He released Brick and transferred the hug to Sevda. "Allah! What a place for Kurds."

Sevda was laughing or sobbing or both. Nothing was clear in the rain. Brick felt his father's hand on his arm and then felt the weight of the pistol as his father slipped it into the pocket of his shirt. Then Ali Sabri said something else that the thunder swallowed, and in another flash of lightning Brick saw that he was laughing. Then they were all plunging into the darkness of the forest together and slipping in the loam and mud and kicking their way through the clinging growth, until they were far enough away from the camp to use the flashlight and the trees gave way to the openness of Hoover Blue's mother's yucca patch.

Brick stopped to let Ali Sabri and his father move ahead into the rows of yucca. He took Sevda's arm and held her back with him, then pressed the flashlight into her hand. "Get them to Blue," he told her. "Wait for me at the boat."

"Don't, Brick, don't," she said. "You won't make it. You can't."

"Leave before daylight. If I'm not there, go anyway."

"She really means that much to you?"

Brick hesitated. "Finding out does."

Sevda took both Brick's hands and pulled him to her. "Then find out. And come back. We'll wait for you, if I have to tie Hoover Blue to a tree. Asshole romantic!"

Brick felt her warmth through the wet clothing. He let his hand move down the smoothness of her back, then kissed her. When he pulled away from her, the rain that replaced the warmth of her was like a blow. "Graduate student," he said, and turned away.

As he had lain in the bushes and listened, he had tried to locate the generator by its sound. It was somewhere past Ali Sabri's hut, not too far into the woods, as best he could tell. He worked his way back close enough to the camp to be able to see power lines in the spillover from the floodlights. He had been right. The main line cut away from the camp between Ali Sabri's hut and the barrack hut just beyond it. He stopped to memorize things: from Ali Sabri's hut, O'Brien's was a straight dash across the clearing—if he could find Ali Sabri's hut again in the darkness. There seemed to be a path of sorts worn from the camp to the generator. But again, could he stay on it in the darkness? It would take the sleeping camp a few minutes to react. He needed those few minutes. He damn well better stay on it. He took it now, hoping his feet would remember its twists when he came back over it.

A single bulb burned over the jerry-rigged generator, which rattled inside a three-sided tin shack. Brick took a last look behind him, mentally aiming himself toward the path. Then he reached for the distributor cap on the old automobile engine that powered the generator, and yanked.

The darkness was utter, as if the last light in creation had snapped out. Brick stayed low as he moved, using his hands like feelers along the path.

364

Twice he lost it, and then lost long seconds finding it again. Without the sound of the generator, the rain was a roar that swallowed the noise of anything more than a yard away from him. And when he reached the clearing, the voices that shouted from hut to hut were swept away into disjointed syllables.

Was it Ali Sabri's hut that his hands found? And when he dashed into the clearing, stumbling through the soggy remains of campfires, was he really running straight ahead? He had never run in such total night before, in a place where he had nothing at all to guide him. He felt his shoulder smash into something. The something muttered *"pendejo"* and vanished in the rain. He slowed, feeling ahead with his hands. He should have reached O'Brien's hut by now, goddamnit! He tripped, and his hands landed in spiny grass that drove into his palms. When he scrambled to his feet, he was in the brush again— beyond the camp.

He backtracked, circling, blind, wanting to touch anything solid. When he did, it was the corner of a hut. He felt his way along it, heard half-a-dozen voices shouting inside. It was a barrack hut, then. Had there been a barrack hut next to O'Brien's? And on which side? Why in hell hadn't he memorized something like that?

He sprinted away from the hut toward the place the next one ought to be, slipping in the mud, nearly losing a shoe to it. He didn't dare sprint too far: he could overshoot again, or slam into the hut and break his neck if he found it. As he slowed, his fingertips brushed the solidity of cane and he knew he had been inches from passing the hut and stumbling into the jungle again. He felt his way once more. Was he at the side of the hut? The rear? And whose hut?

Then light spilled from the window above him, the jerky glow of a flashlight. He flattened himself along the wall of the hut. He strained to hear voices above the clatter of the rain. And there were voices, only too low for him to make out what they were saying. But it didn't matter what the words were. One of them was the husky voice he had last heard on a telephone in London. That was enough.

The glow inside the hut vanished. Brick worked his way to the corner again and saw the light cutting through the rain across the clearing toward the generator site. Two or three others moved to join it from around the clearing. In only minutes they'd find out that it wasn't the rain that had stopped the generator.

He moved the rest of the way around the hut to the steps in a crouch. The wooden steps creaked as he climbed them, but the rain muffled the sound. Inside, his hands found a table, then against the wall a mosquito net.

"Get up, Livia," he said, staying low.

No one answered him. He felt along the mosquito net for an opening. Did she have a pistol? She would have used it by now—but he didn't think he gave a fat rat's ass if she did. He jerked the net back. "Get up. It's Brick, goddamnit." Frustration at the darkness, rage at Livia, at this place, slashed at him. He pulled the revolver from his shirt pocket and with his left hand reached into the bed.

The smell of sex hung in the air underneath the cloying net. His hand found rough sheets, then a naked breast. Livia's hand closed around his wrist and held his hand against the breast. "Is Wolf with you, Brick? Has he come yet?" There seemed to be no surprise at all in her voice, as if she'd lost the capacity for it.

"No."

"Your father's here. Do you know that? I sent Blue's boy with the message. Did Wolf get it?"

"He knows. Get dressed."

"God, I'm glad you're here. O'Brien's a real swine. I had to do this, Brick, you know that, don't you?"

Brick forced his hand away from her breast. "Yeah. Come on." She slid across the bed toward him and kicked the covers away. Her hand touched the pistol.

"You don't need that," she said. Brick ducked out of the mosquito net. "There should be a chair behind you," Livia went on. "My clothes are on it, and my bag. Would you be a dear? Where do we meet Wolf?"

Brick leveled the pistol at the bed. He backed away and crouched again. "I know where you are, Livia, but you don't know where I am. Get your own clothes and find me a flashlight. We're not meeting Brenner."

"Then you're not...?"

"Tony wants you back, Livia."

"Tony? Oh, Christ. Tony! Don't try to tell me you came all the way here because of *Tony*."

"Would that be so stupid?"

"Yes. Stupider than you are. What about Ali Sabri?"

"He's gone already."

"And your father?"

"Him, too."

"Oh, God, God, God." Her feet thudded on the floor with a hollow sound, and her voice was taut with anger. "Then you're so damn right. I don't want to be here when O'Brien finds that out. Neither of us

367

wants to be here when Wolf comes. Do you know what you've done? Do you *realize?*" The chair scraped as she jerked her clothes off it.

"I've got an idea."

"Do you? This whole thing—the Kurds, Grupo Primero, Brenner, O'Brien, Turks, Israelis, all of it—it's like weasels fighting in a hole, Brick, like a snake pit. *That's* what pushes the world around. Finding a safe part of the hole to hide in, that's all. It's not governments and conspiracies and Mafiosi and all of that nonsense that's behind the god-awful things that happen in the world. It's just business as usual that's behind it all. And you don't think that applies to you, too? You think you're exempt— that anybody is? I had it beat, Brick. Wolf had figured the whole system out, and we had it beat. That's what you've done, Brick—you took a safe part of the hole away from me and gave it to somebody else. And what will they do with it that I couldn't? Do they *deserve* it any more than I do? Oh, my God. Nobody *deserves* anything."

Rain lashed in the open door and across the floor. Brick shivered in the wind. "What's Brenner got in mind to beat it with now, Livia?"

"I don't know. But something. He'll have something. Or he would have until you came along." She fumbled with something on a shelf. A glass fell and smashed. "Damn," she said. "You want this flashlight?"

"Roll it across the floor."

"Brick, I need you to help me get out of here now. Don't you see that?"

Brick stood and lowered the pistol. "Yep," he said. "Business as usual. Give me the flashlight."

Brick stepped out into the rain ahead of her. As

he did, he said, "Tell me one thing, Livia. You've got Tony. You've got Tony's money. Why isn't that safe enough for you?"

"I told you that in Turkey, Brick, but I think you heard something else. Tony loves me too much. I'm terrified of that, like a big woolly animal that could roll over on me and smother me and never know the difference. Do you understand that?"

Brick dropped down into the mud. "I do now," he said.

"You loved me, Brick. Didn't you?" They moved off in what Brick judged should be the direction of the main trail. Flashlights cut swaths across the clearing behind them. The whole camp must have been up by now.

"Yes," Brick said.

"Do you now?"

Brick risked switching the flashlight on for a moment. One more wouldn't make any difference. The beam swept the jungle and came to rest on the opening to the trail, a dozen yards in front of them. It was clear! The sentry must have come in when the lights went out. He switched the flashlight off. He didn't need it—he knew where the trail was now, which direction freedom lay in. "No," he answered Livia. "No, I don't."

As they moved onto the trail, the clearing behind them burst into light, as if their leaving had set off some gigantic, silent explosion. "Run!" Brick shouted through the wall of rain to Livia. He slipped in the mud, went down on one knee, and came up running. He knew Livia was somewhere behind him, but he didn't turn to see. He felt weightless, skimming above the mud, untouchable. "Run!"

* * *

He had no idea how long they ran, just that the flashlight had given out and that his lungs were bursting with the sodden air—and it was dawn. Twice they had stopped for breath, and neither time had there been anybody behind them. O'Brien's people would come; he had no doubt of that. But his and Livia's head start had held so far. Brick figured that it would have taken O'Brien ten, maybe fifteen minutes to discover just what had happened and to get organized enough to come after them. There had been no other boats beside the few *bungos* at the landing yesterday. Livia said that O'Brien did have a launch, but that it had gone downriver to Bluefields on the coast for supplies. She didn't think it would be back until midday at the earliest. That meant that Blue's *bungo* with the trolling motor, slow as it was, was the fastest boat available. Once they got to it, they should be safe. They could head for Bluefields, only an hour or so away, not back upriver to El Rama.

But it was dawn. And O'Brien and his guerrillas-in-training were behind them.

Brick looked for comfort, and found it only in the fact that even if Brenner had made it to Managua as he suspected, he couldn't possibly reach them before late afternoon. That, at least, was one thing he didn't have to take into account. Not yet.

They were on the wider part of the trail now. That gray dawn light could penetrate the clouds at all meant the storm was passing; the thunder came from far to the west now and the rain had settled into a steady drizzle. And they *had* to be near the landing. But past each bend lay another, then another, and he ran, trying desperately to ignore the pain in his

370

side. One more yard, one more stretch of mud, one more bend.

And then the landing was before them. A bright macaw dove over the *bungos,* and a family of monkeys chattered away from them into the trees over the stream. Nothing else moved.

And Blue's boat was gone.

Brick let his legs go and they slipped away from him. He went down on his knees, then pitched forward into the yellow mud. He heard Livia gasping for breath behind him, then she was beside him, on her knees, too, heaving as if she were in labor. Brick curled onto his side and raised himself up on an elbow.

"We'll take one of the *bungos,*" he said. "Drift, paddle when we're able."

"He won't kill me," Livia said, her voice coming in half sobs. "You forced me to go with you. He'll believe that. Everything's blown, but he won't kill me." She clutched her bag to her as if it were a stuffed animal and rocked back and forth on her knees, staring ahead of her at the empty stream. "Get out if you can, Brick. I can't help you."

Brick looked at the rain-filled *bungos.* Where would the strength to bail one come from, the strength to push one onto the water, the strength to paddle? He hadn't eaten since noon yesterday. He hadn't slept. He had run half the night. How long ago had Sevda and the others left? She had promised to wait. He had believed her—and he still believed her; she had waited as long as she could. Nobody had forced him to go back for Livia. Nobody but himself. He had had something to settle, and no matter what happened now, he had settled it. He knew who Livia was, and he almost knew who he was. If he hadn't

been able to go all the way, to read the last page, he
had gone as far as he could. And that was far enough.
He dragged himself toward the edge of the trail,
toward the partial protection of the broad leaves of
a banana tree. To wait.

The hands that cupped underneath his arms to
lift him came from behind. He tried to jerk away
from them, as if they were something that had
dropped on him from one of the trees. But then he
heard the voice and the accent and reached to clasp
the hands. "My friend Brick," Ali Sabri said. "Even
though you are heavier than that one, I will let your
father take her." Brick turned to see his father struggling to help Livia to her feet. Yellow mud covered
her, and her soaked clothing clung to her skin like
a kind of membrane. If Brick looked as bad as that,
he didn't want to know. "She has been handled so
much I'm afraid that if I touched her too hard, she
would fall apart. Or I would strangle her if she
didn't."

"Where the hell were you?" Brick said.

"The boat? Oh, down this stream a bit. Did you
want us to wait right here, in the open? Mr. Blue got
very nervous at dawn. My niece felt sorry for him."

"You all right, son?" Brick's father called.

"Just great." Brick made it to his feet. Leaning
on Ali Sabri, he followed his father and Livia toward
a path that ran along the stream bank. "My niece
has a good heart," Ali Sabri went on as they walked.
"She reads too much nonsense and not enough Agatha Christie and she probably can't ride a horse anymore, but she has a good heart. The rest I can repair."

Brick let him talk, too grateful, too exhausted, too
full of his returning sense of freedom to care if Ali
Sabri wanted to recite chemical formulas in Arabic

to him. He leaned into him, stumbling over tree roots and fallen limbs and feeling nothing in his feet, as the shape of the boat and the two people in it took shape out of the gray light and mist, hidden like a log beneath an overhang of vines.

Sevda swung out of the boat. "Brick!" she shouted, then pulled up short as she came face to face with Livia and Brick's father on the path. She and Livia stared at each other a long moment, both equally wet and muddy and bedraggled. "Thanks," Livia said at length.

"Yeah," Sevda said and stepped aside to let them pass. She made a face, a variant of her restroom-attendant look.

"Well?" she said when Brick and Ali Sabri reached her.

"Well."

"I'm here," she said.

"Yep. So am I."

"I waited."

"And I got here."

"Yeah. Get in the boat."

"Move and I will." He shook himself free of Ali Sabri and took hold of a vine to ease himself down into the boat. Blue reached to help him and started to say something.

He never finished.

Ali Sabri heard the sound first, freezing and listening with the same intensity that had surprised Brick when they heard the gunfire in their camp on Ararat. He made a sharp hissing sound to hush them. Brick strained to hear, but it was a full half minute before his ears picked up anything besides the rain and the lapping of the water against the boat. And when he did hear, he couldn't make out if the sound was only one motor or several.

"Launches," Hoover Blue said softly. "A little one, maybe two, three big ones."

"Get out of the boat," Ali Sabri said. "Back into the trees."

The launches were moving fast. The first one, the smallest, came into sight almost before the bushes they had flattened themselves into had quit swaying. Its nose plunged as it throttled back in front of the landing, and the two larger launches—at least twenty-four-footers, Brick estimated—had a chance to ease off more slowly. All three seemed to be full of men in some sort of uniform; through the bushes Brick could only make out that they were vaguely military. But the boats had no kind of government markings on them.

"I thought you said there weren't any launches in El Rama," Brick said to Blue.

"Those aren't from El Rama, sir. I know them. They're for-hire boats from Bluefields."

"Then who the hell's that in them?"

"My guess," Brick's father said, "is that they're irregulars. Every dictatorship in Central America is full of ex-National Guardsmen that Nicaragua kicked out who are training private armies to take the country back. We're picking up their radio communications everywhere."

"Why now?" Sevda said. "Chance?"

The small launch nosed in as close as it dared to the landing. "No," Ali Sabri said. "Not chance. Not at all chance." A man in a sharply creased fatigue uniform with no markings on it climbed out onto the bow of the launch. He leapt into the shallow water of the landing and wrapped a line around a tree.

Behind him, helped by half-a-dozen pairs of hands, Wolf Brenner made his way shakily onto the wet bow. Even in the rain, his stiff hair stuck up as if it were spring loaded. He looked like an accountant, Brick thought. Evil looked like an accountant now.

That was how Brenner had done it, then: he'd never been in Managua at all. He had probably flown to Costa Rica and gotten a boat up the coast and been in Bluefields about the time Brick and Sevda had gotten to Hoover Blue's. Since Ali Sabri disappeared from Mexico City, he'd had plenty of time to arrange this raid through his "connections," the people he'd helped rob the country blind with his phony bank. A quick surprise attack, give his "connections" a welcome chance to wipe out a guerrilla training base, and be out of the country with Livia and Ali Sabri by nightfall. Then he's a hero: Ali Sabri's safe and grateful, Grupo Primero has got its deal back on again a hell of a lot more cheaply than O'Brien would ever have agreed to, Brenner's back in Grupo Primero's good graces—and all that remains is to convince the Israelis and the Turks to put *their* deal back together again. Beautiful. As Livia said, Brenner had the whole system figured. Good business.

Except that nobody involved would touch Brenner with a ten-foot pole. To think that they would, the man had to be as mad as a hatter.

They were all so intent on watching the boats unload that nobody noticed Livia until she was already on the path. She still didn't have much of her strength back; she was wobbly, clinging to any tree or vine she could reach to help her stay on her feet. "Wolf," she shouted. "He's here, Wolf. We've got him!"

Brenner turned. Sevda leapt out onto the path.

"You bitch!" she yelled and started for Livia. Ali Sabri managed to get a hand on Sevda's leg and trip her up, but not to hold on. By the time Sevda was on her feet again, Livia had swung around and braced herself against a tree. Brick saw the .45 automatic come out of her bag even before Sevda did, who was struggling to hold on to her footing on the slippery path.

"Sevda!" he shouted. Sevda looked over her shoulder and lost a piece of a second. Brick rolled out onto the path. His hand fumbled in the pocket of his *guayabera,* found the wet, slick revolver. All of Livia's attention was focused on Sevda; the .45 automatic rose and sighted. Sevda at last saw it, and froze.

When Brick fired past her she lunged to the side as if he had hit her with a whip. He fired only twice. With the first shot, Livia's .45 jerked up and fired into the trees. With the second, Livia spun off the tree she was braced against and lost her balance. She reached wildly for something to grab on to, the look on her face surprised, like a child who has picked up something scalding. Brick turned away before she fell, and bit into the mud to stop his own scream.

He was aware of gunfire somewhere, and of someone shaking him, dragging him. Then the dragging stopped and he felt something heavy crumple onto his back, and then somebody was moaning just behind his ear. He opened his eyes. Brenner stood at the end of the path, a machine pistol pointing down it. Brick shoved at the heavy thing and it flopped off him. He rolled away from it and saw it was his father. And then the gunfire started again, much more gunfire than before. The men from the launches were flinging themselves down wherever they were and firing up the main trail toward O'Brien's camp. One of O'Brien's kids in a fatigue shirt and jeans ran into the middle of them, firing in all directions before the front of him ripped open and he toppled into the water.

Brenner was gone now, too—dead or in the weeds with the others, Brick had no idea. He got to his knees and pulled at his father. His father was still moaning, but his eyes were open and he was trying to speak. "The boat," he managed to say, and Brick nodded and began to drag him. Then there were other hands beside his own, and he recognized Ali Sabri's voice but couldn't make out what he was saying with the explosions filling up all his listening space—not only gunfire now, but louder explosions like hand grenades.

He gave his father over to Hoover Blue and Ali Sabri to lift into the *bungo*. He tumbled in after him and smelled the fishy, wet-wood smell of the boat even in the rain as Sevda helped him to a half-sitting position and rested his head against her shoulder, sobbing and saying things to him in Kurdish that he couldn't make sense out of. Then he was aware of the vines trailing across the boat, and a dishwater sky above, and the sound of the explosions growing fainter, and an olive shore slipping by in the gray light of morning.

"You pay for being a damn fool," Brick's father said. The tourniquet Ali Sabri had rigged on his leg seemed to have stopped the bleeding there; what was going on because of the hole in his side there was no way of knowing. Brick held a wadded, wet shirt over it and tried not to imagine body cavities filling up with blood, organs punctured and withering, his mother's face. "Most people just go bankrupt, or to jail for it, but I guess this'll do, too."

The river was broad and slow here, in spite of the rains. They were approaching the delta. Green islands split the water ahead, and the great spidery roots of mangrove trees marked labyrinths of coastal marshes. Now and again there was a low splash along the shore as a crocodile dove. "How long?" Brick asked Blue.

"Few minutes. If this battery holds, sir."

"Now, Jackrabbit and myself," Brick's father went on, his voice weak and beginning to slur. "We were a couple of hotshots in the Navy. That was the problem, I guess, Brick. A couple of old farts who wanted to be hotshots again. Never was just the money. It was the goddamn desk, and the cocktail parties, and reading all those reports from people who were *doing* things. I always wanted you to *do* something. You know that?"

"Lie still, Dad. It's all right."

"No, it's not all right. I never did talk to you much. I want to now. You know, I guess I always wanted you to be more like Roger—I used to tell your mother that. Well, so much for what I knew. Look at us now."

Sevda sat a foot or so away, cradling Brick's father's head in her lap. Her eyes met Brick's and held them. They gave away nothing; they were simply there. "Yep," Brick said. "Look at us now."

Brick's father blinked, as if he were trying to clear away something in his vision. "There's got to be some local who's the American consul in Bluefields. Find him. I can take care of the rest."

Brick nodded. His father's eyes closed; his breath-

378

ing remained shallow, almost too even. Make it, Dad, make it, Brick thought. Please. Be with me this time.

Hoover Blue heard the launch before even Ali Sabri did, as if his hearing were more attuned to the sounds of things over water and in mist. It came as a higher-pitched sound than before, the whine of a motor at open throttle. And it came from behind them.

The rain had stopped, and the mist had begun to rise over the river so that visibility was maybe half a mile, Brick judged. The launch could be just beyond that—or three miles away, for all he knew. Blue scanned the riverbank worriedly, looking for a place to put in. Would it be Brenner in the launch? Or O'Brien? Maybe neither. Maybe just whoever was left trying to get the hell away from the shooting. None of the possibilities was good.

"How close is it?" Brick asked him.

"Hard to say, sir. Coming pretty quick time."

"Can we make Bluefields?"

"Oh, no, sir. Lucky if we can make the bank. If this river had a bank."

Brick saw what he meant. The mangroves walked out into the water so far that there was no place you could say the trees ended and the land began; the entire shore was a snaky maze of thick, tangled roots, impossible to get through. Only the crocodiles and the water moccasins seemed to know ways through them.

"Then how about those islands?"

"What I was thinking. There's plenty channels in there, sir. Some of them big enough for us, maybe, but not a launch." He cut the whirring motor hard to the left. "Me, I'm heading for them."

The launch came into sight, a dark spot in the

mist, while they still had a good three hundred yards to go before the first of the islands. Brick goddamned the wake that they trailed behind them on the smooth surface of the river—even if they *were* out of sight already, their wake would lead to them like a road sign. If whoever was in the launch wanted them, he had them. Unless Blue's channels narrowed damn quickly.

The mangroves rose in walls around them as they threaded between the first of the islands—walls that were too far apart to be any help. Half-a-dozen launches could pass between them abreast. Blue stood up in the stern of the *bungo* now, sighting for narrower channels. But which were channels and which were coves? Which had outlets? Which were traps? Brick looked back, craning to see past Blue. Blue's channels hadn't narrowed quickly enough. The launch had seen them. And it wanted them. A long rooster tail of water spun away from it as it banked in a hard curve toward the channel.

Blue rounded the island. The shadows of the mangroves cut across the murky water in front of them like shapes of long-vanished docks and ships and fortifications just beneath the surface. The island was no island; the mangroves had grown a wall of themselves along the silt to the riverbank. The channel ended. There was no visible way to go but back, back toward where the sound of the launch told them there was another kind of wall they couldn't get past.

Blue guided the boat in a maddeningly slow circle around the lagoon, searching, hoping for any kind of break. But the thick roots, intertwining like tentacles, were solid as steel fenceposts.

Almost.

"Hah!" Blue shouted as an opening the size of a sidewalk took shape out of the tangle.

"It's too small, Hoover," Sevda shouted back as Blue swerved the boat toward the opening.

"Gotta be, gotta be!" He squatted and took aim as if the prow were a rifle barrel. They slipped into the opening—ten feet, fifteen feet. And then stopped. The sides of the *bungo* wedged between fists of roots with a soft squeal like the sound of a wooden peg twisting and locking into place. The electric motor churned like a blender. Forward. Backward. Nowhere.

The launch sliced into the cove. There was only one man in it. His eyes darted ahead of him around the cove through thick glasses, and his hair whipped in the wind like stiff marsh grass. He skidded the launch in a quick circuit of the cove like a puzzled dog who knows his rabbit *has* to be in this patch of briars. And then again, another circuit, standing up and straining to see over the wet, blurred windshield. Perched like some ugly tropical bird, Brick thought, as Brenner's leaping eyes found the opening and he twisted the launch's wheel toward it, reaching wildly for the throttle to slow himself.

He found the throttle too late. He jerked the wheel again to try to pull away from the wall of roots. But his control was gone: the boat planed sideways, a wave of green water slapping up into the tiny channel ahead of it and slamming the *bungo* another foot further into the mangroves. As the launch hit the roots with its side it nearly righted itself; the prop whirred free of the water for a moment as the boat glanced up into the air, its hull caving in like a plastic toy's. Then it wrenched back into the water and plunged across the cove. Brenner was no longer in it. It had flung him off it as cleanly as a rodeo horse.

He bobbed up, glasses gone, as the launch smashed head on into the mangroves on the other side of the cove. This time it didn't keep going. It somersaulted into the trees, hung, then exploded. Brenner thrashed toward the mangroves. His hand touched the first root just as the water began to boil around him. He jerked his hand back and grabbed at something that looked like a gray stick imbedded in his neck. And then the water was full of the gray sticks, writhing and slashing at him. He went under again, then struggled to the surface. He gasped for air; the sticks were hanging from his face, his neck, his arms.

"Nest of 'em, sir," Blue said, his voice hushed. "Water moccasins."

Brenner screamed. From across the cove, logs began to move toward him. But Brick knew they weren't logs.

"Your pistol, Brick," Ali Sabri said, echoing Blue's hush.

Brenner slapped at the gray sticks wildly. "Rustin!" he screamed. Brick crawled past Ali Sabri to the bow of the *bungo*. He was glad the roots held the boat steady. Of his four remaining bullets, he had three left over to fire at the moving logs after Brenner sank beneath the surface of the stained water.

Epilogue

Brick carefully refolded the thin airmail stationery and slipped it back into the smudged envelope. It had all begun with a letter. That first one had been written here, at Roger's desk, as a summer had just been getting underway. And now this one came, weeks after it had been written in snowy winter mountains somewhere in Iranian Kurdistan, as the cherry blossoms along the Potomac signaled the beginning of another summer. It had come by courier from Ankara, with the return address of Major Erkut Özpamir. But inside that envelope was another one, with no return address.

Brick hadn't heard from Sevda in months, not since she and Ali Sabri had left Washington. He had had reports of "Kurdish offensives" in both Iran and

Iraq from the *Middle Eastern Desk*'s stringers, and
of protests to Israel from Baghdad and Tehran about
arms shipments that were mysteriously making
their way into Kurdistan. The reports mentioned
"new leadership" among the Kurds, but never names.
For Brick they didn't have to.

Brick reached across his desk to drop the letter
back into his "In" box on top of all the others his
secretary had opened and culled for him. Just as he
was about to let it go, he hesitated. He pulled back
his arm and opened the letter again.

Sevda's handwriting was the old-fashioned, ornate script of Europe and the Middle East. It was
partly in pencil, partly in a ball-point that seemed
always on the verge of running out of ink.

"Dear Brick," it began. "I don't know if I will get
to finish this tonight or not, or when I will get to
mail it—if ever. We're moving in the morning again.
I can't tell you where to. I can't even tell you where
I am now, except that there is snow and that I actually find myself longing for a few of those warm
nights in Bluefields. I hope this finds you well. By
the time you get it, I hope it finds *me* well. The
fighting here has been heavy. We seem to be con-
stantly attacking some military outpost or other,
then running to attack another someplace else. I
have even become a pretty good horsewoman again!
Our salvation so far is that the Iranians and the
Iraqis are in no position to coordinate anything
against us, so that as long as we can keep shifting
from one country to the next we should be all right.
Inshallah!

"I wonder if you understand yet. I wanted to stay
in Washington with you, wanted it with all my heart.
I accepted that you weren't ready to plan anything

yet when we got back. There were too many faces
you had to erase first, you said, too many things you
had been putting in a shoe box that you had to take
out and think about. Did you really believe that I
couldn't sympathize with that? What had I been
doing in the ten years I was out of Kurdistan but
taking things out of a shoe box, like seashells I had
collected, and deciding which were worth keeping?
I think I had decided that I would have to come back
here with my uncle as early as Bluefields, while we
were waiting to get your father evacuated, though
I didn't know it yet.

"Does that upset you? Does it make you feel that
even as we were making love that first time in Bluefields, I was planning to leave you? I think once it
might have made you feel that way, but not now. Or
I pray that it doesn't now. I pray that the months
you have had with your thinking since I went away
have made you see what I had such a hard time
telling you: I love you. I think I have loved you since
childhood. So there, asshole romantic! I wasn't leaving *you;* I was leaving a life that wasn't any good for
me anymore. Surely you of all people should understand that."

The letter broke off. When it began again, it was
in ball-point.

"This is two days later, Brick. There is even more
snow than before, new snow that makes the mountains look as if they were covered with white cake
icing. We have ridden for two days and I am very
tired, so if I don't make much sense, forgive me. I
want to tell you this. When you promised Roger's
father and Claire that you would take over the *Middle Eastern Desk* for him, I remember you said to me
that you had no intention of trying to fill Roger's

shoes, that you wanted to be what he never was. You already are what Roger never was, Brick. Even your father realized that in Nicaragua. You are what your father never was. As you told me, there wasn't very much of interest in that "code" of his when you broke it, was there? You can't *find* your own kind of sense, Brick, you have to make it. That's what I'm doing now, and that's what I hope for you, too. In so many ways, you have already begun making it. Don't stop.

"I don't know if I will ever see you again. When you see the return address of the person who is forwarding this to you, you will know who to contact to find us if you should ever want to. There is very little to offer you here but a fight for something that matters—to me, at least. Often there is not enough to eat, and the killing is terrible, though I keep out of that part as much as I can. I'm still too busy issuing proclamations. Please thank Tony Lo Presti for the money he is sending, if you are still in contact with him, though I can understand if you are not.

"My uncle sends embraces, and says to tell you that he thinks he could teach even an American to ride like a Kurd if the American wanted to badly enough. He asks that, if you should happen to be coming this way sometime, would you please pick him up another meerschaum like the one he bought in the bazaar in Istanbul. He lost the other one in a knife fight with an Iranian Revolutionary Guardsman, he says, though I think in truth it had something to do with a woman.

"Mashallah. I love you. Sevda

"P.S. My uncle says to tell you one other thing. He says that Noah's Ark really is up here somewhere."

Again, Brick folded the letter. But this time he

stuffed it into the pocket of his jacket. He looked at the stack of galleys waiting for him on his desk, and at the full "In" box. Then he pulled out a piece of stationery and an envelope. He addressed the envelope to Major Erkut Özpamir, Unified Turkish Army Command, Ankara, Turkey.

"Dear Erkut," he wrote. "Never read your letters twice. There's trouble in that." He laid the pen down. The galleys and the "In" box caught his eye again, and he felt a twinge of guilt. But he would get to them all right, and the person who sat at this desk after him—probably Claire's new boyfriend from the faculty at Georgetown, who would love the job— could read the next batch. They were, after all, only business as usual.

He picked up the pen again. "I won't go into much detail now," he wrote. "Since, *inshallah,* we'll be seeing each other soon. I hope there won't be any trouble with my getting into Turkey again. There shouldn't be. All I need is a transit visa."

The National Bestseller by

GARY JENNINGS

"A blockbuster historical novel. . . . From the start of
this epic, the reader is caught up in the sweep and
grandeur, the richness and humanity of this fictive
unfolding of life in Mexico before the Spanish
conquest. . . . Anyone who lusts for adventure, or that
book you can't put down, will glory in AZTEC!"
The Los Angeles Times

"A dazzling and hypnotic historical novel. . . . AZTEC has
everything that makes a story appealing . . . both
ecstasy and appalling tragedy . . . sex . . . violence . . .
and the story is filled with revenge. . . . Mr. Jennings
is an absolutely marvelous yarnspinner. . . .
A book to get lost in!"
The New York Times

"Sumptuously detailed. . . . AZTEC falls into the same
genre of historical novel as SHOGUN."
Chicago Tribune

"Unforgettable images. . . . Jennings is a master at
graphic description. . . . The book is so vivid that this
reviewer had the novel experience of dreaming of the
Aztec world, in technicolor, for several nights in
a row . . . so real that the tragedy of the
Spanish conquest is truly felt."
Chicago Sun Times

AVON Paperback   **55889 . . . $3.95**